Published by Darlington Press Australia

ISBN: 978-0-9873305-9-8

GUILLAUME

BOOK TWO OF THE
TRIPTYCH CHRONICLE

PRUE BATTEN

Darlington
PRESS
AUSTRALIA

REVIEWS FOR GUILLAUME

"This is for readers who love the historical fiction of writers such as Wendy Dunn, but yearn for the adventure of an earlier period and the excitement and mystery of ordinary people tangled in dangerous politics."
*Gillian Polack, bestselling author of **The Middle Ages Unlocked***

"With her customary elegant use of language, Prue Batten plunges us effortlessly into the mercantile houses, twisted alleys and secret shadowy tunnels of medieval Europe. Guillaume is a riveting tale of twelfth century trade, treachery and intrigue."
*Matthew Harffy, bestselling author of **The Bernicia Chronicles***

CHARACTERS

Guillaume de Gisborne – formally of Anjou, most lately a textile merchant
Cateline – Guillaume's mother
Anselin – Guillaume's stepfather and a reputable bowyer and fletcher from Anjou
Ariella Ben Simon – daughter of Saul Ben Simon
Amée de Clochard – wife of deceased textile merchant, Jehan de Clochard
Luzio Gigni – nephew of the merchant family, the Gigni, from Florence
Alexandrus Gigni – head of the Florentine trading family, resident in Lyon
Mahaut – servant to Amée de Clochard
Dana – more properly known as Jehanne de Clochard, daughter of Amée and Jehan
Michael Sarapion – former merchant of Constantinople
Saul Ben Simon – a Jewish textile merchant and money lender in Venezia
Tobias Celho – troubadour and occasional spy for Gisborne
Sir Guy of Gisborne – disenchanted knight, spy and merchant
Lady Ysabel of Gisborne – wife of the above knight
William of Gisborne – four-year old son of Guy and Ysabel
Petrus – one of Gisborne's spies
Adam of London – Gisborne's Master at Arms
Herviet – de Clochard's guard
Gosse – de Clochard's guard
Roul – de Clochard's guard
Odo – steward and notary in the Gigni house.
Phillip II of France
Reynaud, Archbishop of Lyon
Henry VI Hohenstaufen, Holy Roman Emperor
Pierre Vaudès – founder of the Poor Men of Lyon, also known as the Sandalati
Richard I of England
Eleanor of Aquitaine

'Where a man's heart is, there is his treasure also…'

Saint Ambrosius

PROLOGUE

He sighted along the shaft of his arrow to the needle-sharp bodkin. A beam of light caught on the forged steel and he moved it a hair's width into the shadow of tree and leaf.

The feathers stroked his cheek like a whore's fingers and he closed his eyes, seeing a pers-tinted *bliaut* rucked up, and blood seeping from the folds. And a man lying close by, neck slashed wide – a sword blow of extraordinary power.

He opened his eyes and sighted again.

They came, the two men – riding along the forest path. The dappled light shifted and changed as a breeze skirled around them, carrying the smell of damp earth and fungi and the sweat of horses. The men laughed raucously, and a cuckoo flew up with a sharp cry, battering the air with its wings. One of the horses danced sideways, and on being dragged back to the track, tossed its head up and down, harness jingling.

Its rider sat easily – a man of means and equestrian skill. A man of power.

How easy it was, thought the archer, to forfeit your life by taking an innocent's.

He waited one breath more and loosed and loaded in the time it took for the next breath.

Thwack…

A dull sound – through the skull, front to back.

Loose again!

An even duller sound as the second arrow took the second man through the eye, the force of the arrow carrying on through the brain.

Both men died instantly, falling backward onto their horse's rumps, the horses startled and shying, and then as the men fell lifeless, still in stirrups to dangle about nervous legs, they bolted, the riders bumping along like ill-filled bags of barley.

The archer jumped from the tree.

Revenge, he thought, is not so sweet after all...

CHAPTER ONE

LYON
AUTUMN OF 1193

He coughed and stirred on his cot.

Awareness…

Nose tingling, a smell of scorching. As if he had fallen asleep too close to the hearth and his hose had caught alight.

'Fire! Fire!'

His eyes flew open. Beyond the window, lights flickered and jumped and a crackle and spark sounded loud in the pitchblack of Matins while horses screamed and kicked against wood.

'Fire! Guillaume! Fire!' a voice yelled again

Luzio?

'Fire!' Guillaume roared by return, leaping from the cot. 'Fire!'

Naked, he cursed the time it took to pull on *braies* and chemise and to run to Amée's and Ariella's chamber, bashing on the door, then charging down the stair, bellowing to any who could hear. He threw open the door to the yard where the fires of hell burned and his heart began to pound fit to burst. Despite the heat, a cold tide spread through his body and panic crept higher till he thought he might choke.

Flames spat, hurling embers toward the house. One landed on his bare foot and it jerked him back to the reality of what lay before him. He leaped on the spark, stamping and swearing and grabbing his boots to drag them on.

3

A neighbour, he was sure it was Luzio, disappeared through the smoke with the horses and one of the mules, heading toward the gates. The animals reared and stalled, pulling back on ropes, shrieking with fear, but Luzio held on, shouting at the beasts, dragging them onward by sheer strength.

Guillaume seized a pail by the trough, filled it, threw it.

Again.

Again.

Barely noticing that others had streamed through the gates and were grabbing buckets of water and throwing.

The noise deafened him. Yelling, the fire roaring, twice his height, flames yellow, mad, set to destroy anything in their path. The heat forced him back time and again, burning his face, drying his eyes. The smell of burned hair hung around him – and other odours – charred wood, blistered skin.

The cloth, Jesu and Mary, the cloth!

But he could barely see through the smoke in the yard, his eyes stinging, watering as if he wept for a life past, the smoke choking his breath. All around, men coughing, yelling with rasping voices.

Faces glistened with the heat, blackened with ash – a vision of Hell. More people joined him, a bucket chain, more buckets, more water, a fog of smoke, and still the roaring carmine and umber flame.

Someone, who he did not know, had the foresight to throw bucket after bucket against the house to dampen it down. At some point he heard Amée screaming but could not see her.

God keep them safe. Please…

He stumbled as a neighbour cried out and thudded into him, the fellow's leather gambeson beginning to flame and he threw a bucket of water over him, crashing him to the ground and hitting the last of dying flames with his bare hands.

'You're alright. It's out. Are you burned?'

'No,' the man gasped. 'The leather saved me. Christ's nosehairs, Guillaume, thank you.' He jumped up with his pail still in his hand and raced toward a hogshead.

'It's empty,' he yelled back. 'All the hogsheads are empty!'

'Behind you,' shouted Guillaume. 'The river! There's a bucket chain!'

Fire was the enemy of any town, any village, and the citizens of Lyon and of Rue Ducanivet fought as if it were war. The bells of Saint Jean rang urgently and all the town knew that a conflagration had begun and so many came with buckets from troughs and hogsheads in the street and a chain had formed from the river across the road, bucket after bucket. Men and women, hand over hand…

The smoke filled Guillaume's chest like a wad of foul-smelling wool and he coughed and coughed. Next to him a man dragged in a breath and then spewed yellow vomit across the cobbles, and Guillaume grabbed him, sending him toward the gates.

'Go,' he yelled. 'Matthieu, go! You cannot breathe this. Save yourself!'

Matthieu wheezed his way around the streets at the best of times, assailed by a chest filled with thick, moist congestion.

'Please,' he grabbed the old man by the shoulders. 'I will not have your life on my hands. You have helped enough, now go, Matthieu!'

Old Matthieu looked at him through bloodshot eyes streaming with smoke-induced tears and mouthed *'Sorry'*, then headed toward the gates. Guillaume's last sight of him was a stooped shape swallowed by billowing smoke.

God protect him…

The remaining mule pelted out from the conflagration shrieking, its coat aflame. Someone threw a bucket of water over it but it was too late and the smell of roasted meat singed Guillaume's nostrils. The mule gave one last horrendous wail and then collapsed half out the gates, kicked once but then stilled in a tableau of death.

Mercifully, there was no wind and as pail upon pail attacked, so the flames began to retreat; growling but with less fierceness, now a sibilant hiss of cowed defiance. The people of Lyon began to contain the blaze, keeping it from the house, from any other dwellings. And when the moon had slid to the far side of the sky, misted by mean bands of acrid smoke, and when the bells rang for Prime, they had won a battle, if not a war.

The house stood unmarked, but all that remained on the other side of the yard where had been Jehan de Clochard's storerooms and barn, were blackened frames, bubbled with heat and soot, tumbled stone and puddles of ash-filled water. And a dead mule – rank with the smell of roasted meat.

Guillaume looked around in the grey moonlight. Faces stared at the wreckage – skin striped with soot and exhaustion. Appearing out of the acrid fog, Amée and Ariella moved toward him, long chemises filthy with ash and grime, their expressions shattered.

They huddled against him and he held them to his chest, relief incarnate.

'I thank you, my friends,' he called to the neighbours, his voice croaking. 'Madame de Clochard thanks you.'

'God's breath but you were lucky, Guillaume,' someone replied.

'Maybe…' he tried to smile but his face had set with its coating of drying ash.

'Your gates are burned,' another said with a hoarse, smoke-filled cough punctuating his words.

'Gates and storerooms can be rebuilt,' said another. 'It's lives that matter.'

And our merchandise. God protect the cloth…

But he didn't say that, because lives mattered – of course they did. Fire was a reality that a town must deal with on a daily basis. Every man in front of him was well versed in protecting a town from burning; more well versed perhaps than protecting it from warfare.

'Matthieu?' he asked, a real fear hammering at his heart. To have a life lost for the sake of de Clochard… Lyon would sink the merchant house without a thought if that happened.

It's lives that matter…

'He got out before the gates burned. I saw him,' a young man of solid build and filthy clothes replied as he sat on the ground, hands flopping tiredly over his bent legs.

'Can we do anything more?' one man asked as he wiped his face with the corner of his tunic. 'The fire is out. There's just the mess to clean up.'

'No. No, thank you. Are any of you hurt?'

'Not really. A bit of smoke in my guts…'

'No, thanks be to God…'

'A blister is all…'

'I got me hair burned…'

'You needed to lose some, Jean, we haven't seen your face for a year…'

A chorus of croaking laughter and coughing started up around him and he was relieved that they all survived more or less intact.

'You must go to your homes and get some rest.' Guillaume lifted his voice and it rasped with smoke taint. 'I thank you again and Madame will be in touch with all of you in due course. We are in your debt.'

Tired voices called out night greetings and folk trailed away to their homes in stained and burned clothing, patting Guillaume on the shoulder, nodding apologetically to the two women. Amée and Ariella whispered thanks to their neighbours, their voices almost done, sawed through with smoke and yelling.

The stench of burned cloth hung in the air as Guillaume de Gisborne, Ariella ben Simon and Amée de Clochard stared at the smoking haunches of the mule. Of their storerooms, only one remained and Amée, covered in soot, her hair like a madwoman's, collapsed on the step and wept.

'Did she settle?' Guillaume asked as Ariella walked down the stair after seeing the older woman to her bed.

'I gave her valerian, combed and plaited her hair and washed her face and hands and just stroked her forehead till she fell asleep. She is cut to pieces, Guillaume. She thinks she will lose her husband's business. And I confess *I* am worried. We've lost all except these newly dyed woollens.' She pointed to a pile of folded textiles in the corner. 'All we have saved of Jehan's business, which Amée calls his legacy, is the house and if we are lucky, the ells of the velvet and wool in the far storeroom. She kept saying *Jehan's legacy* over and over again…'

Guillaume washed his hands, the soot wafting in clouds round the bowl to then sink like mud. Ariella passed him a rough linen square and he wiped his fingers, leaving charcoal prints behind. The house smelled of burned everything – cloth, timber, a sorry mule. He could not see how any fabric could avoid being ruined but he would not tell Ariella. Not yet.

'The velvet and wool is purple-dyed,' he said, 'and is to go to the Hohenstaufen court. You know this. It will more than recoup our losses.'

'Do you not think it might reek of smoke? I cannot see the Holy Roman Emperor paying out on expensive cloth that makes him smell of the hearth. I suspect it's more a liability than an asset. This whole godforsaken house stinks!' Ariella flung herself on Amée's upright oak chair. Exhausted, her hair awry, her face smeared with ash, she represented nothing of the contained beauty that organised de Clochard so well. After this latest, Guillaume thought she would have to step up even more to bolster a woman who might be thrown once again into the deeps of grief.

He sat, pulling off his damaged boots and inspecting the soles of his feet, finding a large blister which stood proud and angry. He winced as he prodded it and took up one of Amée's bone needles, drenching it in wine to pierce the blister, the liquid inside running down to drip to the cobbles. He swabbed it with the linen cloth which he dipped in his mug.

'Crusade make-do?' Ariella asked.

'One does what one must and I *have* to move around,' he growled and realised he had been less than polite. But there was something about the evening's events that sat badly, as if there were no such thing as mere accident and so he made no apologies. He thanked God and the Saints for the collegiality of Lyon and the way his neighbours had sprung to the defence of the de Clochard premises. 'We are indebted to a lot of people, Ariella. This will have to be paid back somehow. People have long memories and de Clochard is only just now climbing back on its feet after Jehan's death. That Hohenstaufen cloth *must* be safe…'

'Why don't you rest?' Ariella stood and slipped her arm over Guillaume's shoulder as he slumped on the stool. 'You are exhausted and thinking of all of this does nothing. Tackle it with a fresh mind.'

'You are just as tired,' he said. 'Go now and sleep till dawn in my cot. Amée may be restless. I would keep watch and make sure no coals re-ignite. Besides there are no gates to secure us, and I would not have felons steal anything we have left.'

'Then I shall stay with you…'

He smiled at her for she was a strong-minded woman. '*I* will do it. We need one of us with a clear head on the morrow. And I suspect it won't be Amée. You can think for us all!' He gave her a little push, lifting her hand to his lips as she left. It trailed through his palm like a starburst and he thanked the Virgin Mary for putting this Jewish woman in his path. He watched her climb the stair, her long chemise stained and clinging with damp. She had never been the kind of woman who needed protecting – he knew that the moment he saw her in the Arsenale of Venezia, standing beside Ysabel of Gisborne and young William, protecting them like a wolf-mother with cubs when she flicked the cutting shears into a felon's chest. Besides, a Jewess who had been through the York Massacre and lost her mother in that fated tower and who had fled across Europe to Venezia, was as much armed against life as himself.

Christ's breath! Poor Widow de Clochard – her husband dead, her daughter gone long since and the de Clochard business almost destroyed. And not just *her* business but Gisborne's and Ben Simon's as well.

He rubbed his eyes. They were gritty with tiredness and ash, and sore from the smoke but he'd gone whole nights in the Holy Land without sleep during the Crusade. He sighed, scooped some water from the ewer into his eyes and blinked, then splashed the rest of the water across his face. He dragged on the boots again, swearing as the leather slid over the burst blister, and then headed off to walk the remains of the yard until the new day could shed light upon their dilemma.

The smell of the yard hit him like a sword blow.

He wanted to leave and stand on the edge of the Saône, taking deep breaths, and with each breath forget what lay ahead and indeed what lay behind. He made a tentative list in his head as he wandered in the last hours of night – a mule carcass to be dragged away, buildings to be replaced, stalls, shelving, bolts of cloth, gates…

Damn it to hell! It didn't take long for people to turn their backs on merchants once a supply had dried up, as there were always others to take their place with rapidity. Business in this time of burgeoning trade was cutthroat and traders rarely made old bones.

The sky was softest grey, no longer the ebony nap of night. A few stars flickered lazily as if they knew their time was almost done and as if they really couldn't be bothered about the dramas of the earlier hours in the de Clochard yard.

There was no point in examining the wreckage in the dark, but he felt he needed to guard the corpse. The comparison might be stark but come daylight, he hoped against hope that they *did* still have a business with a pulse of sorts.

He shivered with cold and returned to the door of the house to grab his cloak from a hook inside. Looping it around and pulling up the hood, he sat on the stone step, closing the door behind him and gazing at the smouldering wreckage across the yard, glad beyond belief that Luzio, if it had been he, had taken the horses and at least one mule from the stable. At least they had transport, although harness might be another thing.

He had almost begun to doze when he heard the sound of crunched stone. His neck prickled and he shrank back into the shadows cast by the house and the ancient oak that cloaked the property. He felt for a weapon and gritted his teeth when he realised he had none, not even the *misericorde* that he normally wore at his belt. He felt around his feet for a stone, curling his palm around one that could make a decent enough hole in a skull and as he straightened, stars exploded across his eyes, there was pain and he fell into a black night sky.

Perhaps a sennight had passed and it was evening again, he did not know. He lay face down, warm blood trickling along the folds of his neck. The thumping ache was like the hooves of Saladin's mounted archers pounding across the barren desert of his brain.

A broken and rusted voice sounded close by.

'Where then?'

'Somewhere…' a whisperer responded.

'The *traboule*,' Rusty replied. 'Has to be somewhere in the *traboule*.'

Guillaume turned his mind from the pounding hooves, dragging at vacuous concentration.

Lyonnais accents…

'Where's the entrance to it, then?' asked the whisperer. 'Did he not say?'

'As his feet burned, he said closest to the gates. God rot his roasted soles!'

'There's nothin' beneath the debris – no handles to doors and no stairwells…' the whisperer hissed.

Agitated.

A sick faint flirted with Guillaume, dark and then light and dark again. Perhaps it was the Ferryman, he of the hooked nose and uncharming face. Any moment now, Guillaume would be free and even in Paradise, because the ache behind his eyes and the pooling vomit on his tongue was surely the end…

'We've got nothin' to show for this except a pile of bloody ash,' said Rusty.

Beyond the gate a cock crowed and a horse clopped along the street. Clip-clop – it measured Guillaume's heartbeat, which in turn echoed in his skull.

'Come on,' said the soft-mouthed one. 'This here's trouble. We've nothin' and he's stripped shreds from others for less…'

Their voices moved beyond the gates or perhaps Guillaume fainted because the silence was blessed and deep.

'Wake, Guillaume. Wake!' Something cool dripped down his neck and he dragged his eyes open.

Ariella…

'By the stars, Guillaume, what happened? There's a deal of blood…'

'Someone hit me,' his voice croaked, maybe even as rusted as that of the arsonist and attacker.

'Who?' Ariella helped him to sit up and the yard swirled round like the rope of a church bell in the wind. The soft light of early morning cast a veil over the dramas of the night before, only the smell of burned mule meat, wool and timber reminding him of what had been.

'I'd stake my life on it being those who burned the yard.'

'It was deliberate?' Her voice squeaked and he wondered if she meant the fire or the attack.

''Ella, I have no answers nor the wherewithal just now. Just a blinding pain.' He reached round to feel the bump, grimacing as he glanced at the congealed blood on his fingers. 'It oozes. Does it need stitching?'

'I think not but I'll clean it and have a good look when you come inside. Can you stand?'

He didn't answer, hoisting himself up and glancing at the sky. 'Is Amée awake?' he asked.

Outside the gates, Lyon went about the business of trade and textiles, money and merchandise and the soft topaz of an autumn dawn sun blessed it all, such normality at odds with the scene of devastation before them.

'No,' Ariella replied. 'I made doubly sure she would sleep for some time.'

'Good. I need to clean up and then have a look at what's left in the light of day and I need to send an immediate courier to Venezia.'

'I have already done so.'

Naturally, he thought wryly. She was Ariella ben Simon, daughter of one of the most successful Jewish merchants in Venezia and she had been trained well.

'Of course you have,' he muttered as his knees sagged, but he concealed the momentary weakness by pulling off his boots at the door and walking into the chamber they called the hall, in which they lived, ate and did business. 'This is sabotage; I am convinced. And to find out why, I must question

Amée without any resultant hysteria.'

'Guillaume, under the circumstances, that's unkind.'

'Ariella, we could have been roasted like pigs on a spit last night. I think someone knows something about Jehan, wants something of his and we must find out what it is.' Without ceremony, he stripped to his *braies*, washing himself from a freshly filled ewer on the table, scrubbing the dirt from every inch of his torso and face. Ariella turned her back as he stripped to grubby, tall nakedness, wiping away soot and ash that had collected in secret crevices.

'Do you think it is cloth or money?' she asked over her shoulder.

He grabbed a clean chemise, *braies* and hose from the pile she had considerately placed on the trestle table. 'Maybe none, maybe all…'

'A trifle ambiguous, Guillaume.' She turned as he pulled his hose into place. 'Sit now and let me dress that wound.'

Compliant for once, he sat on an oak stool as she carefully parted his dark brown hair, soaking the dried blood away, and wiping the cut with a cloth dipped in a bowl of vinegar. 'Bruised,' she said. 'A decent cut too. But you will live, methinks. Have you an ache?'

'Yes, and my experience is that I will…'

'Have it for some time. Yes, I know.' She walked to the door and tossed the bowl of bloody vinegar outside. 'Do we possibly talk secrets? Papers of some sort?'

'Ah, you are so quick!' He looked at her with no real surprise.

'I am a Jewess, the daughter of a merchant. Wealth you seem to have passed over, *and* cloth, and rather too quickly I might say. Why burn the yard for a secret? If it *is* a secret of some sort – it must be documents of value to someone, something Jehan had collected for Gisborne. Here, have some bread with some honeycomb.'

Of a sudden he was hungry, tearing at the wastel, spreading wild honeycomb across the crust with his dagger. The sweetness settled on his tongue and energy began to flow once more.

'Indeed. Secrets. One wonders if Amée knows if her husband had secrets,' he mused, slicing more bread and following it with Burgundy wine which Amée rested in casks in her cellar. They were comfortable, the de Clochards. *Had* been comfortable…

'They were very close, Guillaume. In life as well as business. She functioned within Gisborne's spy network as much as Jehan.'

''Tis true and it's not to be discounted...' But something made him think otherwise. It wasn't anything tangible, just something that set his teeth together. 'In any case,' he added, 'she must understand that her life could have been reduced to ashes and scattered on the wind to the four corners of Lyon yesternight. Her bones could well have looked like the beams out there.'

'Then if you want her lucid and calm, might I suggest you refrain from saying that to her? She aches enough with the loss of Jehan and with the disappearance of her daughter. This latest is the Devil's joke, surely.'

'In which case it is the Devil's demons who hit me. Mark me, Ariella, there is something here for which one could be killed. We must find what it is and fast if we are all to survive.'

Above them, the floor creaked and then they heard a ponderous tread upon the stair, punctuated by world-weary sighs. Amée entered the room dressed in a dark green linen *bliaut* as tired and worn as its owner. But her chemise was as crisply white as her wimple and her veil flicked over her shoulders with more energy and purpose than the wearer.

'Amée,' Guillaume ushered her to the table. 'How do you fare?'

She replied with a heavy sigh. 'May God forgive me, good Guillaume, I confess I am lost...' Her eyes filled with tears. 'With no way forward.'

He hastened to reassure her as Mahaut, their maidservant and cook, carried fresh bread into the room from the kitchen, along with another flagon of wine.

'I am not hungry,' Amée said. 'Take it away.'

'May we leave it? Ariella and I have not broken our fast to any great degree and I am starving. Mahaut, could you bring us some of the newly arrived dates and some more wine, if you would. And cheese?'

Mahaut's hairy double chin drew back and she placed the tray on the table with a thump. She gave him the kind of look reserved for street curs and left, muttering insults.

'She thinks you usurp Jehan. I will speak with her.'

'Amée, I usurp no one, least of all Jehan whom we respected greatly.'

'I know, I know,' Amée said. 'But Mahaut has been with us since we took possession of Rue Ducanivet and she is very loyal and does not cope with change.'

He smiled. 'Do not worry yourself,' he said. 'It's nothing in the scheme of things.'

Mahaut placed a second tray on the table with only a fragment more grace than the last time. He watched her stout figure retreat, thinking she did very well in the de Clochard house. Many of her age were skinny and insipid.

'Sit, Amée. I would talk with you.'

She sat, obliging him with her attention. 'Are we to leave? Are things so bad? This business ... Jehan worked so hard to thrive...'

'I'm not sure that it's good, I don't know yet. But I see no reason for you to walk away from your family enterprise.'

The seeds of Ariella's words floated in his head and took root.

You seem to have passed over ... cloth ... rather too quickly I might say.

Perhaps cloth *was* the target...

'If the Hohenstaufen cloth remains untainted, that is your saving grace,' he said.

'It is sealed in a chest, ready for shipment.'

'We will open it to be sure, as there are reputations at stake.'

And lives lost in the effort to procure the purple dye in the first place. Such a risk, such loss. It is inconceivable that it might be for nothing.

When he had received Gisborne's note informing him of Tomas' execution in Constantinople after the purple dye had been stolen from the Byzantines, he could only imagine what pain the remaining twin, Tobias, was going through. The twin brothers were soul mates from before birth as only twins can be. Guillaume had grown to love his own half-brother but that was a lately acquired kinship and had still to grow deep. Tobias and Tomas had a relationship that was ancient by comparison.

Little acorns and big oaks...

'Guillaume?' Amée's voice broke through his thoughts. She gazed at him with less than her usual acuity, her expression blunted with loss, almost as if she looked beyond him to some distressing scene of the past or future.

He cleared his throat. 'Amée, is there anything ... that is, are you aware of anything Jehan might...'

'Madame,' robust Mahaut called from the kitchen doorway. 'That priest is here. Says he has important business to discuss with you from the Monseigneur.'

'Brother Crispianus? He's here?' Amée grunted and stood, smoothing the tired folds of her gown, patting the sharp creases of the veil.

'Yes, Madame.'

'Then show him in and bring the Venetian glass goblets. Guillaume, may we speak anon? I must see to our guest…'

As she spoke, the priest slid into the room, his eyes shifting to take in the scene. Guillaume disliked him, despised the sanctimonious voice and the obsequiously folded hands. His robes never seemed clean, as if dirt and fading underlined his concept of purity.

'Madame…' Scurf sifted from his almost bald head. 'My poor dear child…'

'Ah, Brother Crispianus, we have lost so much…'

'Have you?' He seemed almost energised by Amée's confession.

'The business is intact,' Guillaume broke in, ignoring the glare from Ariella. 'We had a fire which destroyed two stores. Fortunately…'

Amée's mouth opened and closed as if she would comment but Guillaume took her by the arm and led her to the folding stool near Ariella, pressing her onto it.

'Fortunately,' he continued as he passed a wine to Madame de Clochard, 'we have lost nothing of importance. We stored grain and harness in the burned spaces. Our horses and mules were rushed from the barn to safety.'

The monk smiled – a rictus begot of hours on his knees or flagellating in some cell. 'Monseigneur Renaud will be glad that Our Lord saw fit to smile again upon the de Clochard house.'

Guillaume leaned against the wall, one foot braced on a tawny tapestry stool. 'Then, Brother Crispianus, it is our turn to be desolated. We lived in the belief that God always smiled upon His innocent children.'

'Of course, of course. Do the Proverbs not say *I love those who love me, and those who seek me diligently, find me?*'

'Well, we have not stopped seeking,' Guillaume answered.

The monk, however, had a hide of leather and showed no obvious discomfiture. In fact, he looked at Guillaume as if he would remember every hair and every line on his face. Guillaume imagined it would be stored in a long memory.

'Madame,' the priest said. 'Monseigneur Renaud was concerned when he heard of the fire in his good friend Jehan's house. He sends his blessings and will pray for you at Mass, which he hopes you will attend.'

'*L'Archiveque* is kind and I would ask you to thank him,' Amée replied, dabbing at her eyes with a linen square. 'Jehan had a special place in his heart for Monseigneur Renaud, as you know. I will attend Vespers at the Cathedral, you may tell him. In the meantime, I must help Guillaume and Ariella clean up after the fire and deal with the daily business of de Clochard.'

'God will welcome you into His house, Madame.' The monk's clay-coloured glance took in Ariella, quietly stitching under the light of a window and Guillaume who still leaned against the wall. 'Madame, may I speak with you privately, if you will?' His limp hands moved within his cuffed robe and his sandaled feet shifted on the stone floor – a sound like cloth being torn.

Amée's brows drew together and Guillaume waited. This would be an interesting moment.

She sighed as if the world pressed upon her but softened the exasperated sound by a mannered little smile. 'Dear Brother Crispianus, you can speak freely amongst us. Ariella's father is an equal partner in this business and Messire Guillaume is the brother of de Clochard's other partner. Indeed, as you know, Messire Guillaume is de Clochard's manager since Jehan died. Anything you wish to say can be said confidently and confidentially in front of them both.'

Well-played, Madame!

Guillaume could not help a smile and looked down at his feet, all hose and no boots, so that the priest would not see his satisfaction.

'I think, then, it will suffice if I pass you this.' Scarred and scabbed hands passed a rolled and sealed parchment to Amée. The Archbishop's seal swung free on a red silk cord and a sunbeam caught on the brass coin-sized disc. It glistened and anyone more pious than Guillaume would say it truly was a message from God.

He wondered exactly when it was that he had become so cynical and lacking in piety. Maybe that day in La Flèche…

'Master Guillaume, I bid you adieu,' the monk said, a smile sliding to one corner of his ascetic lips. He looked at Ariella and then away, saying nothing. No one could miss the deliberate snub – and certainly not because she was a rich foreigner's daughter. No, she was a *Jew's* daughter. It was enough for an ignorant son of the Church.

Amée hurried ahead of the man to open the door and the monk passed through to the sodden and ash-filled yard as if he were a papal envoy, if not the Pope himself. He left behind the smell of an unwashed body and bad breath, worse than the smell of the fire and Ariella waved her hands about, grabbing a bunch of dried *lavendula* from a pitcher and twigs of apple-wood, thrusting both into the glowing coals within the hearth.

If Guillaume had been less mannered, he would have spat on the monk's tail.

'Jew hater,' Ariella muttered.

'He's a dangerous fool,' Guillaume said. 'A fool for his manner and dangerous for the ears into which he drips his poison.'

Amée hustled back into the room, having ordered Mahaut to admit no one else for the day, *'for God's sake and ours, Mahaut.'*

She held the parchment out to Guillaume. 'You read it.'

'It is for you.'

'Nevertheless, I would prefer you to read it…'

She sat, her head tilted back, eyes closed and jaw clenched, fingers of one hand drumming on the table. Guillaume wondered in what way the priest's visit had sharpened her anxieties.

He began to unroll the parchment, letting the silk cord dangle, the metal seal tinkling as it hit his belt buckle. He sat on the stool and raised his eyebrows as he glanced at the carefully scribed letter. 'Monseigneur Renaud de Lyon writes as if he is your family. Certainly as if he knows you very well. It is quite personal.'

'The Monseigneur and Jehan were acquaintances. They would play chess together at the palace. They were very evenly matched. Read on…'

Guillaume pushed his hair back and began.

'Madame de Clochard, esteemed friend, from Archbishop Renaud de Lyon, blessed greetings.

I am mortified that my friend Jehan de Clochard's business should be so wantonly treated by the Devil's agent…'

Guillaume looked up. 'The Devil's agent? He makes that judgement so soon?' He frowned and continued.

'I would offer you my prayers to God Almighty and should you need it, monetary assistance. My agent and notary, Brother Crispianus, will be available to assist you. You are aware of the offer made to Messire Jehan of course. That offer is open to you, Madame, with God's blessing.

In Pace et Valete.'

Guillaume threw the parchment on the table where it rolled swiftly back upon itself. 'By God, he presumes, does he not?'

'It might seem so to you, but in truth not so. He offered for the property many times as he and Jehan played chess.'

'I think, Amée, you must enlighten me. Is this something of which Saul and Guy are aware?'

'No.'

Ariella put down her stitching, slipping the threaded bone needle through the scooped neck of her *bliaut*. A trail of ruby silk thread lay like a small bloodstain across her gown and Guillaume's hair stood on his neck. 'Why would the Archbishop want this place?' she asked. 'Does he not own half of Lyon as it is?'

Amée indicated with her hand toward the Saône which flowed with a mellow sweep past Rue Ducanivet and the house. 'This house is perhaps only equalled in its position by the rest in our street – four properties in all. All owned by the Church except ours.' She settled to the telling – a kind of soft rhythm in her voice and Guillaume listened intently, wondering why she had never told her business partners of the Church's interest. He looked at the rotund, veiled woman with her apple cheeks. Perhaps such things meant little to her. It was possible.

'We were market travellers,' she continued, 'drifting from one *foire* to another when we were young and just wedded. Selling small ribbons and linens, the odd piece of woollen fabric, whatever we could find with our limited resources. It is how we got our name – Clochard – *vagabond*. Jehan changed it to *de* Clochard when we settled in Lyon. He thought it gave us a kind of gravitas.' She smiled wistfully back at her friends and Ariella reached to touch her arm as she continued. 'We were quite mature when Jehan met Gisborne in an abbey *dorter* in Calais and Gisborne put a proposition to him. We became conduits – as one does for the man – and our luck changed. He paid well for what we could find out on our travels and eventually we had his backing to settle in Lyon and buy this property. We were tired of travelling and wanted to settle down with our daughter, Jehanne, who was old enough to need a home and respectability. Gisborne's foresight at such a young age was truly astonishing. He was *such* a very young man, maybe seventeen years, perhaps less, when he contracted us. So clever…'

She shook her head at the memory. 'But back to this property. It has its own access to a *traboule,* as you know. So we could unload and store merchandise swiftly and without weather damage. We are much better placed than other textile merchants further into the town and so we became successful with moderate speed. A fact no doubt noted by the other merchants and by Archbishop Renaud. The Archbishop is the second most powerful man in the land after all. Only the King of France and the Holy Roman Emperor supercede him, although one would not tell *him* that. Thus, it was an advantage for Jehan to play chess with him on a regular basis. Jehan loved assuming the role of the amiable, naïve ingénue merchant. It secured much information for Gisborne.'

Guillaume thought over what Amée had said. 'I can see it would be advantageous for the Church to own the whole street. Do you think that is *all* that is at stake? Mere pecuniary interest?' He looked at Ariella and she nodded, agreeing with his line of questioning.

Amée paused, opened her mouth, took a breath and then spoke with care. 'I believe so. I can't imagine what other reason there would be. Not a chess game went past without an offer. Jehan said it was somewhat of an ongoing joke. But toward the end, Renaud de Lyon became a little testy over the thing. In any case, Jehan liked being in the ranks of the best – as much a property owner as a merchant. Only the Gigni own their own premises and they have the might of Florence behind them. Oh, and the Vaudès. Madame Vaudès kept the properties when Pierre Vaudès divested himself of his wealth to establish the Poor Men of Lyon.'

'Were you living here when that happened?' Guillaume asked. He knew Vaudès' history – that as a wealthy man he gave up everything to become a selfless wanderer, spreading the word of God. But Vaudès' word had lately begun to cause ripples and the Church muttered in dark places about heresy.

'We had been in this house a bare sennight and we were invited to a dinner at Madame Vaudès' home. Pierre had had his epiphany long before and had left to spread his word.'

'And did you become friends with the family?' Guillaume asked.

'My word, yes. Madame was kind and welcoming. Her daughters had been entered into the convent at Fontevrault at the time Pierre divested himself of his wealth. The Church benefited greatly from the dower, one assumes. Anyway, even though Pierre had left the world of trade behind, he would occasionally visit with Jehan and they would talk. They spent hours together in this very room whilst I sat up the stair in the solar, stitching. That was until he left the city. But the Poor Men of Lyon are still here secretly, and one of Pierre's followers came to visit with a note from Pierre when Jehan died. The man, Hamelyn was his name, stayed to talk with me in an attempt to give me solace.' She sniffed and touched her nose with the linen square. 'He was very kind and I have a great deal of respect for he and his fellows…'

What Amèe had not said, and which Guillaume knew, was that Pierre had found fault with the scriptures and had parts of the Bible translated to the common tongue. He reverted to the essential message of love from the Gospels and he decried idolatry and indulgences. Afraid of his message, the Church declared him excommunicate. Guillaume wondered if there was a deeper issue at stake in respect of Amée – a connection with heretics. But would it be enough to burn a business?

People have been burned for heresy, a business is nothing in the scheme of things. And it would surely force her to sell…

'But in any case, Guillaume,' Amée sharpened, brushing thoughts of her husband and his heretical friend away. 'This is all history and has no bearing at all on our situation. Even if last night's losses *are* underwritten by my lord Gisborne and by Ariella's father, we will have little ready cash to pay for our daily expenses or our taxes. It would take time for bills of credit to arrive from Venezia. You know this. Thus to have a willing buyer…'

'You have jumped too far ahead. Let me see the Hohenstaufen velvets and woollens first. And Ariella, I am assuming you have our ledger?'

She bent and pulled the little wood-covered book from beneath her basket of threads, flipping through the pages.

'Check our outstanding orders,' he said. 'We have a good supply of wools, linens and expensive trims in the cellar and if they are free of taint, they may just satisfy any outstanding customers. Mayhap you can add value to some ells by embroidering them?'

'Oh, of course!' Amée huffed out a breath. 'I was so distraught I had forgotten. There are English wools in very subtle crimsons and greens, and there is fine bleached linen as well. Ah, if only my girl, my Jehanne, was here.

Such an embroiderer…'

Guillaume edged toward the door with a complicit glance toward Ariella. She would handle the problems within the house whilst he investigated the far greater issues outside.

Finally…

He had chafed to examine the debris in daylight, to find something, anything, that would provide answers.

He walked carefully through the ash, watching it puff up in noxious clouds about his boots. He glanced at the charred and disintegrating beams – what he had told the priest was true. One third of the yard was gone, but the rest of the property was untouched.

The burned buildings had been a barn and storerooms. The barn contained the animals, a cart and harness. The grain for the house and livestock was all burned, having been stored in the other half of the barn. It had been a stone and timber building with no windows – what Amée had euphemistically called the buttery or granary, depending on what she wanted Mahaut to retrieve. Now it was a pile of wet rubble topped with snapped and charcoaled beams.

Next to the 'granary', was another storeroom – one that represented a substantial recent investment for de Clochard. Normally, the space would have been filled with bales of quality textiles, with furs and boxes of trimmings. But only two days previous, Guillaume had ordered the goods be removed to a cellar beneath the house to make room for a shipment of raw wool from England. He had found a family who would scour, spin and weave the wool into fine cloth and he had sourced dyers of good reputation. It was a new venture and he had the bales of wool stacked straight from the river into the store.

Huh! He might as well have poured *livres* into a cesspit.

So … two buildings, grain, a mule, harness and a large shipment of wool bought at cost from England.

But there was a third space, an untouched store at the far end of the yard…

He looked around the de Clochard property. It was no wonder the Church craved ownership – if *that* were the case. The yard was big and square and had its own charm, stretching from Rue Ducanivet to La Grande Rue and with three floors. In the centre of the courtyard, an oak tree spread its ancient branches. It was rare to find such a tree amongst the dense housing on the banks of the Saône – someone had a gentle hand, thought Guillaume, when they had built this house, taking care to leave the tree to grow and prosper. Its shade, its shivering leaves, its bare tracery of branches in winter, its deep cushions of acorns and leaves in the autumn – it was as though it held the property in its arms, its leafy canopy reaching far to the eaves. The side closest to the fire had singed and the autumn leaves hung brown and crisp and Guillaume hoped the tree would not suffer.

The gates of the property opened onto the riverside street, Rue Ducanivet. If one followed the street to the southern corner and climbed a gentle slope, one soon arrived arrived at the Cathedral Saint Jean. It was an elderly church, its construction begun at least one hundred years before, and it had assumed a grandeur befitting the Archbishop. But then, thought Guillaume, power had the capacity to erode, and Archbishop Renaud was afraid enough for his assumed authority and wealth to shelter behind the defensive walls of Château de Pierre Scize than reside in the episcopal palace close to Saint Jean's.

Lyon had a framework and history that made Venezia look unformed and haphazard. But that was changing faster than the blink of an eye as Venezia's hold on trade from the east grew more powerful. Which was why he, Guillaume, was in Lyon. The Gisborne house was spreading its trading wing, solidifying it, making money in a time when men wanted to better themselves. Availing themselves of good textiles and funnelling them from the east via Lyon to the rest of Europe was a step up the ladder. Making enough money for Jehan to furnish his house with good oak chattels and with horn windows, and even, in the chamber which he and his goodwife had shared and which Amée used as her solar, there were two glass windows, imported at cost from Venezia.

The house foundation was built of stone from the Roman days of Lugdunum, but then the building lapsed to occasional blocks of stone and unassuming timber, the layers telling stories of Lyon's history. Jehan's thick, bubbled glass windows looked across to the other bank of the Saône – from the east window and past the Pont du Change, one could just see the front of the Jewish quarter with the homes of the moneylenders. On a fine day, Jehan's windows would be thrown wide and one could listen to the honk of river birds, and on a cold day, the windows would be shut fast to cosset and protect those within. An expensive affectation, that glass, but Amée preened with the ownership.

But the property's true value lay in the storeroom upon which Guillaume's eyes now rested. It sat safe, untouched by the fire – its stone and timber façade taking up one whole side of the yard. Guillaume was well aware that it could hold the way back to prosperity for the merchant alliance of de Clochard, Gisborne and ben Simon. The venerable stone was heavily chiselled and uncompromising and the space had no windows, its door chaste in iron and the thick timber stained black with age.

Inside lay the Hohenstaufen wools and velvets, but inside too lay an entrance to the odd subterranean ways of Lyon that led down from the town. These *traboules* led to others, all the way to the River Saône.

Anyone with a good Christian upbringing might believe they trod the path to Hell and worse inside the *traboules*, so dark and steep were they. People never lingered. Goods were carried up and down swiftly to the river barges, and invariably with loud banter. It was this swift delivery to merchants' properties on which the town thrived. From the moment barges arrived from points north and south, merchandise was unloaded, transported into the town and placed on sale, almost before ropes had been looped over the timber moorings.

Guillaume breathed in.

Venezia always smelled musty – as if one's woollen cloak had been bunched up wet in the bottom of a chest. Sometimes, the sea air ameliorated the odour, but it was still marshland when all was said and done. But Lyon had the scent of forest on the wind and it settled Guillaume's soul when his mind wandered to past times. He would close his eyes and breathe in the scent of oak and birch and remember a village called La Flèche – a place with the reputation for making the best bows and arrows in Anjou.

His fingers flexed as he breathed, almost as if he were going to reach for an arrow to nock it. Instead, he pulled the key from his belt where he had tucked it, and fitted it into the door. It was a big cast iron key and it required two hands to twist it. This was the entrance the arsonist had wanted to find and whomever had said it was close to the gates had not been lying.

Because that's what pain does. It makes one admit to things. But why did the torturers want to know?

He had just begun to turn the key when a voice sounded from the burned gateway. 'Guillaume! Guillaume!'

Luzio!

He turned the key back to make sure the storeroom was locked, and slipped it back into his purse, making his way to what was left of the big timber gates. The dead mule had begun to smell rancid.

'Luzio, well met.'

'A fine entrance you have, Guillaume, my friend. It makes somewhat of a statement, does it not?' Luzio laid his arm along Guillaume's shoulder. 'You have survived yesternight's conflagration, praise be. It was a fierce flame. As the poor mule will attest.' He lifted a linen square to his nose.

'It was. And we have all survived. The neighbouring families gave us more support than I thought possible. If we had not had that bucket chain, I doubt the outcome would have been as good. I am yet to run an accounting, but we are not dead in the water, I think.'

Luzio grinned. 'I can see that. For all that you fought fire till nearly dawn, you are remarkably sharp.'

Guillaume felt anything but. Anger festered like an open sore, and impatience gnawed at him like a rat at a crust. The responsibility for de Clochard, for his half-brother's and his friend's investments, indeed for Ariella and Amée, sat heavily.

Until he joined the Gisborne house, he had been responsible for none but himself. To be honest, he had not even felt the responsibility for his fellows amongst the crusaders. He had fought to keep himself alive, nothing else.

Well, almost nothing else…

If perchance he protected others in the doing, well and good, but for months before finding Gisborne and after Arsuf, he had turned inward, maintaining a dour calm to the world. It kept others at arm's length and enabled him to pretend that all was well.

'The animals have survived and rest in my uncle's stables. The remaining mule has a burn which one of our ostlers is tending,' Luzio added.

'The Gigni family are kind,' said Guillaume. 'But tell me, how came you to be here as the fire took hold.'

Luzio looked at Guillaume from the corner of his eye, a faint smile upon his lips. Satisfaction, Guillaume would say. Luzio was too good looking by half – eyes fringed with women's lashes and silky black hair that waved upon his nape. He had a chin marked by an angel's thumb – a cleft that sat in the middle of a powerful jaw. Everything about him exuded moneyed masculinity. He held up a finger and tapped the side of his nose, replying in his seductive Florentine accent. 'A woman…'

'Of course,' Guillaume responded with conscious irony.

'A Madonna of the Angels,' Luzio sighed. 'Mature, soft, knowledgeable and…'

'Enough, Luzio. 'Tis your business. For me, I thank the stars you leaped to our aid.'

'One thing, though,' Luzio said quite seriously. 'How came your gates to be unbarred at night?'

'Indeed.' Guillaume sat on a bench beneath the oak. 'I barred them myself at dusk…'

So who must I not trust?

'Someone unbarred them?' Luzio's brow furrowed and then he sucked in a breath and leaned forward to fix Guillaume with an astonished gaze. 'God in heaven, you think the fire was deliberate?'

Guillaume closed his eyes; he had hoped to keep such deductions to himself. 'We do not know. But the gates were barred when I went to my bed. Beyond that?' He shrugged, hopefully curtailing any further interest. He examined the burned buildings. 'I want everything rebuilt before the sennight is past.'

Luzio frowned. 'The sennight! Then I wish you much luck. Most carpenters are at the Cathedral Saint Jean, working for the Archbishop. He has … delusions of grandeur. But anyway, a sennight is a demand too far, my friend. Look at what has to be demolished…'

Guillaume growled. ''Tis not what I want to hear, Luzio. I have a business to run…'

Luzio stood, pulling at his fine scarlet tunic, settling the handsome leather belt with its silver buckle and patting the scabbard that hung by his thigh, resting his hand on the pommel of his sword. Guillaume had only ever seen the weapon as an affectation, but watching the Florentine's fingers settle easily at the grip, he wondered.

Can you fight, my friend? Because I may have need of you…

'Guillaume, don't fret so. I could approach my uncle, if you would like. He has two carpenters he divides between the Forez forest manor and Rue Tramassal.'

Guillaume accepted the offer because now was not the time for stubborn pride, but he told Luzio he would like to approach Messire Gigni himself; it was right and proper. He would find the cash to pay the carpenters somehow. Besides, in Lyon the Gigni were considered successful and highborn, despite being foreigners, and they mixed with the nobility and Church with ease. It was best, Guillaume thought, not to alienate them.

He gripped Luzio's hand in acknowledgement of the offer – he liked the Florentine's easy manner after all. It made for an uncomplicated friendship, despite that to others the man seemed irresponsible, conducting very little business for his uncle. However, Guillaume felt, rightly or wrongly, that there was a genuine nature behind the louche behaviour. But right now, and despite it all, Guillaume wished him gone and it showed, because Luzio took a step toward the gates.

'I can see you are distracted by what confronts you and I beg your forgiveness for interrupting. I shall leave and if you need anything at all, send a messenger. And do get rid of that mule! By the way, did you know you have a clot of blood at the back of your head?'

Guillaume's hand flicked to his skull and came away stained. 'I tripped back over a fallen beam and struck a paving stone. But Ariella cared for it, it is a mere surface wound.'

'They breed them tough in Anjou, do they not,' Luzio said as he passed through the gates. '*Valete*, my friend. And don't be too concerned about the carpenters.'

Guillaume saluted and watched as the Florentine strode along Rue Ducanivet toward the Pont du Change, whistling as he went.

They don't just breed toughness in Anjou, Luzio. They breed much else besides...

And he wondered why he had lied to his friend about his head injury.

CHAPTER TWO

<u>x</u>

Relieved at his solitude, he unlocked the storeroom door, slipping into the darkened space, pushing the door wide to allow the light to enter. The chest lay before him, the oak glowing and satin smooth, iron latch and lock glistening darkly. He removed the lock and lifted the lid.

Inside, the cloth lay folded in unbleached, course linen that caught on the roughened skin of his fingers. The aromatic tang of *lavendula* filled the chamber and he bent and sniffed the linen, as sure as he could be that if there was smoke taint, the linen would smell.

Nothing…

Carefully he eased the wrapping away from the first bundle, running his fingers over the nap of velvet. It reminded him of rabbit fur, or the soft plush of a dog's ear. He lifted a fold to his nose and sniffed once.

Twice to be sure…

Nothing but lavendula. *By the Virgin's robes, thanks be!*

He lay the fold back down, wrapping it back in the linen as if he swaddled it, placing it in the chest and scooping a handful of the *lavendula* flowers over the goods. He unwrapped the second package, the magnificent fine wool dyed with Tyrian purple. He sniffed. Sniffed again to be sure. It was subtly scented with *lavendula* and he rewrapped it, laid it in the chest and swiped his hands together in satisfied relief. Lowering the lid, he pulled the latch down, slipped the lock through and clicked it shut.

Henry Hohenstaufen, the Holy Roman Emperor, son of Frederick Barbarossa, would pay well. His agents had liked what they saw and after some bartering over price, had agreed to eight ells of the ebony velvet and six ells of the purple wool for more *livres* than Guillaume had thought possible, but he had emphasised its value to the Byzantines, of the way it denoted imperial power through history. Mostly he emphasised its rarity throughout the known western world. The courtiers had salivated on Henry's behalf.

'The Emperor will be the only ruler inside of the empire and out, who will have clothing made from this. A statement, I think...' the stringy one had turned to the shorter one for agreement and the shorter one had breathed, *'Indeed...'*

As Guillaume recalled that moment with the courtiers, he also had a sharp series of thoughts...

Richard of England had been hounded across the seas from Outremer and subsequently through the lands of the Holy Roman Empire until he was caught by Duke Leopold of Austria and finally imprisoned for ransom by Henry Hohenstaufen. Eleanor of Aquitaine, the Lionheart's furious mother was breaking England's back as she raised the ransom monies and it was believed the exchange of coins for kings would take place in the new year.

Was the purple cloth to be cut to clothe the Emperor so that neither Eleanor nor Richard would ever forget the imperial power? Such was surely the mindless way of the nobility. A small chest of *livres* would be handed over when the agents took possession of the cloth and that must happen soonest because somewhere in Guillaume's mind a chain rattled.

Were the arsonists looking for the purple cloth? Did someone wish to prevent the select cloth reaching the Hohenstaufen court by burning the de Clochard yard? That de Clochard had purple cloth to sell had been a closely guarded secret, but secrets can be discovered. Perhaps this was something vile between rulers of men...

Once in Anjou, he had seen a nobleman's jeweled ring – a smooth semi-precious purple globe but with the sanguine tint of *rubinus lapis*. They called it *amethystus* and perhaps it was but it reminded him of the *rubinus lapis* he had seen often upon the Jews' scales in Outremer. *That* was the hue of this wool – a godly blend of purple and scarlet, a colour so regal and so remarkable men would bend knees before a king who wore it. Henry the Sixth, the Holy Roman Emperor, would be unique and every ruler, even every petty nobleman, would try to match the colour the Byzantines had protected for so long

And then of course there was the fact that velvet had been purchased for the Emperor, a rare fabric woven by the Moors in Al-Andalus in a history that went back more than four hundred years. Saul had found the Moorish velvet weavers and purchased the cloth in times past because its rarity gave it a value beyond belief.

Ah, so much in the casket for which men might feel envious…

Guillaume lifted the bar to the *traboule* entrance and hastened down and around the stone stair. His feet tapped and echoed and his fingers trailed in an unconscious fashion along the cold inner wall of the spiral. The air smelled foetid with the humid aroma of the autumn river. He unlocked the bottom door and and light bled through.

He blinked as he stepped out – the sight of a silver gold river, moored wooden barges, some rafted together with others. Directly in front was the barge he sought and he hurried to it, seeing a group of men bent over a game of chance. The dice rattled as the small wooden blocks struck the deck – a collective groan from the players wafted up the stone river walls.

Only one man was silent – a giant with broad shoulders, thick arms and a chest the depth of an ox's. His hair fell down his back in a ragged blonde waterfall and he had the mark of a slave burned into his forearm.

'Petrus!' Guillaume shouted and the giant saluted back after slipping silver coins into his purse.

Petrus spoke to his gaming colleagues, his voice a volcanic rumble and then he hoisted himself over the wale of the barge, landing lightly on huge booted feet and stepping with ease along the mud and rocks of the shore. He wore a thigh-length red-ochre tinted tunic with the hem embroidered in symbols of the far north from whence came the Varangians. Perhaps he had once been one of the Byzantine guards of that name but no one dared ask about that or the slave mark. Petrus might pick them up by the throat, slam them against a handy wall so that all their life's breath flew out, and rasp,

'Who wants to know?'

Such a brutal manner belied the small tooled, almost feminine purse hanging from his belt. But the accompanying war-sword that many said was beyond the lifting strength of the strongest man, affirmed the man's volatility.

'Messire Guillaume. You have work?'

Guillaume reached to clasp Petrus' forearm in greeting. He often wondered if his own arm would be crushed, but Petrus was gentle with those he liked.

'I do,' Guillaume replied. 'Do you want to go north?'

'This is for Sir Guy?'

'Yes.'

'How far north?'

'The Hohenstaufen fortress. You might need more men. I want the Hohenstaufen courtiers and the cloth they have bought to reach the Holy Roman Emperor intact.'

'Ach, 'tis not so far north, then. River or land?'

'River as far as possible and soonest. Leave before dawn I think.'

Petrus twitched his bottom lip and then he nodded. ''Tis done,' the words rumbled out. 'You will pay half now and half when I return.'

Guillaume agreed, privately wondering if Petrus might meet his match one day and never return.

'I *always* return, Guillaume,' the giant said with a glint in his fierce eyes. 'Always. And I think *you* need guards as well. Someone wants to get rid of de Clochard.'

'Maybe. Have you friends you can recommend?'

'Petrus has good friends, yes. I will send them to you before dark.'

They discussed the imminent departure and then Guillaume climbed back up the *traboule*, happier than he had been before speaking with Petrus.

Petrus was one of Gisborne's men, another member of the clandestine cadre across Europe that was used for the gathering and unravelling of information. He would drink with the Hohenstaufen household, would talk and play games and pretend to be drunk and no doubt he would return with a secret or two that Gisborne could manouevre to his advantage.

Guillaume was about to head into the street when Ariella called him. She ran across the yard, her wine-coloured hair streaming behind. She eschewed veils – *'a nuisance'* – and despised tied and piled hair – *'I might as well cut it off'* and Guillaume admired her spirit. He had respected her courage since he met her and they had like minds and spoke freely about many subjects. Her thinking had a seductive quality, coming from the kind of educated mind he valued.

Would he wed her?

In a heartbeat if her father would allow her to wed outside her Faith. For Guillaume, Faith was superfluous to a relationship; what mattered was what emerged from one's heart and one's soul and it had little to do with which god one might worship. Faith and souls were not intrinsic; he had learned that during the Crusade.

Right now, he waited for her to speak her mind.

'And?' she asked with a petulant sigh – exactly what he expected.

'And what?' he replied. She could be referring to anything after all.

'The cloth, Guillaume. Don't play with me. I am not of a mind and I am surprised *you* are. Is it tainted?'

'No, 'tis perfect. I go to the agents now and have organised for Petrus to accompany the courtiers and the order to Germany.' The oak leaves shivered in the breeze and a few fell, one or two settling in the autumnal glory of Ariella's hair. He picked them off. 'It must leave soonest, 'Ella. There must be no further risk.'

'You think they wanted the cloth?'

He heaved a sigh. 'I wish I knew. What else would it be? Amée was not forthcoming of anything of Jehan's that may be coveted, was she? Perhaps the cloth was not meant to reach the Holy Roman Emperor. A thousand things race through my mind – repairs, orders, deliveries, monies, reasons why. And not least, I must inform the agents they leave by barge before dawn *and* with a guard. You must excuse me, my dear. I have much to do.'

'Of course,' she kissed his cheeks and stepped aside and he left the yard, stepping over the stinking mule carcass and hoping no one would call at Chez de Clochard in his absence and confound a day that seemed to march to its own melody.

He had always valued his solitude.

Of course the Crusade gave little solitude to any man, but he knew how to shrink inward. It was easier than engaging. But then he had entered the Gisborne house, the home of his half-brother, and solitude became a figment of his far imagination. So that as much as he valued his place in the family, as much as he valued the respect and affection of the men with whom he worked, as much as he craved Ariella's company, right now he revelled in being alone. It gave him time. Time to sift through his thoughts, to think and plan without the constant tidal flow of household emotions. The streets were quiet because everyone had made their way to inns and booths – anywhere that sold food and it had been a long time since dawn and the breaking of fasts. As he walked, he glanced at the busy river, acknowledging that there was the very occasional time when he wondered if he should just jump aboard a barge and head upstream without telling anyone.

Just leave…

But then why had he bothered to seek out his half-brother in the first place? Surely he knew it would mean an end to a solitary life.

Of course he knew.

And he knew also that after the Crusade, he craved 'family'. It was undeniable.

As undeniable as the sound behind him…

Almost a footstep or two.

He stopped.

The sound stopped.

Unconsciously he had turned into the lane that shortcut his way to the Place Saint Jean and it was ill-lit in the alley, houses leaning down over the rough cobbles, bare soil indicating where cobblestones had been lifted and stolen for the building of a new house wall, a new street elsewhere.

The houses on either side were high walls of stone and wood, no doors, nor windows. No one could see him.

He turned a circle. No one there…

He headed forward again, the sound behind continuing to pace with his own step and as his hand reached for his *misericorde*, he sensed someone so close that he bent double, down to the dirt, and swung the blade quickly.

A leg, if I can slice a leg…

A miss and a return stroke from his assailant which he parried, swinging his arm up and catching the attack sword at its grip, right on the bone of his forearm. He grunted, annoyed with the sound. By return, there was an exhalation of breath from the stranger and it gave him a mere moment in time. He stood swiftly and swung again, this time with the needle sharp point of the dagger leading the swing. It entered cloth, and he cursed as he tried to free his grip from the folds of the attacking cloak.

His assailant had a sword and it whispered its way toward him, a skein of words that meant death in any language and if not death, then veins open to stream blood on the cobbles. He jumped back and the *forte* edge flew past him, hissing through the air. He locked his gaze on the eyes of the man who would kill him, the face shielded by a cloak hood.

'Coward,' Guillaume uttered. 'Show your face!'

The man laughed, a sour sound, flipping his hood back to reveal an unfamiliar and pockmarked face framed by greasy hair. He swung again and Guillaume leaped away, the attacking sword edge catching the wall with a sharp crash.

Let him come on…

If he could get the fellow close in, he could use the dagger.

He whirled to the other side of the alley, knowing the man would follow, heard the grunt as the sword was lifted.

No room … use it to the advantage.

He ducked down again, it seemed he tripped, the fellow moved in, raising the sword higher for a death stroke upon the neck. He slashed with the *misericorde*, found some flesh and twisted the blade up.

A leg, yes! The blood flooded down over his hand as he withdrew the point.

The man shrieked, then growled, lifting the sword again, but already Guillaume stood, thrusting high this time. The stomach. He ripped the knife upward, hard and angry, tearing cloth, skin, muscle and sinew and then pushing in, in, in…

The sword dropped, the attacker fell against Guillaume, looking straight at him, blood seeping from his mouth. Guillaume flung him away, his *misericorde* pulling out, a further gush of blood and terrified hands grasping at the wound.

Guillaume ran.

He rushed into Place Saint Jean, into daylight, threading into a small crowd that mingled in front of the church. His breath heaved in and out and he looked down at his clothes. Blood everywhere.

Christ and Jesus!

He grabbed his cloak folds and dragged them across his clothing, looking for the horse trough that stood in front of the church.

There!

He took a breath, deep down. Another…

Calm…

He bent over the trough and used the linen kerchief Ariella had placed in his purse, to wash his bloody hands. A horse tied nearby sniffed the stained

33

water and snorted. Guillaume held his breath for a few heartbeats, waiting till the pounding slowed, and then he dried his fists on his hose, relieved that he could cover the blood that lay on his boots with dust. He pulled at his cloak folds to check for stains – nothing!

Thank you, God.

Standing straight, he shook his hair back over his nape and drew the persona of de Clochard back over himself. Someone wanted de Clochard gone and any who worked there.

Later, Guillaume...

He turned across the square.

The Inn of the Golden Fleece befitted agents of the Holy Roman Emperor. It also betrayed an irony – an apt name surely when all de Clochard's newly purchased fleeces had been torched in a golden flame. The inn sat prosperously opposite the Cathedral, the bells of which had just chimed for Sext, and the two courtiers chided Guillaume for not coming earlier, that they had heard of the fire and wished to return forthwith to Germany to inform the Emperor of the loss of the cloth.

'It is why I am here, my lords.' He held his cloak tight. 'The cloth is perfect. It was packed and stored far from the blaze and is in fact ready to leave and soonest, with an armed guard organized by de Clochard.'

'But we will not allow it to be conveyed to the Emperor without confirming for ourselves that its condition is as perfect as you say,' the small fat one spoke through a squat nose and with a piece of rabbit stew nestled in his beard.

Guillaume invited them to accompany him, giving a coin to an urchin to go ahead and inform the house they were to expect honoured guests. If he did what was required, there would be money at the house for him. The child's eyes gleamed and he bit the coin, then ran as if the Devil were behind.

'My lords, when you see the cloth is perfect, you will agree it must leave for the Hohenstaufen court immediately. I have arranged for a barge to leave before dawn with de Clochard's most able guards.'

Of a sudden, they could see the need for careful behaviour and so decided to leave all bar their cloaks and weapons behind. After all, they had much to gain on their successful return to Henry's arms.

They left without paying their bill, Guillaume thought it was best, saying he would arrange payment on the morrow and then he guided them the long way home, past the subtle finesse of Rue Tramassal, past the crowded yards and houses of La Grande Rue, and finally to Rue Ducanivet and the burned entrance to Chez de Clochard. The breeze had cooled to clip at their heels, reminding them that late summer was well and truly done and winter only weeks away.

The short courtier whined, hoisting his cloak collar higher and skirting round the dead mule with a fold to his nose. 'Indeed, Messire Guillaume, if your cloth is pure, we must be gone immediately. We will be travelling slowly and need to be well done before winter closes the rivers and roads.'

Guillaume smoothed the fellow's feathers and was relieved to find Petrus' huge bulk inside the gates as they entered and so he was introduced to the courtiers as the captain of de Clochard's guard. They assessed his height and muscle and pronounced themselves well pleased. Petrus by turn, bowed in a suitable fashion and asked if they could ready themselves to depart before dawn. The short courtier sniffed, and in an effort to reclaim the ascendancy, said the cloth had first to be approved and Petrus bowed again with deference, turning to Guillaume and saying with good manners,

'Messire, I shall return at dusk with my men. Do you need aught else?'

Guillaume thanked him. 'Yes. Can you organize the removal of the mule and soonest?'

'It will be done, sir.'

Guillaume led the courtiers to the oak trunk and its valuable contents, blessing the fragrance of *lavendula,* hoping they couldn't smell the iron odour of blood upon him.

The cloth passed the olfactory test, soft hands holding the folds to Germanic noses, the courtiers' lascivious fingers smoothing the nap. After taking the men into the house, he requested clothes from a bemused Ariella, asking that she entertain their guests until he was changed. He opened his cloak and she saw the blood and he whispered,

'Ask no questions, 'Ella. Not now. Go to them quickly. I shall be a moment only. Can we give them a bed for the night?'

'Of course. Amée will sleep with me and she can give them her marital bed. It is big enough and she will use her best linen for them.'

He nodded and in a few rushed heartbeats was back with the envoys, his clean hose twisted uncomfortably in his haste.

The courtiers drank smooth Burgundy wine from Amée's busy Venetian goblets before kissing the ladies' hands and retiring to the glass-windowed chamber. She would send them their dinner and they could sleep, ready for an early departure.

Guillaume knew that their presence placed a huge burden on Amée, Ariella, and Mahaut, but he thought it was safest for the successful outcome of their biggest sale yet.

The sun was sinking as he leaned against the house wall listening to the crisp rattle of oak leaves and the occasional patter of acorns on the ground. He had a sick intuition and it had served him well on the Crusade.

Ah, he knew he would not sleep well this night.

Ariella met him at the door when he turned round. 'Before I ask what happened, I would like you to see what we have done. Although stitching in the face of such gore seems of little interest.'

'I would rather see stitches a dozen times a day or more than what I confronted earlier, Ariella. Someone wanted to kill me, but I gave back more than the attacker bargained for. There is nothing else to say but much to think on. Do not tell Amée. Not yet.' He put his arm around Ariella's waist and guided her into the house.

The women had been busy whilst he'd fought for his life. With sharp-as-a-dagger bone needles and using fine red and gold silk thread, they had stitched decorative bands along the tissue-fine linen. The woollen cloth had been trimmed in blue and green thread. Each length of fabric was folded neatly, embroidered edges to the fore and stacked on the table.

The aroma of a stew laced with *rosmarinus* and *thymum* drifted from the kitchen and for the first time the acrid aftermath of smoke and flame drifted away from the house.

Guillaume washed his hands in a bowl, using a bar of soap that Ariella had purchased from an Arab trader at a *foire* – a hard bar filled with the dried heads of *lavendula* and which scoured the day away.

'These are exceptional,' he said, examining the cloth, displaying a knowledge he didn't have. 'You've done well.'

Ariella was winding threads onto an oak bobbin that he had whittled one sunny summer hour in Venezia and the polished wood glistened in the light of a candle tree that flickered behind her. Dusk had enclosed Lyon with speed and Rue Ducanivet became lost in the encroaching shadow. Amée obviously had no qualms about the cost of good beeswax candles.

'We did our best,' Ariella replied with a faint edge of irony. ''Tis fortunate we are able to handle a needle. The designs are different enough from the norm to attract attention – the gold thread especially.'

Amée sat back in her chair. 'So with the Emperor's cloth and with these lengths, we are viable?'

'I believe so. Ariella, have you seen my list of suppliers?'

'By your cot. I will get it.'

She hurried up the stair and Guillaume sat on a stool with a sigh, leaning his head back against a wall.

'A long day, dear boy,' Amée's voice was kind. 'I am grateful to you, Guillaume. You took control as I unravelled. 'Tis good that you have persuaded the Emperor's men that we are a solid investment.'

He shrugged with a touch of diffidence as Ariella walked back into the room with a small leather-covered book. She moved with the grace of a woman with breeding, her hips swaying subtly as she flipped a lock of hair back over her shoulder.

He took the book from her and cast a glance over the course parchment pages. He could not afford good paper and his writing was rough but at least he *could* write, a rare thing in an archer. He had learned quickly in Venezia where it was the norm for a merchant family to read and write. Already he knew the names of de Clochard's suppliers:

Geoffrey and Gilbert from England; woven wools of a firm nature that sold well at the bottom end of the cloth market. Balwiinus and Ericus from the Low Countries; again, woollen cloth but a finer grade, and soft linens of the kind women favoured for chemises and undergarments. There was Gaspare of Florence – expertly woven linens and the odd length of velvet, legacy of the Moorish trade.

He relied on Saul, Ariella's father, for the superlative silks from the East and for which both women and men salivated. There were as many male aesthetes as there were women of fashion in the town. He noted there were six bales due any day from Venezia. The nobles of Lyon would chitter like birds around the baker's stall when he offered ells up for sale.

'We have a shipment from Venezia due in the next few days if the weather continues to hold. So I suspect we might just be able to trade out of this. We must let Lyon know that de Clochard is as strong as ever.'

Amée clapped her hands together. 'Then I shall go to Mass and give thanks. Shall you come with me? It is dark...'

'Do you really need to go? I have employed guards for the business but you are not familiar with them yet.'

'Guards? Huh.' She frowned. 'The Archbishop and Brother Crispianus expect me, Guillaume. It will be noted if I do not attend.'

'Women are oft ill after a tense time, Amée. Do you want to go?'

'Not tonight. Not at all, if I am honest.'

'Then send a message to your friend the priest, begging his indulgence and asking he and the Archbishop to pray for your imminent return to good health after your experiences. I suggest you do not tell them we have the Hohenstaufen courtiers here.'

She clucked, a disturbed little hen scratching in the dirt to turn up something good after a less than gentle night and day. 'If you say...' She took up a quill and began to write a note in her hasty merchant's hand. 'And he is *not* my friend. I just think it is good, politically and diplomatically, to keep him on de Clochard's side...'

Not just a merchant's wife, then, are you? Methinks you know more than you are saying.

'And,' she continued. 'I have concerns that you have employed guards. I feel it makes de Clochard look tentative and afraid. We have never had guards and people will talk, thinking we are a bad risk.'

Since he had said they might trade out of their problems, Amée's manner had changed. She sat more upright, her eyes exhibiting a glint that had disappeared during and after the fire. Her tongue was once again as loquacious as ever.

'Mahaut,' she called. 'Mahaut, leave our meal!' She allowed her voice to shake and tremble, the epitome of an ill woman, and signalled for Ariella to support her as she stood.

The maidservant entered, a look of dislike directed at Guillaume.

'Mahaut, I am unwell. Take this,' she held out the folded parchment, 'to

Brother Crispianus at the Cathedral. Ariella will help me to my bed and you can attend me when you return. Go, go.' She made a shooing movement and sighed as if life squashed her down.

Guillaume, amused with her little act, walked to the door and held it open for Mahaut as the woman pulled her cloak from a hook. 'I will wait at the gate for your return. Shall you be alright alone?'

She snorted at him, mumbling something angry and bitter, but he ignored the vitriol as they walked across the yard. He wished Johannes of Lübeck, a Gisborne guard, had not returned to Venezia after seeing he and Ariella to Lyon. To have one more man amongst a house of women. Just one...

Mahaut's face was a picture of annoyance and she huffed petulantly as he stood at the burned gates.

'Mahaut, I have no claim upon your mistress, nor de Clochard. I am an employee, just as you are. If I order you to do something, it is because I am the manager, the steward. And like as not Madame has asked me to give you orders. I do it with respect for Madame but I do it with respect for you as well, because you have been in this house far longer than I.'

He fixed her with as conciliatory a glance as he was able and she stared back at him, her irregular, widely-spaced eyes assessing. She hefted half a nod in his direction and squeezed her ample bosom and buttocks past him.

The street was lit by a few torchères and braziers and folk hurried past. He watched her until she vanished, a skirl of nightbreeze blowing crunchy autumn leaves along the cobbles, flicking fanciful words at him as they passed the gates, *'Eyes at your back. Eyes at your back.'*

'Messire Guillaume,' said a voice behind. It vibrated from a cavernous chest.

He spun round, flicking out the *misericorde*, the needle-sharp blade between himself and whomever may threaten him.

'Your wits are as sharp as the blade. Put it away,' Petrus said, towering over Guillaume and knocking his hand down so that it ached.

'Christ Jesus, Petrus! Don't creep...'

'It is good to have eyes in the back of your head,' the big man replied. 'You are on edge I think. Is there more reason than I have already noted?'

'Maybe. I meant to tell you when you returned with the men but I wasn't expecting you so soon.'

'I said I would come imminently. I have five men. Three for Germany and two to leave here.'

'So six of you to sleep here tonight? We are short on room, Petrus. We have the Hohenstaufen envoys with us.'

'You have a storeroom and a cellar. I see no problem.'

'Food?'

'We have eaten but will require food for travelling. As to those who stay with you, that is for you to manage.'

'Of course. To be honest, I am glad to have your men here.'

'You are tense…'

'I was attacked.'

'But you hit back?'

'He will die.'

'Good. It is as it should be,' the big man said. 'Now I will introduce you to the men.' He whistled and five shapes loomed out of the flickering dark and one by one, entered the yard. 'Albus, Simon, and Bayard. They will accompany me to Germany.'

Each man nodded as they passed Guillaume and he was struck by the evenness of their height, big men who threatened by size alone. He noted weapons as well – swords hanging by thighs, bows over shoulders, small bags filled with a costrel no doubt and perhaps a change of hose or tunic.

'And for de Clochard we have Herviet…' the man was tall and thin and hefted a pike to his other shoulder to shake Guillaume's hand. It seemed he had an index finger missing but his eyes were bright and he smiled. 'Messire,' he said. 'Have no worry. I'm left handed and good with it.'

'And finally,' Petrus interrupted. 'Rufus.'

Guillaume looked more closely at the hooded man who brought up the rear. He knew a Rufus once…

'Christ on the Cross,' he exclaimed. 'It *is* you!'

Adam of London grinned, throwing back his hood and revealing the fierce red hair for which William of Gisborne had called him Rufus. 'Aye, 'tis me.'

'But how…'

'Long story short. When Johannes returned to Venezia, he mentioned a few things about de Clochard – the *traboules*, the vulnerability – and Sir Guy sent me. I arrived yesternight and sought out Petrus which was my charge from Sir Guy. From what I've heard, seems Sir Guy was right. You *do* need me.'

Adam had been Gisborne's Master at Arms when Guillaume was welcomed into the family in Venezia. In those early days, he chose to live and train with the guard and liked them all.

More importantly he trusted them.

Guillaume led the way to the storeroom, torches flickering round the yard, elongated shadows climbing the walls of the house as though souls of the dead were rising from the ground.

As they passed the door to the house, Ariella greeted them, smiling widely when she saw a face she recognized. 'And you, Adam!'

'And me, *Dameisele*.'

'It's so good to have you with us. It's been a difficult time.'

'I've heard. But we are all here to help. *Dameisele*, I have a letter from your father…'

Ariella's face lit up – it was as though the moon had slid from behind a cloud to shine its dulcet light upon her. There was a faint sparkle in her eyes, tears unshed by the only child for the father she missed. Guillaume wished he could hold her. He had escorted her to the Jewish Quarter a number of times to see those who knew her father. It was the closest thing to being with family – sharing the views of her fellow Jews. And yet, she had asked to come to Lyon, leaving her father far behind.

'Go,' she said. 'I'll bring wine and food and blankets. Guillaume, there's a brazier next to the storeroom. Perhaps if we lit it?'

'She is a good lady,' Petrus observed as Guillaume unlocked the door and pushed it wide, placing a torch in the bracket on the wall.

'She is,' he replied. 'Madame de Clochard could not do without her. Madame wishes her daughter was here; you know she went missing?'

'I heard. Murdered or picked up for the slave trade.'

'Who knows? It is a sad thing for a mother to lose her child and her husband over a quick three years. Petrus, we need this chest moved to where it will have no taint from brazier or torch. This is your cargo on the morrow. Can you organize it? I must wait at the gates. Madame's servant carried a message to the Church of Saint Jean for her. I must see her return…'

'The Church!' Petrus spat into the courtyard and then pushed Guillaume forward. 'Do what you must, my friend, and then we will talk.'

Waiting outside the yard, Guillaume could not help but lean against the wall and close his eyes. Christ, he was tired and still so much to sort through. The thump to his skull beat like a war-drum and the muscles in his arms and legs were starting to bellow, but he had been exhausted before. Even so, he tried not to think of his cot and the wool-filled pillow Ariella had stitched for him – down that path lay inattention.

'Messire Guillaume!' his arm was punched as the redoubtable Mahaut hove into view.

'What took you so long?'

'Brother Crispianus was busy and I had to wait,' her voice was like turgid mud. Jesus and Joseph, he tried so hard to like her because she was a hard worker...

'Did he send a message by return?'

'For Madame yes. Not for you.' She stalked off like a disgruntled sow and Guillame hurried back to the storeroom; there was something in Petrus' tone, something of import.

'We have placed the chest outside under covers. It should suffice. Now come, we will speak outside,' the huge northerner said after ordering Adam to the gates till dawn. They followed Adam who had shouldered a stave and whose sword rattled mutely by his thigh as he walked.

'He is well-armed...'

'It is better to expect trouble and be prepared than to think all is well and find a knife at your throat. Messire Guillaume, I will be fleet so do not speak.' A meaty finger was held up in warning. 'Listen to me. One of us...'

'Us?'

'I said do not speak. *One of us* was in Rue Ducanivet just before someone yelled fire. He was keeping watch. Your gates were indeed unbarred and two men slipped through, were there briefly and then slipped out again. It was assumed you had business with them but then smoke was smelled and flame appeared and it took little to imagine who started it. Our watcher ran from house to house shouting *'Fire!'* and helped with the bucket chain as long as he was able. Unfortunately, he was burned badly on the hand and went to the infirmarian at Saint Nizier to be doctored. It was during that time you were attacked within the yard. And more particularly, as our watcher hurried to Saint Nizier, he saw a monk.'

'A monk?'

'A man of the Church.' Petrus spat; he was evidently not a Believer...

'Brother Crispianus, that creeping turd of a man!'

'Perhaps. Perhaps not. His robes were in shadow and there was nothing to identify him. But you should know.'

Events finally sharpened Guillaume to a knife point. 'I should know a lot more,' he snapped. 'Who is this watcher of yours? Do I know him? And why does he watch de Clochard without my knowledge? And why did Gisborne send Adam without informing me? Does he not trust me?'

'Gisborne does what he wants and in any case, a letter would arrive at the same time as Adam. It is of little import,' Petrus growled. 'Perhaps you should think that he does what he does to protect his brother and the ladies.'

'He protects his investments.'

'Then he is a wise man and you are stupid with tiredness and make little sense. Go to your cot. All is taken care of.'

'I will get your half-payment...' Guillaume seethed with a tired impotency.

''Tis done. Your good lady has seen to it and much besides. Methinks the Germans will be treated like kings under her care. Go.' Petrus turned away to the storeroom, forestalling further conversation, acorns and oak leaves crushed to powder beneath his tread.

Of a sudden, a wave of exhaustion rolled across Guillaume and he didn't want to think or digest any of what he now knew. He felt his way through the darkened house to his cot and crashed down upon it, the rope slings cracking and sighing as he stretched fully dressed, boots and all, and closed his eyes.

Sleep claimed him, but not before a vision slipped through his mind of a man strapped to a trestle, dirty rags binding his mouth. His body arched and an inhuman cry gurgled beneath the filthy folds as a flaming brand burned his soles to a crisp...

'Wake up, Messire Guillaume. Wake up!'

A voice sounded, muffled as though the mouth were covered in the middle of a gritty sandstorm. Guillaume turned in the cloying darkness.

A hand grasped his shoulder and he sat bolt upright, grabbing the forearm to twist and snap it. But another hand reached down and that same forearm was crushed hard against his throat so that he couldn't breathe.

'Leave it, man! It's me, Adam.'

'Jesus and Joseph!' Guillaume coughed and pushed Adam's arm away.

'I tried to wake you gently, sir, but you were somewhere far away in your sleep. Not here, that's for sure.'

'I was tired. And I thought … never mind. Is aught wrong? The gates?'

'Herviet is at the gates in my stead and there's nothing at all wrong except Petrus said to wake you so you could farewell the envoys in as dignified a manner as becomes de Clochard. His words not mine. He speaks pretty when he wants.'

Guillaume swung his legs over the cot, surprised to see he was still booted and clothed. Some crusading habits died hard. 'Where are they?'

'The Germans? Breaking their fast. And Petrus and the men have been loading the barge with supplies. The chest will be loaded last for safety, after your guests are aboard.'

'Ariella is awake?'

'Aye, although Madame still sleeps. But *Dameisele* Ariella ordered that grumpy old sow, Mahaut, to lay a good table. The Germans are eating like princes, which is just as well as I think Petrus will be pushing his men hard. He won't be stopping for riverbank refreshment.'

Guillaume washed his face, scrubbing sleep away before it reclaimed him. Ariella had left a wooden comb and he dragged it through his hair, tearing at the knots and wincing as the teeth slipped over the scabby lump on his skull. The aching bruise reminded him of all the issues that had plagued him yesternight before he had crashed onto his mattress, issues that sleep had finally drowned in a dank blackness. He pulled his tunic and hose straight and grabbed the belt he had shucked off the night before.

Adam hustled him. 'Come on, messire. You'll do. They are not royalty.'

'They might as well be, Adam, for what they are purchasing. To be truthful, a chest of *livres* doesn't even begin to cover the expense. Ask Tobias next time you see him. I think he might agree. The dye used for the cloth is creating its own chaos.'

'Can't be sure we will see Tobias anytime soon, sir…'

'How so?'

'I'll tell you after the Germans have gone, messire.'

Guillaume buckled the belt and led the way to the stair. 'And don't call me messire. I was one of your men once.'

'If you say. I was just being polite – your brother is a nobleman after all.'

'My brother is a merchant and a spy. If you asked *him*, I think he would disown the nobility outright.'

'Aye,' Adam whispered. 'Have to say he's only Sir Guy when he thinks it might pay. Right then, *Guillaume…*'

They entered de Clochard's main room where Petrus was chivvying the Germans to finish. The envoys grabbed some bread and shoved it in sacks, along with costrels filled with watered wine that Ariella handed them. She must have been tired, overseeing Mahaut and making sure a table fit for courtiers was set. Instead, she glowed with a morning dew freshness, charming the envoys, subtly flirting with them as Guillaume had seen noblewomen do with knights and troubadours. The envoys stood and bowed to her, taking her hand and kissing it, thanking her profusely for her generosity and wishing Madame de Clochard prosperity.

'My lords,' Guillaume said. 'You have all you need?'

They turned toward him and mouths opened to reply but Petrus intervened. 'Good sirs, dawn approaches with speed, we must be gone before light. If you value the secrecy of your departure…'

The men fussed and Petrus pushed them toward the storeroom and the *traboule* door. Guillaume cast a thank you over his shoulder at Ariella and he and Adam followed Petrus, the chest and the envoys down the stairwell, their feet brushing the steps in quiet whispers and the old walls damp beneath their palms. Adam had grabbed a torch as they filed through the door and it was the only other light they had, Petrus guiding the envoys with his own sputtering flame held high. For safety, he dowsed it as they passed through the low arch onto the riverbank and Adam left his inside the *traboule*. Beyond, a quarter moon cast a pallid light over the river and a damp mist twined amongst the reeds and over the stones, muffling any sound they might make. Guillaume thought that just this once, God might be on their side.

The barge slapped back and forth in the night breeze and cloaks began to flap, Petrus urging the envoys to be silent. Along the banks all was quiet, barges moored but with crewmen in the town taverns until dawn. The river sat at mid-height and the envoys climbed aboard, their feet almost slipping on the night-damp plank that stretched from wet stones to the wales of the vessel. The chest was heaved on board and lashed down after a covering of a heavy hemp cloth was laid over it and finally Petrus stepped across the plank, the piece of wood bending with his weight until Guillaume thought it might snap. He wondered what brute force the men would need to shift the barge along the river with its cargo – and Petrus – but then the northerner sat opposite the chest at an oar, and the boat balanced evenly on its flat hull.

'Cast us off, messire, when you are ready,' he spoke in hushed tones. 'And listen to what Rufus might have to say. He is well-informed.'

Guillaume cast a quick glance at Adam and Adam grinned back.

'That's me,' he whispered.

The thin German edged to the side of the barge, speaking directly to Guillaume. 'The payment is with *Dameisele* Ariella. We will send a note with your man, if we require more cloth from you.'

Guillaume hoped to God the Emperor would be pleased with the quality of the purchase and nodded his thanks, wishing them well. '*Valete*, my lords. Safe journey.'

He and Adam untied the bow and stern lines and pushed the craft out from the shore. The oars rattled out as the four men, Petrus and his chosen three, began to pull. Not a word was spoken as the craft moved silkily away on the river and as they disappeared into the rivermist dark, Guillaume found that breath he had been holding gushed away.

'Nervous?' Adam asked.

'To a point. There are a lot of souls resting on the cloth reaching Henry Hohenstaufen intact, Adam.'

CHAPTER THREE

×

'Living and gone,' he added but hadn't meant to speak thus. Perhaps recent events greased the wheels.

'You talk of Tomas,' Adam unhooked the torch from the *traboule* wall and they began to climb.

'Yes. And Toby. How does he?'

'Who knows? He arrived from Constantinople and departed on the same day. Took his horse and only spoke to William and to Gisborne and I think even that might have been by accident. Gisborne says he went to his family in Pigna but there has been no word and when we asked Mehmet to tell us what happened, he said *"It is Tobias' story to tell, may Allah give him peace…"* Methinks the old man grieves.'

They had reached the entrance from the *traboule* into the storeroom and as he stood there, Guillaume had no trouble drawing up an image of Mehmet, that quiet, considerate physician with the soft manner and the iron will. He could even hear his mellow voice with its throaty Saracen accent, *'It is Tobias' story to tell, may Allah give him peace…'*

He turned and locked the gate behind them, Adam placing the torch in a bracket and hefting a bar across. 'Huh, these *traboules* – a great strength for Lyon, I think. But a weakness as well…'

'As you say,' Guillaume said, frowning as he added, 'Adam, I think Mehmet grieves justifiably.' If he chastised the Englishman, he made no apologies.

Adam held up his hands. 'Don't take me wrong, Guillaume. We all grieve for Tobias and Tommaso. We are family in the Gisborne house.'

Guillaume nodded, feeling as empty as the hogsheads in the yard.

We need rain to fill the barrels…

He looked at the dawn sky which was overcast, with heavy clouds sitting atop Lyon.

But if we have rain, the yard will be a heaving black mess, the carpenters unable to re-build…

They walked out of the storeroom to see Herviet standing at the entrance, his pike angled across, blocking entry to any who might try. The smell of singe and scorch was less overpowering and the mule had been carted away – Petrus had been as good as his word.

Had he the illusion that managing de Clochard would be easy? Not at all. It required ears to the ground and he liked that – the challenge of bringing something to the market before anyone else and making money from it. But there was a certain amount of obsequiousness required. He found that hard, especially knowing that the Church and the nobility frowned upon the merchant class here in France – used them for sure, but frowned upon them. So different to the Italian states where merchants were a force with which to be reckoned and where noble families enjoyed the mercantile life as much as the traders themselves – especially in Venezia, in Genova, Pisa and lately Firenze.

Did he *expect* cutthroat behaviour? In the back of his mind there had always been the thought, because where money was made, men's need to avail themselves of it was overpowering. Perhaps he had hoped against hope that de Clochard was a mild-mannered little business that offended nobody. Not so little though, and with powerful neighbours like Monseigneur Reynaud of Lyon and the Gigni.

But no…

In truth, he knew part of his crusader's soul would begin to thrive on the threat that now surrounded them. He needed the call to arms to jerk him out of the profound lethargy he had been feeling since he was wounded in England as he protected his half-brother from a vengeful assassin. He wanted to succeed in Lyon for Gisborne's sake and for Ariella's, but maybe for himself as well. He needed to find a new life away from the mire of the past and this was it and he would defend it against all comers. Ah, perhaps his battle-lust had not died a death after all. It was something he would not tell 'Ella, not yet – although she might understand, from the viewpoint of her own vile history.

'Dark days, Adam,' he said.

'Which brings me to this place. Deliberate arson and two violent attacks upon yourself. Someone doesn't like you.'

'Doesn't like me or de Clochard?'

'Christ's toenails, Guillaume, you're one and the same. What we have to do is find out who doesn't like you and why.'

'An easy task by the Saints,' mocked Guillaume. 'We will have solved the mystery by Prime.'

'Ah, get off. You're a moody bastard when you want. You and Sir Guy come from the same pot, that's for sure.' Adam could say anything it seemed, especially since Guillaume had reminded him of his superior status over Guillaume in the past. 'And yes, we will find out. And then we shall play a little game of retribution.'

Guillaume shook his head, rational argument sifting Adam's words. Sometimes when he debated reasoned ideas with himself, he felt he should have been born to the law, not archery. 'Retribution is well and good, Adam,' he said, 'and it would truly give me pleasure to play the game back. But I have the widow to consider, as well as Ariella. And not to mention the Gisborne and ben Simon investments.'

'Payback can be carried out in the dark,' said Adam. 'It's called subtlety.'

'Then having achieved payback, one hopes and prays it stops dead there.' Guillaume pushed the thought of a place called La Flèche away. No matter how much he tried, it raised its phoenix head in everything he did.

'Indeed,' said Adam with sage irony. 'Herviet!' he called and the man turned. 'Have you eaten?' Herviet nodded, waved and turned back to guard the gates. 'Good,' said Adam. 'I'm tired and hungry and wasn't looking forward to relieving him whilst he ate. Do you think *Dameisele* Ariella could spare some food for us until we can supply the store-room?'

'Adam, there will only be one of you eating at a time, so the house is yours. We would be a poor place if we could not sustain you as you protect the house. This is your new family.'

Adam bobbed his head. 'Thank you. Very kind.'

They entered the house and the smell of fresh baked bread pervaded every corner – that moist smell with the sweet edge of ferment. Guillaume's mouth watered. Mahaut sighed and slapped down pitchers of watered wine, a pewter plate of blush-red apples – stalks and dried leaves still attached, and a block of cheese. Each platter vibrated with bell-sound as it hit the table and Adam screwed up one eye at the offensiveness of it.

After Mahaut had left, he cut himself bread and cheese, saying, 'Ah, she's a breath of fresh air, that one!'

'If you say,' Guillaume grinned. 'Although one must give her dues – Madame de Clochard swears by her loyalty and service to the house.'

'Well there has to be something to be said for her because her nature's as pleasant as a week-old carcass. And she doesn't like you – *which* I shall be remembering. Who else might you have offended in Lyon?'

Guillaume sat back and poured some watered wine into a mug, noting the bleached colour and deciding that Mahaut would further penalise he, Adam, and Herviet by giving them more water than wine.

'Christ knows. I've read back through our order book to see if there might be someone who received low quality or delayed orders and there is no one. We have good relationships with everyone, the Jewish quarter, with other merchants and trades. We pay everyone in cash on time and have no debt outstanding. They all came to our aid during the fire and the Gigni are stabling our animals. Does that not imply trust and respect?'

Adam frowned, puffing out a disturbed breath. 'Then there is only one area we haven't examined.' He took an apple and began to peel it carefully, loop upon loop of ruby-striated skin falling in a pile at his feet. He bit into the apple, crunching the sweet flesh, juice running freely down his chin.

Guillaume waited, knowing full well what would come but in no way wishing to anticipate the Master at Arms. He'd rather not discuss it at all.

'So, Guillaume. The Church…' The Englishman wiped his chin with the back of his hand.

'Indeed. The Church.'

Adam raised a sandy eyebrow.

'I *have* no relationship with the Church. Brother Crispianus, the Archbishop's notary, and I do not get on and as for Monseigneur – I have never spoken with him. He is merely a figure by the altar at Mass.'

'And…'

'And what?'

'That is not all, I think.'

Guillaume grunted. 'And when did you begin to see what might not be there, Adam?'

Adam grinned, tapping the side of his nose.

'Jehan de Clochard and the Monseigneur were friends and played chess regularly,' Guillaume said. 'After the fire, he sent his godforsaken notary with an offer to buy this property.'

'Ah. This now becomes interesting.'

'Enough to burn the property? Or to attack me? Enlighten me.'

'True. But maybe Guillaume, we are dealing with two separate issues here. Which makes such a coincidence providential for each enemy.'

'You make it sound like a war.'

'War isn't always massed troops and border clashes. It can be much more insidious.'

As an image of the blood-soaked sands of Arsuf floated before Guillaume, he asked, 'How do you propose to unveil who *are* the enemies? Church, state – an enemy is an enemy. All *I* want to know is why?'

He debated telling Adam about the man whose soles had been burned. But he wanted to carry out his own discrete investigation; de Clochard was under his aegis after all.

He sat back with his watered wine in his hands, pushing at the tension which once again climbed up his body. It was as if the fire had reignited a smouldering ember that had sat buried since he had left the bloody fields of war. There was a fragrance drifting from his mug, the faint aroma of spikenard. Perhaps Mahaut had placed one or two drops in the bottom of the jug to disguise the fact that it was lesser quality than would have been offered to the envoys. Amée's spice chest was a thing of great beauty – many of the spices came through Saul's trade with the east and they were privileged indeed to have food that was delicately spiced. Like the glass windows, it was another mark of Jehan's increasing prosperity … until the fire. He sipped and then waited for Adam's blinding common sense to flash forth and Adam bent to the task readily.

'Let's start with the Church,' he said. 'I am assuming Madame de Clochard can tell much of her husband's relationship with the Monseigneur?'

'She has indeed done so.'

'Ah – but not enough, patently, or you would surely have more to say.' Adam laid the apple core on the table. 'Tell me about your relationship with this Brother Crispianus that pits him against you.'

'I disagreed with him.' Ariella's image vacillated between he and Adam – her lovely manner, her questioning intelligence, her outrageous courage. 'And I consort with a Jewess. *That* is enough to enflame his zeal. You would not like him, Adam. He's as cold and shadowy as a mountain ravine. If he lives by any creed at all, I doubt it is one professed by the Church.'

'Another Jew-hater within the Church is not unusual. How did you disagree with him?'

'I sold cloth on a Sunday. And argued the point with him.'

'But if he is a zealot, Guillaume,' Adam tapped his mug, 'and if he has the ear of the Monseigneur, should you not be a little more wary?'

'You think the fire was caused by him? That it is *my* fault?' Guillaume's eyebrows rose.

'I didn't say that. But I think the man bears watching. Especially as Petrus said one of his men saw a monk at the time of the fire.'

'But the monk was not identified…'

'True. But we have some interesting facts, do we not?' He flicked his gaze from his mug to Guillaume's face. His eyes were an intense blue and they pierced Guillaume, and he almost felt himself revealing the rest of the story about a tortured man.

Almost, but not quite…

The sound of yelling penetrated the walls of the house, Herviet shouting, angry voices in reply.

'Jesus and Mary, what goes?' Guillaume threw his empty mug on the table and hurried to the door with Adam who muttered with irony,

'Ah, 'tis surely the revolt!'

Herviet stood at the gates with his pike pointing at two men and two ox-carts loaded with heavy timber beams and planks. The men argued back and forth until Guillaume yelled for quiet.

In Rue Ducanivet, passers-by had stopped, forming an interested knot that scrutinised the entrance to Chez de Clochard, and a small dog ran back and forth barking shrilly as the men traded insults. Standing tall in his dark tunic, Guillaume was aware that people watched with curiosity and he knew he must handle this with care. De Clochard's reputation had stood on a knife-edge over the last two days and it must be seen to be functional and organized within.

'Stand down, Herviet,' he ordered.

Herviet turned and being a military man to his core, shouldered his pike in an instant. 'Messire...' he bowed his head.

'My good men,' Guillaume addressed the carters, 'This is the de Clochard yard. Can I help you?'

The older one wiped sweat from a flushed face. 'Messire Guillaume?'

'I am...'

'We come from Messire Luzio. We are the carpenters to rebuild your burned chambers and gates and we bring timber and tools from the Gigni house. Your man would not let us in.'

'But I haven't spoken to Messire Gigni nor ordered timber...'

'I wouldn't know, Messire. Perhaps you should read this?' He passed Guillaume a roll of parchment.

Unravelling it, Guillaume glanced quickly at the name at the top and the seal at the bottom. The wax was honey-coloured and still smelled fresh. It bore the imprint of a machicolated tower and the name, of course, was Luzio's.

Was he ordering his uncle's men and supplies on a whim? Guillaume felt a surge of anger at his friend's bald behaviour. The crowd, seeing that the excitement had stilled, moved on, the little dog giving one defiant and hopeful bark. Guillaume began to read.

Guillaume de Gisborne, from your good friend, Luzio Gigni greetings, with an offer and an invitation to mark our friendship.

In respect of the carpenters and timber which you have received, I informed my uncle of your dire situation and he deemed it right to send our carpenters and timber at no cost. I hope our efforts meet with your approval and that the measure will be new gates and store space by the end of a sennight.

I would also invite you to attend my uncle's spectacular hunt in the Forez at the end of the sennight. It is a chance to show Lyon that de Clochard thrives, is it not? Please come, my friend.

Valete...

Guillaume rolled the parchment, held it tightly and with a smile and gritted teeth he urged the carpenters to enter, apologizing for the confusion. The men clicked their tongues, urging the oxen on and the carts and the animals made their ponderous rumbling way into the yard. Ariella watched from the door and smiled broadly as one beast lifted its tail to fill the yard with the sweetly green reek of steaming ordure.

'As you can see,' Guillaume said. 'We have not begun to clean up the debris, but at this point, it is paramount for me to have the gates repaired and soonest.'

'Indeed it is, sir, and if you will allow us, we can easily pull away the burned timbers and have the gates repaired by nightfall.' The older carpenter laid his hands on the uprights. 'These are untouched. 'Tis only the gates themselves that are scorched,' he said as he pulled one of the gates toward him and burned chunks of plank fell to the ground. 'Even though this looks bad, it will take no time to pull it apart and repair it. Mind you, we can do nothing about the damaged ironwork.'

'It doesn't signify. All we need are gates that we can bar. If you can do that, we shall be well-pleased.'

'Then we will begin. And if we can get it done fast, then we can clear the yard ready for a clean start on the morrow. One thing – it will be a very basic repair, sir. There are stone walls which have tumbled. Have you found a stonemason?'

'No...'

'Then if you wish for stone walls again, I can speak with a friend. But the repair will take longer.'

'Do what you can then, to give us weather-proofed storage for our animals and feed and the stonemason can follow later. Is that possible?'

'Indeed it is, sir. We'll just start then.'

Guillaume liked the no-nonsense manner of the tradesmen as they rapidly unloaded the carts, unharnessed the oxen, tethering them and pulling sheaves of hay from the cart to keep the beasts content whilst work was carried out. In a short space of time, the sound of cracking and dismantling was replaced by the sound of hammer upon timber as thick, heavy planks were attached to the gate frame.

Relief coursed through Guillaume like a mountain stream. By dusk this night, they would have the gates secured and they could all sleep a little easier,

Adam included. He turned to see the Master at Arms leaning against the wall with arms folded, yawning widely. It occurred to him that Adam probably hadn't slept for days, having arrived in the dark and gone straight to Petrus and yet not once had the man complained, taking his role as seriously as he had at the Venetian villa.

'Adam, take to your cot. It will be *your* watch before you blink, if you are not careful. Was it not you who told your men to take sleep when they could, that it would be the difference between life and death if one was fogged with tiredness? We will continue our discussion this evening.'

Not that I shall be relaying anything else…

Adam yawned again, his square jaw opening wide. 'Right you are. Call if you need me.'

'Hopefully we won't need you and by the time you wake we will be significantly more secure.'

'As you say…' The Englishman headed to the storeroom, dragging his unremarkable tunic over the red hair. His chemise rose up with the effort, revealing a body striated with muscle tone.

Forceful…

As Guillaume stepped inside, he crunched the parchment into a rope-like skein. He hated debt of any kind and especially to a family that was considered almost noble by the Lyonnais' citizens. Nobility, power and corruption – they all went hand in hand; he had seen it often enough. And being indebted put one in their power. And the note patronised him, he was sure. An invitation to a hunt to show what particularly? That de Clochard now played with the big houses?

Damn Luzio!

To him it was just a game. Despite that Guillaume liked him and they had an evenly weighted friendship, *this* – he screwed the parchment into a ball and little flakes of dried wax fell onto the stone floor – tipped the scales the other way.

He walked up to his small chamber, the space whitewashed like a monk's cell, indeed it might have been one and Brother Crispianus would surely have approved. A cot, folded blankets and a good oak chest with clothes folded military fashion inside and then another smaller chest on the top. It was into this that he inserted a key, lifting the lid and dropping the parchment ball inside.

As he relocked the chest, he knew he had little option but to request a meeting with Messire Alexandrus Gigni. He would ask for the costs so that he might pay. With what he had no idea and it made him feel petty and churlish to think thus, but he would not have de Clochard beholden to anyone.

As to Luzio, he would find him and explain. They were well enough acquainted now for him to speak plainly and surely to have Luzio understand. If not…

They had met by the river at the *traboule* entrance that led up to the town. The *traboule* passed the de Clochard subterranean door as it wound upward, opening onto La Grande Rue and then down and up again to Rue Tramassal, home to the Gigni. Had anyone any doubts as to the scale of Gigni's wealth, they had only to look about them. Rue Tramassal *was* the Gigni, the façade of the buildings blended in honey-tinted stone and timber to look like one extensive house. Some would say that it rivalled the Episcopal Palace, but in truth it was a step down and Guillaume had no doubt that was deliberate. Better, like Jehan, to set oneself below the Archbishop than to compete.

Both Guillaume and Luzio were ordering the unloading of barges and their men had arrived at the *traboule* entrance together. Luzio looked at Guillaume and grinned.

'Shall we toss for who goes first?'

Guillaume's eyebrows lifted. Single-minded and serious about his position as a merchant, he was surprised someone should gamble with the right to proceed into the *traboule*. But he was new to Lyon, new to his mercantile employment and had no wish to antagonise.

'If you wish,' he agreed.

'My name is Luzio Gigni. You know my uncle? From Rue Tramassal?' The fellow opened a soft leather purse hanging from his belt and extracted a silver *livre*.

Guillaume nodded. 'I know *of* him but have not had the pleasure of his acquaintance. A worthy family…'

'Indeed,' Luzio smoothed back a flop of black-silk hair with a hand whose skin was smoothly olive, except for a scar that laced proud and erect right across the top. 'Worthy enough to presume to settle *me* down apparently.

Backs or fronts?'

Settle him down? And he gambles in the course of business?

Clearly the might and wealth of the Gigni had not yet won the battle with Luzio's glib approach to life. He flashed the *livre* in his fingers, waiting for an answer and smiling the charming smile of a man used to beguiling his companions. One couldn't help liking him…

'Backs,' Guillaume said.

Luzio shook his fist with the coin enclosed and then flipped the piece onto the back of his hand.

'*Madonna Mia,*' he laughed with a flash of white teeth. 'Backs it is.' He sketched an elegant bow, indicating the *traboule* entrance, the stones and mud of the river incongruous against his silken appearance and satin-smooth manner.

They had been friends ever since –and in that time, Guillaume had become as proficient as the most learned notary from Bologna or Paris. He had met with other merchants, excluding the Gigni, although the illustrious family acknowledged him in passing, and besides, their nephew, Luzio, had formed an acquaintance.

Luzio was often at his side when he was out and about in Lyon – Guillaume decided the man was bored amongst the Gigni but he had yet to discover what was Luzio's fascination with a small trading house and himself in particular. He was amused to watch the Florentine's smouldering manner as they traversed the Rue des Trois Maries, past the bath houses, the whores leaning against the doors. They would call '*Luzio!*' in breathless voices. '*Good day to you…*' He would blow them kisses and they would simper, whilst toward Guillaume, they would whisper '*Et tu, Messire de Gisborne, et tu…*' as if they were even more familiar with every part of him.

He would frown from his substantial height and walk on and a skein of laughter would chase after his cool indifference.

'You know they flirt with you, Guillaume,' Luzio said one day. 'They say a tough nut has the sweetest meat.'

'Is that so, Luzio? Then if I am a tough nut, what might you be?'

'Ah, a plump date from the east. Decadent, tender and promising much…'

Truthfully, no one but Ariella was able to soften Guillaume's hard edges since he had arrived in Lyon but Luzio always tugged at the corners of his mouth. Occasionally he actually felt a belly laugh daring him to let it fly free

– almost but not quite.

Guillaume was about to leave his room when there was a soft knock.

'Yes?'

'It is I,' Ariella pushed the door open with her hip, her hands filled with a heavy little casket which she laid on his cot, the mattress dipping. 'From the envoys, and here is the key.'

She passed him a plainly forged key, like the Germans themselves – no nonsense. He unlocked the casket, raised the lid and inside lay six open linen bags filled with silver and gold French *livres*.

The Gigni debt is paid...

'Half a king's ransom,' Ariella breathed, her fingers stroking one of the bags. The coins shuffled and shrank from her touch.

'At the very least ours,' he replied and if there was any relief or even concern in his voice he let it lie. 'I must go to town to do business.' He counted out more than a handful of coins and placed them in his purse, a black leather one that hung from the handsome ebony leather girdle Lady Ysabel had given him before he left Venezia. 'And we must sequester the rest away. At the moment, it's all that stands between us and a certain amount of disaster.'

'But we will sell the embroidered cloth tomorrow and you said we have the silk coming. Or had you forgotten?'

'No. I hadn't forgotten. It is just that I must pay a rather substantial debt today.'

'A debt? But we have never been in debt...'

'Indeed. But we now have guards, carpenters and timber to pay for. Above and beyond our daily expenses.'

'Guillaume...' she pressed his hand. 'Do you not think that whatever we make tomorrow will refill this little bag and then when the silk comes, we will be secure again? If you are so very worried, I know my father's friends in the Jewish Quarter would make us loans. There are times when we need operating capital to tide us over. I am sure Joshua...'

'I have no doubt, Ariella, and we may have to avail ourselves of his services, but let's try not to. I would prefer the company to sink or swim on its own than be beholden to anyone outside of our current partnership. Danger lies down that path. The Gigni have given us timber and time, with no cost to us, they say. But it is a debt in any other language and debt puts us on a weak footing. Gisborne and your father would agree with me in this instance, I think. Someone is endeavouring to destroy de Clochard and I will not give them any help. Now come…'

They moved the chests out of the way and Guillaume pierced his knifepoint into a gap between the wall and the frame, easing part of it away. It was an odd thing to hide something from Amée who was the main partner in the business, but her mouth was sometimes too free. It was worth noting. And of course there was the redoubtable Mahaut…

Be honest, Guillaume. You don't like her.

But then liking had nothing to do with trusting. He liked Amée, but sometimes he wondered if he could really trust her. It was why money was hidden, after all.

They lay the linen bags in the musty darkness of the wall cavity and then replaced the loose frame, big chest and small chest which he unlocked to retrieve Luzio's note. He pushed it into his purse as Ariella picked up the envoys' casket and they prepared to leave the room. But she turned back to him, her face furrowed.

'Ariella?' he asked, stepping toward her.

'Are you afraid?' she asked.

Such a simple question.

Am I afraid?

There was no dissembling with Ariella. From his first conversation with her after his arrival from Outremer, when they had discussed the vengeful attacks upon the Gisbornes, he knew obfuscation was not her way and that it showed her deductive powers little respect.

'For myself, no. I have faced worse. But for de Clochard…' He took the casket from her and then rubbed her upper arm. 'But for you and Amée, yes.'

The furrows on her face had hardened as if with winter frost. Not bitterness, but almost. 'You needn't worry about me. I'm a Jew, remember? I am used to being threatened, it is how we live.'

'Nevertheless, 'Ella. I worry for you. Not because I don't think you can handle yourself but because I don't want you to have to. I deal in practicalities. We have fire damage, I will fix it. If I am attacked I fight back. And I will never let those who matter be harmed.'

'It's odd,' she said. 'I would not have thought a mercantile endeavour in

Lyon would require *fighting back.*'

'I confess, the whyfors of the last two days defeat me. But in the meantime, Herviet and Adam are here and I intend to employ another guard so that with myself, we shall always have two on, two off.'

'Do you think it is somewhat of an over-reaction?'

He denied that it was, saying that better to be over-guarded than burned in their beds. Her hand covered his as she replied. 'I am glad Adam is here.'

'Your hands are cold. Warm them at the hearth. Is Amée awake?'

She opened the door and they could hear the cluck and fuss of the widow as she ordered Mahaut around. 'Need you ask?'

Together they walked down the stair to begin the day again, despite that they had been up since before the cocks had crowed. Guillaume knew the day might unfold in ways that would require sharp eyes and ears because someone had indeed thrown down a challenge and he intended to meet it full-on.

'Good morning, Amée. You are well?' he asked.

She looked up from the table where she had the order book laid out in front of her. 'Huh. The envoys have their cloth and I imagine a large payment will be forthcoming. Yes? Good. We go to market tomorrow with lengths that others can't match and Saul's silks arrive any day. Outside I can hear repairs being carried out and we now have guards. By the Virgin, I think we've turned the fire on its head and Lyon will look at us with something akin to awe. And when people are in awe, they admire and it is a short step to crave what one is admiring before one's neighbour buys exactly that which one is craving. This is exactly how Jehan would want things to go. So yes, *I* am feeling remarkable!'

Cocky, plucky. All of those...

'Indeed,' he agreed, amused at her bravado. 'We are safe and we can breathe again. Do you go to Church this morning?'

'I do. But to give thanks to God. Not to pay respects to l'Archiveque and the notary. Just in case you are wondering.'

'If you wish, I can escort you,' Guillaume said. 'I have business in the town.'

'Blessed boy. That would be a fine thing and good for de Clochard to be seen out and about.' Amée's apple cheeks glowed with something like the vigour of the past and her eyes were bright. As always, her veil and wimple were crisp and businesslike and a foil for the soft woollen folds of a russet gown. She wore a girdle of embroidered cloth and it surrounded her rotund middle like the girth on a horse.

'I am ready to go now, if you wish.'

'Then I shall get a cloak and we will be gone.' She hurried away with a broad smile toward Ariella who picked up a piece of embroidery, tucking the order book away from Mahaut's eyes beneath her threads.

Guillaume sat before the fire, taking the brief respite to watch an unaware Ariella. Her luscious hair fell over her shoulder as she threaded a bone needle with green thread and her fingers nimbly plied the same needle back and forth with that soothing shushing sound. He could imagine the comfort of a life less fraught but perhaps it was not to be the pattern for a child born of rape, or an adult who had seen murder many times over.

Born of rape…

That much he knew. His half brother's lady mother had sent he and his own mother to her former home in Anjou many years ago as a precaution. The senior Gisborne knight, Sir Guy's father, the man who had so thoughtlessly and cruelly lifted Guillaume's mother's skirts was not to be trusted. When Guillaume found his noble half brother, so many years later, he found that even the true son had been badly treated and his lady mother even worse. Guillaume's own mother had always said it was God-given that the wronged servant and her infant were removed from the soiling temptation of a knight who barely lived his creed.

He loved his mother.

Cateline was her name.

Such a beautiful name and such a beautiful woman…

She may not have been sculpted from ivory with an image to match the Virgin's, but her nature was as pure. Even the village priest had acknowledged that much when he prayed for her soul. She could have been a saint.

Was a saint…

And he thought, looking at Ariella, there were not many other women like her – with perhaps one or two exceptions. Ariella brushed back her fire and brimstone hair, looked up at him and smiled with seductive collusion. He loved the contradictions in her manner.

Amée rushed back down the creaking stair, the wattles of her chin wobbling. She had slung a fine grey woollen cloak around her body and the hood hung at the edge of her veil, catching the neatly marshalled folds. Outside, a breeze had begun to blow and leaves flew past the open door, rustling across the cobbles like the sound of people shuffling.

'Ariella, I shouldn't be too long and when I return, we can decide on how to display the stall for the market. We want it to be a showpiece. It is my belief that we should sell some of the trims as well whilst the cooler weather does us favours. Come Guillaume, I will discuss *which* trims whilst we walk.' She sailed out the door like a ship, her cloak billowing back as if it were a filling sail. 'Mahaut,' she called back. 'Make sure those hares are enough for six at the dinner table.'

A disgruntled *'Oc',* came from the kitchens as Guillaume wrapped himself in a cloak and shifted Amée into the yard and toward the gates where she continued her loquaciousness with comments on the ox-dung ('Good Gracious, what *do* they feed the beasts?'), the carpenters (she nodded and waved as if she were a *duchesse*) the quality of the gates (approval), Herviet (another wave), the trims ('We must sell the squirrel as it becomes the green wool so well and the mink from the Russias enhances the crimson so that it is *almost* regal!')

Guillaume wondered if she would take a breath, longing for the gates of the Cathedral to appear. In the meantime, as she smiled and waved to neighbours, so he followed her example. It was a valuable playact to make de Clochard seem so confident. He looked around, casually inspecting those who might watch back. But the sight seemed innocent of threat. Merchants in expensive clothes made of fine wools, bakers dusted in flour, or perhaps they were stonemasons, peasants hauling baskets of fresh produce in from outlying estates. Along the butcher's lane, blood ran down a stony gutter and into Rue Tramassal.

Amée clucked and turned up her nose, lifting the folds of her cloak and *bliaut* and stepping clear of the gore. 'It shouldn't be allowed,' she muttered as a woman followed her example. The breeze sniped harder and she wrapped her cloak more tightly. 'Guillaume, I am concerned we only have silk ordered. With winter at our doors, I wish we had more wool…'

So did he. The plan had been to process the fleeces that had been in store, but of course they were a pile of ash now.

'And I hope we can find more furs than we expect, when we begin to unpack those stored in the cellar. They will sell,' Amée continued. 'Did you see Messire Ricard?'

He had – the man who had an eye for fine skins and leathers, which he sold at great profit.

Does he *crave de Clochard?*

He had been wearing a long brown tunic lavishly hemmed with rich chestnut squirrel. His boots could barely be seen beneath the luxuriance. Guillaume felt Ricard was overdressed for autumn but then posturing was part of the game.

As they climbed the gentle rise to Place Saint Jean and the Cathedral, the bells began to toll for Sext.

'We're in time. Come, come!' said Amée as the monks began the plainchant, the melodic timbre of *Alleluia* chasing away the rippling echoes of the bells.

'No, Amée. I've important business to conclude. You go to Mass and I shall wait for you after I am done.'

She tapped him on his chest. 'You refute God too often, Guillaume. He will desert you in your hour of need if you are not careful.'

'Amée, my God and I had words long since about responsibility. He knows where I stand, don't worry yourself. Now go. I shall be waiting at the doors when you are done.'

She assessed he and his words with curious eyes. Whilst she may not yet know the context of his words, it satisfied her and she nodded, then turned and entered the Cathedral doors with the last of the worshippers. The plainchant faded as the doors were closed and the busy sounds of life in the square once again surged to the fore.

He debated going straight to the Golden Fleece to pay the account but thought better of it, crossing back over the square to Rue Tramassal, walking along in front of a handsomely constructed façade, home of the Gigni.

A palace?

In some places perhaps. In the Italian States it would have been a grand villa. It announced its importance in the elegant subtlety of its stonework – one block chiselled neatly to fit upon another, a keystone carved with the family crest sitting in the arch above the yard gates. Apart from the third floor, where any windows were horn, all windows were glassed with heavy oak shutters. The floor at street level had no windows at all.

Sensible precaution...

A woman swung open one of the horn windows on the third floor and without looking, emptied a pot of excreta into the street and Guillaume jumped backward, avoiding the odorous splatter. He thought the Gigni would surely have rules about the despoiling of the entrance to their property and business. They were merchants after all, with visiting clientele. The maid-servant caught sight of Guillaume, her hand flying to her mouth. She dragged the pot inside, slamming the window as she realized her mistake.

Certainly at de Clochard, they had a rule. Amée hated the cobbled way being soiled. 'Who in their right mind wants to feel silk in their fingers when their boots are shit-stained?' She, like Petrus, could have a way with words.

At the Gigni gates, he gave his name, requesting an audience with Messire Alexandrus. Mere breaths passed and he was led into an expansive yard, as big as a good-sized keep. Servants hurried past, horses nickered and a blacksmith hammered a percussive beat, dogs fighting lethargically over a trough of genteel scraps laid out before them. He had known Luzio's family were wealthy, had known their superior position amongst the merchants of Lyon, but this ... this reduced de Clochard to a plaything.

A servant in a neat, dark tunic urged him through a rather majestic door that he assumed was not for the servant's use and bid him wait in the main hall. The fellow's boots click-clacked over evenly paved flooring and the echoes bounced from walls which reached to a gallery on the first floor. Trestle tables and bench seats were pushed hard against the walls, candle trees stood sentinel, unlit like the pile of kindling and logs in the hearth but waiting for the family's meal times to approach. Unusually, there was a dais, just big enough for two stools and they stood regally cross-legged and fine with crimson leather.

If there were any doubt at all that the Gigni were not descended from nobility, then this chamber must surely convert the unbeliever.

Alone now, and interested, Guillaume walked to the dais, climbed to the throne-like stools and surveyed the room. His lip curled but he quickly schooled his face to its habitual neutrality. A door opened behind the dais and a man of mature years walked in.

'Messire Guillaume de Gisborne,' he said in a well-modulated voice. 'It is a pleasure to meet you in person rather than to merely nod from across the crowds.' He spoke with the accent of the Italians but it was softened with the elegance of his manner as he reached out with his hand to shake Guillaume's, placing his other hand possessively on top. He smiled but Guillaume, adept at determining expression, noticed the smile stopped beneath the sharp cheekbones, the eyes remaining almost devoid of any animation.

Letting go of Guillaume's hand, he lifted a palm to flip a piece of his finely brushed silver hair away from his forehead, and unconsciously, the hand then moved to smooth a beard that vied with Mehmet's for perfectly clipped submission. Those unreadable eyes were shadowed by storm-grey eyebrows; had the man's manner not been so suave and charming, one might feel nothing but intimidation.

He was of a height with Guillaume and whip-thin, a fact exemplified by the long folds of his dark velvet tunic. And Guillaume was sure that in the smallest gesture of power-play, the double-handclasp had been designed to pull him off-balance.

'Messire,' he said. 'We have left it unforgivably long and beyond the bounds of etiquette…'

'Not at all,' the Florentine replied. 'It takes time to come to terms with a town and its business. Aside from that, you are friends with my nephew, so we are in fact quite familiar with you. As I am sure you are with us.

Ah, thought Guillaume, if only you knew how little Luzio speaks of his family, and then only in mocking terms.

'My nephew speaks highly of you, Messire Guillaume, and I am sure his family will be glad that he spends time with someone who has more steadiness than himself. Come, we shall take refreshment.'

He led the way through the door and along a narrow hall that was painted Virgin-blue with gold stars and moons across the walls. Light bled softly from the yard through horn windows and dogs barked with energy as someone shouted.

'We prepare to take part of the household to the Forez,' he said. 'We leave tomorrow after the market and it takes a lifetime for the women to pack.'

Guillaume asked if it was for an extended stay.

'No. We go for our annual autumn hunt. Boar, deer and so on. The women will seek fungi, nuts, and berries. It is an occasion and as you know, gives us a winter food supply. The kitchens will be busy...'

But Guillaume had swallowed on a knot of bile as an image of another hunt floated into his memory. He almost missed the Florentine's next words. 'Messire Guillaume, you must join us. Luzio would be delighted. It is a wonder he did not invite you himself.'

'He did, messire, in his note. But I suspect he knows how involved I am with de Clochard, especially since the fire. Which is why I must politely decline.'

'I insist on mine and my nephew's behalf...'

Guillaume shook his head. 'Messire, it is about the fire that I am here.'

Gigni led the way into a pleasant room that looked through thick glass to the yard. He sat on a chair in front of a large table liberally piled with parchments and rolls. A quill straddled one such sheet and a pile of seals and sticks of honey-coloured wax lay close by. In the yard, there was now bustle. Two carts had been pulled from the stable and chests were stacked on them. Grooms had tied four mounts at rings and were brushing them down. They had strong bone of shoulder and leg and de Clochard's plain rounceys were no competition.

'Here. Sit, sit.' Gigni passed Guillaume a pewter goblet of wine he had poured, and leaned back, pulling a vast black bearskin from the Russias over his knees. 'I feel the cold in my dotage. I should have ordered a brazier lit but I try to forestall the inevitable onset of the cooler days. It flattens my spirit. But I ask your pardon. You were saying something about the unfortunate fire at de Clochard?'

Guillaume took a sip of the most excellent wine and detailed the fact that Luzio appeared to have organized timber and carpenters from his family's supplies without settling it with de Clochard in the first instance.

'It also seems as if it is a gift.' He passed the now-smoothed note from Luzio to the older man.

Gigni flicked his eyes over it. 'Perhaps a little precipitate but it is no problem. In fact, I am quite relieved that he saw beyond the kind of life he lives, to see the plight of others. I knew the cost of his offer before he made it as I intended the same offer.'

'The point being, messire, that whilst I accept the generous honour you have done de Clochard, I must insist that we pay.'

'Pfft!' Gigni waved his hand. 'It is unnecessary.'

'Nevertheless, sir, and with respect, it is the way *I* do business. If you could tell me the value of your offer, I will settle with you this moment.'

Gigni sat as still as a marble statue and his eyes examined every inch of Guillaume's bearing. The intensity of that gaze may have raised hairs on anyone-else's neck. But Guillaume had stood up to authority in the past. It wasn't hard. Meet the scrutiny, don't flinch, believe in what you do and use your height to advantage.

He stood, placing his goblet on the table, and looked down upon the merchant. The man broke first, turning to the papers on the table and flipping through until he found a wax tablet covered in numbers. Running his finger down it, he frowned and then handed it to Guillaume.

'If you must pay, there is the value. But the Gigni honour their gifts, Guillaume.' He dropped the 'Messire', sounding like a father chastising a son.

More power-play?

Guillaume glanced at the figure, loosened his purse and counted out the silver *livres* onto the table. 'We are grateful beyond doubt for the kindness you have shown, but this, messire, is how *I* must do business for de Clochard.'

Another frown and then a chuckle. 'By God and the Saints, Luzio said you were a serious and focused businessman with success in his sights and I can see that he is right.' He scooped up the money and clinked it back and forth in his hands before pouring it into a leather bag lying behind the seals and wax sticks. 'But you must have some balance in your life, my boy. Life is not all work. I shall accept your payment readily if you accept Luzio's and *my* invitation to come hunting with us. You need stay only for the day of the hunt and the night of the feast. Thereafter, you can return to the riverside with alacrity if you feel the business cannot cope without you.'

Cannot cope without me?

Maybe he, Guillaume, felt so.

He disliked the vaguely patronising arrogance in Gigni's words. De Clochard may be small, but it had the weight of great commodities behind it. It was a burgeoning trading house to be protected at all costs. And by its most recent success with the Holy Roman Emperor and with the supply of the most unusual and sought after silks from beyond Byzantium, de Clochard had the potential to knock the other traders out of the marketplace. Gigni however seemed to want Guillaume to play. Like Luzio. And he wondered if this was part of the game – to remove him from de Clochard whilst lasting damage was done.

But he had Adam and Herviet to guard the place and by this night he would make sure there was an extra guard. Perhaps, as Amée said, it must be seen by other merchants that de Clochard was as vital as its most recent sale had been. In its way, it was its own game of chance.

'*Can* they cope without you?' Gigni sat with a self-satisfied smile playing round his lips. 'The hunt itself is not for a sennight. We go early to prepare as we have many guests on the day of the hunt and for the feast afterward. So you could organise your household and make sure it is in order before you leave. If you doubt me at all, see this as a gesture of gratitude for your friendship with Luzio. He is … a troubled young man.'

He is? That, I have missed. Misguided yes, but troubled?

'Messire, of course de Clochard can cope. I am merely being over-zealous…'

And I have Herviet, Adam and one other…

'The market will be done and we shall almost be at the end of the river season,' he continued. 'Your men will be finished with the repairs. In truth, it will be an honour to attend your hunt. I thank you.'

Gigni stood and slapped Guillaume on the back. 'Excellent,' he said. 'Luzio said you were an archer with Richard of England's army in Outremer. Your skills may very well bring down a good-sized deer.'

'Perhaps. It is better to expect nothing, messire.' Guillaume moved with the Florentine to a door in the passage and out into the yard.

'They say you have been extremely fortunate in a sale of great magnitude, Guillaume. Are they right?'

'I am not sure who *they* are, messire. Nor what sale is meant. We have many sales.'

'They say it was to the court of the Holy Roman Emperor. Something about purple-dyed cloth?'

'Indeed, messire? Whoever *they* are, they tell a story that would entertain halls.'

'It is not true, then?'

'We made a sale of rather excellent velvet from Al-Andalus to some German nobles who pass through Lyon currently. That much I can tell you. Purple dye? If de Clochard could get hold of purple-dyed cloth, the house's fortune would be made.'

Is this why our yard was burned?

A change of subject was needed and fast. 'Is Luzio here?'

Gigni frowned, patently annoyed that the line of questioning had been halted. 'He left for the Forez this morning. He had a desire to leave the town rather quickly. I suspect he had troubles with women again.' Gigni sounded disappointed in his nephew and ready to admit it. 'He can be a trial sometimes, but I love my brother his father, and am prepared to give him a chance.'

Guillaume felt an air of discomfort at this revelatory speech and cut it short by reaching for the man's hand, shaking it and bowing his head. Turning, he walked away through the busy yard, a hunting dog sniffing at his fingers as he passed by. He knew if he turned back, Gigni would be watching him, he could feel it through to his spine, and bumps raised upon his arms in consequence.

The Golden Fleece was almost empty, perhaps in deference to the service within the Cathedral, or perhaps that it was mid-morning and the clientele were busy and not yet thirsty or hungry. The innkeeper took the payment Guillaume made, his eyes sparkling as his fingers ran across the banked-up *livres*.

'Messire, we expected our honoured guests back to their chamber yesternight…'

Guillaume explained that the envoys had had a late meal with the de Clochard company and after discussing business and with more yet to discuss before they left on the morrow, they had decided to stay in Rue Ducanivet.

'They will send for their chests, then?'

Christ on the Cross! I had forgotten…

But he barely missed a beat. 'One of my men will come with a handcart before the day is done.' He added another *livre* to the pile on the trestle table. 'Thank you for attending so well to our esteemed visitors.'

He was bowed out of the inn, amused that he was receiving the kind of treatment that he had just used with Gigni. It was all relative, he thought, as he noticed the Cathedral doors swinging wide.

As he began to cross the square, a gang of rough young men with barely a whisker between them, had begun to chase each other, pushing and shoving with much shouting and ale-fuelled laughter. Between one blink and another, he was enclosed in their midst, the laughter roaring in his ears, together with a heartbeat that spoke of fighting, not fun.

His hand closed on his dagger as he felt someone shove him backward, a sharp point pricking through his tunic and cloak. He stepped hard on the foot behind him, grinding his heel down and shoving his elbow back full-force into a soft midriff. The knife-point pulled away from his back as the fellow sagged forward and Guillaume pushed out of the mob, whispering furiously, 'He wants me?' gesturing back to the man who was doubled over and coughing up dawn's food. 'Then tell him to seek me like a man. Not in the back.' He had let his own knife hang on the belt and instead, with a hard fist, punched the nearest neck, leaving a young man gasping for air, his friends dropping away and Guillaume walking to the Cathedral unimpeded.

He reached under his cloak and rubbed at his lower back, annoyed that it hurt. His fingers when he glanced at them were stained red.

'Guillaume,' Amée hurried over and he wiped his hand swiftly on a cloak fold. 'I'm sorry I took so long. I was speaking with Monseigneur and the notary. Were those young men annoying you?'

'Not especially,' he said. 'Just lack of control. They will remember their manners next time.'

Hired thugs who care little beyond the coin they are paid…

'Did you know any of them?'

'In truth, none. I suspect they are felons passing through Lyon. It happens close to market day, does it not?'

'For shame, it does, and a shame too that they are gone. They needed a lesson served. You have concluded your business?'

'Indeed. And now we can go home and plan how to take Lyon by surprise on the morrow with our stall. Did you ask for God's blessing?'

'Enough of your teasing, Guillaume.'

He took her arm through his own. 'I apologise. Do you need to tell me anything from the Archbishop or the notary?'

She made a mew, a fat little cat expressing displeasure. 'I'm not sure, if I am truthful. Monseigneur asked me about my beliefs, did I share the view of the Church on the Gospels? I said of course I did, else I would not be at his services. Then Brother Crispianus said they were concerned that the heretical view of Pierre Vaudès had such strength in Lyon. I wanted to say for them to look to the Church's wealth, but instead I asked why they should think I would countenance such a view and they said such people as the Poor Men

70

of Lyon would prey on those in distress. I replied that my Church is a solace to me and I have no need to listen to others.'

Amée's voice had dropped as she spoke, and Guillaume suspected she was remembering Jehan. 'But then the Monseigneur pushed me further and he looked as if he were sucking lemons. He was certainly unhappy to be speaking to me about such things, or so it seemed…'

'*Madame de Clochard, I am loath to say so, but Jehan was a close friend of Pierre Vaudès and in addition, it is well-known that after Jehan's death one of Pierre's followers visited you…*'

'*Yes. With a message of kindness and condolence from Pierre. Not to convert me to his thinking.*'

'*But Madame, the heretic was nevertheless in your house,*' Brother Crispianus interjected.

'*Yes. He was…*' Christ, I was angry. '*And I welcomed him into my home as Pierre's wife welcomed us to Lyon. It has nothing to do with beliefs but everything to do with kindness. Will you burn me at the stake for common decency? Brother Crispianus, I am ashamed of you! Where is your Christian charity? Monseigneur, I am incensed,*' I turned to the Archbishop. '*Your notary seems to be implying something for which I have no taste.*'

'*Madame, I apologise on his behalf…*'

'And Guillaume, I have to say the Archbishop *did* look as if he meant it. Sometimes I think that foul-smelling monk is the power behind that throne. But anyway, the conversation continued and I confess I got madder by the moment.'

Her round face had reddened and the stain bled under her wimple, her words quite clipped.

'*Madame,*' said the Archbishop. '*Vaudès has copied the Bible into Provençal and slanted it away from the true Church's teachings.*'

'*You mean that the wealthy, by his teachings, cannot buy their way into Heaven by plenary indulgences…*'

'I tell you, Guillaume, the Archbishop looked as if a rat had climbed up his backside at that point.'

Guillaume had to laugh. 'You're a brave little thing, aren't you?'

'And Brother Crispianus jumped in then, and said any teachings from Vaudès were heretical, that all heretics will burn here and now if they are caught and that the copied teachings are believed to be hidden in Lyon.

I almost exploded with wrath at that point. God forgive me.' She crossed herself and continued,

'If I did not know better, Brother Crispianus, I would say you are implying that a copy of the Vaudès Bible is hidden in Rue Ducanivet.'

'The monk had the sheer audacity to look me straight in the eye and say *Yes.* I looked him straight in the eye back and said, *Then you are utterly wrong. I hope you will beg God's forgiveness for what you have said to me today. Good day, Brother Crispianus.* I turned my back on him with as much flip and force as I could muster and took the Archbishop's hand in my own and kissed his ring. And I tell you, and God forgive me, I wanted to spit on them both.'

Guillaume allowed her breathing to settle and her colour to fade a little before he spoke. 'Amée, *do* we hide the Bible at Rue Ducanivet?'

'No,' she replied, a simple response accompanied by a breath filled with the release of accumulated tension.

Did Guillaume believe her? Perhaps. But the truth was it would explain the man being tortured, the misinformation given by the poor unfortunate and then perhaps the fire itself.

He took Amée's hand through the crook of his arm, wishing the pain in his back would go away. 'I'm hungry. Come on, let us go and make short work of Mahaut's excellent hares.'

'If it is excellent,' Amée said as she hurried beside Guillaume with short but frequent strides. 'It is because I gave her the instruction. If it is not excellent, it is because she did not listen.'

They continued along Rue Ducanivet, Guillaume's wits as sharp as the pain in his back. But all was quiet until they stopped at a fruit vendor where Amée wished to purchase some apples. As he stood waiting for her and staring toward the Pont du Change and the Saône, a man knocked against him. His hood was up and his face shadowed, but he uttered one word. There was nothing polite in it and it lacked the gravitas so lately referred to by Amée when describing the change in their name and fortunes.

In a wild dog snarl, he whispered at Guillaume's neck, his breath hot and sour, 'Clochard!'

Chapter Four

×

'Adam,' Guillaume's mouth lay close to Adam's ear. 'Adam!'

Adam lay stretched out on his stomach on the cot in the storeroom. Looking around, Guillaume could see he needed to order more cots, chests and bedding, so that each man had their own space. But right now, his own needs were greatest as he attempted to wake the Master at Arms. Adam's mouth was open, lips slack, and dribble trickled down the pillow he had made of a folded cloak. His snoring sounded like pigs in swill and he coughed as Guillaume shook him.

'Adam!'

He rolled over, opening one eye. 'Christ's beard, Guillaume.' His voice was husky with sleep.

'Sorry, but I need you to help me.'

'I've barely slept for a heartbeat and you were sure all would be well. What is it?' He swung his bare legs over the cot and rubbed at heavy eyes before scratching at his wild red hair so that it stood on end.

'This…' Guillaume had removed his cloak and thrown it on the bed, pulling up his tunic and chemise to display a wad of bloody fabric tucked into his *braies*.

Adam reached for the wad and pulled it away. 'Jesus wept…' he said as blood began to trickle. He hastily padded the wound again.

'You have to stitch it closed as I don't want Amée or Ariella to know.'

'I can see I do.' Adam was wide awake now and bright-eyed at the escalating drama. He reached for a costrel, pouring wine over a cloth, peeling the stained wad away and drenching the wound. 'More attacks?'

It took as long as threading a bone needle for Guillaume to explain to Adam, finally closing with, 'That needle's sharp, isn't it?'

Adam just grunted as he fingered the wound closed, pushing the needle in and pulling it through. 'I might lack the *Dameisele's* fine needle style, but invariably my embroidery holds together.'

'Glad to hear it,' Guillaume said through gritted teeth as the needle dove in and out, tugging at the flesh and periodically being punctuated by little dabs with the wine-soaked cloth.

"You know, another push and that dagger would have pierced something important. You were lucky he sagged over his belly and dropped the weapon, rather than falling against you and pushing it further in. Did you ever get wounded in Outremer?'

'Not so you'd know,' Guillaume replied, closing that point of conversation down.

'Well, the time for thinking here is done. We need to take action.' Adam knotted the final stitch, over, under and through and cut the thread with his knife. He grabbed a pad of linen from a leather bag on his cot and placed it over the wound, saying 'Hold it,' whilst he took a roll of linen bandage torn from some unlucky woman's bed sheet. Winding it round Guillaume's middle, he slapped the flat stomach, saying 'As well you're not rotund else I'd run out of bandage.' He tied it off neatly and stood back.

'From now on, wherever you go you'll have a companion, and next time you're attacked, and you will be, that's for sure, we will take him down and get the goddamned truth from him.'

'It's exactly what I thought. But I want to increase the guard on de Clochard as well.'

'Petrus has given me names. I'll organise two more immediately.'

'And I need someone with a handcart to collect the envoys' chests from the Golden Fleece.'

'It's done.'

'Adam, there's something else. I heard about someone being tortured…'

He laid the story out, including Amée's confrontation at the Cathedral.

'Does she tell the truth about the Bible?'

'I don't think so.'

Adam blew a breath out. 'Nose hairs of the Saints but she's a brave little thing then. Wonder why she didn't tell you the truth?'

Guillaume shrugged his shoulders, having wondered the same thing, but if Amée had told anyone at all, it would have been Ariella and he would ask her and soonest. 'There's one other thing,' he said as Adam pulled on his tunic, hose and boots and washed his face in a bowl of water no doubt left by Ariella. He told Adam of the man in the hood and that whispered word.

'*Clochard*. It means vagabond and the thing is whether it was directed at me or the business, it was an open declaration. My life, or the lives of those here, are forfeit.'

'True. And whether it's you, or Gisborne, Jehan or Amée that prompts it, it makes no difference. Do you think Messire Gigni showed a hand today?'

'If he did, he was remarkably subtle.'

'Well if you aren't attacked tomorrow, then you will needs watch yourself on the hunt.'

'It seemed expeditious at the time to agree to go. If he is the instigator of the troubles and I *am* the focus, better I am away from Lyon. I can handle myself if you can manage here.'

'My guards will manage here but if you think to go to the hunt without me, then you're mistaken.'

It seemed ridiculous to Guillaume that they would jump from a house of three to a house of eight in a heartbeat; and not only that but a house that had been wrapped in silk transformed into a house bristling with iron.

When he explained the house changes to the women, Amée was quite blithe. 'I rather like having a house of men. It's exciting and it shows a degree of prosperity. That said, I do wonder how we will feed everyone and pay for it…'

With money we don't have. And I think you are wrong – rather than showing prosperity, it may show panic…

Later, when he and Ariella had a moment alone, he asked her about the Bible.

'No,' she replied. 'Not at all. I wonder why she would keep such a secret from her business partners. Especially now, after the fire.' She gave a petulant little sigh. 'You know, I don't think these incidents are about de Clochard the company as it was at all. It's more about what it is now. Something else entirely.'

'How so?' he asked as they stood in Rue Ducanivet, the day sinking around them. Opposite, the newly repaired gates stood open and they could see the additional guards settling in. Cots had arrived and the storeroom now had the appearance of military billets. There was just enough room to squeeze past the cots to the door into the *traboule*, although Guillaume had no idea how bales of cloth would be carried through and into the yard. But it was surely temporary. By the end of the sennight, the carpenters would have the barn and another chamber built, albeit rough timber. The guards could then move, leaving the storeroom free for what it was intended and for access to the river.

'I can't explain. It's an intuition. Nothing substantial,' she said.

And for some reason the word *'Revenge'* slid through his mind and he shivered.

'Guillaume, we will have to go to the moneylenders now. There is nothing else for it. We are a house of eight and that chest of Holy Roman money won't last more than two sennights with such expenses.'

'I'm forced to agree. After the market tomorrow, shall you come with me to visit Joshua?'

She nodded. 'He is a nice man, a good friend of Father's, and he will not charge high interest rates. Besides, this is merely until monies come through from Venezia.'

They watched a barge come upriver from the junction of the Saône with the Rhône. The vessel sat low in the water as the oarsmen pulled hard across the current to reach the moorings below. The last of the daylight lit upon muscle and bulk, but in the rear of the craft, a hooded couple sat watching as lines were thrown out, grabbed and looped off.

'Hoy!' yelled the bargemaster to Guillaume. 'Is there anyone from de Clochard about?'

Surprised, Guillaume called back, 'Yes. I am with de Clochard.'

'Messire, I have a load of silks from Marseille for you.'

'Those are our silks,' Guillaume said, before shouting out, 'I'll get men and we'll come down the *traboule*.'

He ran across the road and through the gates with Ariella on his heels. 'Ariella, we need to pay the bargemen, can you get the coin from my room? I'll get the men and open the access to the *traboule*. Have Adam shut the gates behind me. This need not be a public affair.'

In moments, de Clochard was sealed off from prying eyes and Guillaume, Herviet and the two new guards, Gosse and Roul, were running down the stairs of the *traboule* to the river. Guillaume had the forethought to bring a lighted torch and proceeded to strike a flame to further torches lining the walls.

'My name is Balduino, messire, from Marseille,' said the bargemaster, a tall, slim, broad-shouldered man, 'And I have this for you.' He passed a parchment packet over and directed the men from de Clochard to start unloading the bales. The oarsmen sat quietly, waiting until the barge was emptied of the cargo. There were six bales, a number of timber crates and two barrels from which a heady fragrance emerged.

'All of this is for us?'

'That's what I was told, sir,' replied the bargemaster as the last barrel was toted up the stair. 'And this is the bill for the shipping but it was paid for in Marseille by a friend. You may know him – Ahmed?' He passed over a single sheet of weatherworn parchment and Guillaume glanced at it.

'Yes, I know Ahmed – a good man and as you say, a friend. Then this is extra,' Guillaume said, counting four silver *livres* onto the bench, 'for honesty and for a fleet arrival of the goods. I thank you.'

The bargemaster nodded and ordered the crew to tidy the vessel whereupon they could head into Lyon, and after shaking hands he turned away, but then quickly swung back. 'Oh. We have two passengers for you as well. Madame? Messire?'

A man and woman walked along the larboard side of the craft to the plank leading to shore. It was too dark now to see their faces but Guillaume nodded to the man as he jumped ashore and he held his hand to the woman as she stepped carefully along the plank before jumping onto the river stone.

'Messire? Madame? I am Guillaume de Gisborne, manager of de Clochard. Can I be of service?'

'I believe so,' said the man. 'My name is Michael Sarapion, formerly a merchant of Constantinople and this,' he said stepping back to allow the woman alongside, 'is my wife, Jehanne de Clochard.'

'*Jehanne!* But...'

'I know,' the woman replied. 'My mother?'

'Inside. She will be shocked.'

'And happy, I hope. The business does well?'

'It does…'

'But?'

'We have problems currently.'

'Trading problems?'

'Not especially. No, this is something more insidious. Madame, I need you to sit with the Master at Arms and talk, but now is not the time. You must first see your mother.'

'Master at Arms? By the Saints…'

'Come. It gets dark and cold, these estimable oarsmen need to rest in the town, and we must lock up the *traboule* gate.'

Guillaume could barely believe who followed him up the stair. He knew of Michael Sarapion, the merchant who had managed to procure the Tyrian purple in Byzantium and the man whom Tobias, Mehmet and Tomasso had travelled to meet. He wanted so much to talk of that journey, to find out what had happened in Constantinople that led to Tommaso's death. Tomas had been the difficult one of the twins to be sure – damaged and explosive, but no one had foreseen his demise, no one at all. As for Jehanne, for so long Amée and her departed husband had assumed their daughter was dead. She had disappeared on a market day, just like the one they would attend on the morrow. By her mother's side, serving people and then gone. No one had heard of her nor seen a sign anywhere. She had been an attractive young woman and it was assumed she had been abducted. Maybe worse…

Although, thought Guillaume, Gisborne would admit to a woman called Dana, an embroiderer in Constantinople, who had access to the imperial house and who reported on the politics between Komemnid and Angelid families and the way in which the Byzantine empire was beginning to close in upon itself. And that woman, Dana, from France…

When had Gisborne beguiled her with the exotic life in Byzantium? *How* had he beguiled her? For beguile her he must have done, to leave Lyon without a word to her parents.

Guillaume thought less of his brother in that moment. Why could the man not admit to Amée and Jehan that their beloved daughter lived and was of great value within his web of spies? Was his underground business of information gathering more valuable than a mother's feelings?

Christ, not by Guillaume's reckoning!

The Sarapions waited whilst Guillaume closed the *traboule* door and barred it. Adam arrived with a flourish, saying in a loud voice, 'Got everything stored in the cellar for now. Bloody back's brok… Oh, begging your pardon, Madame.'

'Adam, this is Messire and Madame Sarapion come to stay. Messire, Madame? This is our Master at Arms, Adam of London, from Gisborne's own guard.'

'Sarapion?' Adam asked in some wonder. The name resonated like a high-pitched bell.

Sarapion nodded, assessing Adam with a quick glance. He was sharp man, observant and looked able to make swift judgements. Guillaume knew the type straight away. The kind one would want at one's back in a skirmish.

As for Jehanne, she said immediately, 'Once I have spoken to my mother, I would like to speak with you, Adam, and with Messire Guillaume. And I would like to do it tonight.'

So. A strong woman who had survived the insidious courts of the Byzantines and lived to tell the story. With the dip and rise of an oar-blade, the dynamics of de Clochard had changed. And it seemed adaptability was the name of the game.

'Madame Sarapion…' Guillaume began.

'Please. Call me Jehanne.' She half-smiled at him but he recognised that merriment would not come easily and that she would suffer no fools in her life.

A kindred spirit?

In the light of the torch that he held he could just make out her even features and she was of a height with Ariella, but any more detail would have to wait for the candletrees of the little hall.

'Jehanne, do you think it wise to surprise your mother? She has lived with your *death* for a long while.'

'Guillaume. May I call you that? You know my mother well. Presumably then, you know she is no wilting wildflower. Besides, what other way is there but the open and honest way? She will cope, mark you.'

Ah, Jehanne, you have been away too long. You did not see how the grief of

79

your father's death and the arson attack on de Clochard affected your mother. True, she pulled herself together. But even so...

They turned as a small group to enter the house. Adam stayed behind with his men but watched with curious eyes. Guillaume nodded to him, unable to help his lips twisting with irony. Above their heads, the clouds had momentarily parted, a pallid moonlight dropping briefly to the yard. But an iron grey mist had already begun to rise from the river, over the roofs of Ducanivet and into the yard, catching on the branches of the oak. It was the kind of mist from which soft rain might leech, drenching everything. For the first time in many months, Guillaume asked the Virgin to intercede and make the morrow a perfect market day – so much depended upon it.

In the hall, a pleasant warmth emanated from the fire burning beneath the side-hung chimney. Two candletrees lit the room and the table was filled with the remains of the hare pies, with fruit and cheese and bread. And on a large platter was a golden pile of honey and almond cakes. Amée had her back to the door and she and Ariella were gathering empty plates and remains to return to Mahaut in the kitchens outside.

Guillaume led the way, looking to Ariella, sending a message. *Stand by Amée, stand by her.*

'Amée,' he said gently. 'We have visitors...'

'We have? And with a table that is a mess of remnants. They will have to excuse us...'

'Mama, of course we excuse you.' Jehanne said baldly.

The pile of wooden and pewter plates fell from Amée's arms and her face bleached to the white of her wimple. Her mouth opened and nothing came out, but her eyes...

Her eyes opened as if she had observed Heaven and Hell in one. And then she just stood there, tears beginning to trickle, her mouth twisting as if she hurt with all the pain of a new death. Ariella's arm encircled her and held her tight.

'Mama, 'tis I,' Jehanne said. Guillaume would later say that she was bemused. Surprised at her mother's pain. But he was not. He had seen maternal pain at its worst.

'I can see that it is my daughter, Jehanne,' Amée finally said. 'And yet for three years her father and myself were led to believe that she was dead.'

'It was necessary for me to assume a new identity, Mama.'

'Necessary for whom?' Amée's colour had returned and begun to escalate dangerously, her voice lifting. 'For you? Definitely not for your father or myself.'

'Mama…'

'We went through a living Hell, Jehanne. And I would venture to say that the pain helped kill your father. He adored you and the loss he suffered scoured his very soul.'

'Mama, do not say so.'

'I *will* say so! A word, Jehanne. One or two words. It was all we needed.' A sob eked out and Ariella held her tighter.

'But Gisborne said it was too dangerous.'

'Gisborne!'

'He employed me to spy for him in the Byzantine court. I was an occasional embroiderer for the imperial ladies and their tongues were very loose.'

'*Gisborne* took you away from us?'

'In a way…'

'What way?' Amée uttered through clenched teeth. '*What* way?'

'I hated my circumscribed life in Lyon. Sometimes I felt I might as well have taken holy orders. I was neither noble nor peasant because a merchant fits nowhere and I hated selling cloth to fat, opinionated women. I heard Gisborne talking to you and Papa of what his men did, of what you did for him. I heard him talk of Constantinople and I desperately wanted to see it for myself. He didn't know I had left you until I turned up in Venezia…'

'You travelled *alone*? *That* far?'

'No. I travelled with pilgrims going to Rome.'

'And he sent you to Constantinople. Without a word to us. By Christ and the Saints, I had so much respect for him and…'

Jehanne butted in with haste, '*He* sent me home. But I stowed on a ship called *Durrah*, sailed by one of his men – Ahmed. They found me on board when we reached Crete and I had become ill. Ahmed sent a message back to Venezia but had to keep to a sailing schedule and to leave me alone in Crete was not suitable. When we reached Constantinople, he sent for an Arab doctor, Anwar al Din, a friend of Gisborne's, and I lived with he and his wife until I was well. It was all very seemly. But by then I had proved to Gisborne that I could be of as much service as any other of his men. And that is exactly what happened. I sourced information for three years.'

'*Gisborne* knew you were alive,' Amée sneered, 'and never said?'

This is bad...

'Amée,' Guillaume butted in. 'Please sit. Can we all sit?'

Ariella pulled out stools and benches and hastily retrieved the dropped kitchenware, hurrying it out to Mahaut and then shutting then door firmly.

'Amée,' said Guillaume as gently as previously. 'You above all people should know that it is how Gisborne works. People must be assumed dead or lost to maintain a veracity...'

'No!' Amée spun round to look at him, her eyes filled with flaming ire. '*She*,' her finger pointed and with each word, she stabbed the air, her words collapsing in a welter of tears. '*She* ... is ... my ... daughter.'

'*Maman*,' Jehanne went to hold her, but Amée leaned back.

'Do not touch me...' She held a hand up.

'*Maman*, I am sorry. But did you never wonder why so much money came back to you from Gisborne? It was far more than you and Papa earned through your secret-gathering here. It was earned by me for information about the Angelids that he eventually sold to the Holy Roman Emperor, to the Venetians, to whomever would pay the highest. But I tired of the subterfuge and in the end, after the Tyrian purple had been retrieved, it became exceedingly dangerous as the Byzantines looked for cracks in each other's faces. I asked to leave, to return here where I belong.'

'Belong?' Amée laughed bitterly. 'You think we haven't got on with de Clochard without you?'

'Amée!' Ariella rounded on her. 'Enough! I am a daughter who has left my father for another place and I recognize Jehanne's need to push away, to be more than a woman in a man's world, to find something new. Sometimes, one does what one has to. Do not be so bitter. Be prepared to listen to her as my father did to me.'

Amée sat back, looking down at her lap, her tears dripping onto her *bliaut*, darkening the cloth in spreading splotches. 'She said she wanted to travel to Constantinople to buy cloth and we listened. We even thought to arrange for her to travel with merchants and their wives. But she was gone before we could talk with her. Just gone!'

'It had to be that way, Mama...'

'We held a Mass for your soul. *That* is the kind of pain we lived with. Gisborne had only to let us know you lived. We were owed that and would have kept the secret.' She looked at Jehanne, studying her. 'You are become very beautiful…' she whispered.

Jehanne reached out and held her mother then until the tears eased and some semblance of rational quiet fell upon the room. Through all the emotion, Michael Sarapion had sat, not saying a word.

Clever man, knows when to hold his peace.

Guillaume nodded to him. 'I think wines for us all.' He poured rich Burgundy wine into the treasured Venetian goblets and handed them around. As he passed Sarapion his, he said, 'Michael?'

Amée turned at that. 'And who is this? I beg your pardon, sir, for my excesses…'

'Madame, you are forgiven. It was such a shock for you and I am deeply sorry. My name is Michael Sarapion and I am a merchant from Constantinople. I am your daughter's husband.'

'Oh,' Amée's breath sucked in. 'This is true?' She pushed Jehanne away. 'You are *wed*? For how long? And Gisborne sought not to tell us that *either*?'

'We met when I arrived in Constantinople but we were married when we arrived back in Venezia,' Jehanne said. 'We waited for Saul to put a shipment together for de Clochard and then we travelled with it immediately.'

'Oh by the Virgin's robes, I am exhausted with what I am hearing. I … I…'

'Hush, *Maman*. There is little more to tell except that when I arrived in Venezia to hear that Papa had died, I was heartbroken. And beyond guilty. I am profoundly sorry for *your* pain and for my dear father's pain.' Jehanne's regal face stayed smooth although her voice had the faintest tremor.

Even so, Jehanne, you manage to hold your tears…

Guillaume scrutinised her and found her compelling. Such behaviour seemed as familiar to him as the lines on his own palm – as if a lock on one's heart has jammed and the key lost. It had happened to him, except at night when the demons unlocked the doors of memory with a key of their own and haunted him with the pain.

Amée began to settle as the wine loosened her angst. She reached out a hand to her daughter's cheek and held it there.

'I cannot forgive him, Jehanne. Gisborne lost his son, he knows what that torment is. And to be honest, I cannot forgive you immediately either.' She sighed. 'I wish Jehan could see you...' And then she shouted, 'Mahaut! Mahaut, come quickly!'

The kitchen door was flung back hard and the ugly bulk of Mahaut stood at the door like Beezlebub or Belial.

'Mahaut,' Amée said. 'We have visitors. Even one you may know...'

'Madame, we have no room left and the food is done for tonight. I am sorry... Oh! Oh Lord! By the Blessed Virgin...' the stout cook stumbled from the doorway, her wide-apart eyes shedding tears. 'My little Jehanne. Oh my sweet Jehanne, you live! You are here! You see? I never gave up hope. God answers the prayers of true believers. Oh my dear little child.' She patted Jehanne's cheek as if the woman was an infant and Guillaume exchanged a surprised glance with Ariella. For them, Mahaut had only ever been a wound with daily salt applied.

'Now now, Mahaut, calm yourself,' said Amée. 'My Jehanne is here to stay, and so too is her husband. This,' she added in a proprietorial fashion, 'is Messire Michael Sarapion and they will have Ariella's chamber. She can move to the chamber next to yours on the next floor...'

And in a heartbeat, Ariella was reduced to the level of servant when she had once been Amée's friend, treated like a daughter – all changed now that the true daughter had miraculously risen from the dead. Ariella's colour changed, a flush running up her neck. Was she insulted, Guillaume wondered? Did she feel a measure of usurpation?

'No, Madame,' she said. 'Guillaume and I shall take rooms in the Golden Fleece.'

'But this is not right,' Jehanne said. 'This house is partly yours, the two of you, through your brother, Guillaume, and your father, Ariella.'

'Indeed this is true, Madame Jehanne,' said Ariella, maintaining an interesting distance from the interloper. 'But the house has no space, we have lost even more through a fire and our cellar is filled with all our merchandise. It is what it is. In the meantime, I shall go with Mahaut and help her make your chamber ready, so that she too may retire for the night. She has worked a very long day.' She chivvied Mahaut up the stair and Guillaume eased his back as his stitches began to throb in a warlike manner.

'I am uncomfortable with this,' Michael said. 'We have discommoded you all.'

'There is little to be done, Michael,' said Guillaume. 'In a sennight we might have repairs enough done and everyone would have room to sleep, even our guards.'

'Then Jehanne and I shall stay at the Golden Fleece until the sennight is done. No, Madame de Clochard, it is as it must be. These people have a share in the property and business. They have worked tirelessly to support you in your hour of need and we have thrown things awry. Besides, it is only for a sennight and we will be here from dawn to dusk every day. Can we make our way to the inn without breaking curfew?'

Guillaume watched Amée's mouth open and close as she subsided meekly. It surprised him because meek was far from an apt description of the widow. 'I will light you and we shall take two of the guards,' he said. 'If we are stopped we have a legitimate excuse – your barge arrived late on the river.'

'But Guillaume, before we leave for the night, I would like to know what problems have occurred here. You mentioned them as we came up the *traboule*.'

'Indeed. But I think Adam, our Master at Arms should be here as well.'

'Then fetch him if you would,' said Jehanne.

The imperiousness of her tone rubbed at Guillaume but he tried to ignore it, reasoning the woman had been fierce and courageous in Constantinople and had lived with a degree of independence that made her what she was.

He had known worse folk in his time…

Adam and Guillaume settled how much should be revealed as they walked from the storeroom. A skeleton briefing, both men agreed. They sat together in front of the dying fire, taking turns to lay down the bones, but when Guillaume mentioned the initial attack upon himself, Amée sat up, her chin wattles sagging over her wimple.

'You did not say!'

But he held up his hand, shook his head and together he and Adam pressed on – avoiding the most recent attack completely until they reached the point where the market of the next day needed to be discussed. Ariella came quietly down the stair and stood behind Guillaume and Adam, her hand lying on Guillaume's shoulder.

'Someone doesn't like you, Guillaume,' Jehanne mused.

''Tis what I said, Madame,' said Adam. 'And it is rightly what one would think. But none of this is at it seems and so we must also assume that the attack on Guillaume might not be because he is who is, but because he represents someone else entirely.'

'Ha!' said Amée. 'You mean because he represents Gisborne, don't you? And I'm not surprised. The man makes enemies easily.'

'You may be right, Madame,' Adam said. 'In any case, we can't afford to ignore the possibility.'

'And thus my business is under threat because of *that* man,' she said quite baldly.

'*Maman*,' Jehanne said. 'You forget. This is no longer exclusively your business. It's now a triumvirate of yourself, Gisborne and ben Simon. If it wasn't, then you would have lost it when Papa died. And on that point, how do you know it is not a vendetta against Saul?'

Michael placed his empty goblet on the table, standing and stretching, rubbing at a leg that obviously pained him. 'Then do you not think, Jehanne, that *Dameisele* Ariella would have been the target?'

Jehanne frowned, digesting the thought before speaking. 'Mayhap. In any case, how do you plan to find out who and why?'

Adam took control, detailing strategy. 'Tomorrow is the market – a perfect day to attack us whilst our attention is elsewhere. Except it won't be. I shall have this place guarded by Herviet, Gosse and Raol. Myself and Messire Guillaume shall be at the market. I shall be amongst the crowds close by. Messire Guillaume will stand in front and will greet customers. He will be seen and he will be vulnerable. Madame Amée and *Dameisele* Ariella shall serve customers as normal. If an attack is made, I shall move in from behind…'

'I shall be in the crowd as well,' Michael said. 'No one knows me and I am handy with a knife.'

'I too…' Jehanne said.

'Jehanne!' her mother responded.

'I am good with disguise, *Maman*, and with hand weapons. I have had to be. I shall dress as a youth. That means, Adam, that there shall be three of us to defend Guillaume, should he need it.'

'By all means, Madame. I have no reason to doubt your abilities if you worked for my lord Gisborne. Then we are done. It is just a matter of waiting.' Adam stood up. 'Oh, one more thing, Madame,' he turned to Amée. 'We have not talked about your conversation with the Archbishop and Brother Crispianus today. By all accounts, it was very pointed.'

Amée shrugged. 'A moment of insanity by the notary and a lack of management by Monseigneur.' She brushed her fingers across the sleeve of her chemise, as if she removed a troublesome fly. 'It is no matter. I do not care.'

'*Maman?*' Jehanne's brow creased. 'You have had words with senior men of the Church?'

'Pfft,' Amée puffed her lips in apparent disgust. 'The monk is no senior man.'

'Madame,' Adam broke in. 'They almost accused you of being a heretic and of hiding a copy of Pierre Vaudès' Bible. Those are not *little* things.'

'I proved them wrong, left the notary to stew in his juices and Monseigneur to clean up the mess.'

Adam didn't look in Guillaume's direction as he asked the next question. 'Madame, *do* you have the Bible?'

Amée snorted. 'If I did, do you think I would make it common knowledge? Of course I don't have the Bible! If Pierre had any sense, I imagine he removed it the moment the Church's attitude toward him began to change. As to his disciples, they don't give the books to just anyone.'

Adam sat for a moment before saying 'Good,' and then turning to Jehanne and Michael, added, 'Might I suggest we escort you to the Golden Fleece, Messire and Madame. It is getting late.'

'Interesting times,' Ariella remarked as they stood at the door, allowing the night quiet to soothe the ruffled feathers of the evening.

'They are two very strong women,' Guillaume replied. 'And Michael is an enigma. It will be as you say … interesting times.'

'My heart broke for Amée and yet I was able to understand Jehanne's needs fully. It is exactly how I felt for so long. We women are required to fit a mould, Guillaume, and if we so much as whisper that we seek more, we are branded foolish and wayward, if not entirely insane. Women of your faith are sent to the Church to have sense knocked into them and yet, the world has great women who achieve much despite society's opinion.'

'I have no quarrel with a woman seeking to improve her life, Ariella…'

'And what about following her dreams?'

'A woman alone in this world is a dangerous thing.'

'You think I don't know? I am a Jew,' she replied tartly.

For a moment they said nothing and then he looked down at her and she grinned.

'I disturb your equanimity sometimes, don't I, Guillaume? Tell me, do you believe Amée?' she asked.

God's breath but he loved the way she managed the *voltare*, switching from one subject to another with such acuity, it sometimes made his head spin. 'About the Bible? I want to but my gut says no, but Adam will tell you, my gut is oft wrong.'

Above them, the evening sky had broken into a dark patchwork. '*Echiqueles*,' said Ariella, looking up. 'Grey and black. Almost like a chessboard, but with no pieces. No stars, no moon.'

The river mist had dissolved but the air smelled moist. Ariella shivered. 'Winter comes too fast.'

'Go to your bed, 'Ella. It's been a murderous long day. We must be well up before cockcrow to select the new silks for the stall. And besides, methinks you would like to read your father's missive.'

She reached up to kiss him on the cheeks, but this time he wanted no chaste touch and turned his head, meeting her lips with his, hand lacing strongly through her hair, cradling the back of her head. She didn't fight, leaning in and pressing hard against him so that he felt a stirring. When they pulled away, her eyes burned into his.

'Wed me,' he said, his hand on her neck.

'I am a Jew, Guillaume, you are a Christian. We have rules. My father…'

'Then I shall ask *him*.'

Her face twisted as if she faced a dilemma and then she kissed him quickly on the cheek and left, a floral fragrance hovering behind, but then the aroma was surely his imagination. He cast a glance around the yard. Gosse stood at the gates – a big man in breadth and height, and Raol walked the boundaries of the yard like a deathly shade, taking a position in deep shadow against the wall of the storeroom where he could observe the roof of the house. All was quiet except for snoring from Herviet across the yard in the make-do billet.

Guillaume shut the door, leaving his boots against the jamb, feeling Adam's stitches pull as he bent over. Then he climbed the stair as softly as he could to the small space he occupied beyond Amée's chamber. He would move in with the men when the repairs to stable and storeroom were done. It seemed sensible.

But he burned with indignation at Amée's dismissal of Ariella. Such behaviour on Amée's part caused a memory to itch like a scab and he knew if he had been in Amée's employ, and not Gisborne's half brother with the responsibility for an investment, he would have taken Ariella and gone.

And he knew why.

Amée's arrogance reminded him of the nobility – people he despised, and whilst Amée might hold a position of regard amongst the merchants of Lyon, she was not at the top of that particular tree. Perhaps she needed reminding.

Yes. He was angry, but it didn't surprise him that such familiar antipathy was aroused. Sometimes he thought he sat on the knife-edge of emotion. Did people snap from reining it in so hard?

And what about Ariella's response to his proposal? He had felt her fire and he knew that their minds melded like damascened steel. But she persisted in holding back from him for that final commitment.

Why so?

Because he wasn't Jewish?

But then he could barely even call himself a Christian these days...

He had reached his room – the tiny cell that filled with his rangy bulk the moment he shut the door. He would move the chests and the money when it was time and the cot could stay there. This could be Ariella's room. Better than sleeping near the moody bulk of Mahaut. He would buy a woven blanket for her – a soft-coloured dye, something from his heart, perhaps at the market.

She had left a candle lit for him, as she did every night, a bowl sitting on the chest with a jug of water on the floor. He stripped to his *braies*, washed his face, hands and neck, thinking he wanted her as his wife.

Sitting on the cot, he drew the small chest onto his lap, taking a quill, a small flask of oakgall ink and a folded sheet of parchment from inside. He shut the chest, using the lid as a flat surface, smoothing the sheet out, feeling the doeskin surface of the paper. He had rescued the evenly edged remnant from a sheet Amée had cut in half. It was good quality, more so than he could probably afford, the quill an old one that he bought from Venezia, the ink a flask he had purchased on a trip to the Jewish quarter with Ariella. He thought for a moment, looking into the faraway distance of possibilities and then dipped the quill into the un-stoppered flask. Thus he began to write in his laborious hand:

To Saul ben Simon, from his servant and friend Guillaume de Gisborne, greetings.
I write to request your permission to take your esteemed daughter, Ariella, Lioness of God, to be wed. I have a deep affection for her which I believe she shares. I await your reply in the knowledge that spiritual differences may intercede. Your daughter will accept your decision though it would pain us both should you decide against such a union.
By the Grace of our Gods sir,
Valete.

He read it back. It was perfunctory, he knew, and his relationship with Saul was owed more. He had met him in the same place he had met Ariella. Moments after she pitched those cutting shears in a deft sally against attack in the Venetian Arsenale, her father ran into the warehouse yard, stricken with the thought he might have lost his only child. But Saul and his wife had named their daughter well – Ariella, Lioness of God. Guillaume tapped some sand over the letter as he thought.

No. Better to be honest and direct, as he had always been with Saul.

He rolled and tied the parchment, sealing it closed with a thick drop of plain wax into which he pressed Gisborne's seal, the three arrows dividing the wax palewise. He would take the missive to one of their trusted couriers before dawn, knowing that his wait for a reply would be long and testing.

As he looked at the roll, he wondered if he held a kind of fate in his hands, because if Saul denied him, he knew he would leave Lyon, leave Ariella and take to the road again. There were all sorts of courage but sharing the table with a woman you wanted but could not have was a step too far.

In any case, now that Jehanne had returned, he wondered how the management of the company would change. Perhaps there was no place for either he *or* Ariella, despite their intimate connection to the shareholders.

But that was yet to be seen so he laid the scroll down upon the chest, pulled off his *braies* and climbed into the rough linens that were the sheets on his bed. He lay very still, his stitches throbbing with the pressure of lying on his back and he fingered the bandage around his middle, wondering for how long he must wear it and thinking Ariella must not see him without a chemise.

He wasn't sure why he wanted to protect her from the knowledge that he had been attacked again because it was not as if she wouldn't be able to handle it. Perhaps it was more his problem than hers – this need to keep things close. It had been a matter of life and death once…

He waited for warmth to creep around the cot and loosen the knots of a difficult day, but it was tardy and so he grabbed a cloak from the door, wrapping himself like a shrouded corpse, and slipped once more into the bed.

He thought of the Bible and wondered if it was indeed why the house was torched and why he had been knifed. Crispianus was capable of organizing such things, he was sure. There was a stinking morass behind the monk's murky eyes. Adam might say there were other reasons for this current volatility around de Clochard, but in Guillaume's mind it came down to a Bible the Church considered heretical and a zealous priest who would stop at nothing to remove it from life, let alone Lyon.

The Vaudès Bible lay somewhere in Chez de Clochard and he would find it. What he would then do with it was yet to be considered and as he debated flames, deep holes in forests, or dispatching it with cargo to Venezia, the warmth he had longed for laid itself over him like a soft bodied whore and his eyes shuttered down.

The courier was not pleased to be woken when the sky was still black but he was a trusted man. Sighing, he took the scroll and his instructions with a nod, saying he would ride at dawn. Walking back to Ducanivet in the dark, Guillaume gave a brief thought to the note to Saul, wondering if there was any way it could have been handled differently. Deciding not, he was glad he carried a flame as he wiped sweat from his hands. Every dry leaf crushed, every cough behind closed shutters made his heart jump across his chest, reminding him of desert nights – dark skies with brilliant stars and the banshee wail of the wounded.

He was glad too that the Watch strode toward him, armed and carrying their own light.

'Messire Guillaume, you are about too early,' the one with a black beard said.

"Tis the market, you see. I am concerned our space is too small. I had to check.'

'But you break curfew…'

'I will pay any fine. It's just that after the fire, you know about the fire? Well, after the fire, I want everything to go well for Madame de Clochard. She has suffered much.'

'Aye,' Blackbeard said. 'She has, with her daughter missing and then her husband up and dying. She looked after my missus with good cloth that rightly we couldn't afford, but she reckoned the colour suited my woman and dropped the price. I haven't forgotten. She's not one to fleece the coin from a man's pocket.' The man looked to the east where a pale line the colour of peaches from the orchards of Persia bled upward into the night sky. A cock crowed, the strident call forcing a dog to retaliate.

'Go on,' the Watchman said, his fellow Watch yawning. 'It's dawn.'

By the time Guillaume reached the gates, the yard was busy, all guards about, Adam briefing everyone. In the hall, two bales had been carried in for the women to investigate. A rainbow of silks of which kings and queens might dream were revealed and somehow the women decided which might suit the stall and which might entice further customers to visit de Clochard's premises.

The second bale was slit open and Amée clasped her hands to her chest, whispering 'Praise *be* to Our Lord!'

Inside were fine woven woollens in *pers, cramoisy* and puce.

'A wonder…' Amée uttered as she unrolled an ell of the *cramoisy* and held it to her chest, the tint almost matching the apples of her cheeks. 'What a colour!'

Ariella's smile was broad. 'My father is nothing if not prescient.' She turned to the door. 'And where have you been?'

'Sending a letter to your father,' Guillaume replied as he picked up some of the unrolled fabric.

Ariella held the *pers* cloth to her chest and it looked as if she held a piece of the deep sea there. She looked down at the fabric and then said, 'Then let us hope he responds with due haste.'

There. It was said and it was done. And no rebuke.

'Is the cart outside?' she continued just as Adam knocked at the door to inform them that indeed it was.

'I have no doubt *you* ordered it,' Guillaume remarked as Ariella placed folded cloth into his arms.

'Of course. You were otherwise engaged yesterday and without our own beasts and harness, I thought it necessary.'

'This business thrives on your organization, Ariella. You know that, don't you?'

'I protect my father's investment, Guillaume, and in so doing protect myself.' She piled more of the woollens into his arms and he began loading the cart.

Finally, all that was left were the fur and ribbon trims. They were bagged in hemp and under Amée's forthright direction, placed at the front of the cart where she insisted she would sit with Adam who took the reins. 'By the way,' she called to any who would listen. 'I think we have a large debt to pay to our neighbours after the fire, and I was thinking to have an event – a feast perhaps. And I thought what a thing it would be to have it at the convent if the sisters would agree. I doubt it will be a problem if I offer money.'

Guillaume's eyebrows climbed and he cast a quick glance at Adam but the Master at Arms merely looked heavenward and clicked his tongue, flicking the reins on the horse's back. The cart rolled forward with Ariella and Guillaume following.

The carpenters were coming the other way and nodded, calling out that by nightfall, the frame of the barn would be constructed. A stringy youth sidled up, passing a message to Guillaume for the payment of a coin – Michael Sarapion thought quite rightly that it was not advisable to be seen with the household before the market. He and Jehanne would break their fast at the inn and then begin to mingle with the market crowd.

The market stretched in two long rows amongst the trees and scythed grass of the Monasterium Sancti Petri Puellarum on Presque L'ile. It was set back into the corner of the estate and customers and merchants entered through double gates set in the high wall. Old hemp awnings, much faded and limp with age, covered the rows and gave shelter and a sense of separateness to each stall, and the market also had a sense of history, as if it had been the same since Roman times.

The path between the rows was well trodden and smelled of late clover, but the only moisture was the previous evening's dew, waiting for a tardy sun to shine. The day promised to burn off to a brilliant blue, one of those autumnal days where dawn air is as sharp as cut glass, a light-as-cobweb mist hovering between the sun and the land, promising to reveal the detail of life at any moment.

By the time the food-sellers had set out their booths, the customers were filling the market space. Tall and short, fat and thin, guilty and innocent, ancient and new – they came because the market foretold excitement and a change from the hard routine of existence that was their everyday life. And if nothing else, at least they could break their fast with something other than pottage.

If they had coin…

As Guillaume walked along the aisles of booths, he heard a sweet voice calling to him and he turned. 'Soeur Marie! Good day to you!' he said.

An elderly woman with soft white skin and blue eyes redolent of the autumnal sky smiled back. 'A good day indeed, Messire Guillaume. I wish to thank you for the lengths of *brunete* wool. Our Sisters will benefit from it as winter approaches.'

''Tis nothing, Sister. You have always been kind to Madame de Clochard, especially since her husband died, and it is a way of honouring that kindness.'

She bowed her head in acknowledgement. 'It is God's will that we help where we can, Messire. Well, I must be gone. We are endeavouring to provide alms for those in need today…'

'Sister, can I ask something?'

She stopped, an interested look in her eyes.

'You embroider off-cuts from us to sell on the convent's behalf, don't you?'

'Yes…'

'I wish to buy a blanket for a woman's bed. Something…'

'Something womanly,' she said. 'And might we be talking about Ariella?'

He felt the stain of a blush creep over his face and she laughed, a clear tinkle amongst the rising noise of the market.

'I have a length of *verdalet*, not quite a blanket but almost. Madame de Clochard thought it might cut into a number of things, but we could not bear to slice it up. It is embroidered with a simple design on the hems.'

'Can I buy it?'

'It seems odd to buy back what de Clochard once owned…'

'Even so, it is what is right. And have you any girdles or purses made from other offcuts?'

She thought for a moment and then lifted her hand. 'In fact, we do. I have a small purse made of a suede offcut from Messire Ricard. One of the novices is an excellent stitcher and she embroidered it. It's *vermeil*, very bright.'

'It is a gift for Madame de Clochard before I leave for the Gigni Hunt and somehow, her nature requires brightness.'

'You are right and she will like it, bless her. You are very kind.'

'May I send for the goods tomorrow, Sister, perhaps before Sext?'

'Of course.'

'And the price?'

She shrugged. 'I cannot...'

'Then let me donate to the convent.' He dug into his purse and dragged out three silver *livres*, taking her hand and dropping the coins into her palm. 'Is this enough?'

Her eyes widened. 'Good gracious, yes! Our almshouse needs food money and this will do admirably. God keep you, messire! I shall offer prayers for you.'

'*Valete*, Soeur Marie, and I am very grateful.'

He bowed and then watched as the nun walked away, head tilted over her stooped body, nodding and smiling graciously to all she met. If only there were more in the Church like her.

He turned the corner and surveyed the market, now heaving with folk. Every cloth and fur merchant who could, sold their wares, but so did the artisan bakers, leather craftsmen and blacksmiths, women selling baskets of roadside herbs – hogweed, nettles, rosehips, plantain and more. A woodworker sat whittling toys, surrounded by a pile of soft golden curls – the shavings from a tree branch that he then fashioned from the mystery of his mind. Little dolls and tiny, rough flutes lay in a heap and in a short while, many a child ran wild with piercing peeps from the fresh made pipes. Jongleurs tumbled, tooted and strummed and a wandering puppeteer played his stringed dolls to tell a fable, children following him as if he were a figure of enchantment.

Guillaume looked about, charmed at this, his first Lyonnais market. It was easy to forget the violent possibilities of the day but his wits sharpened as he caught a glimpse of the Sarapions and he straightened, the stitches catching on the linen that wrapped him tight.

Women had initially been the first customers at the de Clochard stall and ell upon ell of cloth was quickly cut, folded and exchanged for handfuls of silver counted out willingly. But then men began to examine the cloth and Amée greeted them like old friends. Perhaps they were, for all knew her well enough to commiserate over the fire and compliment her on the array of quality merchandise.

Ariella merely smiled as if she had a secret. There was nothing patronising in it – men and women alike engaged with her as if she had been living in Lyon all her life and she responded to their questions honestly. She spent time giving the cloth its glorious provenance and customers' fingers developed the same lasciviousness the German envoys had displayed.

Guillaume leaned back against the tent-poles and listened, impressed at the mercantile skill that seemed life's blood to Ariella.

'Really? It came from the land of oliphants?'

'The Doge of Venice has this? This same cloth?'

'Mink from the Russias – oh, it is so very soft…'

'*La Reine* Eleanor wears this particular colour? I must have it then…'

She looked over the top of a man and woman bickering politely over a white fox trim from the north. Her eyes sparkled and she smiled broadly at Guillaume and he knew in that one glance, that if Saul gave his blessing, she would come willingly with all the fire of her mind and body.

For the first time in months, he allowed himself to experience a precipitate joy.

There was no harm in it, surely…

He turned to survey the scene and just at the moment, the crowds split apart, allowing a sliver of a view to the opposite side of the *allée*. A man bent over his bench, attaching feathers to an arrow shaft. The arrow had a bulbous nock, and the sunlight caught on gleaming white feathers as the fletcher bound them with dark string. The sharp steel bodkin flashed in that same sunbeam and the weapon might as well have pierced Guillaume's chest, so painful was the memory that scorched across his mind. Just prior, there was a fleeting moment when he wondered why an arrow maker at a market would be fletching arrows with a warhead rather than a common hunting bodkin but then the blood drained from his face like a fast flowing ebb tide and he became lightheaded as he remembered a time in the woods of La Flèche in Anjou.

His fists curled into tight, white-boned bunches as he sought to push memories far away…

CHAPTER FIVE

×

'Ansel,' Cateline stood close to her husband, tapping him on the shoulder. 'Teach him. He is interested.'

'I can see that,' Anselin replied as he prised three white flight feathers from Guillaume's hands.

He had been young the day his mother had urged his stepfather to teach him and make him an apprentice, but like his mother's marriage to the man, Guillaume's and Ansel's partnership was strong. Anselin of La Flèche was a bowyer and fletcher whose skill was recognised not just in Anjou, but further afield in the kingdom of France. He crafted curved arcs of yew or beech, crossbows, arrows and quarrels and he made knives and needles – the handles of the daggers carved from horn or bone and the needles from remnant bone slivers and tough hog bristle.

Anselin was proud of his stepson's willingness to learn and the two maintained La Flèche's reputation as a village of great bowyers and fletchers. However, as he grew, it became apparent that Guillaume had another skill…

His father had given him a light bow, one that he had traded from an Arab at a foire. Quaint and made of horn, it had upturned nocks and its size appealed to Ansel who had heard of the deadly Saracen archers at Hattin during the Second Crusade. He had his stepson nock an arrow, drawing until the feathers flirted with his cheek.

Guillaume pulled with ease and at the command 'loose', the arrow sighed away to hit the target. Ansel passed him another arrow and then another, each flying true, and at the end of ten Guillaume was neither tired nor strained. Ansel clapped him on the shoulder, remarking 'Good' as he retrieved the arrows. But he kept his son's prowess a secret.

'There are vainglorious noblemen who would find it insulting that a mere vassal could be a better archer than themselves or their trained men. Your skill is the kind that will make men jealous. Use it wisely.'

Guillaume always listened to what his softly spoken, almost deaf stepfather would say and time passed with Guillaume taking more of the responsibility of the crafting. Whispers began to reach La Flèche of a new holy crusade. And the orders came for weaponry, orders from the Comte d'Anjou, and suddenly the words changed from whispers to shouts.

'The Cross…'

'Jerusalem…'

'Holy Crusade!'

Young men swaggered as they prepared to join Richard I, Duke of Normandy, Duke of Aquitaine, Duke of Gascony, Count of Poitiers, Count of Anjou, of Maine, of Nantes, Overlord of Brittany and Lord of Cyprus by the Grace of God.

When Father Dominic enunciated the titles to those assembled, men preened at the thought of serving such a man of power for they were simple men who believed in the lustre of majesty. Now they lived in a state of perpetual battle fervour, where young men saw fighting as a right of passage with no real care that slaughter was implicit. The same call to arms went out in France, as Philip Augustus prepared his army, and to the Holy Roman Empire and the Italian states.

'It's such a sad irony,' said Anselin, 'that a bowyer scrapes to keep his head above water in peacetime, but come the war wherever it is, monies flow readily.'

As a vassal of the Angevin Comte, Guillaume would be required to join King Richard's army, but Ansel was an aged liability. He could barely hear his beloved Cateline or his stepson, and he had become frail over the years. He confessed to being glad.

'I may not receive forgiveness for my sins but I cannot condone killing men. Not even for God and King Richard.' He crossed himself and then picked up a sliver of ash and began to fletch it. 'They say there will be three thousand archers –three thousand men who march because they want to fight for their King. Or perhaps because they want expiation for their sins. Huh, three thousand – that's a lot of sin.'

Hours were filled with feathers and wood, bodkins and string and there was *never enough time in a day. But then the final sennight was upon them with painful suddenness, accompanied by an odd request.*

Guillaume had been hunting and as he laid bird carcasses on the trestle to pluck, Anselin said, 'You must go to Chinon tomorrow.'

'Chinon? In Christ's name why?'

'King Richard orders the best bowyer and fletcher in the County of Anjou to attend him. He was told that it was you or I…'

Touraine appealed to Guillaume.

He found the Vienne river valley, close by Chinon, cool and shady in the early June warmth. He was not at all anxious about meeting the King – Richard Plantagent was surely just another man like himself, sprung from between the legs of a woman equal to his own mother. But he had no doubt the King was probably arrogant, most certainly filled with the idea of noble privilege. Since he was a small boy, Guillaume's opinion of true nobility lay at the feet of Anselin of La Flèche. No purer man could exist, despite that he had no crown. Ordinary men suffered at the whim of their leigelords – across Anjou, across France, the Holy Roman Empire and further if what they said was true. This merely confirmed Guillaume's belief that the nobility had little compassion for men, women and children beyond their walls. Did they not say that every man in England had to pay monies to the Monarch's treasury to allow Richard Plantagenet to go to war against the Saracen? Did the Monarch himself not say, as he raised scutage, 'I would sell London, if only some one should buy it?'

Where was the noblesse *in such a sentiment? If Guillaume felt anything about going to this Holy War, he knew he would have to hide his temper in the face of the arrogance of nobility. He could never suffer fools gladly.*

As he was led through Chinon Castle by a steward, the courtiers looked him up and down meaningfully, smirking and whispering behind hands. But it barely scratched his skin, because there were few who matched his height and it gave him a perverse pleasure to look down upon the insolent privileged.

He was taken to a pleasant arbour where the sounds of doves laced with the seductive belly laugh of a mature woman. Older than Cateline but younger than an ancient, she sat on a cross-legged stool – her burnished beauty a thing of pleasure to look upon. Guillaume was a man who had lain with women and he knew beauty when he saw it. This then was the great Eleanor, mother to a king…

'Majesty,' a young woman of pleasing countenance drew Eleanor's attention to the new arrival.

Eleanor of Aquitaine turned and he dropped his head in obeisance.

'You are the archer?' she asked, her voice stroking every part of any man close by. Christ she had a presence!

'No, my lady. I am the fletcher.'

The Queen's courtiers sniggered and Eleanor's gaze flew round, scorching them into obedient quiet.

'Of course you are an archer! Show me a bowyer and fletcher who has never tried his own weapons and I shall bestow a county upon you!'

He grinned at her. ''Tis true what you say...'

'Your name?'

'Guillaume, my lady.'

'Guillaume of?'

'Guillaume of ... Anjou.' He felt no discomfort at labelling himself thus because it was a simple truth. And it sounded better to his ear than Guillaume de La Flèche, despite the latter had a more suitable ring to it.

'The King my son has ordered you here, Guillaume of Anjou... ah, he is come...'

A sunrise-sunset presence swept into the arbour and there was an immediate rustling of cloth, like a breeze passing over a field of summer barley. Knees and waists were bent and Guillaume bowed his head again as Eleanor said, 'This is the archer, Guillaume of Anjou...'

Richard stood shorter than Guillaume, with a cropped beard and head of tawny mussed hair, as if he had walked through thorns backward. His clothes were filthy, his hose with holes and the tawdriness illuminated action and energy.

'Ladies and sirs, leave us. Maman, you will stay?'

'If you would have me, Sire...'

Richard stood in front of Guillaume, examining him.

'Are you English?'

Am I? I was born in England...

'No, Sire. I am from La Flèche.'

'You have no family in England?'

I will not tell you my history. It is my mother's and mine alone...

'No, Sire...'

'Christ Jesus, Maman. There is an unholy likeness...'

'I am not sure that it is unholy, Richard, but yes, I do see. It is amusing. His name is Guillaume of Anjou…'

Richard shook his head. 'I should like to stand you with a knight of my court because there is a haunting sameness. His name is Guy of Gisborne. Hah!' He slapped his hand on his thigh, shaking his head in amused disbelief. 'So, Guillaume of Anjou – you are touted to be one of the best bowyers in all my duchies and counties.'

Guillaume's heart crashed against his chest. His mother had told him of his noble half-brother, of his roots. But to have the King of England drop the name into a casual conversation… He dragged his sensibilities back to the King's presence. 'An honour, Sire, but there are many as good.'

'The humility does you proud and is refreshing after a morning with Welshmen. Do you come to Outremer with me?'

'Of course, Sire. It is a duty to my liege and to God, is it not?'

'Indeed it is.' He laid his hand along Guillaume's shoulder. 'Now, master bowyer, I have had the misfortune to listen to the Welsh who brag incessantly of their archers. They are loyal to our Holy Crusade but given to misplaced embellishment. They say their fellows are better archers than my own. That if we all used a curved bow instead of a crossbow, Jerusalem would be ours in a heartbeat. What think you?'

The King stood in an errant sunbeam and it lit his tangled hair with a golden halo but with his common appearance, he was hardly kingly. A man of the people they said…

But which people? Those in England whose lives had literally been sold to raise monies for the Cross?

'My stepfather would say so, Sire. He has never been a lover of crossbows. He calls them widow-makers.'

'But according to the Welshmen, good fletched ash can make widows as well. Piercing armour through to the heart.'

'Indeed, my lord. The right bow, the right arrow and the right man – a swift and deadly delivery.'

'Then my army of crossbow archers are useless?'

'Not at all. But a good archer can loose five arrows, maybe more, from a curved bow in the time it takes to load a crossbow. I am sure you know all of this, Sire.'

Richard frowned, his handsome features as creased as his clothes. 'Of course. And indeed it is what the Welsh say, but I like to hear what the men of the field think. What weapon shall you use?'

Guillaume looked at Eleanor and her mouth curved as if she knew Guillaume's answer.

'My lord, I am a bowyer and fletcher, not an archer. I will arm your men, not fight.'

'By God, you will fight, Guillaume of Anjou!' King Richard exploded. 'No man travels to the Holy Land with me who does not wage war on the Saracen!'

Guillaume bowed his head. 'As you wish, Sire.'

'I do wish, Guillaume of Anjou, and you will heed me. I expect to see you with my army in Lyon and thence we shall proceed to Marseille.'

He turned his back on Guillaume and taking his mother's arm he walked away. Guillaume thought what a waste of time the visit to Chinon had been when he could have been helping Ansel. Richard, tempestuous 'man of the people', had the word from his Welshmen so he hardly needed the word of a lowly Angevin. Everyone knew of the magic that hung about the Welsh archers. Richard Plantagent was just toying with time – filling in the idle moments until he could lead his army to meet the French in Lyon. Did he plan to re-arm the archers? Hardly likely. Not that Guillaume cared. Nevertheless, Cateline would enjoy the tale of the day. It would serve to lighten her mood as she counted the hours until her son left for the Crusade.

As he rode home on the horse borrowed from the blacksmith, he wondered at his own attitude to this war. The morality of it stank like a dung heap in his mind. Try as he might, he could not believe that it was godly, no matter that popes and prelates said otherwise. Surely God did not condone the slaughter of innocents, whatever their faith.

Guillaume knew he should fear God more but the truth was that whilst he respected his God, he had little to no respect for those who ministered in His name. They took much and gave little, and for vassals like the folk of La Flèche, Chinon and any other place, there was no redress. Not if they wanted to die shriven.

His horse ambled past the inn that had overflowed for weeks now with travellers making their way to Lyon to join with Philip Augustus or Richard Plantagent. Men were so caught up in the crusading spirit – even now he could hear German and Italian voices, routiers from across the country. In another day, he too would be a part of it all – a reluctant soldier under orders from his king.

He halted at the rear of the blacksmith's, dismounting and removing the saddle, seeing a sweat mark on the horse's back and wiping it with a knotted grass wisp. He worked rhythmically and the animal pushed against him, enjoying the pressure on its coat as clumps of thick winter hair floated off in the spring breeze. As Guillaume clicked his teeth to get the beast to straighten up, he heard shouts from within the smithy and he dropped the wisp and hurried round to the front. Two men appeared at the entrance, swearing and threatening. One held a horseshoe and hurled it away in a fit of rage. It hit a rock on the other side of the track, the collision ringing on the air. The man was broad and of middle height, his woad-dyed tunic spattered, the sleeve torn and he pushed at Guillaume, snarling, leaving a scent behind of stale breath, sweat … and something else…

Jean One Eye, the blacksmith, came after them, his face puce with temper as he fingered his neck. 'Bastards! Ignorant bloody foreigners!'

'Soldiers? Routiers?' Guillaume watched the men hurry away, pushing aside folk in their path.

'Arrogant piss artists more like. They're Pisans heading to Marseille from Paris, they said. They want a horse shod now, this instant, and when I explained I still had a shipment of arrowheads to be forged by dark, the taller one took me by the throat and then threatened Alaïs. They saw her when she bought in my food, you see. I said to bring the animal at first light…'

Guillaume commiserated and thanked the blacksmith for the horse, passing him a livre that had been pushed upon him by one of the Queen's ladies.

'The Queen says thank you, messire,' she had said and now Jean One Eye took it from Guillaume, slightly mollified.

'The carts of weapons leave in a convoy at first light, Guillaume. Anselin hasn't bought in your last shipment.'

'You say? He said he would load the handcart and make two or three trips whilst I was away.'

'Nope, hasn't been…'

'I will bring them, never fear. He had an ague not long since and tires easily.'

'He is lucky to have a son like you to take over, Guillaume.'

'I am as lucky to have him as my father, Jean. Be careful tomorrow and send Alaïs away for the morning. Don't tempt fate. They have the look of danger about *them, those Pisans.'*

Guillaume walked on, wanting to reach the bowyer's cottage before dusk. He wanted time to stand still whilst he farewelled a life well-lived. He was under no illusions as to the dangers he would face.

He called out as he strode along, but there was nothing but the evening call of birds and Cateline's fowl pecking amongst the wild herbs of the path.

'Cateline? Maman?'

Nothing…

'Ansel?' He poked his head into the workshop.

Arrows were tied in bundles of ten, both plain and crossbow. Unstrung bows had been piled into the handcart.

The silence irked him.

This was not what he wanted – not on this last night. He wanted to remember the sound of a family.

'Maman, Papa! Where are you?'

A deathly quiet pervaded, even the birds silencing as a breeze stirred unfurling buds with a shuffle. His skin began to prickle, his breath quickening as he hurried past the woodheap to the rear of the plain dwelling.

He saw her foot first. Her boot was missing – those fine little chamois boots that Ansel had bought her, and her bare white toes looked so vulnerable. He ran toward his mother as she lay twisted on the ground, her bliaut rucked up brazenly, blood smeared on her pale thighs. Her head was turned away and he gasped, falling to his knees, pulling the folds of her gown down. He put his hands tenderly on either side of her head and turned it towards him.

Her face could have been no whiter, not even if she was a spectre. She had been thrashed across the mouth and had bitten her tongue and blood had flowed down her chin. Her cheeks were contorted with swelling so that one side of her face seemed not to work at all as she took one breath and then another, spaced so far apart that Guillaume thought she had died in between.

'Maman,' he whispered, grasping her clenched hand.

Her eyes fluttered open and she stared at him. He knew her body was broken and that the pain had skewered her and he knew he could do nothing.

'Guillaume…'

'Hush, Maman.'

'Anselin,' she mumbled through her swollen mouth. 'Ansel…' With inhuman

effort she turned her head toward the copse of trees and he then saw what she had been facing toward as he arrived.

His gentle stepfather lay in a pool of blood, his neck almost severed. In his hand, he clutched one of his daggers but it hadn't saved his life as he had tried to save his wife's.

A sob tore from Guillaume's throat and he glanced down at his mother, holding her hand and shuffling on his knees to block her view.

But her eyes stared into a distance far beyond the carnage. In that brief moment, her soul had flown and all that remained was a single tear sliding down her cheek. Guillaume scooped his index finger beneath it and held it for a moment, watching the setting sun reflected in the miniscule crystal clear globe. Christ, he hurt. He kissed the tear, then closed his mother's eyes.

One of Cateline's fowl stood tall and flapped its wings as he smoothed his mother's fist out, finding a scrap of cloth crunched there, and in just one beat of the bird's wing, Guillaume, who had been as kind and gentle as his stepfather, hardened to sharpened steel.

He wrapped his parents in blankets and took them to the priest at the little Church of Saint Pierre. He banged on the door, caring not that he was covered in blood, or that he disturbed the priest at his meal.

'I want a Mass,' he said, words forced from his mouth. His hands trembled. 'I want them shriven. I want them buried in holy ground before I leave because they were murdered when I wasn't here to protect them and they deserve better.'

'It will take time,' the priest grumbled. 'The graves...'

'I will dig them myself. Right now.'

By the time a pale grey dawn sky had replaced the somber night, Anselin, the bowyer of La Flèche and his loved wife, Cateline, were blessed and laid side by side. The priest had asked of the murder but Guillaume was sparing in the detail — what was there to tell beyond the loss of two lives?

The priest said, 'An unfortunate thing but a common one. God has them in His care now, my son.'

Guillaume threw some money on a plate on the altar. 'He should have had them in His care always,' he sneered and stormed from the church, slamming the door behind.

He delivered the remaining shipment of weapons to Jean One Eye, telling him nothing of his parents' violent end. The priest would do that, he was sure, and he wanted to be well gone. It was the overt sympathy he could not cope with. Better to leave now…

'I leave for Lyon and the King's army immediately, Jean, and I need a horse. I have money…' He opened his purse.

'Take Colle. He knows you. Did you meet the King? You didn't say…'

'I did. 'Tis why I can pay you for Colle. I received monies for yesterday's journey.'

Jean pulled a face. 'Then King Richard is generous. I had heard he counts every penny for his army.'

Guillaume cinched up the girth on Colle and the horse tossed his head up and down. 'The coin came from Queen Eleanor, not her son. Have the Pisans been?'

'Yes. I sent Alaïs to her aunt's on the other side of La Flèche yesternight, which was as well, because the Pisans were here before light and pushed their way into our house.' Jean spat. 'God's beard but they reeked, Guillaume. Of money and wine and much else besides. Good riddance.' The blacksmith buckled the bridle. 'Worse than Saracens.'

Guillaume said nothing, his mind filled with his parents' suffering, an ugly grief poisoning his blood to black. As he mounted, Jean took hold of the reins.

'Take care, Guillaume. For your mother and for Ansel. Come back for them and for us all. We wish you well.'

Guillaume nodded and forced a thank you through teeth that chattered. 'Valete,' he managed to call over his shoulder as Colle settled to a steady trot.

As he left the village, he acknowledged no one and didn't look back, closing his heels on Colle so that the surprised old horse squealed and then began to gallop. Guillaume held the reins in one hand, feeling his purse at his girdle – a purse that held a scrap of woad-dyed cloth that belonged to the sleeve of a Pisan who reeked of wine, sweat, blood…

And rape.

The road in the direction of Lyon from La Flèche was less a highway, more a forest track and Guillaume knew it well, knew the other tracks that wove and bent through the forest and it was one of these short-cuts that he took, pushing Colle through the spring-clad trees. Forest detritus muffled the hooves but inevitably, a hoof would crack a fallen branch and birds would fly up in alarm.

A few leagues and the track looped back and he slowed Colle, the animal snorting and breathing hard. He led him behind a rise, to a dense copse of trees, hobbling him and hoping that the animal would graze, even doze. Anything rather than neigh to approaching horses.

He took Anselin's Saracen bow from the saddle, along with two arrows. They were fletched in a hawk's flight feathers, unusual for their workshop. Mostly white feathers were used but these were the tawny colours of a predator. It suited Guillaume.

Back by the road, he climbed a sturdy beech, concealed by the spring canopy, the watchet green discs flirting and flitting in the light morning breeze. Dew still hung on a web by his shoulder and a spider squatted balefully, shifting a leg as the web shivered in the puffs of air.

He sighted along the shaft of his arrow to the needle-sharp bodkin. A beam of light caught on the forged steel and he moved it a hair's width into the shadow of tree and leaf.

The feathers stroked his cheek like a whore's fingers and he closed his eyes, seeing a pers-tinted bliaut rucked up and blood seeping from the folds. And a man lying close by, head and neck almost severed.

He opened his eyes and sighted again.

They came, the two men – riding at a shambling walk along the forest path. The dappled light shifted and changed as a breeze skirted around them, carrying the smell of damp earth and fungi and the sweat of horses. One of the men laughed loud, and a cuckoo flew up with a sharp cry, battering the air with its wings, one of the horses dancing sideways. On being dragged back to the track, the animal tossed its head up and down, harness jingling. Its rider sat easily – obviously a man of means and equestrian skill. A man of power.

How easy it was, thought Guillaume, to forfeit your life by taking an innocent's.

He waited one breath more and loosed and loaded in the time it took for the next breath.

Thwack…

A dull sound – through the skull, front to back.

Loose again!

An even duller sound as the second arrow took the second man through the eye, the force of the arrow carrying on through the brain.

Both men died instantly, falling backward onto their horse's rumps, the horses startled and shying, and then as the men fell lifeless, still in stirrups to dangle about nervous legs, they bolted, the riders bumping along like ill-filled bags of barley.

He jumped from the tree.
Revenge, he thought, is not so sweet after all...

'Look out! Look out!'

Shouting, scuffling, a pain as something hit him in the back and he staggered as he turned.

The crowd pulled back as he grabbed at the fleeing youth who had almost knocked him over.

'Thief, thief!' an accented voice called from amongst the people and the crowd parted further, allowing a small bearded man to rush up. 'The pile of pig shit stole my purse. Look – it's in his hand. Christ's nosehairs, you little goose-turd!' He swiped the purse back from the youth's filthy hands as the Watch took him from Guillaume's grip.

Guillaume's back throbbed with a ferocious tempo but he was glad. Glad too that the thief had knocked into his wound so hard it had probably split the stitches. Because the multi-coloured memories that had flooded into his recall were as quickly banished as he had grabbed the youth.

'Pile of loose shit!' the small man yelled after the Watch in what sounded like a Spanish accent. 'Put him in a prison cell!'

He reminded Guillaume of Tobias with his foreshortened height and his swagger and there was a tone in his voice. But of course he looked nothing like suave, silk-covered Toby who never had a hair out of place. This fellow's face was covered in an untrimmed black beard and his hair was streaked with grey above his ears.

But his eyes...

They told stories and right now, they pinned Guillaume to the stall's poles. '*Toby?*'

'Christ Jesus, Guillaume,' Tobias hissed. 'Has your mind dulled to mud since you have been a merchant? Be quiet!' He looked around and said in a louder voice and with a bow, 'My name is Sens di Dia, from Spain. And I thank you for your swift actions. He had taken my whole purse. All my money. I would have been a pauper, reduced to beg...'

Guillaume broke in, 'You are welcome, sir. I am your servant, and if I can be of further assistance, come to the cloth merchant's house, de Clochard, in Rue Ducanivet. It is easy to locate. We are quite well known.'

'I thank you again, sir. It may be that I do need some cloth for a new tunic, maybe a cloak. *Valete…*'

Tobias twitched a one-fingered salute and walked away, whistling.

Guillaume, amused and happier than he could have thought possible, turned back to the stall, Ariella sidling up to him.

'Was…'

'Yes,' he replied with speed, immediately changing the course of the conversation. 'How do we do?'

'Very well,' she gave Guillaume a sideways look, but caught on swiftly. 'We are almost done. There is so little left, we could close now and return to Ducanivet.'

'Then do it.' He rubbed his back. 'We are safer in our own home than in the open air here on Presque L'ile.'

His back hurt and under his cloak, he felt dampness. Adam must do more doctoring when they got back to the house. And like the wound, his memories rubbed at his consciousness as he tried to ignore them.

Grief is my companion, he mused, and I am a changed man forever. Only those who have lost like I have, or seen what I have seen will understand. He looked across the crowds and his gaze met the steadfast eyes of Michael Sarapion. With the slightest lift of the man's eyebrows, he seemed to ask if all was well and Guillaume nodded, a barely there movement as like to come from a man who was thinking about something.

Directly in front of him, his back facing Guillaume, Adam of London stood examining his nails, sliding one under the other as if cleaning them. But his calves were bunched and he stood lightly on his feet so that he could spring in any direction.

'Guillaume!' Amée called and he swung about, walking to the trestle, noting it was as naked as a new set of planks. 'We are done!' She slapped the wood and held up two clinking linen bags. 'Excellent morning. Now, where are the guards to see us home?'

The time for concealment was done and he called to Adam, to Jehanne and Michael and together with Ariella, they moved to their cart. The women climbed in, the men following behind as Adam led the horse.

'No problems,' Michael observed. 'Apart from the young thief.'

'No. And yet we were sure…'

'Perhaps too obvious a place and time? Perhaps they think to catch you more off guard?'

'I thought the same,' Guillaume agreed. 'They choose to catch us when our defences are down.'

'An interesting scenario, Guillaume. I am not sure I thought to be walking into something like this when we left Venezia. It smacks of Constantinople.'

'Was it desperate there?'

'In a word? Yes. And a sad end. I saw Tobias today, didn't I?'

'Yes.'

'Shall he come to us?'

'I suspect so. In his own time.'

'I like him. He's a good man…'

'More than good, Michael.'

As the cart rolled out under the arched gate of the convent wall, a priest moved in front of them and Adam dragged the horse to a stop. It stood chewing its bit with temper and tossing its head up and down.

'A successful day, Madame de Clochard.' Brother Crispianus smiled like an angel from Hell.

'Oh indeed, Brother Crispianus,' said Amée, her face reflecting the joy of a day well done. 'God continues to smile upon us. You have obviously petitioned for us in your prayers and we thank you.'

The smile thinned to the width of a piece of string, and almost as limp. 'Indeed, my child. Always.'

Adam clicked the horse ready to move on but the priest reached for the cheekstrap, holding it back. 'You forget your dues, Madame. A percentage of takings to pay from your stall.'

'But I paid in advance, Brother Crispianus. The money was paid by Ariella to the Sisters in order to reserve our booth. In addition, we gave them some ells of burnet woolen cloth for cloaks.'

The monk's face twisted to a grimace, 'Then they did wrong in accepting both the payment and the cloth. All rentals are paid direct to the Archbishop's notary.'

'Since when?' Amée snorted. 'The Benedictine convent owns this land.'

Brother Crispianus skewered Amée with a look as sharp as a *misericorde*. 'They are answerable to the highest priest in the land. That is Archbishop

Renaud. You surely know this.'

Guillaume hated the priest that little bit more. 'Madame de Clochard did what she and Jehan have always done, Brother Crispianus. They paid direct to the Sisters. I would ask *you,* surely *you* must know this.'

'The rules are changed.' The priest stood his ground.

'Without notice,' Guillaume replied. 'As is your God-given right, it seems. And how much would the Archbishop like? A half? Three quarters?' He had moved to stand directly in front of the priest, his lean height overshadowing the man so that he must look up.

'A quarter,' Brother Crispianus replied in his nasal voice, folding his scabbed hands into his cuffs.

'Then shall we count our takings here on the road and give you your share now, or shall you trust us to return to Ducanivet and do it there? Perhaps you would prefer to attend us to make sure we are honest?'

People had stopped, curious at the tense voices, at the man fronting the priest that no one liked. They listened with expectant hope, wanting to see him belittled. The priest noticed them and with a little sneer, lifted one side of his string-like mouth and Guillaume wondered if the Devil had pulled it.

'The Archbishop has always trusted de Clochard. I see no reason why that should change…' His muddy gaze fell upon Ariella before he continued. 'I am sure you will conclude an adequate accounting and pay the Church what it is owed.'

'Of course,' Guillaume bowed with as little sincerity as he could muster. 'Less what was given to the Sisters.'

Crispianus' eyes settled back upon Guillaume and he too bowed his head with false humility. 'Of course. God keep you.'

Guillaume turned away, calling over his shoulder, 'We shall call upon you just before Vespers. Adam, move on if you will.'

The horse was clicked on and the priest had to step out of the way. Guillaume knew that as they headed toward the bridge from Presque L'ile, the man would be calling down God's disfavour upon them all.

They made their way in silence across the Pont du Change. Below them, the water quickened about the bridge, parting angrily round the spans to run on and if they listened carefully, they could hear the splash and splatter of a weight of water against stone. The sky gazed at itself in the quieter reaches further on, a clear blue reflection that spoke of a still autumn day. Here and there, fallen leaves no doubt floated on the river current like strange little vessels from another world.

Halfway across the bridge, Amée uttered a wrathful curse. 'Seed of the Devil! That's what he is! How Monseigneur Reynaud can have that monk representing him, I will never know. A quarter of our takings indeed! How dare he? It's never been so high. I'm of a mind to speak to the Monseigneur about this. I lay my life down that he does not expect a quarter of anyone's takings.'

'Probably not,' Ariella said. 'But there is little point in making a scene because Brother Crispianus would make sure he got back at de Clochard in other ways.'

Jehanne pulled off her veil and smoothed her hair, tossing her plait back over her shoulder. 'He doesn't like us, does he?'

'Well I can't think why that would be,' Amée was still puffing with ire. 'I am a regular churchgoer. I pay my dues. I honour the Archbishop and all that he represents. What more does the damned monk want?'

'Me,' Ariella answered and all eyes swivelled toward her. 'You all consort with a Jewess. By his laws, I deal in usury and am a disbeliever. He would consider anyone who has contact with me to be a sinner and me the biggest sinner of all.'

'Then he can deal with it,' Guillaume snapped. 'Do you not think so, Amée? After all, Ariella is a partner through her father and she has been a bulwark in tough times.'

Amée's eyebrows lifted in surprise at the vehemence with which Guillaume spoke. But he was determined she should not shove Ariella aside now that Jehanne had returned. He wanted her to remember back...

Amée had the grace to blush and she leaned forward and patted Ariella's hand. 'Indeed you have, my dear, and I have been remiss not to appreciate your strength and assistance these past months. Jehanne, this woman has been at my shoulder when I had no one else.'

It was Guillaume's turn to be surprised. But then perhaps not, because Amée obviously still hurt at her daughter's perceived disloyalty at leaving her parents alone, ignorant of her fate and grieving. He also wondered how Jehanne, so self-possessed and strong, would accept another woman of equal power and accomplishment within de Clochard.

'Then I am glad, *Maman*,' she said. 'And Ariella, I look forward to working with you in moving my family's business forward.'

'You are not afraid of disturbing the monk's equilibrium?'

'Not at all. Living with jealousies and insecurities in Byzantium was as bad, if not worse.'

Ariella responded with her customary dignity. 'Thank you, Jehanne. Because like my father and my lord Gisborne, I believe de Clochard has great scope for the future.'

They had almost reached the gates of de Clochard. Guillaume had allowed the women to play their hands with each other because he needed to know how the land lay.

'A strong group of women together can be a problem,' observed Michael.

Guillaume answered with a wry grin. 'Indeed and if this gathering of cats ever turns on each other, then it won't be pretty. But they have everything to gain from working together. I don't know anything of your Jehanne but I can vouchsafe Ariella.'

Michael rubbed at his thigh as if it pained him as the cart turned into de Clochard ahead of them. Gosse stood at the gates and saluted. 'Jehanne is self-sufficient and she has survived in a violent and reactive city. She must get used to being within a partnership again and to trusting people. She is not by nature a vicious woman.'

Guillaume heard the note in Michael's voice. 'She impresses you.'

'Enough to make her my wife, yes. And she saved my life.'

Envy ran like molten tar through Guillaume and he hated it. 'You are a lucky man,' he said.

'You would wed Ariella, I think.'

'But I am not Jewish, Michael. It matters.'

'To you or to her?'

'Not to me, no.' He didn't add any more, he did not know Michael well enough. 'In any case, I suspect all will be well with our women and we must help by making it so. Businesses are apt to fail when egos get in the way.'

'I understand. A process of adjustment for us all.' Michael smiled and walked up to the cart, putting out a hand to help the women alight.

Adam spoke kindly to the horse as he unbuckled the harness, busying himself with the animal's comfort. '*Dameisele*,' he said to Ariella. 'I will return the beast to the livery later if you agree.'

'Perhaps when Guillaume takes our dues to Brother Crispianus? Additional protection?'

He nodded and gave her the slightest wink which Guillaume caught. He liked the way the two had slotted back into their Venetian friendship. It made for solidarity within de Clochard.

Amée and her family had walked into the house, the widow's voice filling the space with life as she ordered Mahaut to set the table for a hungry household. Mahaut's reply was but a sullen rumble, like a far-off thunderstorm.

Ariella and Guillaume stood side by side watching Adam make a last swipe at the horse's coat with a wisp.

'I look forward to bringing our animals home,' Guillaume noted. 'The carpenters are making swift progress. By the end of this sennight, I suspect we will have a barn, if not Amée's beloved buttery or whatever she calls it on any one day.'

Indeed, the frame and roof supports were raised and planks of timber were being nailed along the walls.

'You have a damp patch on your cloak, Guillaume,' Ariella said. 'Methinks it is blood...' She touched it and looked at her fingers. 'That youth was armed?'

'No...'

'Tell me,' she ordered.

'*I'll* tell you,' Adam said at his most phlegmatic, shifting the horse over so he could move around it. 'He was attacked in the square when he took Amée to Mass.'

Ariella's eyes widened.

'And he would not tell you for fear of worrying you.'

'What a considerate man he is,' she said, irony sharpening her tone. She lifted his cloak and looked at the stained tunic. 'And so stupid. We have shared much, so this is just another.'

'I will tend it for him, *Dameisele*. Whilst I am no physician, I can look after men.'

'In war, yes. But this is...'

'War. Or as good as. If we only knew who the goddamned enemy was!' He ran his hands over his freckled forehead, pushing ruddy hair behind his ears.

'Ariella,' Guillaume said. 'We shall not tell Amée. It makes for quieter times.

114

Michael and Jehanne on the other hand, are worth including. Their history makes them commendable assets to us and most definitely to de Clochard.'

'I agree,' Ariella said. 'But I feel for Amée…'

'She has had shock after shock for weeks now. Let her mend a little and enjoy her daughter's homecoming. We can manage. It is after all why we are here, is it not?'

She sighed, her mouth twisting in the smallest of grimaces, but he knew that she would agree. He kissed her on both cheeks, saying 'Adam will see to me and then we shall come in and begin the accounting. Or shall you start on it?'

She laughed, the soft sound from deep in her belly that set his manhood tingling.

Christ she is beddable. If only…

'I'm a Jew's daughter, Guillaume. Doesn't everyone think we count coins in our mother's wombs? No, I shall wait. Don't be long.'

He sat on Adam's cot, the bed rocking on the cobbles. 'You need to chock the legs, Adam. It's unsteady.'

Adam nodded, unwrapping the bandage around Guillaume's middle. 'But then I am hardly in the bed long enough for it to matter. You lot in Lyon are worse than them in Venezia!' He pulled the wad of linen away from the wound and swore. 'Jesu wept, Guillaume. Half the stitches are split!'

Guillaume sat still, trying not to wince as Adam plied the bone needle back and forth again. He thought of the last few days and begged any angel or saint to give them a pattern – something, anything so that they could discern who was their enemy. It made no sense, none of it.

Adam wrapped him up again with brusque efficiency. 'Well, like I said, I'm no physician but I reckon if they pull again, you'll have no use of me, Guillaume. You'll need a proper field-surgeon. The wound's torn now, although mercifully free from infection. More by good luck than your good management I think. You attract trouble like bad meat attracts flies. I never would have thought. Makes life interesting although Christ knows what my lord Gisborne'll say!'

Guillaume shrugged, pulling on his stained tunic, saying he was hungry and that it was time to eat.

Mahaut had filled the table with a stew of pork and herbs with root vegetables. As always though, and under the widow's direction there was something for the Jewess in their midst – a fish pie this time. There was fresh wastel and ale, and the wine had improved. Guillaume was under no illusions that it was because the daughter of the house had returned. Every time Mahaut bought a salver to the table, she almost simpered past Jehanne, even patting her head as though she were still a child. But to Ariella, Guillaume and Adam, she was as ill-mannered as always. The food however was filled with the taste of autumn pickings and was welcome.

Once bellies were full and the long table had been cleared, the accounting began. Ariella had been insistent that a list be made of the goods going to market and as she and Amée were the ones selling the cloth, they knew exactly what had sold and to whom. Amée kept up a running commentary, telling everyone what position this or that purchaser held within the town as Ariella crossed off the list and counted the coins.

'Did you see Messire Gigni, Guillaume?' Amée asked. 'He bought the thick trim of white fox for his wife's cloak. An ebony velvet he said, bought at great cost from Al-Andalus. I was surprised he purchased fur trim from us and not Messire Ricard, not that I'm complaining. Mind you, I wonder that he doesn't have such trims amongst his own merchandise. He said you are to leave at the end of the sennight to hunt with his family in the Forez? Is this true?'

'Yes. He invited me yesterday. I declined but he was insistent, and I didn't want to offend, given his position in Lyon. I am taking Adam, if you don't mind.'

'The guards are your responsibility, dear boy. If you think it is necessary then do it. By God and the Saints, you have climbed the tree quickly. Hunting and feasting with the Gigni is akin to being part of a noble court. You have made your mark, I think! And tell me, where is the showy Luzio? I saw no evidence of he or his women at the market today. He is normally an entertainment in his own right.' Amée liked Luzio and had always made him welcome, but then Luzio would flirt with her and she would be melted butter in his sunlight.

'He is already at the Forez *domus*, apparently. So Messire Gigni said.'

'He will keep everyone amused.'

'Who will keep everyone amused?' a voice said from the door.

'*Toby!*' Ariella jumped from her seat, a little pile of *livres* tumbling with a silvery sound. They hugged and she kissed the top of his head. 'I *knew* it was you,' she said. 'Despite that you are not as glossy.'

'No. So it seems.' He glanced down at his dust and travel-stained clothes. 'Madame and Messire Sarapion…' He bowed in acknowledgement.

'Tobias,' Michael said. 'It is good to see you. How do your parents?'

Toby shrugged. 'Sadly accepting of the news, for in this violent world in which we live, what parent doesn't think they will lose a child, Michael?'

Amée spoke up. 'Indeed. You are right, sir. I thought I had lost mine and thus my heart grieves for your parents. I know a little of your story. My name is Amée de Clochard.' She held out a hand and he took it and made a chivalrous point of kissing it.

'Madame. I have heard much about you and your late husband. Sir Guy speaks highly of you.'

'Huh! Sir Guy of Gisborne! The man has no respect from me at all and we will *not* talk of him here…' Amée's cheeks filled with colour.

'*Maman!*' Jehanne said. 'You must excuse my mother, Tobias. She blames Sir Guy for the fact that I vanished for a three year. Despite that she knows it is the way his company of information-seekers is run. It is good to see you. How *do* you?'

'I carry the weight of Byzantium on my back like a snailshell, Dana…' he shook his head. 'I'm sorry. I mean Jehanne, of course. My mind is back at Saint Akyntos, at Tomas' grave and I hate it. Truth? I run from the memories daily. Did not Euripides say *the fiercest anger of all, the most incurable, is that which rages in the place of dearest love*? Jehanne, I did love him.' He sighed. 'Now tell me, who is the amusing person of whom you speak?'

'Luzio Gigni, a friend of Guillaume's,' said Amée. 'And nephew of the most successful merchant house in Lyon. Luzio has the knack of amusing everyone.'

'Except his uncle,' Ariella commented. 'He finds him a trial. Tobias, did you see who else is sitting here?' She pulled Adam from the shadow at the end of the table.

'Adam! By the hems of the Virgin! How many more are here from Venezia! God but it's good to see you!' He pumped Adam's hand and then turned to Guillaume. 'And you, Guillaume. I see you and I see your brother

– there is a sameness. He was very kind…'

For a moment the depth in Tobias' eyes was unfathomable and Guillaume wondered if they now shared something in their souls. Guillaume had never been one to talk of his losses, not even to Ariella, although they had talked broadly of the York Massacre and of Acre. But he had never mentioned Cateline and Anselin and he wondered if the time was approaching. There had been too many nightmares, too many moments where his palms filled with sweat and he trembled…

'May I come on your hunting trip?' Toby said. 'I can pay my way with music if someone finds me a lute or a *vielle*.'

Guillaume and Adam looked at each other. 'Not such a bad idea, I think,' said Guillaume. 'Amée, have you a lute that our minstrel can tune?'

'Somewhere…' she yelled for Mahaut, and the long-suffering woman was given orders to find the instrument and bring it forthwith. Mahaut looked at Toby and crossed herself, her fear patent.

Guillaume muttered, 'Ah Tobias, you are another reason for her to hate all we interlopers. I swear she thinks we are here to fleece the widow.'

'No matter. I am used to it. But she is hardly the face of an angel herself, is she? Are you sure she is filled with the milk of human kindness. Must be curdled if she is.'

'Curdled, sour and bitter as gall, but we are used to it. Do you want a mug of ale? Wine? Just while we finish our accounting? We must take a tax to the Archbishop's notary in a short while or he will storm the house with the flame of God in his hands.'

'A nice man, is he?'

'Pious and poisonous. You'll like him…'

Tobias laughed. 'By God's grace it is good to be amongst you.'

Thus money was counted to the soft plucking of Tobias' fingers on the found lute with his gentle voice singing the words of the beautiful *Carmina qui Quondam*. Guillaume thought how apt it was, for all in the room had faced loss – he counted the lost souls as the little pile of money grew upon the table. Ariella's mother, Guillaume's parents, Amée's husband, Toby's brother. As Toby's lament filled the corners of the room, he wondered what losses had torn through Adam's life and as he looked across at the carved face of Michael Sarapion, he knew there was loss there that might never be revealed.

Finally, the accounting was done and Ariella sat back.

'Well?' Amée burst out. 'Can we pay for our needs? The repairs, the guards, new harness? Tell me!'

Guillaume took the final figure from Ariella's hand, glanced at it and then smoothed the muscles of his face, speaking with a confidence that he hoped would beguile the widow.

'We have done exceptionally well. If you add that to what is left from the German envoys' half payment and taking into…'

'Guillaume!' Amée growled. 'Tell me…'

'Almost, but not quite. We may need a little short-term trading capital.'

'We must borrow?' she squeaked. 'Jehan never borrowed.'

'*Maman*, it is short term. As soon as we have funds from Venezia, we can pay off the debt.'

'Oh my goodness,' Amée's cheeks flushed red, a sure sign of emotion. 'Funds from Gisborne! It makes me puke to think I must accept it. Jehan would roll in his grave.'

'Papa had great respect for Gisborne, Maman.'

'But then he didn't know that the man kept your existence a secret, did he? No. I will not borrow. We must trade out of difficulty.'

'Maman, it is not possible with the fire. We have to do this.'

'Amée,' Michael took the widow's hand. 'I borrowed frequently for my business. Sometimes, when markets dip or there is an unforeseen event, it is what we have to do. Risk-taking is part of mercantile endeavour. You know this as well as anyone. Spend, borrow. In the end they are one and the same. And just remember that you are in a better position than most with insurance to come from your Venetian partners. You must trust in them and trust in Guillaume and Ariella.'

'But any borrowings will have to be paid back with interest,' she replied gloomily.

'Joshua is a good man,' said Ariella. 'He loaned my father monies when he was establishing himself as a merchant.'

'But he is a *moneylender!*' Amée snapped back. 'They charge like boars for their services.'

'*He* will not.'

'But he is a Jew!' Amée' said without thought.

The comment hung in the room like Damocles' sword.

Finally, Ariella said very softly. 'As am I, Amée…'

Amée realized the hurt of her words the minute they left her mouth and her hand slapped across her lips, her expression horrified. 'I am so sorry, Ariella. That was unforgiveable. I am just overwrought…' Her eyes filled with tears.

''Tis no matter,' Ariella said as she placed the coins from the market into a small linen sack. 'But if you would feel more comfortable to forgo the borrowing with Joshua, then I will accept that.'

Toby began to pluck a little *carole* upon the lute. 'Come, Amée. Where is your spirit of adventure? The spirit that took you and Jehan into trade in the first place?'

Amée looked at her hands as if she were trying to see the past written there and eventually she looked up at Ariella, before finally saying 'I trust you to do what is right for your father and for Gisborne and thus for me.'

Toby's little melody wound round them all. Whether it banished the unfortunate moment, Guillaume couldn't tell. He took the bag of church taxes and nodded at Adam to follow. Best to leave the house to sort itself out, he thought, and wasn't a little glad to be departing.

The late afternoon sun had a mellow warmth to it as Guillaume and Adam walked toward the livery, leading the horse and cart.

'That was unfortunate,' Adam said.

'Indeed,' Guillaume replied. 'Ariella has exploded for less. She handled it with diplomatic care.'

'Do you think the widow is a Jew hater?'

'No. I think she still hurts from Gisborne's lack. She grieved for three years for her daughter. Any mother would hit out. She's had many shocks in a short space of time and so we must be lenient.'

They clipped along in silence, the only noise the horse's shod feet on the cobbles.

'I don't mean to pry,' Adam ventured. 'But are you paying a fortune to the Church, Guillaume?'

'Too much. I think the priest lines his own pockets.'

Adam snorted. 'Do you think the Archbishop is aware?'

'If he is, then my feelings towards the Church are justified. They say Renaud de Forez is a cowardly and avaricious man. 'Tis no doubt why he locks himself behind the defensive walls of the chateau rather than live in the episcopal palace.'

'Do they not say the Archbishop is one of the most powerful men in Europe?'

'They do. Behind the Holy Roman Emperor and the King of France. I might add a third contender to the list, though. What about the Pope? Perhaps Renaud de Forez has leanings toward the papacy. Certainly he will need money and much of it to tread that road.'

'I don't like priests,' said Adam. 'Never known an honest one. It's easy to hide behind the scriptures, don't you think? Point is, they offer me nothing, especially the flea-bitten monk we are seeing today. What a turd!'

Guillaume said nothing by return, even though he shared Adam's dismissive view of the Church.

But God?

He frowned as he answered his conscience, *'No, not God…'* and could not help the automatic sketch of a cross. He was glad Adam was fussing with the horse's reins and had not seen. This lop-sided relationship with God was something he could never explain.

He believed in a God who would receive Cateline and Anselin into Paradise and love them for eternity. He did not think God required money and idols as part of worship and he believed in a God who could care.

He did not believe in a God who gave His name to a crusade and allowed more than two thousand Saracens to be beheaded in a day and a night in Acre.

That was Richard Lionheart's God. Not his.

CHAPTER SIX

×

Outremer stank.

Despite the vast blank stretches of baked and powdered earth, and night skies that rivalled a king's crown. Or green swards and banks and folds of trees that defied the imagination in the seering heat. Or skies bluer than pavonalilis, *or* pers *or* paonace. *And despite horses that were finely chiselled, with curving ears and small scooped heads, and which could gallop in the heat forever and never falter. Or the fact that Lord Jesus had trod these pathways with Peter and Matthew, Mark, Luke and John.*

Despite all that, Outremer stank.

It clung to Guillaume's clothes – the sweat and urine. And then even more odious was the smell of shit and vomit from weak men, those who had caught the sickness of warfare when water is tainted and men become crazed.

But most abhorrent was the smell of rotting flesh – the smell of death upon the living. A sweet smell that cloyed and offended and made one gag and then puke until one's insides had nothing left to give. Every time Guillaume stripped his hose and chemise, he would check every scratch to make sure Death hadn't hooked a fingernail into him. He learned the value of cleaning a wound and binding it with a strip of fresh cloth, to provide a barrier between the wound, the stink and the flies – those fast, annoying, sticky beasts they called cincelles.

He sometimes wondered why he bothered to protect himself. There was no one who would care if he succumbed – no one at La Flèche who mattered to him anymore, and no one in Outremer who would mark a grave for him.

As he trekked with the army, he thought of nothing but placing one foot in

123

front of the other, his independence of spirit lacerated and bleeding. He took orders from knights on destriers that plainly suffered in the desert heat – big cumbersome brutes that made the Saracen horses seem like spirits of the air.

If he thought at all on his condition, he would say he had lost his mind, shelved it, blinkered it, locked it in a casket, so that his existence was defined by the man in front and those to his sides. They were men he chose not to engage with or befriend. He had no feeling for his brothers in arms.

Except for one…

He was young – a tall, willowy archer who had probably not seen thirteen years but was a prodigious bowman. He used a warbow as if it were an extension of his body and his speed at nocking and loosing arrows rivalled Guillaume's. They stood next to each other, that first day on the shore of the Holy Land at Tyre, and as Guillaume cast a glance at him, waiting for the order to loose, he noticed the boy's complexion was grey and that his arm shook and his teeth chattered. Some were made for war, and some, despite them having a God-given skill and deadly aim, were not. This one was a shy boy with little speech and no confidence and Guillaume said to him as they waited. 'God keep you, my friend. Have faith.'

The boy looked at him, and a tear slid down his cheek, the smell of urine drifting from his clothes. He said nothing and Guillaume gave him a smile of fortitude enough for them both. Caring for the boy – sheltering him from the bullying of the others, making sure he ate and drank – it gave him a purpose between volleys of arrows sighing off like a flock of sparrows into the skies. He hadn't realized what a bowman the boy was until he turned his back to pick up an arrow he had dropped because one didn't waste weapons. One moment's inattention, and the mounted archers of Saladin swooped toward the crusaders, picking off men like soft peaches from a tree, never missing.

The arrow meant for Guillaume never came because the boy, Alain, nocked, aimed and caught the Saracen archer in the side of the head as he wheeled past. Another arrow in the horse's head, a shaft of ash with a sharp bodkin made for war, and the animal went down squealing. Guillaume felt that Death had pointed at him that day but then moved on, and he vowed that Alain would live to survive this godforsaken crusade, 'so help me, God.'

The crusading army moved onward along the coastline of Outremer, harried and harrying, finding themselves in heated desert plains and then amongst forests of cool trees and on green swards that would keep many an ox or horse happy. It was a land of hideous contrast – so marked that men with fevers would see what was not or what might have been and they would succumb to their madness unless someone grabbed them and took them kicking and yelling to the Hospitallers.

'Why are you here, Alain?' Guillaume asked one day. They were camped south of Tyre, the army resting as Richard negotiated with emirs and mamluks from Saladin. Phillip Capet, or Phillip Augustus depending on what day it was for the soldiers, kept a watchful eye on Richard and his negotiations. Rumour had it that he was unhappy with a Christian king speaking to the Saracen enemy.

'I lived with my mother in Poitiers and when I left, she was very sick and like to die. King Richard is my king. They said I was a good archer and as I owe my allegiance to the King and God, the priest said I must support my king. The priest said that Maman might be spared, or at worst, die a blissful death knowing I am fighting for God and Jerusalem…'

'All of us have been told of God's blessings upon us if we fight in God's name,' said Guillaume, not believing for one minute that he would be blessed. He'd murdered two men after all.

'And you?' Alain asked. Guillaume noticed his voice still held the high edges of childhood and there was no sign of fluff on his chin. A boy…

'The same as you. It was noted that I was a good archer and I had an allegiance to the Count of Anjou. I met him one day and he ordered me to join his men in Lyon.'

'You met the King?' Alain was like a child as he listened to Guillaume's story of Chinon. He told it quietly, away from other men – it was purely to allay Alain's nerves, to allow him to forget for one minute that he could die tomorrow or the next day or if not then, the day after.

'They say his hair is red…'

'I would say russet or perhaps like a field of straw in the red of the setting sun. You've seen those autumn fields, have you not, after a harvest?'

'The King wears a helmet on the battlefield and never comes close enough. He rides in front and has no fear.'

'Indeed. He is a warrior king.'

'Guillaume, every day we are out there, despite they say I'm a marksman, I'm so afraid, I can barely string my bow, let alone nock and loose.'

'A soldier who isn't afraid is a bad soldier, Alain. We are all afraid.'

'Are you?'

Am I?

'Yes. Like I said, it is a bad soldier who isn't afraid of his enemy. Tell me, did you like being on the ships?'

As often as not he would engage the boy in good memories and experiences, so that the sights and stink of war did not wear him down. In a wholly perverse way, it helped Guillaume as well, drawing up memories of a life well-lived and images to be cherished. They even laughed together over childish misdemeanours.

'Once,' Guillaume said, hoping to raise a smile on Alain's gaunt face, 'when I was too young to know better and having watched my father, the bowyer, fletching arrows, I caught one of my mother's hens and pulled out its tail feathers. The fierce screeching of the bird brought my mother running.'

'Did she beat you?'

'No. But I was roundly abused. My father laughed, fletched an arrow with the pulled feathers and told me that when I was old enough I should use it.'

A grin appeared on Alain's face and fear and sorrow were erased for a heartbeat. 'And did you?'

'Yes. It was less than useless. I did not know at that early plucking that I needed flight feathers. Maman and Papa laughed about that story often. What about you, Alain? Surely you weren't forever a good child.'

Alain stopped biting his fingernails momentarily and then widened the grin that had appeared at Guillaume's revelation. 'I loosed an arrow into the cloister...'

'The cloister?'

'My mother worked for the nuns at L'Abbaye Sainte-Croix in Poitiers.'

'Ah. And your arrow? My heart is in my mouth!' Guillaume tried to hook back the grin that had disappeared the moment Alain mentioned his mother.

Alain relaxed and chuckled, a small sound as if he had forgotten how and was surprised that he could. 'It skimmed across the top of a pile of parchment being carried by one of the Sisters from the scriptorium and lodged in a bench. She screamed. The parchment scattered across the paving stones, the doves in the dove-cot flew up into the sky with much clacking of wings and I had to learn the Pater Noster by heart. I had just seen six years.'

His faded blue eyes sparkled as a youth's should and he looked up at Guillaume. 'The Sisters were good to me.'

'Did you live on convent land?'

'Yes. Close by. Maman was a lay worker, working for the Infirmarian.

126

She knew about herbs and plants, you see. Her *mother was a village midwife and healer. The Sisters liked my mother. She worked in any weather and never complained. They could trust her.'*

'Are they caring for her now?'

'They said they would. I hope the monks don't interfere. I don't like priests.'

Neither do I, but that's another story.

'And your father?'

'I have none.' Alain's face shut down and Guillaume said gently,

'Neither do I. My parents were murdered the day before I left for Lyon and the King's army.'

'Guillaume! I am so sorry.' He crossed himself, muttering 'In nomine Patris, et Filii, et Spiritus Sancti... *Do you know the murderer?'*

'There were two. They were routiers. Maybe even noble routiers. They acted like noblemen. You see that I have little respect for those above me, but take no notice. Sadly I am an embittered old man.' He said no more.

The bond between man and boy became stronger after that. Guillaume considered him a younger brother. The two would line up behind a shieldwall and always, they would look at each other as the first arrow was nocked.

Alain would always whisper, 'Ave Maria, gratia plena, Dominus tecum. Benedicta tu in mulieribus, et benedictus fructus ventris tui, Iesus. Sancta Maria, Mater Dei, ora pro nobis peccatoribus, nunc. Et in hora mortis nostrae...' *And the two together would say,* 'Amen.'

And time after time, as the army moved toward Acre, Guillaume would wish that Alain had taken holy orders. He was so much more suited to following an horarium than loosing arrows from fly-driven dawn to fly-driven dusk.

They could hear the noise of a fully-fledged assault on Acre, even before the city was sighted. For days, weeks and months, siege engines had pounded the walls, knocking through the stone whereupon Saracens would stream out, fight, and then stream back in again, leaving the Christians to retrieve their dead and wounded and finish off any of the enemy whose souls might not yet have left for Paradise.

It was the random nature of it all that disturbed Guillaume and he could see Alain's sensibilities developing more cracks as they came within range of the horrendous cries of men dying or wounded.

They had skirmished before, but Acre was another world entirely. A huge city that had stood through an age of war and the Plantagenet and Capetian monarchs were determined it should fall.

It was relentless upon the senses – day in and out. Noise, blood, orders roared by harassed knights, and the supply of weapons diminishing so that they must go out into the field under cover of dark and retrieve what they could, even if it meant plucking arrows from the dead and wounded.

'But it is in his leg. If we pull it, he'll bleed to death.'

'He's a Saracen, he'll die anyway if the knights find him…'

And they would pull the arrows and leave men to die swiftly as the last of their blood watered the parched soil.

Guillaume had learned to look no one in the eye on these sorties – dead or alive. But Alain would stare and offer a blessing and then vomit. The boy became as thin as a blade of grass outside Acre and Guillaume despaired that he would see beyond the sennight, let alone the crusade. He found one of the camp-followers, a cheery woman called Matilda, and offered her a silver dinar if she could make a good pottage daily for Alain.

'And Matty,' he said. 'If you find some wine, I shall give you another dinar.'

She was as good as her word and didn't ask where the dinars had come from, just passed the pottage and wine over each day. The dinars had come from a Saracen's purse – his eyes had been glazed and his black turban lay in folds all around, his entrails curled amongst the cloth. Guillaume reached for the purse – he was beyond caring about robbing the dead because the living had more need.

Alain at first could barely eat. Guillaume took to getting him to drink a mug of wine beforehand as they sat together, and then, when the boy's speech had softened at the edges, he would urge him to eat the pottage and the colour, what there was of it, began to return to the boy's cheeks.

The battle for Alain became more important to Guillaume than the battle for Acre and he wished that the two of them could just keep walking one day, to the water and onto a fishing boat and sail away beyond the sound, sight and smell.

No more did the sound of flight fill him with joy. He would forever hear birds on the wing and be reminded of flocks of arrows flying away, darkening the sky to black with their multitudes. No more would he enjoy hearing trees bending in the wind, because it would remind him of ranks of archers drawing their bows – that creaking sound and then the yell, 'Hold, hold!' and 'Loose!' Followed by inhuman screams and panicked equine shrieking. Like Alain, he would begin to tremble when he heard drums and horns. No more would a foire *with pipe and tabor thrill him because he would see the mounted Saracen cavalry pelt down from the hills each time a wall was breached. And he would never want to feel the earth shudder like it did when the siege engines lobbed the stone into the walls of Acre so that men, women and children were crushed.*

Even though the crusaders and their kings prevailed, Guillaume could not care. He and Alain found an inn behind the now opened gates, where a tired man and his wife placed mugs of fruit syrup in front of them and bowed before slinking, frightened, into a corner.

'They think we will rape and kill,' Alain said.

'Then they have nothing to fear while we are here, do they?' Guillaume sucked long on the syrup and beckoned for another, asking by signing, if there was flatbread to be had. He fell on what they were given, starving hungry now that the sound of the siege had quieted. 'Drink, Alain. Drink long – it will wash away the dust and dirt.'

Alain swallowed the cordial but Guillaume knew the damage to the boy could never be repaired and he wished he had the power to send him home, perhaps to holy orders. Alain had talked with animation about the Sisters who worked in the scriptorium. If he could have the monastic life, surely it would go partway to heal the ills of war.

But they had yet to breach Jerusalem. Acre was a message to let the enemy know nothing would suffice until Jerusalem belonged to the Christian world again. And Guillaume was tired of it.

'We shall find some new clothes and a bath-house, Alain. Get rid of the stink.'

Days passed with an ennui growing upon them both. They slept, walked and ate, and Alain found a tiny church that monks had begun to rebuild and he would pray there often. It seemed to settle his nerves.

But the order came for men to begin to train within their formations again. Richard Plantagenet had no plans to march on with an army of soft soldiers. A whisper became a roar with the news that Phillip Augustus planned to return to France – aware of the heavy French losses in front of the walls of Acre, slighted, ill and tired of Richard's posturing. Richard's men poured vitriole upon the French and Guillaume and Alain kept clear of tension, walking further from the city centre, spending time looking out over the sea.

Guillaume had been sitting in the shade of a rock by the water whilst Alain had gone to find bread. He watched fishermen leave in small battered boats, knowing they would return with the sardines that he had grown to like. The Arabs called to each other, seabirds wheeled and life could have been normal…

'Guillaume, Guillaume!' Alain came running along the road that edged the shore, his voice broken, a sob on the air.

'Here! I am here! What is wrong?'

'He is going to kill them all, every one! They start now…' Alain dashed a hand across his cheeks.

Guillaume knew what he meant – the two thousand, seven hundred men who were prisoners to be ransomed to Saladin. Today was the day, the hour had come and passed and Richard – fiery, red-haired Richard – would execute them all in the sight of Saladin's men who hid in the hills behind Acre. More than two thousand lives to end with a sword stroke.

Oh, to be sure, this was war and no doubt Saladin would have done the same to any prisoners he might have taken. Wouldn't he?

Guillaume took Alain by the arm. 'We will go to the church and pray.' He could think of nothing else that might calm the boy and he knew if they were seen, they would be expected to to cheer from the walls and gates as the blood was spilled to become a lake, a sea … an ocean.

They sat in the quiet of the little church, its stone walls repaired and two candles lit upon a simple altar. There were only four benches either side of the miniscule nave and the damaged door stood wide, allowing the heat and sound of the city to filter into the space in small drifts. Alain said the Pater Noster, *the* Ave Maria *and the* De Profundis.

But nothing could stop the keening and then the screaming. Nor the cheers of the Christians. Nor the sound of drum and horn from the Saracens in the hills and the yelling of 'Allah Akbar!' *as they poured down to avenge the dead and dying. Alain jumped up, but Guillaume grabbed his arm.*

'We will stay here, Alain. Pray. It has more meaning than anything we would be ordered to do out there.'

Alain looked at him and Guillaume began, 'Pater Noster, qui es in caelis, sanctificetur nomen tuum…' *and presently the youth's voice joined in. His eyes were squeezed tight shut and his hands clasped so white, Guillaume could see nothing but bone. He left Alain to begin the* Ave Maria, *then the* de Profundis. *And they went round and round in circles, until Alain's voice drifted to nothing* and Guillaume could see he was asleep on his knees. Carefully, he picked him up, the youth mumbling, and he laid him on the bench and covered him with his cloak, sitting to guard him through the long and bloody day.

Did he believe the prayers he uttered with Alain? Yes. Somewhere, he knew his God was watching and keeping account. But to what end, he asked himself. If it is mine, then am I exonerated by caring for this youth?

A priest came rushing in and noticed him, becoming angry, urging him in stuttering Latin to take the boy and leave. 'This is not an inn and today is not the day to sleep off your drunkenness in God's house.'

Guillaume woke Alain, helping him stand, guiding him from the church, back to the gates and toward the tents that were their billets and which they shared. Beyond, the executions continued and Guillaume tried to shield Alain from the sight as they wove through the camp. A few were around, not many, and they looked shattered, covered in blood and dust from the latest sortie.

Without warning, Alain began to puke and Guillaume held him whilst he emptied and then with an arm round his shoulder, took him to his makeshift cot.

'What ails the weakling? Still not standing the sight of blood?' sneered a Welsh archer.

'I know not. He sweats. Perhaps it is the tertian fever…'

The fellow backed away, leaving the two alone and Guillaume felt Alain's forehead which was slick with damp.

It was not such a lie then. He was ill and Guillaume tried to find a Hospitaller who wasn't already overworked with the wounded being carried into the camp. But there were none free and so Guillaume's night was spent sponging the lad, stopping him staggering outside, listening to his feverish ramblings.

The order to move on came swiftly. Alain had barely the strength of an infant and Guillaume cursed the Plantagenet pigheadedness. He only ever sighted the King surrounded by his hunting pack of knights who looked down upon the foot soldier and he wanted to yell at the Monarch for his selfishness. That he was a strategist and brave, that the common men loved his fooldhardiness was all very well, but men were dying in droves and for what reason?

That wasted journey to Chinon – for what? And why had Guillaume ridden on to Lyon to join the army anyway? He could have ridden to Venezia, mingled with the watery crowds on the watery islets and just disappeared. Instead, caught up in grief and a bloodlust that defied any rational thought, he had joined the army and marched to Outremer, so that he could be burned, baked, pricked like a bladder and left to rot!

'Matty, Matty!' Guillaume called. The camp follower turned, her clothes thin and frayed. Her wimple was clean however, and her veil blew about her shoulders in the breeze off the water. 'You do not stay in Acre?' he asked.

'Ain't no business for me here when you all leave. I shall ride on one of the carts with the other girls.'

'Is there room for Alain on the cart, do you think?'

She frowned. 'If he's caught lying about on a cart by them Templars, they'll boil him in oil. Only Satan's scarier than them red-crossed knights. Alain's an archer and a good one and they'll say he should be with the men.'

'He's been so ill, Matty. It could be the tertian fever or it could be the analdia that the king has had. He's very weak and can barely walk.'

'I...'

'I'll pay you a dinar a day.'

'A dinar a day! Well how can I say no?' She grinned at him, some of her teeth blackened stumps. But if her teeth were black, her heart was not. 'How came you upon a wealth of dinars then?'

Guillaume looked out at the vast array of an army packing to move off. 'I robbed the dead,' he replied with no emotion. He had felt nothing as he picked purses from belts slick with gore. If he hadn't, someone else would have and he knew the money would have a use – for the boy. He still could find no reason for his brotherly care of Alain – as if it was almost spiritual. Almost as though he was trying to reach out to his lost parents by caring for the living and this one lost like a lamb.

Matty's eyes slitted. 'Them or us?'

'Both,' he answered. 'Is it too stained with blood for you to accept?' He reached into his purse and extracted a gleaming silver dinar.

She took the coin. 'Well... not too stained.' She flipped it over in her hand. 'You're a wicked man, Guillaume from Anjou and I ought to report you if it weren't that I thought your heart was good.'

Later, he walked back with Alain, supporting him under the arm, the boy leaning heavily.

'Lordie,' said Matty. 'I hope no one breathes on you because you look as like to blow away! Reckon we'll have to fatten you whilst you sit with us. Like one of *them emirs who they say quaffs fruit syrup and grapes and throws out orders like the knights throw out their washing!'*

They settled him on the cart, his eyes drifting down, the girls watching over him as Matty walked a little distance back to the lines with Guillaume.

'You can see he's in a bad way, Matty. Perhaps he should have been with the Hospitallers but they are so busy with men off the battlefield. I meant what I said, I shall come every day with a dinar, maybe two if you can care for him and get him up and about. We move to Arsuf next, so you may have time.' He passed over an extra dinar on account.

'You must have done some serious stealin' to have that treasure.' She tucked the coin into a small purse that hung off a girdle beneath a thin surcoat. 'You'll be goin' back to Anjou rich, methinks.'

'I doubt it. I'll be lucky to survive the march to Jerusalem. Why did you decide to come on with us? You would have been safe in Acre. You could have set up a small business...'

'Maybe after lookin' after young Alain, I could. But I haven't enough coin yet, and my man was killed in Sicily when there was the brawl with Tancred's men. As to goin' home... to what? Me and my man were peasants workin' the fields. All I knew was pickin' up stones in the fields at ploughin', then sowin' and then scarin' the birds after sowin', then the harvestin' and so on. I lost two babes before we came here.' She rubbed her stomach, and Guillaume noted she was with child, the early stages but nevertheless. 'Here, I get pennies for laundry and for mendin'. I even cut hair for them's who want it. They pay me more for a hug and more again for a swive and sometimes, if I wipe their tears an' listen to their fears, then they are very generous indeed.'

'There's a lot to cry about here, I think,' he said. The air hung around them – thick with odour. The Hospitallers called it a miasma, the stink of death that caused death and if nothing else, he would be glad to walk away from the stink that was Acre.

'Most of 'em cry. Only a few don't. Seems to me those that don't have their souls tied in knots. I wish I could help the poor things.' She looked sideways at him. 'Do you cry, Guillaume?'

He heard the calls from the lines and looked down at the little woman who was probably younger than himself but seemed ancient in experience. 'I haven't the time to cry, Matty. Not now. But you will hear Alain often. Wipe his tears for him…'

He hurried away and it became a pattern that once each day, when he could, he would find the camp followers, and the cart with the women and his young friend. He would pay the daily dinar because Alain's cheeks had roses for the first time and he even laughed with the women. But his hair had thinned, falling out in clumps so that he looked even younger and more innocent.

'The Saracens are harrying us, Guillaume, but the Hospitallers and Templars have us safe. I am frightened, but I can't let the women see. They need me to be strong for them, do they not?'

'Indeed. How are you feeling?'

'My hair has fallen out. Do you see how Matty has shorn me like a ram? And my nails fall out as well. My fingers are sore – how do you think I shall handle bows and arrows?'

'Perhaps you must wear some leather gloves. I shall see what I can find. I think you have had analdia, like the King. They say Philip Augustus has had it too, only the French call it leonardie. *Can you walk?'*

'I shudder like a sapling in the wind. Do I have to go back?'

A part of Guillaume wanted to run. Both he and Alain. Far away. Instead, 'Yes. Your skill was noted and it is missed. Most know you have caught the analdia and they make allowances, but not for much longer.'

During the days after that, Alain's face again became pale and he no longer joked with the women, so Matty said. Like many of the soldiers, he had become fatalistic, with no hope of surviving to see Jerusalem, as Saladin's fleet archers galloped down upon them from the hills and then disappeared like a swirl of sand, something mythical, and always leaving a trail of bloodshed behind.

Just before dawn at Nahir-al-Falik, Guillaume hurried to the cart. He owed Matty her daily dinar and was determined she should have that and more before the army's move to Arsuf began.

As he approached, by the light of torches, he noticed a Templar knight walking by, his white cloak with its red cross partée snapping around him like a nasty statement. His mail coif was flung back, his hair cut neat but lifting in the pre-dawn breeze off the water. Nothing could disguise the exhaustion and the resultant temper of the man – not a man to cross. He stood in front of Alain with a bull's stance and balled fists and demanded to know what good reason prevented a young soldier from leaving comfort for his duty.

'You swive, perhaps. A little whoring?' he sneered, glancing at the women as if they were the Devil's brides.

'Hardly, my lord.' Guillaume strode up, a head taller than the knight and using the difference to best effect. 'He has had the analdia, like the Kings of France and England.'

'And yet King Richard still found the strength to appear on the battlefield,' the Templar spat.

'Indeed sir. From a litter. This man is an archer and could barely stand to piss, let alone draw a bow. Begging your pardon, my lord. In any case, I have come to fetch him to return to our lines.'

The Templar's expression barely eased at the quiet explanation, a puce tide flowing across his face. 'You waste time, then. Get moving!' He stamped past Guillaume, pushing him away, his cloak flapping against Guillaume's arm.

'My life's debt to you, Guillaume, for lying on my behalf!' Alain lay back, breathing hard.

''Tis no lie, my friend. I have come to pay Matty what is due and to escort you back to our lines. See?' He waved his arm to encompass the army. 'We march on Arsuf and I cannot protect you from the likes of the Templar any longer. The Angevins have been placed under the command of Robert de Sablé and I will keep you by my side.'

'De Sablé? The Grand Master of the Templars?' But he barely listened to Guillaume's response as he slid from the cart. 'We shall be in the thick of it then, God save us.' Dawn was bleeding across the night sky and in the early light, it was possible to see that his tunic hung off his frame and that his legs were like twigs. So much for Matty's efforts.

Guillaume called to her and she came like a hen wanting grain. She took the dinars readily and kissed Guillaume on each of his cheeks. 'I tried, Guillaume. But he worries his food away.'

He nodded, thanking her and advising her to leave the army as soon as she safely could. She clicked her tongue and then hugged Alain as if he were her son.

'You be careful, my boy. Rumour has it that Saladin's emirs won't negotiate with King Richard's envoys, so this next fracas will be a big one.'

Alain said nothing, his hands working feverishly one over the other.

They left the women to fend for themselves with the other camp-followers as the army began to move – a vast panoply of war-mongers in an ever-growing cloud of dust. Out to sea, Richard's fleet kept pace, loaded with supplies and with the many wounded.

As Guillaume and Alain walked with the army, Guillaume looked around at the drawn faces amongst the Angevins. He and many others were under no illusions that Saladin would attack the flanks hard and that the archers were depended upon to protect the army. A kind of fatalism drifted on the air, where men doubted they would see the end of the day, let alone Jerusalem.

The army stretched for leagues in the hard desert light, from the first to arrive in Arsuf, to the flanks and to the rear well behind as from the hills came the Hell-sent beat of drums, the clash of cymbals and shriek of horns. The sounds of battle that every Crusader had learned to hate and which sent bellies writhing, bowels and bladders emptying, and cold shivers across bodies.

'Allah Akbar!' was screamed from the hills as the emirs pushed down against the Crusaders, arrows sighing through the air, darkening the sky to a shade of Purgatory. Spears flew back and forth, men skewered and screaming, soft targets all. Guillaume's hand had stopped shaking as he reached time and again for arrows pricked in the ground beside him.

'Pater noster qui es in caelis, sanctificetur nomen tuum…' he muttered as he loosed each arrow, with barely a breath to check that Alain still stood beside him. The Saracens' fleet horses flashed past time and again and for some reason, every time one of the pert, elegant beasts crashed to the ground with spear or arrow impaled, Guillaume's heart cried for the bravery of an animal in a fight that wasn't theirs.

'Allah Akbar!'

'Beau Sante!'

'Saint George!'

'Allah Akbar!'

'The King!'

Shouting, yelling, screaming, clashing, the thunder of hooves – Arsuf crashed and roared around him. He could barely see an arrow leave his bow in the dust cloud, nor could he see Alain and when the mêlée began, and despite his hatred of close combat, he drew his sword, slashing and slicing to save his own life. This wasn't about God, nor wresting Jerusalem from foreigners.

It was about survival.

The battle noise faded about his ears and all he heard was the grunt and rasp of his own voice, the greedy sucking in of air and the explosion of a breath outward from a chest that burned with effort. Twenty times, a hundred times he ducked and bent, blocked and turned. He was cut and punctured, but suffered no killing blows. In the muted battle for his life, he asked himself for what was he being spared? And as the thought flew through his mind, so a young Saracen man, olive of skin with glittering dark eyes, his mouth hidden by a trailing scarf, his head bare, turban gone, pounded toward him, unhorsed and filled with fear and fury. His curved kilij swung back, no sparkle in the dusty mist, no cry from the shrouded mouth. Just desperation in the eyes and Guillaume wondered if his held that selfsame desperation.

Kill. Or be killed.

He flipped back wide with his own sword and with a double-handed grip swung it back hard and swift through the air, a defiant scream as he took the Saracen across his waist, opening him, so that he fell to the ground lifeless.

Guillaume stood still, vaguely hearing the Saracen call to retreat, feeling the pounding hooves fade through the earth, his senses returning, filled with the cries of the injured and the shouts of knights.

'Re-arm! Be ready! They'll turn!'

But he had no arrows and there were others like him. A Templar cantered past, 'Collect the arrows. Hurry.'

And once again, archers collected arrows – pulling them from the earth, from the dead, from the injured.

But Guillaume just looked for Alain, calling, rolling bodies over. His mouth was tacky with thirst, tongue cleaving to the roof, eyes gritty and sore as he rolled over the emaciated body of the young man from Poitiers. He was pierced in the thigh with a Saracen arrow and bright blood pumped out of the entry point. His eyes fluttered and he groaned.

'Alain, 'tis I.' Guillaume knelt, holding the boy who had tried to be a man, whilst awful sounds filled the plain of Arsuf.

'Guillaume, it's over.' Alain's eyes sparkled with misplaced relief. 'I heard the call to retreat…'

'All over,' Guillaume replied, not looking at the wound but feeling the pooling blood beneath his knees.

'Am I hurt?'

'A little…'

'Take me to the Hospitallers,' he grasped Guillaume's arm. 'I have to get home to Maman. *She waits…'*

'Yes, she does.'

'Archer!' A voice cracked from above him like a thunderstorm. He looked up. Grand Master de Sablé sat astride his horse. 'Pull the arrow.'

'But…'

'I said pull it! Now!'

Guillaume ripped a part of his tunic and tied it round Alain's thigh, dragging it tight. 'Yes, my lord,' he sneered through gritted teeth. Alain moaned, his eyes closing as he fainted. Guillaume grasped the arrow shaft, ready to pull.

De Sablé's horse danced on the spot, nervous with the blood and mortality all around. The whites of its eyes were large, ears flat back and it snorted. De Sablé held it tight in check. 'Do it!'

What did one arrow matter? The nobleman was surely mad with battle lust. Guillaume hoped for the man's death. Rather him than young Alain.

'Do it!' De Sablé screamed and Guillaume pulled the arrow. The blood spurted over his hands for a while, then bubbled like a slow fountain, then trickled like a little stream, to finally fade like an ebb tide. 'Shieldwall!' De Sablé yelled as the horns and drums began again. He wheeled his horse away, sending a skirl of dust across Guillaume and Alain. 'Shieldwall!'

Guillaume shoved his bow to the other shoulder and picked Alain up, cradling the boy across his arms. He began to carry him away from the battle, behind the army, down toward the coast. No one stopped him and he didn't care that the fight for God and Jerusalem went on without him.

He carried Alain to the cliffs at the edge of Arsuf and laid him down, the boy's eyes closed, his limbs in the loose state of death. In a little cove below, a small boat had been beached and in front of him, a narrow track, two goat hooves wide, snaked down between tussocks and rocks. He hoisted Alain over one shoulder, the wound staining his chemise and tunic.

Finding boulders, he laid the boy down again and sat, the sky darkening to the clear ebony desert of the night. He straightened Alain's tunic like a mother, wiping his face, smoothing a hand over the roughly shaved skull.

And then when stars pricked the sky, he laid Alain in the boat, filling his hose with stones, laying more in the hull and then towing the vessel beyond his depth where he hammered at the planks with another stone until a hole appeared and the boat began to fill.

He swam back to shore to his bow and sat, shivering with pain, with sorrow and with the horror of this god-awful thing they called a 'crusade'. Through chattering teeth, he managed a Pater Noster *and then when he could see the boat no more, he stood.*

Up the cliff and to the south was Arsuf, Jaffa and Jerusalem and more of the same.

He gave the idea no thought.

He struck out north…

'Guillaume!' Adam's voice broke ranks with his memories and he was glad. 'Saints and sinners, Guillaume, where the hell *were* you then? By the look of your face, I'll be bound it was Outremer.'

Guillaume turned with surprise to the Englishman. 'How did you know?'

'I saw it on many faces during my time there.'

'You were in Outremer?'

'Wasn't everyone?'

'Gisborne never said so.'

'Why should he? I tell you, Outremer's when I lost my Faith. You were at Acre, were you not?'

'Yes.'

'Ah. That's when God and I became enemies.'

'Strong words.'

'The look on your face when I disturbed you tells me you share my view.'

Guillaume shifted the bag of money to his other hand. 'God and I have an arrangement, Adam. It is more likely to be kings and their egos who are my enemies.'

Adam digested this and one could see him laying the Acre Massacre over Guillaume's words. 'Hmm,' he answered.

They had reached the Cathedral of Saint Jean and pushed through the big doors. The Cathedral interior fluttered and jumped with candle flame and the cloying smell of *olibanum* cloaked the air. Their footsteps echoed on the flags of the nave and there was no one about. No supplicants, no novices, no nuns – no monks. Adam hissed at the gold plate on the high altar.

'There's your taxes,' he whispered.

Guillaume said nothing, just looked for a door to a chancery. He had never been this far into the Cathedral, nor this far into any church since his parents had been killed. He'd stood behind the worshippers here at Mass, but right near the doors, as if he needed to know that he wouldn't be trapped in a place where he was at odds with his beliefs. Outside, he and God could communicate. Here, in a manmade edifice, no matter how well-crafted, it seemed to him it was all about Man's glory to God and not God's love of Man. Out in the woods, or on the river, even the ocean, he felt God might listen more readily to his thoughts.

'Messire Guillaume...'

They hadn't heard the monk move in behind. The priest was bare-footed on the cold paving stones and the tops of his feet were bleeding.

'Brother Crispianus. We did not hear you.'

'I move quietly out of respect for God the Father.' They could barely see the man's eyes in the wavering light but his skin appeared yellow and wax-like.

'Herewith the taxes...' Guillaume held out the bag. 'You can trust that we have given you exactly a quarter of our takings, less what we paid to the Sisters.'

The priest reached for the bag with hands that had lately run with fresh blood and as his fingers curled around the sack, he sucked a very subtle breath, as though the effort pained him. 'Thank you, my son. I shall offer prayers in your name this evening.'

Guillaume nodded, turned and walked away. He wanted to get as far from the insidious man as possible. Adam hurried behind him and they pushed open the doors and entered the clear air of a blue Lyonnais day.

'Thank the bloody Lord. Fresh air!' Adam sucked in the breeze.

'I thought you and God were enemies.'

'I blaspheme. 'Tis all. That man in there, he stinks of rancid evil. Did you see the blood on his fingers and feet? I reckon he's crucifying himself. Nails and wood. Christ!'

'I need a drink,' Guillaume pushed on into one of the smaller squares that faced west and where the sun shone down in the late afternoon. Around them, small finches and chiffchaffs scavenged, their warbling easing the distrait of the men after their confrontation with the monk. They asked for wine and sat in the sun, surrounded by others who sought to finish the day in the same way. Nearby, a small group of men sat having a quietly intense discussion, but the ambience of the square was calm.

'Nails…' Adam said and swallowed a large mouthful of wine.

'He suffers for his God. That's how those of his ilk see it. Pain to reach some sort of ecstasy and elevation, close to the Almighty. I've seen it with other priests. You would see the bloody stains on their robes.'

'I ask you. Why would I even want to return to God when those are the messengers of His word.'

Guillaume agreed but merely supped his wine. His village priest had shown no empathy as his parents had been buried. The lapsed Templars who had kidnapped little William of Gisborne in an act of retribution were beyond any Christian redemption. And where was the compassion of the great nobleman, Grand Master of the Knights Templar, Robert de Sablé, who had ordered Guillaume to pull the arrow that killed Alain? Where was God in any of those men? He saw gold and jewels, venal living, indulgences paid for by the sweat of an ordinary man's brow. He did not see God.

'I deserted, Adam,' he said, wondering where the statement had come from.

'Many deserted, Guillaume. So what?'

'I wanted you to know.'

'Why? In case I think you are cowardly? You who took a wound trying to protect your half-brother in trying to rescue little William? Hardly! Let it go, friend. It matters not. What matters is that priest. He's unstable and we must surely consider him a prime suspect in the fire.'

They drank their wine, allowing the autumn sun to cleanse their minds and to warm their bodies. A small breeze of no account skipped leaves back and forth across the square and there was the murmur of voices, the occasional laugh and the clatter of a mug falling to the ground from within the tavern.

If Guillaume closed his eyes, he knew he could fall asleep but then there might be the sound of hooves and drums and he would be at Arsuf again, so he preferred not to doze in a public place whereas Adam rested his head against the chipped stone of the tavern wall, closed his eyes and thus his mouth fell open and a soft snore emerged.

Without warning, birds flew up with an audible flutter of wings. Shouts sounded from a street nearby and running feet clattered ever more distinctly. The adjacent table of men jumped up, mugs scattering, and they disappeared to be swallowed by the shadowed lanes and back alleys. As one of their number ran past Guillaume, he brushed Guillaume's shoulder, hissing 'I am Hamelyn,' before running on. Then like the Saracen archers at Arsuf, all who were there had gone.

Adam woke as a *quadrum* of burly men thumped into the square, swords drawn and blocking the exits with intimidation. A yellow-faced, odoriferous monk came hard on their heels.

'You've lost them, you fools!' His searching eyes settled on Guillaume and there was an incipient satisfaction in the slipping of hands into worn monastic cuffs and in the way he walked across to the trestle. 'Messire Guillaume, should I be surprised that I find you here?'

'I don't know. Should you?'

The monk bent down and hissed in Guillaume's face. '*Don't* play with me, de Gisborne...' Two of his men placed themselves at either shoulder and Adam jumped up, his sword sliding from the scabbard.

'Stay you, Adam,' Guillaume said mildly. And then, 'I play with no one, monk, least of all you. You intimidated Madame de Clochard today. You insinuate our house does wrong. Say what you will and be done because,' he stood, finishing his wine and looking down upon Brother Crispianus. 'I want to return to my home and my friends.'

But as before, the monk was not belittled. 'You consort with heretics.' Spittle sprayed through the air as he enunciated the words through his string mouth with its foul teeth.

'And I say to you, I do not. Is that all?'

'The widow and her husband were members of an heretical faith. You are here where was a gathering of the Poor Men.' He held up a worn wooden cross dangling from his waist. 'Tell me you did not come here to meet them.'

'We did not. We left the Cathedral to return to Rue Ducanivet and on the way decided to have a wine. Ask the serving wench or the innkeeper. We met no one.'

Crispianus' face flushed with an ugly stain. 'God has told me to root out all heresy and evil. It sits in your house. Divine right shall prevail by the grace of the Lord God.' He spun around, a maleficent odour hitting Guillaume and Adam, and stormed off with the guard, in pursuit of his quarry.

'Jesu!' Adam sheathed his sword.

'Another blasphemy, Adam?' Guillaume began to walk because his fury with the monk had lit a taper that he had long thought buried. Walking hard might just pinch the flame out...

Adam hurried up next to him. 'He has us well in his sights.'

'He does.'

'It worries you?'

'Of course. Adam, we must find that Bible. It's imperative.'

'And what then?'

'I'll think of something. In any event we must protect the house.'

Adam pulled at Guillaume's sleeve and he slowed. 'I'm not sure how to say this,' the Englishman said, 'so I shall be blunt. *Dameisele* Ariella lives in that house and the monk has marked her. He has no boundaries.'

It was true and Guillaume worried about her safety every day. He knew she would make the standard argument of being able to protect herself, but even so, he hated that she would be under threat for the selfsame faith that might keep he and she apart. Perhaps, rather than taking Tobias to the Forez, he should take her. Between he and Adam, they could...

But no. It would be improper.

'Adam, I want you to stay here and command the men. Toby and I can go alone.'

Adam drew his chin back in surprise. 'You think Petrus' men aren't capable? You should rest easy as Petrus chooses very wisely. Besides, Michael will be in the house. Do not he and Madame Sarapion move from the inn whilst we are gone? You need to trust in your men. You know as much as anyone that it's the sign of a good leader.'

But Guillaume could only think of de Sablé and it left ashes in his mouth.

CHAPTER SEVEN

×

The house was calm when he walked back into the little hall. The long trestle shone in the flickering light of candle trees and a fresh-lit fire, Toby strumming and then humming in counterpoint to the plucked instrument. He always preferred to pluck any stringed instrument than use a bow. He called it 'teasing the woman to perform'. Guillaume smiled at the memory of such evenings in Venezia; balm to any troubled soul.

The de Clochard women plied needles on some of Saul's rustling silks and Ariella and Michael played chess.

'Done?' Ariella asked, looking up from studying the board. The light caught her luxurious hair. They called Richard Plantagenet a red-haired man, but his was surely sandy. Adam's was fiercely red – even young William had noticed and called him Rufus. But Ariella's? It reminded him of a stream of rich red burgundy in some lights and in others of the lustre of chestnuts. It could never be copied by dyes or by a painter's pigment. It could be called tawny perhaps, or dusky. Any of those...

'Done,' he replied. 'And what have you been doing?'

'Amée, shall you tell him, or will I?' Ariella's voice held a note. Not patronising, but perhaps the knowledge that like the carpenters and stonemasons at work outside, shoring up the buildings, she and Amée had accomplished something just as important.

Amée had removed her wimple and veil and her hair hung in a storm-grey plait down her back. Without the constraints of the wimple, her face had relaxed and her apple cheeks glowed from the warmth in the chamber,

145

and from the half-full goblet of wine beside her.

'Ariella and I went to see Joshua, the moneylender.'

'Alone?' Guillaume asked.

'Of course not! If we were to bring monies home with us we needed guards, so Michael and Herviet attended. Jehanne and Tobias remained here under the tender care of Raol and Gosse.'

Guillaume unbuckled his sword and laid it across the table, the buckles chuckling and jingling as they rubbed against each other. 'And what was the outcome?' he asked with caution. There would surely be a complaint about borrowing at exorbitant interest.

'He's a most accommodating man. I was extremely surprised to find that he knew Jehan and that de Clochard have borrowed from him in the past.' A confused expression flew across her face and was gone, lit instead by the zeal of the merchant she was. She lifted the thread to her teeth and bit through it, then re-threaded the eye of the bone needle with silk the colour of spring leaves. 'Anyway, he made us a loan. Ariella thinks that with what is put by, it will tide us over until the German envoys send your man back with the rest of their payment or until Gisborne sends some funds. Whichever reaches us first. Joshua gave us half today and the remainder will be made available as we need it. When we returned here, Ariella paid what we owed our doughty tradesmen.' She smiled, an expression of satisfaction, as if she alone had discovered the solution to their troubles. She took a few more stitches, her thread sighing in and out, the fire crackling and Toby strumming a handful of notes.

'And?' Guillaume asked. 'The interest?'

'Tuh,' Amée replied as she held her embroidery away, squinted at it and then proceeded to unpick the last two stitches. 'None! He says he owes Saul far more and that this is his way of paying a life debt.' She looked up at Guillaume and shook her head. 'Life's very odd, isn't it? And don't you spoil my good day by telling me about that odious monk. I don't want to hear.'

Guillaume caught the amused expression on Ariella's face as she moved her bishop across the board and was glad she and Amée were once again friends on an equal footing.

Toby stopped playing and stroked the neck of the instrument as he laid it down. 'My friends, I must go before dark.' He took Amée's hand and made a great play of kissing it. 'I thank you for your company and I look forward to seeing you all on the morrow. Mayhap Mahaut and I can sing for you.'

Guillaume followed him out and as he closed the door to the house, he said, 'You and Mahaut?'

Tobias pulled at his sagging hose. 'She was like melted honey when I began to play whilst the house was empty. It was in truth rather miraculous. One moment I was plucking away and singing a song. You know William's favourite? *Somer is y Comen*? She was standing at the entrance to the kitchen and she sang the melody although she didn't know the words. She has a beautiful tone to her voice and is an instinctive singer. Seems God felt guilty when he gave her that wretched face and decided to give her a voice to make up for it. Bit like me really.' He indicated his diminutive size with a wave of his hand.

'I'm in awe, Tobias. She addresses me as if I am a murderer-in-waiting. Did she speak to you after that?'

'Yes. We sang a hymn first, *Veni Redemptor Gentium*. She loves Church music. She asked where I learned to sing and I told her my history of attending the College of Minstrels in Paris, of singing for Richard Plantagenet and Queen Eleanor. I think that was when she realised perhaps I wasn't a spawn of Satan after all. At any rate, she said she loved singing and that the only way to do so was to become a nun but her family were too poor to pay a dowry to join a convent.'

Tobias and Guillaume walked to the gates. The sky had been stained the colour of pomegranates and the breeze stilled. Across from Rue Ducanivet, the Saône flowed onward. Barges were moored and the only movement was a flotilla of waterbirds. Crewmen sat round braziers, playing at habitual dice or a form of tablemen.

'It's a scene worthy of the art of an illuminator monk, isn't it?' said Tobias the aesthete. 'I don't take much with the big Church painters. I think the scribes are cleverer and more mindful of their surroundings.'

Guillaume agreed and then said, 'Toby, Mahaut may be a threat.'

Toby frowned. 'Why?'

Guillaume laid an arm across his shoulder and the two crossed to the riverbank away from ears that might hear. He informed the minstrel of the Poor Men of Lyon, of the monk's insinuations and of the Bible, and of Mahaut's hatred of Ariella.

'So then, methinks you have something you want me to do.'

'Charm Mahaut. If she ever mentions anything about Ariella, try and draw her out.'

'And this is because you think Ariella is in danger?'

'It's a feeling Adam and I share.'

'Adam too?' Toby frowned. He looked into the distance and bit his thumbnail, an old habit when he was disturbed. 'Lord. Danger from Mahaut?'

'Maybe…'

'You are so economical with words, Guillaume. Whereas I…' He shifted on his feet, a little agitated dance. 'I thought our troubles were done after the Tyrian purple had been retrieved.' He chewed his nail again and then, 'Of course I will do what you ask. Ariella is my good friend, more like a sister and I love her dearly.'

'I thank you.'

'Tobias! Tobias!' Voices shouted from the gates and they turned to see Jehanne and Michael hurrying toward them. 'Toby, we'll walk back with you. Better for us all to return to the inn together.'

The three walked away and Guillaume watched them leave, Tobias between Michael and Jehanne. There was a degree of comfort in their solidarity – as if their arrival at de Clochard had bolstered spirits that had flagged. There was no doubt they all belonged in the household – just as much as they had all slotted into the household in Venezia or Constantinople. It was as if borders didn't exist, that the houses were interchangeable. And with the familiarity, Guillaume allowed himself to relax … just for a moment.

Herviet and Gosse fetched the horses and the mule from the Gigni house the day before Guillaume's departure for the Forez. The animals shone despite the fledgling winter coats, and their manes held not a trace of scurf. There was no doubt they had been cared for beyond necessity and there begged the question – what will be the cost?

Guillaume ordered new harness and arranged for grain and flour to be delivered and stored in the newly repaired barn. The buttery would store wine and future shipments of cloth and thus the overcrowded *traboule* storeroom could be emptied to make room for the increased household of guards.

Guillaume however, set up his own quarters in the stall that had belonged to the dead mule. He liked the idea of sleeping in the heady smell of the barn.

When the doors were closed it was warm, and the animals were tolerant of his presence as he carried his possessions from the house. He had asked the carpenters to make him a rough cot-frame and he strung it and placed a decent mattress atop. For bedding he had cloaks. He had left his own coverings for Ariella and had departed the small monastic chamber without a backward glance. He had learned that a bed was where one found it while marching with Richard Plantagenet's men. It did not pay to become attached. Raol helped him carry his chest to the barn and now he clipped down the stair with his small locked casket, a spare cloak draped over his shoulder.

The house was quiet this day. Amée had gone with her returned family to visit a friend on the far side of the town, Michael and Jehanne more than capable of protecting the trio. Ariella and Tobias had gone to the *lavoir* near the *Quartier* Saint Jean, taking Adam as a precaution. Toby had clothes that needed washing and Ariella agreed to help him – and as they left, Toby began singing the *'Women'* song, in the English tongue, finishing as they walked through the gates with,

> *Some cane whister, and some cane crie,*
> *Some cane flater and some can lye,*
> *And some cane sette the moke awrie,*
> *Yet all thei do nat soo.*
> *Sume be lewde,*
> *And some be schreuede,*
> *Go where thei goo…*

Adam, who knew the song and understood the English full well, burst out laughing, joining in the chorus, and Ariella pretended to be scandalised, their voices cheerily fading as they walked along the street.

Guillaume revelled in the solitude and took note of his surroundings. With the house almost empty he seized his chance, leaving the cloak and casket by the door, beginning a search for the holy book that could so change their lives. He proceeded swiftly round the hall, watching for the door beyond which stood the kitchens and where he could hear Mahaut banging kitchen tools. He checked door frames, the hearth, the wall stones, under the table, chairs and stools. He began to climb the stair, noting if any tread squeaked, observing the walls, lifting the two tapestries that hung heavily to warm the space.

But there was nothing…

He hurried to the top floor, under the eaves, and repeated the process all the way down until he reached Amée's chamber. He had just run his hands down the side of the window surrounds when he felt, rather than saw someone behind him. Turning, he beheld Mahaut, her face puckered and pinched with disdain.

'Why are you in Madame's chamber?'

He replied with barely a thought. 'I heard shouting on the riverbank on the way down the stair and went to Madame's window to see.' The lie came easily as he glanced down at two fellows yelling and pushing at each other. 'Look…'

She waddled over and looked through the glass. The noise had become louder and a punch headed for a chin.

'Huh!' the servant said with disdain. 'Dice. They fight over debts.' Her voice held no echo of the supposed beauty Tobias had mentioned. 'They should avoid such a sinful thing.'

Guillaume cursed the woman for the omnipresent nuisance she was.

Not nuisance. Malfeasance…

But he recovered with speed.

'Mahaut, I leave on the morrow with Adam and Messire Tobias, for the Gigni hunt…'

As he spoke she turned from him, muttering, and picking up blankets to fold.

A red vein of fury began to trickle about his body. So much of the last few days had aroused something from Outremer that he wished to forget. 'What did you say?' he asked.

If Mahaut had known Guillaume at all, she might have realised that when his voice quieted so obviously, and that when his jaw set hard, he was not someone with whom to be trifled. She kept her back to him but her response was clear enough. 'I said the house will be as it should be.'

'You tread dangerously,' he warned.

She swivelled her bulk toward him, her eyes closed to harsh slits. 'You think I am afraid of you, an upstart archer with pretensions to be something he is not?' she spat. 'You have no place here. This is the de Clochard residence, not de Gisborne. And take your heretic whore with you. She shames a God-fearing house…'

The trickle became a torrent and he strode to her, grabbed her arm in a fierce grip and held a finger in front of her face. 'Enough. Madame Jehanne and *Dameisele* Ariella are old friends, Mahaut, with a strong history. If Madame Jehanne knew what you said, she would turn you out in an instant. And she shall know…'

She paled, and pushed at his hand and he let her go. He wanted to slap her, so angry was he with her blind beliefs. And the way she spoke of 'Ella, it was as if she could betray her in a breath. It was written in her eyes, in the way her mouth spat 'heretic' as if it were poison.

She continued to fold the blankets but her hands trembled. 'If Madame Jehanne sided with that unbeliever rather than me, she is not the woman I took her for.'

Guillaume stood over the servant, preventing her moving, looking down at her. 'Perhaps you do not know your scriptures, Mahaut. *Dameisele* Ariella is a Jewess, just like Mary, our Lord Jesus' holy mother, and in addition, the *Dameisele* stood by Madame de Clochard when she had no one else.'

'She had me,' the servant cried out, hitting her chest. 'Me!'

And in that moment, Guillaume felt pity for a woman with neither looks, intelligence nor fortune and who merely wanted to sing holy songs, and whose loyalty by her own calculations, was being ignored.

'She could never have run this house without you, Mahaut. You are her mainstay. But I am talking of Messire Jehan's legacy, the trading arm. *Dameisele* Ariella was there for Madame when she needed help to keep that legacy alive.' He said reassuring things but the look she gave him was filled with hate. 'Do you wish to stay in this house or leave?' he finally asked.

She didn't answer but her bottom lip jutted threateningly and she slammed down the lid of the coffer in which she had placed the folded blankets.

'I shall take your silence as a yes, shall I? In which case, in order to ensure your position here, you will run an errand…' He waited for her to respond but she merely extended the furious and jutting lip further. 'Soeur Marie at the convent has a package waiting for collection. It is a gift for Madame de Clochard. Collect it if you will, and return here as soon as you can.'

She turned her back on him and began to walk out the door. 'Mahaut?'

'*Oc*,' she muttered. 'I will go…'

After he heard the door to the yard close and watched her cloaked shape disappear through the gates, he allowed himself the briefest moment of shame for threatening a woman so. It was never in his nature in the past … before … and he hated that his temper seemed to be shorter and his anger quicker to burst into flame. But there was Ariella to protect and he knew for sure now, that Mahaut was a danger to her. He cast a quick eye upon the dice players but they had resolved their differences and were once again gambling and so he began to search Amée's room. Driven, he thought, by the selfsame strength of zeal of which he accused the monk and Mahaut.

But of course the search yielded nothing and as he stepped down the stair, Amée and her family returned, basking in the glow of a good day. The widow said her friend, Berta, had on a grey *bliaut* of exceptional wool that she had purchased in the weeks before Jehan died.

'And we almost had to pick her off the floor when she recognized Jehanne. I can tell you, the news will be across Lyon by Prime. Are you packed and ready, Guillaume, for your sojourn with the rich and infamous?'

'Almost. Not much more to do.'

'Then we shall celebrate with a meal and wine. It must almost be ready. Mah…'

'She has gone to run an errand for me. She won't be long.'

'She's doing something for *you*? Then she has seen the light, as I told you she would after I had spoken with her.' Amée sniffed the air and pulled off her cloak, laying it on a stool. 'Well at least the meal is cooking. She has become so preoccupied of late, and given to praying over-much. Where did you send her?'

'To the convent.'

'Lord,' Amée replied. 'She's so holy these days, she might stay there.' She hurried off to the kitchens from where the smell of rich meaty juices had begun to drift.

Jehanne took up where her mother left off. 'She *is* devout. A pity she could not become a nun.'

If only…

Michael leaned against the hearth, kicking at a log with a toe, watching a skein of red sparks fly up. 'Why don't you offer to pay her dowry then, if you think she might be happier in the convent?'

'Michael, I don't think we have the coin. But it is something *Maman* might perhaps consider later.'

Sooner rather than later…

Guillaume listened to them discussing Mahaut, envying them their closeness, the thought that they might retire together at night and hold each other…

'God's breath…' The door was pushed open and held by Tobias as Ariella rushed in huffing on her hands. 'There's an edge to the air out there for all that the dusk is as pretty as a woman's skin. Have you noticed?'

They looked out the door where the soft colour of a Persian peach rippled across an egg-blue sky. 'But it is a sign of a cold night, I think,' he said, shutting their view away. 'Winter is coming.' He pulled at his cloak and laid it over Amée's on the stool. 'Guillaume, we met a Gigni man at the gate. This is for you.'

He held out a packet and Guillaume once again felt the suede-like skin of quality parchment beneath his fingers. He flicked a nail under the wax seal and unrolled the note.

To Guillaume de Gisborne from your loyal friend and servant Alexandrus Gigni greetings. It occurs to me that you must leave your horses behind for the use of the de Clochard house when you depart for my hunt. Two of our own shall therefore be harnessed for your use on the morrow. Please accept this offer as gift of friendship for which no payment is required. My family look forward to welcoming you to the Forez. Valete.

The man was right but God damn him anyway. The sense of patronage that emanated from the Gigni irked him – it smacked so much of feudal largesse. Nevertheless, he read the note to the room. Tobias appeared somewhat rueful.

'I will rent a mount from the livery as there are only two horses.'

'If you wish,' Guillaume said. 'Or ride behind me.'

Tobias laughed. 'Guillaume, remember? I am not the best horseman. Even less so if I have to hang on from behind. I will get my own horse because I would like to feel safe … not that you don't inspire confidence, of course. I mean no insult but I am what I am. And besides, I will have the lute.'

Whilst Amée was engaged in the kitchens, the five sat discussing the next few days, Michael assuming a' leadership with ease.

'Nothing changes,' the Byzantine said. 'The house must assume it is still vulnerable and under attack. Guard and be guarded. We have four men of extensive experience here, so have faith in us, Guillaume.'

'He does,' Ariella chipped in. 'Don't you, Guillaume?'

She pushed at his weak spot and he frowned. 'Of course. I have faith in you all.'

'Ah, dear Guillaume,' Ariella tucked her hand through his arm. 'There is always a *but*, isn't there? You are so like your half-brother.'

The 'but' hung in the air – the unknown, the undiscovered, the act of surprise – all of those.

Michael crossed his leg, resting the calf on his knee and idly pleating the folds of his hose. 'It's interesting that the past few days have been devoid of anything beyond the priest's ongoing zeal. I suspect they lull us. Guillaume, I'm used to this tactic. I may not be able to ease your concern but we *are* all qualified.'

Guillaume held up placatory hands. 'I know, I know. I am frustrated at playing with phantoms. 'Tis all.'

Michael stood and pressed Guillaume's shoulder, saying, 'I can fight phantoms too, believe it or not.' He walked to the door, closing it quietly behind him.

Guillaume noticed the casket and cloak lying at the door and excused himself to remove them to the barn. There was no sign of Michael outside but Herviet and Gosse stood at the gates.

'All's well,' said Herviet, leaning against the wood for a moment. 'Mahaut should be back soon.'

'Let's hope it stays like this,' Guillaume said. 'Do you want food sent out?' The guards shook their heads, indicating they only had till dark before their shift finished and Gosse held up a slab of bread and cheese.

'For all that she's the grumpy bitch from Hell, she keeps us fed.'

Guillaume walked on to the barn, the workmen having downed tools and gone. One of the rounceys, Bett, looked up and flicked her ears. Lorenz, the gelding, ignored him and continued to chew on a wad of sweet hay while the mule, Obby because he was obstinate, stood, eyes closed, one hip dropped and hoof resting and his ears loosely horizontal.

Guillaume moved into the stall next to him, noticing the animal's bottom lip dangling. He pushed the little casket under his cot and reached over the rails to rub Obby's rump. The mule jerked his head once before his eyes closed again. There was such an air of contentment and calm in the barn. He thought how easy it was to be lulled into a false state of security. The late afternoon air wafted and the horses' ears pricked as Michael walked in and leaned over the side of the stall.

'Better than a military camp.'

'To be truthful,' Guillaume replied, 'Better than my old chamber within the house. A different kind of warm, a calmer atmosphere and no women's voices chipping at the air.' What he didn't say was *'And when I have a nightmare and wake shaking and wet with sweat, or if I cry out in my sleep, there is no one to hear me.'*

Michael laughed. 'Too many hens…'

'Indeed. All the cockerels sleep outside.'

'Guillaume, is there anything else you wish me to know before you go?'

Guillaume stepped out of the stall and leaned next to the Byzantine, easing his stitched back carefully to rest against the partition. Michael's dark hair was threaded subtly with grey like Gisborne's, and Guillaume wondered if his own was the same. It had been a long time since he had seen his face reflected.

Sarapion had shaved since arriving in Lyon and it suited him, revealing a strong chin, but his eyes held shadows of pain. And Guillaume had never noticed before, but under the dark hair at the temple, Michael had a puckered scar which he guessed by its colour was only a couple of years old. He ran a hand under his own hair to feel the scab from the first attack.

'You know about the monk and the fact that he has marked the house as a source of heresy. But it isn't all just about the Poor Men and a bible and Jehan's past history with Pierre Vaudès. There's also Ariella. The monk believes that as a Jew she fouls the house and is a candidate for the fires of Hell. What compounds it all is that Mahaut is zealously devout and believes Ariella places the whole house at risk. I believe the monk has made Mahaut an acolyte and drips poison in her ear.' He hit his fist against the wood, suddenly feeling impotent and angry. 'This is not the time to go hunting…'

'Then why did you agree to go?'

'After the attacks, I believed I was the target and that by accepting Gigni's invitation, I would draw the enemy away from the house. To a point Adam and I still believe that, but the monk's attentions have increased in strength and that concerns me greatly.'

Michael grunted. 'So you think that by going tomorrow, the threat will be halved. But what if you die? What of Ariella then? I know you are probably right in your thinking but I'm glad Adam and Toby go with you. Toby proved himself more than capable in Byzantium and the respect your brother holds for Adam precedes him. But I have to say, Ariella *is* right, you know.'

'She generally is…' Guillaume pinched the bridge of his nose.

Michael punched him softly on the arm. 'She said there is always a *but* with you. Will you tell me?'

Guillaume sighed. 'It's the Bible. I have searched the whole house to no avail. If there is a bible, I would remove it beyond harm's way.'

'You would? How?'

'Burn it, bury it, drown it. Whatever it takes to keep the house safe. I was about to search the *traboule* this night.'

'Then we shall. Easier with two. Now come inside and let us make a semblance of normality.'

Mahaut returned as they reached the door, her face coloured with the dusk cool. She thrust a package into Guillaume's hands and pushed in front of the men. Michael snorted and picked up an armload of wood from beside the door and carried it inside to begin stoking the fire as Guillaume unwrapped Soeur Marie's goods. Ariella's coverlet was like the buds of spring woven from wool, not redolent of the Church at all. And the little purse burst into the light like a sunbeam at the end of the day – a beaten gold orb staining the sky to a fierce orange, like fruit that arrived from Al-Andalus.

He carried the goods to the table, calling for the women to come. Ariella ran down the stair and Amée came from the kitchen.

'Is aught wrong?' The widow flustered like a hen flapping feathers, wiping her hands on a piece of linen.

'Not at all,' Guillaume said. 'I merely bought you both a gift each, because I depart tomorrow.' He doled the presents out.

'Oh! How lovely,' Amée pulled at the rolled leather strings and opened the purse. 'It's the colour of the setting sun. And look, there is gold stitching.' She wrapped Guillaume in her arms and squeezed and for one brief traitorous moment, he thought of his mother. Cateline always squeezed as if she couldn't bear to let go.

Ariella unfolded the coverlet, running her hand over the light embroidery and then holding the wool against her cheek. 'I shall feel as if I sleep under the oak tree in spring, just as the buds begin to burst. Where did you find these? We shall have to look to our skills for there is competition here.'

'Soeur Marie. She and her novices make things from the off-cuts we give them. The green wool was ours once and the leather was Messire Ricard's.'

Amée laughed. 'Clever Soeur Marie!'

Mahaut glowered from the kitchen. 'Madame Amée, the food is ready.'

'Then let's eat, shall we? And toast de Clochard's return to good fortune and Guillaume's success at the hunt.'

Later, Guillaume and Michael ventured outside. They walked past the oak tree to the storeroom, tiptoeing past Herviet and Gosse who now lay snoring. Guillaume eased the key into the *traboule* door and turned it as Michael lifted a flame from the wall sconce.

Together they began, feeling stone upon stone, step upon step.

Once, a stone wobbled in the wall and Guillaume used the tip of his dagger to ease it out enough for fingers to pull. His heart beat faster. But behind the stone was a small rotted parcel of faded silk. When he unwound it, threads catching on the roughness of his skin, a golden ring lay on his palm. The stone was the blue of the deepest ocean and as smooth as a finch's egg, tiny as a tear. The setting was wrought with intricacy and Michael immediately pronounced it early Byzantine.

'Is there anything else in there?'

Guillaume felt around and pulled at a rotting leather pouch that jingled as it slid across the rough stone. He unstrung the leather and a handful of silver coins fell out.

'I wonder of this is Jehan's?'

'Do you know, I doubt it. I believe they are *denarii*. Look at the heads on the coins.' He bent and scrutinized under the flame. 'Is it Justinian? I can't see it clearly. These are very old and I suspect some trader felt the need to hide goods hundreds of years ago. Lugdunum was always important in trade. Who knows? In any case, Guillaume, it's yours. You found it.'

'Not at all. It's the widow's property. You take it.'

Michael held the bag with the coins. 'I will take this for the widow and she can take them to Joshua, the moneylender. I suspect a good deal will be struck. You take the ring … for Ariella.'

Guillaume wrapped the ring back into the frayed silk. To slip it onto her finger would be the answer to his dreams. Not his prayers, because God never played fair. But dreams were another thing entirely. 'We'll see,' he said and slipped it into his purse.

They continued working their way down the stair until they reached the bottom of the *traboule* where the de Clochard entrance stood locked and barred. They could barely see the need to unlock it but did it anyway, just on the offchance that the door frame outside might yield something. And besides, there was still one bend of the *traboule* left before the riverbank was reached.

Guillaume pushed at the door but something barred it on the other side and there was a faint sound as Michael eased alongside him.

'Was that a voice?' Guillaume held the door still.

Michael leaned his head out. 'Jesu! Quickly, someone's wounded.'

He squeezed through and gently moved the body aside, the fellow moaning weakly. 'Guillaume, bring the flame…'

But as Guillaume began to squeeze through, a figure leaped out of the shadow of the bend upon Michael, a dagger lifting in the torchlight. Guillaume brought the flame down on the attacker's arm, the smell of burning wool filling the space. The felon gagged, swiping at the glowing cloth and turning with a snarl toward him. Guillaume held the brand between he and the man, waving the flames across his face, moving forward, pushing the flame ever closer as the man stumbled back against Michael.

Michael's arm encircled the man's shoulder and chest, his dagger held against the windpipe, the fellow sucking air in and out, the torch flame so close to his face that he turned his head sideways. 'Who are you?' Michael hissed.

The man mumbled, arching against Michael's chest, the blade digging deep enough for a trickle to form across the throat. The felon's eyes opened wide.

'*Who* are you?' Michael growled close to the man's ear.

A garble emerged.

Michael went to push the blade deeper but Guillaume noticed the man's open mouth. 'There's no tongue! He can't answer!'

'He deserves no kindness, Guillaume…'

'Agreed. But he can nod or shake his head. Can't you?'

The fellow nodded.

'Do you work for Brother Crispianus?'

A nod.

'Did he ask you to do this?' Guillaume indicated the man lying at his feet.

A nod.

'Is this man a Poor Man?'

Questioning eyes.

'*Sandalati?*'

A nod.

'He pays you for this?'

A nod.

'Did he cut out your tongue?'

A tear escaped the man's eye and ran down the scarred face. A nod.

Guillaume looked at Michael and then bent to the fallen figure at his feet. In the light of the flame, he recognized the face. 'Hamelyn?'

Hamelyn's eyes opened. 'You…'

'We will look after you. Have no fear. He lives, Michael, but barely.'

Michael drew his knife instantly across the felon's throat and let the man fall. It was a quick movement, awful in its unmitigated delivery and yet, Guillaume knew he would have done the same – they wanted no one who could run to the monk and betray them because there was a more important individual at their feet.

'I know this man,' Guillaume ripped off his cloak and laid it over Hamelyn. 'He was at the tavern yesterday and spoke to me.'

Together they lifted him carefully through the door and lowered him to the ground upon Michael's cloak. Guillaume locked the door and then went to move Hamelyn's hands from his middle to tuck them into the extra folds of the coverings, but the itinerate preacher cried out.

They saw the blood all over his hands and saw what Hamelyn was trying to hold together. Both had seen men's guts spilled before – it went with battles and all that was foul in men, but the shock was as great as the very first time and so they left his hands where they were and pulled the folds around him more securely, knowing his life ebbed fast.

His eyes focused on Guillaume, his face already as pale as death.

''Tis me,' Guillaume said.

'The Bible...'

'We can't find it.'

'*Traboule.* Here. Valuable. First one copied by Bernard of Ydros.' With effort, he licked his lips and whispered. 'Must go to Piedmont...'

Guillaume and Michael flicked a quick glance at each other.

'Tell us exactly where?' Michael bent toward Hamelyn.

But Hamelyn's eyes had stilled with a desperate pleading therein, as if he stood before his God and asked for kindness. His face was ashen and his mouth agape, revealing teeth that were surprisingly healthy. If he had ever smiled, Guillaume knew it would inspire trust.

''Tis no use,' he said. 'He is done.' He noted how thin Hamelyn was, but that his beard was tidy and his clothes decent. He looked far better presented than a man just arrived from Piedmont where Vaudès had found sanctuary as an ex-communicant. He found his own hand wandering to Hamelyn's and stroking it, his mind blank of thought. Death did that sometimes – aroused memories and it was better to shut the door than allow them in.

'What shall we do with them both?' Michael's voice broke the chilled silence of the *traboule* and Guillaume blinked the emptiness away.

'Wrap them in the cloaks, weight them with stones and sink them downstream in deeper water. There will be a skiff outside.

'But Hamelyn might have family...' Michael said.

'He might. And we will deal with it at some point, but not now.'

'Of course...'

They pulled the cloak out flat and wrapped Hamelyn as if he were in a shroud, opening the door again and carrying him round the *traboule* bend and to the skiff pulled onto the shore. The air smelled of smoke and mud, reeds and bird excreta, fish entrails and many other things besides and the sky was darkest black, making their short journey to the skiff slippery and cumbersome. Once they had laid Hamelyn's corpse in the boat, they opened the cloak and pushed stones into the man's bloody hose, into his *braies* – wherever they would fit – and then wrapped him tight once more. They did the same with the felon, their hands slippery with gore from both bodies and Guillaume felt as if he floated, almost a faint, and he hated what he had become since Outremer, but he drew in a deep breath as they pushed the skiff into the water and climbed in carefully at the stern, for the weight had lowered the vessel dangerously. Guillaume poled as Michael balanced the craft, sitting in the bow and they slid across the current. As they entered the deep-reeded shore of Presque L'ile, someone called from the Pont Du Change.

'Halt! Who goes there?'

They eased the craft in amongst the rushes and sat quietly, barely breathing. The Watch moved on and they pulled themselves hand over hand through the thick water plants, the sluggish current helping the craft slide along. Once they disturbed a flock of wild duck that quacked a frightened cacophony, pelting out from the reeds, and Guillaume and Michael hoped the Watch would think it was a cat on the hunt.

Nothing followed and presently they were far enough away to heave the felon to the wale, sliding him into the water. They moved a little further on with Hamelyn and hefted him gently to the wale.

'Sad…' Michael observed.

CHAPTER EIGHT

×

They let him go and Guillaume whispered, '*In nomine Patris et Filii et Spiritus Sancti...*' and the two crossed themselves.

They poled as silent as water spirits back to their own shore and in a breath had pulled the skiff onto the stones and hurried up into the *traboule*, through the de Clochard door, closing it behind and shoving the bars across, with Guillaume turning the big key and passing it to Michael.

''Tis yours now...'

'For the moment.' Michael weighed it in his hands. 'When you return, 'tis yours again. This book – what do you think?'

'I know of the original Bible. Vaudés paid two ecclesiastical scholars to copy it into the vernacular from the Church tongue.'

'The whole Bible? Do you think the one we seek is it?'

'Not the whole, no. Just the Gospels and some of the Saints. And in answer to your question? Yes, I think it might be.'

'And Hamelyn is saying that original is here, in the house...'

'So it seems. No wonder the priest wants to find it. I imagine the Church would make a great show of disposing of it and not only that, de Clochard would be ruined for secreting it. The family would be excommunicated and the business would collapse.'

'Do you think the Archbishop wants this house for that reason?'

'Possibly. But more likely, I suspect for pecuniary reasons. He has a mind for fortune-building. No, I think the monk wants the Bible and he is the one who wants to make a show to his Archbishop and to Rome, that he is protecting the house of the Lord.'

'Mad, I would say.'

'Yes.' Guillaume looked to the door, recalling Hamelyn's expression upon his death and as he began to lead the way up through the dark *traboule*, he said. '*Life is short, the times are evil, prepare for Heaven.* They are the words of Vaudès and his followers.'

'Why is the Church afraid of them?'

'Vaudès made the word of the Bible accessible to every man and he also expressed that word in a way that made the way of churchmen seem vulgar and self-centered. He took up the belief that *'Blessed are the Poor'*. And of course Church wealth was undeniable. It was no wonder he and his preachers were excommunicated. And yet they still manage to flourish, even now.'

Michael sighed, observing, 'A difference in beliefs. Our own culture has seen little better. Over the centuries, men were murdered because of the presence or not of icons within our churches. Ultimately it became the decision of two empresses to reconstitute the icons within the Church and those two events a hundred years apart.'

They continued upward, feeling along the stone with their hands, the interior of the *traboule* as shadowed as the Styx. Guillaume could hear Michael breathing close behind.

'I always felt sad,' Michael continued, 'that something so beautiful and representative of God's Heaven as an icon, painted with loving veneration by a monk, should be so worrisome to the Church and State. Nevertheless, that is what happened. One could draw a faint parallel.'

They had reached the upper door and pushed it open quietly, entering the dulcetly lit space of the storeroom, locking the door as quietly as they could. Herviet still snored and Gosse lay on his belly, his lips squashed sideways. In the torchlit yard, they stopped and looked at each other.

'You have blood on you,' Michael said.

'And you. Come to the trough…'

They slipped past the oak and as they bent to the trough to scrub, a woman's voice sounded behind them.

'There is a bath in the barn.' Ariella's voice was impartial. 'Toby and Adam have already bathed so that they are ready for tomorrow. I ordered clean water for you, Guillaume. But it seems you must both share the water.

Blood is hard to remove…'

'Ariella…' Guillaume caught her eye.

'Later. Get clean. Tobias has returned to the inn for this night and said he will meet you at the Gigni gates tomorrow morning. Mahaut and Amée have retired and Jehanne is making up a bed for you and she, Michael, in Amée's chamber.' She turned and walked inside and the two men took a breath.

'She's sanguine. One could almost say she is Jehanne's sister.'

'She's strong.'

The two friends walked into the barn where a tepid half-hogshead sat waiting.

'You go first,' Michael said. 'You need to be pristine for your time with the well-shod. I need only sponge myself clean.'

The two stripped off, broad-shouldered men with scars and scrapes.

'And this is?' Michael indicated the wound on Guillaume's back.

'Ah…'

'Ah indeed. What happened?'

'Another attack. After I had left Amée at the Cathedral before you arrived. I have not told anyone. Not even Ariella. It's this that makes me think I am a target.'

'But not connected to the Vaudès Bible.'

'I don't believe so, no. As I told you.'

Michael grabbed a handful of the lukewarm water and splashed it over his face as Guillaume sank down into the hogshead. 'This is such a puzzle…'

More than a puzzle…

Guillaume lay in his cot in the barn, hands behind his head. Outside, a fractious wind rattled the last of the oak's largesse and snickered underneath the door, shaking it so that Bett snorted, facing her rump to the door.

The Bible had been an enigma till now but surely Hamelyn had given them tacit acknowledgement that the book lay somewhere here – the book that the Church wanted, that the Poor Men wanted and that de Clochard wanted.

Guillaume would destroy it if it meant the house and the business could live on. What else could he do? Hamelyn had been his only link to the Poor Men, the so-called *Sandalati*. If he found the book, how would he find the other followers to give it to them? It was inconvenient that they vanished into walls like ghosts into graves.

Shadow men who could take the bible away with them...

Hamelyn had been disembowelled for a book and his beliefs and if Guillaume were honest, he would say it would happen forever more into time beyond memory. Hamelyn had been a kind, decent man and Guillaume wondered what had led him down the path of a preacher, moving from town to village two by two, always keeping ahead of the Church, always vilified and finally excommunicated.

Two by two...

He sat up.

Hamelyn's preaching companion must surely be one of the men at the tavern. Which meant the man was most likely still in the town.

I have no time to find the shadow man, so Michael must do it...

He shivered, bumps rising over his skin so that he slid rapidly back down under his cloaks, thinking of the one that had become a shroud and which now lay amongst the weedy roots deep in the Saône, tugged ever onward as the river flowed south to its confluence with the Rhône. He wished sleep would tug at his eyelids but there was so much to think on to brood over.

Next to him, Obby shifted, farted and there followed the sweetly pungent slop, slop, slop as the beast soiled. Guillaume breathed in – it was a clean odour – the smell of sunshine, of the silver, green and umber of new cut hay in stooks, of men and women laughing as they tossed the stooks onto a cart.

He lay on his side, the cloaks hitched to his ears but he was still cold. Should he clothe himself? But the chill nakedness whilst he searched for garments in the dark was not appealing and he slammed his eyes shut in frustration, perhaps the better to imagine summer warmth. But he could only feel the heat of the desert, hear the flies and the screams...

He hated it – the cruel fear. It crept up on him swiftly from nowhere. Always a hot flush, then a cold sweat and a body as taut as a bowstring. His breath began to quicken...

'Guillaume?' A soft voice spoke from the dark and the fear receded like a serpent's tongue.

'Ariella?' He flung himself over. 'Why are you here?'

She hunkered down next to him, smelling of lavender and lemons, the soft wool of the coverlet he had gifted her, draping across his knuckles.

'I think you have things to tell me and I would say goodbye with privacy rather than under the scrutiny of the household.'

'I shall only be gone for five days…'

'I know. But it is important to me to do it this way. Tell me what happened tonight.'

He sighed. She was too astute for her own good and she had seen the blood, so he told her.

'But you haven't found the Bible?'

'No.'

'Then I shall hunt while you are gone.'

He took her hand. 'I would that you didn't,' he said. 'Let it stay hidden until I return. I would hate the monk to know you had found it.'

'Me above all others, you mean.'

He was silent, the only sound the single snort by Lorenz, followed by the continued snark of the wind.

'Yes. Jewess that you are, the bane of his miserable Christian life. He does not wish you well.'

'Of that I am aware. And neither does Mahaut. In fact, I think she is worse because I must live with her all the hours of the day.' She shivered and pulled the coverlet tight around her shoulders. 'Move over, I am cold.'

He was naked beneath the cloaks and propriety concerned him.

'Tuh,' she replied. 'If you would wed me, I will see all, so what does it matter? Besides, there is very little of you that I haven't seen.'

Nothing if not forthright…

He couldn't help a wry grin emerging and shuffled over. She lay down next to him and he flicked the cloaks to cover them both. They talked of the bible and of his desire to remove it and destroy it.

'If you can't find the *Sandalati* to hand it to.'

'Yes.'

'What is it that the Church finds so threatening?'

'It is the simple rule of life, love and care, devotion apart from wealth. Blessed are the Poor. It is the rule of the Gospels and of the Saints. Vaudès interprets Faith to be above wealth, above plenary indulgences – so there goes a vast treasury for the local bishops. The bishops have lobbied the Pope to see it their way and the Poor Men of Lyon are considered heretics. 'Ella, you must be cautious when you go out and always take one of the men. In the case of Mahaut, there is little to be done except don't trust her. Her devotion to her God is a little too zealous. That said, I think you are safe in the house.'

'Unless she poisons me…'

Guillaume's heart jumped. He had not thought Mahaut would stoop to murder. Informing, yes, but killing, no. 'I think not. But to be sure, I have talked with Michael about Mahaut and she will be watched so that you will be safe.'

'Huh,' she said with open irony. 'And you, my Guillaume. Are you safe?'

'As safe as I can be.'

'Well, you see, there is the rub. I need you to return to me…'

His heart jolted again. She had rarely ever been so personal. That they had feelings and were close was never acknowledged openly. They always talked of other things – of philosophy and life, of culture and trade and men. But they never discussed their feelings. She had talked of the York Massacre and of the humiliation they suffered as they trailed across Europe as Jews. It was all she had known until she and Saul reached Venezia, and then life took on a calmness that anchored her a little.

But as foreign goods passed through her father's warehouses and as she read invoices and talked with him about the exotic places he visited to find these goods, something began to stir and it was unassauged. It was a longing to move beyond her father's house, to be independent of mind and spirit. She told Guillaume that Ysabel of Gisborne had understood and had argued her cause with her father.

Lyon was the compromise. Travel, learning the merchant's calling, all under the guise of supporting Amèe. She knew that should the day come, she could manage Saul ben Simon's trading house. And she was sure her father recognised this as well. He could have married her off at any time to a Jewish man – a marriage of convenience – but as his only child he allowed her this one moment to become the woman she wished to be. There were plenty of others who ran estates in the absence of the head of the household. There were plenty of others who spoke from a position of strength and knowledge – Eleanor of Aquitaine was one such. Hildegard von Bingen, Heloise D'Argenteuil. They resonated with her and Guillaume could see and hear it every time they had a conversation.

Thus their affection grew and whilst *he* had admitted it lately, tonight

168

was the first time he had heard an intimate acknowledgement from her. He reached down to the little casket beneath the cot and pulled out the rotted silk.

'This is something to remember me by whilst I am gone.' He placed the small parcel in her hand.

'I need a taper…'

He scrabbled under the cot once more and found a candle, struck tinder and lit it. It was poor quality, smoking more than flaming, but it shed enough light for her to unroll the ring from its ancient covering.

'It's beautiful. In fact, it's quite exquisite.'

'It has a history.' He told her of its discovery and of Michael's opinion of its provenance, took the ring and slipped it onto her finger before kissing her hand.

She lay very still and they heard the wind and the animals' breath and then,

'I would marry you in an instant, Guillaume. But my father is all I have and I need his blessing because in the eyes of my people, it would be a difficult marriage.'

'Which is why I wrote to him.' Guillaume replied.

She leaned over and placed her lips upon his. They kissed long and she wound her fingers through his. The ardency of her moves sparked a torrent of explicit desire in Guillaume and he hardened, rolling her gently onto her back, half lying over her, seeing her eyes darken to something new and dangerous. She arched her hips slowly against him, the movement blatant and he kissed her again, one hand gathering up the folds of her chemise toward her breasts, the other hand playing across her silken skin.

As he slid into her, she gasped and he pushed a little harder until she moved with an even rhythm beneath him, tying the lovers' knot that bound them for eternity.

'I am yours,' she said afterward, her voice lazy with the effort of loving.

'And I am yours,' he replied. 'Forever…'

She smiled and kissed his knuckles and he rolled onto his side, so that she curved in behind him – crescent moons, large and small.

Her hand found his wound. 'And this?'

He told her of the attack.

'I fear for you.' Her hand slid over his ribs and across his chest.

'Never fear for me, Ariella. I have been through much worse and am still here.'

'And you will tell me about those times?'

He frowned and pulled her hard against his back. Revealing the bloody past of his life was like opening a suppurating wound. And yet, if she had told him so honestly of her own life, it was surely what he must do. A shared life based on honesty. 'I promise. Everything on my return.' He turned toward her and kissed her. 'You must return to the house before Matins. They must not know you are out of your bed.

Her hand slid from his, fire in its wake and her chemise fell in ethereal folds as she stood, her body almost lost in the fine linen weave.

Almost … but not quite.

She turned to him, no smile, just an intense gaze, as she whispered, 'Always.'

And then she disappeared beyond the light of the candle like a night wraith, there and then gone.

He shivered, a prickling at his neck, but the fire in his palm banished it and he rolled once again onto his side, his eyelids dropping as he answered the echo of her whisper with his own, 'Always…'

'A God-given day, my friend.' Michael indicated the cloudless blue above Rue Ducanivet. 'On such a day, to be riding out into the country would normally seem a pleasure than a penance.'

Guillaume hoisted his saddlebags to one shoulder, adding his precious Saracen bow and tucking six arrows into his girdle at his back. 'Indeed. At any other time…'

'Six arrows only?' Michael asked.

I would take an armoury if I thought it would serve. If I need them, I must make every one count and then retrieve them afterward.'

He told Michael to look for the preachers, there was little else to be said. The household stood at the gates to farewell he and Adam, all bar Mahaut, who loitered at the door of the house like the pestilent malevolence she was. Amée hugged him and wished he and Adam safe, saying 'Bring us some gossip, young man, else there is no point in you going.'

Ariella placed a hand on his upper arm and said in her usual manner, 'Stay safe, Guillaume. Adam, watch out for he and Tobias, for all that they think they can conquer the world.'

'Aye, *Dameisele*. You know me.' He grinned in his usual disarming fashion.

The ring glinted shyly on Ariella's finger as her hand left Guillaume's arm. He held the imprint of her touch in his mind, the soft pressure that spoke of love shared and hopes finally laid bare. It was the most perfect thing – perfection had not touched his life since before the day Cateline and Ansel were murdered.

He and Adam left with the women's chorus of farewells drifting down the street after them like a blessing. As they rounded the corner into Rue Tramassal, Adam grunted, shifting the saddlebags from one shoulder to another.

'Your bags are overly heavy, Adam. Too many clothes?'

'A little heavy, yes. A couple of extra daggers as it pays to be safe, but clothes? Not really.'

They had tramped along the slight rise but Adam stopped before they reached the Gigni house. Above them birds were in full song, and in the street, women walked past, baskets on their hips. Shouting children skirted around them and one mother coddled a fretting babe, looking for somewhere so that she could sit and feed. The child's reedy cry filled the air but it stopped suddenly as she pulled it to her breast and it began to nuzzle.

A man edged past with two alaunts on short chains. The dogs' coats were a fine shade of *bege,* their legs, muzzles and ears shading to black, beautiful animals, proud and brutal with sharp eyes and ears tense with interest. Guillaume expected them to enter the Gigni gates but instead they kept walking to Place Saint Jean where they disappeared from view.

A rat hustled along the cobbled pathway, hard against the house walls, and then dashed into a finger-width gap between the Gigni house and its neighbour. Guillaume doubted there would be a rat alive which could survive in the Gigni yard with its coiffed neatness.

'Then what?' Guillaume asked. 'A couple of daggers aren't that heavy, surely.'

Adam hoisted the creaking bags off his shoulder and patted them down, apparently deciding the left one held what he wanted. Unbuckling it, he fossicked inside, not withdrawing his hand as he quickly checked the street. 'See?' he held the bag close for Guillaume to examine.

Inside lay a book with a plain unassuming brown leather cover. His heart pounded as he opened it. The text was written in boldly aligned script in the brown-black that was oak gall ink. The first letter of the book was illuminated in reds, greens, and blues. It was a mastery of understatement and it began with the words, '*The book of the generation of Jesus Christ, the son of David, the son of Abraham...*'

'Can you read Latin?' Adam asked.

'It's not Latin. It's the Lengua Romana – the people's language. What you and I speak here every day. It's the Gospel according to Matthew. Jesus and Joseph, Adam, this is the Vaudois Bible. Where did you find it?' Guillaume closed the cover and then strapped the saddlebag shut, handing it back to Adam, his heart still pounding.

'You said my cot rocked, do you remember? Well, last evening, after I had bathed and packed, I decided to put something under the leg of the cot to even it up. I noticed one of the pavers was loose, in fact loose enough to lever up, which I did. And in a hole underneath, there it was with a piece of timber over the top to protect it from pressure. It was dusty, but that's all.'

'Did anyone see you?'

'No.'

'I must get a message to Michael...'

'Then you need to be quick. Tobias approaches.'

A leggy horse jogged sideways down the street toward them, over-tall for the diminutive minstrel as its bouncy stride threw him about. His lute hung down his back and he had a leather bag rolled and strapped behind the cantle of the saddle whilst a small sword hung at his side. A door slammed behind the Gigni gates and the horse shied, Toby white as he hauled on the reins.

Adam laughed. 'If you don't come off that before the day is done, then I'm a Frenchman.'

'If I come off this damned thing, then I shall *kill* the Frenchman who hired the brute to me.'

'What's its name?'

'I don't know and I care even less. I shall call it *Diavolo!*' Toby fingered the reins as the horse snatched at the bit, dancing on its toes, the sound of the shod hooves loud on the morning air.

Guillaume heard their banter but was too concerned at Adam's discovery to join in. Was it too dangerous to send Michael word? Because he had to be told...

The Gigni gates opened and a man with neat hair cut to his chin and the long black tunic of a notary stepped out. He looked left and right and then spotted them, signaling before hurrying over. 'Messire Guillaume?' he asked.

'I am he…'

'Messire,' the notary lowered his head in greeting. 'I am Odo, Messire Gigni's steward and notary. I have two mounts saddled for you in the yard. Please,' he indicated the gates which had been opened. 'Come in.'

'I thank you, Odo,' Guillaume replied as he examined the two horses quietly hitched to a rail. They were plain muscle-bound beasts but with good legs.

'God's holy heartbeats,' Toby muttered. 'And I get this…' Diavolo let out an ear-splitting neigh, Toby being physically shaken as the cry reverberated through the horse's body.

'You can have mine, Toby,' Adam said kindly. 'I'll have the Devil.'

'Odo,' Guillaume said as he strapped his bags to the cantle of the saddle. 'May I prevail upon your kindness for a moment?'

The steward nodded. 'Of course, Messire. In any way…'

'I find I must send an urgent message to Madame de Clochard's son-in-law. Have you writing material that I may use?'

The steward barely blinked. 'Of course. Come to my desk.'

Guillaume followed the notary's swinging black tunic to a narrow door in between a grain store and a stable filled with stalls. There was a trestle table and a chair, basket of candles and a used one which had dripped down into the pewter dish on which it stood. The steward indicated a small pile of parchment, the quill and an inkhorn balanced in a pewter mug.

'Will you require wax?'

'If you could,' Guillaume answered, 'I would be grateful.'

'It is no problem, messire.' Odo reached into a small chest on the floor and took out a stick of plain wax. 'I will leave you to compose your note.'

'No, please. I would that you stayed because I have a further entreaty. Just let me quickly write this…'

'As you wish, messire.' The steward busied himself at the chest, sorting, whereupon he took up a quill and began to shape the end with a sharp knife.

Guillaume smoothed the parchment, hastily dipped a quill in the inkhorn, tapped it to remove the excess and began, the scratching of the quill over the parchment's surface the only sound other than the measured scrape of Odo's knife as he worked at his quill.

'To Michael Sarapion from your friend Guillaume de Gisborne, greetings. In haste I write to inform you it was in Adam's saddlebag all along. Valete.'

Michael was no fool, and used to the shortened code of spies. He would decipher the meaning in a heartbeat.

'Odo, I have a further favour to ask,' as he spoke to the notary, he rolled the note, taking the stick of wax, dipping it in and out of the gutting candle flame and then applying the melted end to seal the roll shut. He unpinned the Gisborne fibula from his cloak and pressed the three moulded arrowheads into the wax to complete the seal. He blew on it and pinning the fibula back at his shoulder, he said, 'Is it at all possible that you could deliver this to Messire Sarapion at Rue Ducanivet personally? This morning?'

'Ah…' The steward frowned.

'I understand you may be busy…'

'No, not at all, you mistake me. I was merely thinking that I must go to Presque L'ile before Terce, so I can deliver it then.'

'I thank you,' Guillaume reached into his purse and pulled out two of the Germans' gold livres. 'And please take this.'

Odo took a step back, holding up his hands. He had an ascetic face, almost a younger version of his employer, but also not unlike any notary Guillaume had seen in any of the cities of Europe. Always half-starved, always pale, their lives spent slumped over documents. 'Messire, I could not. I do it because Messire Gigni is my master. He said to look after your needs and thus what I will do is surely part of my duty. Messire Gigni would expect no less.'

'Indeed,' said Guillaume. 'And this is to buy a good wine between Presqul'ile and Rue Tramassal, where you can sit briefly and enjoy the sunshine while you can.'

Odo met Guillaume's frank gaze and Guillaume smiled. He needed the man on his side. Odo reached out with his hand and gripped Guillaume's in a long-fingered clasp. 'I thank you, sir.'

'It is my way of repaying a favour. Now, we must away or it will be Terce before we reach the city gates and Messire Gigni will think we have ignored his invitation. I thank you for your kindness.'

The two men walked back to the hitching rail where Guillaume mounted, noticing Toby and Adam had swapped horses and Diavolo had settled to the more confident hand of the Master at Arms. Tobias sat slumped on the

Gigni rouncey, colour once again returning to his cheeks.

'Odo, God keep you and I shall be sure to mention your kindness when I speak with Messire Gigni on the morrow.'

'Oh, that reminds me,' Odo dug into his purse and pulled out a small square of parchment. 'These are the directions.'

Guillaume reached down, taking the folded sheet and pushing it into his own purse. Then the threesome turned their horses out of the yard, the iron shoes clattering like a bell to warn passersby that someone was coming. He hoped he could trust Odo – so much at stake, and in the meantime they carried the Vaudois Bible and he hoped they could find a deep and angry torrent into which he could lob the troublesome text.

They passed through the streets of Lyon at a jog-trot, the horses happy to be moving, their gait sharp and pacey, ears pricked and tails swishing. At any other time, Guillaume would have enjoyed the clarity of the sky, the many women who smiled up at him, the clothes and regalia that passed him by. But his mind twisted and turned on the book that Adam carried. Instinct told him to destroy it somewhere between Lyon and the Forez, for surely something so divisive had no part in life. He could preserve calm on many accounts by so doing – the house of de Clochard would be safe from harassment, the business secure. And on a wider level, people could live their spiritual lives without confusion – accepting of the Church and its word.

You hypocrite!

His conscience mocked him. Castigated him. He who had given up on the Church's teachings the day he had found his mother and father murdered. Reinforced even more by fighting a war, apparently in God's name.

Some zealous priest had mouthed the words of Matthew to Guillaume's face in Outremer, *'Come to me all ye who are weary and burdened and I will give ye rest,'* and Guillaume had laughed sourly and turned his back.

So what do you want then? he asked of his conscience. *What would you have me do? Give the book back to the* Sandalati? *Cause mayhem for them and for my family's business, for my friends?*

But there was no answer and they passed beyond the city walls as his thoughts went forever round in circles. He didn't notice the old Roman fortifications, nor the sturdy double gates – massive pieces of wooden joinery and ironmongery that had been pulled open to allow access in and out. A stream of carts pulled by oxen and mules rolled by, loaded with produce from outlying villages. Men and women on all manner of mounts rode back and forth – palfreys, rounceys, mules, even a curtained litter carried by four overlarge men.

Once, a mounted destrier as black as ebony had cantered past, an escort of four horsemen behind. The destrier was devoid of trappings and no banners flapped but there was no mistaking the quality of harness, the arrogant toss of the animal's head, nor the haughty expression of its rider.

The horse's rump knocked against Adam's horse in the exiting crowd and Diavolo leaped sideways, trying to get his head down between his forelegs, the better to buck Adam off. But Adam shortened his reins and kicked the horse on hard, laughing.

'They're mad, of course. The horse *and* Adam.' Toby's exchanged rouncey plodded on as if the world hadn't just exploded around him.

'Huh?' Guillaume looked around.

'You heard. But I presume you think on other things.' Toby twisted to watch Adam fighting with his nervous mount and Guillaume followed his gaze.

'Adam will sort him out. In any case, my apologies, Toby. There is business I was unable to resolve before we left which is why I had to send a note back to Michael.'

Tobias laughed. 'If you say so. But the business you mention isn't cloth, is it? Nor fur, nor pretties for the ladies. No, I think it's about some parchment. Mayhap a book?'

Guillaume laced his reins through his fingers and place one hand, fist clenched, on his thigh. 'Mayhap indeed. You are sharp.'

'I'm a Gisborne man, Guillaume. Have you forgotten?'

Guillaume gave no reply, merely tapped his horse's flanks with his heels and pressed it into a canter on the sward at the side of the worn and pitted road, leaving the city and its crowd well behind.

The outskirts of the city were lightly wooded, small dips and rises giving the horses a chance to expend some of the pent-up energy that town living had given them. They cantered past cleared pockets of fallow soil waiting to be tilled and sown. In some places, an ox pulled a plough through the soil, the ploughman stepping through the turned clods, the odour of fresh earth hanging heavy in the air. Behind, came women and children with baskets, picking up small stones that had been upturned and carrying them to heap on cairns in the corners of the open fields.

A buzzard flew high above, its circles a thing of lazy grace, and crows cawed their displeasure at life. But within the copses, where late berries grew in the sunshine and funghi grew in the shade, tits and robins flew with quick delight, turning in a flash of wings, trilling and tweeting. The sound was filled with such clear beauty that Tobias sighed.

'Perfect,' he murmured and Guillaume smiled at the simple joy of the man.

But the perfection of sound was quickly destroyed as a small pig shot out squealing from the undergrowth. Guillaume's mount propped but regained its footing and trotted on, Tobias' horse following close behind. Diavolo however, shied prodigiously to the other side of the road, Adam's feet slipping from the stirrups as he swore with colourful energy. The animal spun and Adam lurched against the pommel as Guillaume and Toby halted their horses to watch. The Master at Arms kicked the horse on, his heels causing a further series of bucks back along the road.

'He's good, isn't he?' Guillaume said as a skein of curses drifted on the forest air toward them. Adam finally got the horse under control, and urged him back to the others.

'Christ's toenails! This isn't a horse, it's a damned trebuchet. All he wants is to pitch me against something hard.'

'You're very good,' Toby grinned.

'Only just, Tobias.' Adam wiped his forehead. 'He almost had me out.' He rubbed gingerly at his groin. 'You'd have been pitched long since I think.'

Tobias laughed. 'A sure bet, my man. 'Tis why I owe you my life for swapping mounts.'

'All's well?' Guillaume asked.

'I've had worse,' Adam rubbed the horse's neck back and forth as the animal tossed its head up and down. 'By the time we get where we're going, I think we shall understand each other.'

'Or else you'll be minced beneath his hooves.'

'Maybe – but I like a challenge and this *is* one.'

They continued on, slowing to a more sedate trot so that Diavolo would settle. The journey to the Gigni estate would take a day and a half and all Guillaume required was that they manage to reach shelter this night with the animals fit – no leg or hoof problems.

The map Odo had provided showed a small priory, Prieré de Pommiers en Forez, almost at the foot of the rise of hills that grew to become the harsh ridges growing out of the Forez. It was surrounded by barely a village, Odo had said, but it had a small *dorter*.

'Tell the friars you travel to Messire Gigni's estate and I think they will treat you with respect,' he had said.

But it was past Sext and approaching None and Guillaume's stomach rumbled. He called a halt and the horses stopped readily by another field being tilled. 'The horses need to rest, and I'm hungry…'

Tobias nodded. 'I though you'd never say! A minstrel cannot possibly perform at his best if he starves.' He unhooked his feet from the stirrups and slid down, his back against the horse's middle. He took a few steps, groaning. 'Riding does not become me,' he whined. 'I wish it did.'

'Do you hurt?' Adam asked.

'Always, Adam. Always. It's the price I pay for being what I am.'

The horses shook themselves with a rattle of metal bits and buckles and the men tied them loosely to overhanging branches, breaking out staples from their saddlebags. The Gigni horses dropped a hock and dozed placidly and whilst Diavolo seemed as if he might want to, in fact he stood with ears pricked, eyes overlarge.

'And you think he will settle,' Guillaume broke off a chunk of bread and cut a slice of cheese.

'I believe so. He's young and has probably never been beyond the city gates since he was broken. He's utterly the wrong temperament to be at livery. But I like him. He has energy and spirit but just needs time and a familiar hand. I would buy him…'

'*Would* you?' Tobias dropped the windfall apple he had been quartering. 'After he almost unmanned you?'

'With good feed and training to muscle him up, I think he would make a good campaign horse. I like his legs and he has good shoulder and isn't too long in the neck or back.'

They continued to eat and then sat watching the scene unfold in the field opposite, so that when Tobias spoke, the impact of his question was like a stone from a siege engine landing in their midst.

'What about the book?'

Guillaume started. Such a bald question and it rendered him lost for words momentarily.

'What do you mean?' Adam asked carefully as he packed his portion of cheese and bread back into his bag.

'You carry a heretical text out of Lyon, Adam. I'm not blind. And if I guess rightly, it's the one that mouldy excuse for God's messenger is looking for.'

Adam sat very still, then shrugged his shoulders and looked to Guillaume for help.

Guillaume owed Tobias the respect of being a Gisborne man. If anyone at all was trustworthy it was the little man who sat next to him, calmly peeling another apple. 'I thought to toss it in a deep ravine where there was a fast-flowing river, or maybe even bury it in a hole on our way to the Forez.'

'I see,' Tobias said. 'But?'

'But men have lost lives protecting it, so why should I undermine what they went through by showing it such little respect?'

'And?' asked Adam. 'I'm very curious.'

'Somehow, I must find a member of the *Sandalati* and return it to them.'

'Somehow…' Adam snorted.

'Yes, somehow. And I hope, Adam, that you and Tobias, Michael and Gosse, Herviet and Raol will help me.'

The two companions looked at each other and then at Guillaume.

'Of course.' said Tobias, as if it should never have been in doubt.

'Aye. That's it. Solidarity,' Adam added and Guillaume felt the air leave his chest as the Master at Arms spoke, as if he'd held his breath for too long.

They left the touchy subject of the book alone then, and continued desultory conversation about horses remembered, and watched with lazy interest as the plough, ox and man turned at the top of each row to head back, tilling a new furrow, the young son walking behind, collecting stones into a wooden pale. The bucolic scene had a soporific rhythm and with the sunshine, it would have been easy to just let go for a moment, to shut one's eyes…

But Guillaume made a move, standing and brushing himself down. 'We must find this priory before dusk and Odo's map doesn't mark which of those two tracks we take. I'll have to ask the ploughman.'

'I will,' Toby pushed himself up and ambled across the track to the furrows, hailing the man at the top of the field.

They could hear the odd word on the air, *'domus'*, *'Gigni'*, *'Pommiers en Forez'* and as they tightened girths and untied horses, Adam said, 'Guillaume, we need to keep our wits about us now. I think trouble approaches.'

'You think we enter the Devil's lair?' He only mentioned it as a joke but Adam didn't laugh.

The Master at Arms pushed out his bottom lip. 'I think we are between passes from the enemy, that's all. You would be a fool to think otherwise. How well do you know the Gigni?'

'Beyond reputation? I don't. I have told you. Apart from Luzio.'

A burst of childish laughter came from the field and the young boy looked at Toby with curiosity and interest as Toby no doubt told him a joke or pulled a trick from his repertoire. He had the knack of beguiling children and they gathered to him like bees to a honeypot.

'Luzio – the errant nephew and your friend.'

'Affected, egotistical, lazy but well-meaning and generous to a fault. A good enough friend.'

They heard Tobias calling back to the man and his son, *'Mercies grazis.'* He hurried back to them and asked for a leg-up and as he settled himself back in the saddle, he said, 'Left path apparently and the priory does have a *dorter* for travellers. The fellow has heard of the Gigni *domus* as well. Said that it's a big place – very noble, he said.'

They began walking with a creak of leather, the horses' blowing down their noses. The road, although wide track would have described it more suitably, led into a shadowy copse with immense shading trees of darkly interlaced and skeletal branches. Guillaume shivered. True, there had been no more attacks; Adam was right. But anyone who knew Guillaume would know he travelled to the Forez. Amèe had the habit of gossiping if it improved her standing and she would want everyone to know the de Clochard manager had been invited to the famous Gigni hunt. As Adam intimated, wits must be foremost. He touched the little *misericorde* at his girdle, his stepfather's Saracen bow hanging from his shoulder like a piece of anatomy. Sometimes he thought of it as angels' wings – for sure it had saved his life often enough.

The priory appeared out of gloom, as clouds had drifted in and darkened the shadows of the woods even more. They smelled smoke before they sighted it, but eventually a small stone church appeared, with a cluster of houses in varying states of dilapidation. The sound of a cockerel reached them and a child yelling. Dogs barked and behind the priory wall an indistinct male voice sounded. To the side of the priory was a field, tilled neatly but with crows scavenging across. Wives and children should have been running with sticks to keep the birds off, but there was no one.

They halted and dismounted at the priory gates which were shut to the world.

'This doesn't look promising,' said Toby. 'Maybe there's been an illness through the village.'

Guillaume lifted a fist and knocked hard on the gates, calling for attention as dusk crept toward them with speed. A woman came to the door of a dwelling opposite and leaned on the frame. She was poorly clad and spoke in a thick accent they could barely understand.

'Priest's ill. The other two look after 'im. What do yer want?'

'To stay in the *dorter* overnight.'

'Go into the church, door's open. Bell for Vespers'll be ringin' soon. One of 'em'll be there then.'

Toby looked at Guillaume and shrugged and the woman, seeing the minstrel for the first time, crossed herself and rushed inside her house. 'Hey ho,' said Toby with resignation. 'Here we go again!'

They walked to the church, towing the tired horses behind. As Vespers began to ring from a cracked bell, Guillaume handed his reins to Tobias and walked into the stony dark of the place. The smell of tallow candles greeted him and he could vaguely see two sputtering flames on a small altar. A young monk hung off the bell-rope and looked at Guillaume with surprise.

'Greetings,' said Guillaume. 'I'm a traveller to the Gigni *domus* with my two friends. We were told we might perhaps be able to stay in your *dorter* overnight.'

The novice let the bell-rope hang and it swung gently back and forth. 'Father Jerome is ill...'

'We don't want to impose. We need shelter for the night for ourselves and our horses. We will pay. We don't need food, if that's what worries you...'

But the novice's eyes lit up. 'You will pay? How much?'

'Two silver *livres* each for us and one to cover the three horses if you can spare hay and water.'

'That is...' He counted on his fingers, where ragged nails had been bitten almost to bleeding. 'Seven *livres*!'

'Indeed.'

'Come to the gates and I will let you in.'

He ran along the nave and through a door in the small transept, leaving Guillaume remembering a small church in La Flèche and hating the memory.

The tired gates of the priory yard creaked open and the companions walked in, leading the horses.

'Messire,' said the novice. 'My name is Brother Hugo. My fellow brother sits with Father Jerome...'

'What ails the priest?'

'He had a fever. Since then he coughs and fills pots with *fleume.* He eats nothing or precious little and grows weaker each day. We think he will die and we don't know what to do...' The boy's eyes filled and Guillaume felt pity.

'Is there a midwife in the village, a healer? Someone who understands herbs?'

'No.'

'Then I pray that God watches over you all. Where do you wish us to rest?'

The novice pointed to a door leading off a chipped and weedy cloister.

'And the animals?'

His finger pointed again to some stalls under a sagging roof where a solitary mule watched them with interest. Tobias pushed alongside Guillaume and asked if they could wash, but no answer was forthcoming as the novice took a step back from the minstrel, crossing himself.

A stifling anger rose in Guillaume's chest; that fury that lay just beneath the skin. 'Brother Hugo, this is Tobias, formerly one of King Richard's minstrels. He is very good at his job and might sing plainsong for you, *if* you ask politely.'

Brother Hugo reddened, explaining with a stutter that since Father Jerome became ill, they conducted no services at all. Neither of the two novices had the authority.

'In that case, we shall keep to ourselves and not trouble you. We will be gone before dawn.' Guillaume passed the coins into the quivering palm of the unfortunate young man and led his horse to the stalls with Toby and Adam following.

'That was perfunctory and a little cruel, Guillaume,' Tobias said. 'I am quite capable of handling that sort of thing myself and usually without making someone who lacks worldliness or confidence feel worse.'

But Guillaume fired back, 'They make me sick, all of them. I have met none who are good.'

Adam mumbled in agreement as he bent to undo Diavolo's girth. He began rubbing at the sweatmarks with a wisp of knotted straw as Guillaume found some good hay. He and Toby filled waterbuckets from a gurgling water fountain in the center of the yard.

'You know, if you look around, I suspect this was once quite a prosperous little place. I wonder what happened?' Toby observed.

'Don't care,' said Adam. 'I just want to be gone. Houses of God depress me.'

'You're a fine pair,' Tobias replied. 'You should travel through the Adriatico and on to Constantinople. There are priests of the Eastern Church who would restore your faith in Christ and God.'

They left the horses and mule content to eat the sweet hay, washing themselves in the fountain before crossing the yard to the *dorter* as the soft *amethystus* of dusk began to change to the harder ebony of night. They could just make out the cots standing two by two along the walls.

'Do you think the mattresses are lousy?' Tobias asked.

'We'll know tomorrow, if not tonight,' Adam said and Toby shuddered.

But the mattresses smelled of lavender and rue and were clean and free of damp so that all three men sank into them with a sigh.

'We have no candles,' Toby remarked.

'Nor blankets, fire nor any decent food.' Guillaume lay with his hands behind his head. 'We'd be warmer with the horses. But it's safe here, and dry.' As he spoke, the door rattled and he grunted as he levered his tall frame off the low cot, shuffling in the dark to avoid tripping over the others. Brother Hugo stood illuminated by two odoriferous tallow candles.

'I thought you might need light,' he stuttered. 'And if you would like to break bread with us, Brother Francis and myself can offer you some broth.'

'Thank you, no. We have our own supplies,' Guillaume replied. 'But the candle is welcome.' He reached out to take the light.

'Messire,' the novice's voice had become high-pitched and breathless. 'I offer my apologies for offence. But Brother Francis and myself...'

183

'Are about to be left alone with no guidance on what is to be done,' Guillaume said, seeing an image of Alain standing behind Hugo, frowning at the situation. In a heartbeat, he placed Alain in Hugo's position in the priory, the brave young archer who would have been content to live the circumscribed life of the Church.

Because at least he would be alive…

'Join us for a moment,' he moved back to allow the monk to enter whereupon the extra candle was placed on the floor in its holder. The fellow was more boy than man with a round face, but he had no sign of manhood upon him, no beard, no fleshing out of the bones. And his voice dipped up and down with irregularity. As the two candles illuminated the room, shadows flickered and danced on the walls and the faces of those within seemed spectral – hollowed eyes, shaded cheekbones, nothing of humanity. Something stirred in the air and Guillaume's skin crawled with untoward prescience.

'Tell us – why are the church and village so decrepit?' he asked.

'A fever ran through the village and the priory about five years before I came here. Many died. There used to be ten in the priory and now we are three.'

'But you have a bigger house which cares for you in time of need? There is an abbot somewhere who knows of your straightened circumstances?'

The monk nodded, his fists locked together. 'Out there,' he waved an arm loosely toward the door. 'We are part of the Forez family demesnes and the village owes allegiance to the family. But we owe our spiritual living to Archbishop Renaud of Lyon.'

'Renaud de Forez!' Adam sneered under his breath.

'Does Monseigneur know of your dire straits?'

'Of Father Jerome? No. But everything else…'

Guillaume had known the amswer even before Brother Hugo had taken a further breath.

'The Archbishop's notary visted a half year ago, at Father Jerome's insistence. He walked around the village, noting things on a wax tablet. The same in the priory. He took our silver candlesticks and crucifix and some of the scribed texts from the scriptorium. The priory's small scriptorium had a reputation before the fever swept through. The notary said he would send help but nothing came.'

'When did you come here? And from where?' Tobias asked.

'I am from Lyon. I was sent here from the Benedictines in Lyon.'

Guillaume nodded.

'And the villagers? Where have they all gone?' Tobias persisted.

'The men who survived the fever went to the crusade. Those who returned saw the state of our village and left almost immediately, seeking work in the bigger towns or at the Forez *domus*. We are now a village of the elderly, of a few women and some very young children.'

'But food... How do they live? How do *you* live?' Tobias was engrossed whereas Guillaume felt nothing but disgust for the way in which a community had been left to rot.

'The women grow vegetables, and harvest things from the wayside and the forest. They snare hare and wild fowl and we help when we can. One of the women is skilled with bow and sling and a sennight ago, brought down a hind. It fed us all. But winter is coming...'

Guillaume bent forward and touched Brother Hugo's arm. 'I will speak with Messire Gigni. He has the ear of the Archbishop. Perhaps there may even be a member of the Forez family at the hunt. Don't fret – look after Father Jerome as best you can.'

Adam sat back and puffed out a breath. 'The notary – you didn't say what his name was.'

The candles flickered and outside the mule brayed twice, and then quiet crept around the priory once more.

'It is time to ring the bell for Compline. I must go...' Brother Hugo bent to pick up his candle. 'The notary's name? A strange name – an old Latin name. Crispinus? Cris...'

'Crispianus?' Tobias asked with a bland expression.

'*Oc*! That's it.' For a moment he looked perplexed but then, 'I must go...' He hurried out the door, his flame bending as he shielded it from draughts, his sandalled feet slapping along the tiles.

CHAPTER NINE

×

'Crispianus is a pile of pig shit,' said Adam. 'I'll lay odds the silver was sold and that in his cell, he has a casket of money to rival a Templar's.'

'And what of the books? I shudder to think,' added Toby. 'I hold church scribes in the highest esteem. They capture the beauty of the scriptures in measured black ink and then laud that beauty with God-given artistry. To have such books in that turd's hands is a sin.'

'I think the books will be in Reynaud's hands, safely ensconced in the library of the Chateau Piere Scize,' Guillaume mused.

'Seems to me both men are just piles of pigs' turds, so it makes little difference,' growled Adam.

The off-key bell began to toll above them and talking ceased. When the crooked echoes had died away and the velvet stifle of night had returned, Adam added, 'Funny how Crispianus stalks us wherever we go.'

Guillaume said nothing but reached into his saddlebags to pull out some cheese and stale bread. The others followed his example and when stomachs were eased, they all slid down onto the cots and snoring followed with speed. All except Guillaume, whose mind pulled everything he had heard apart and then reconstructed it with all he knew, wondering the whole time why his skin prickled and a sense of unease caught at his breath.

He fell into a cloying sleep, one where he sweated then chilled and couldn't breathe. Such things had become the norm of night since the crusade and as he heard the bells mark the hours, he finally eased himself from his cot, wrapped his cloak tight around, and crept from the *dorter*.

Outside, a drear moon washed the yard with a frosty tint. Looking up he saw the round the moon that implied rain might be close. The fountain burbled, comforting with its idle chatter, and he scooped a handful of water over his face and then slurped another handful, grateful for its coolness.

He sat on the plinth, breathing the night air, listening to the sound of silence. Not even a dog barked in the village and he sighed deeply, laying his head back against the stone of the fountain, staring at the heavens, thinking about Ariella, about a life of peace, of marriage, children and normality. He could almost feel the soft silk of her hair through his fingers and heard her saying not to concern himself with the future of de Clochard, that between those in the house, they could survive whatever was thrown against them. He knew she was right. De Clochard *was* strong – a force not understood by those who prevailed against them. He sat until the chill began to creep through his hose and was just about to move when a small mew sounded near his ankle along with the warm pressure of a sinuous body pushing back and forth, followed by a demanding grumble.

He reached down and slid his hand across the soft fur of a cat, its back arching beneath his hand, the tail curling with pleasure, the grumble becoming a rumble.

'Huh, little cat, what it is to have such easy contentment,' he said as he stood, crossing to the stalls of the barn, the cat lacing between his legs and punching his ankle with a determined head.

He moved into his horse's stall, the animal snorting at the disruption, but he pushed its rump, moving it over so that he could sit in the fodder-rich warmth of the byre, content with the sound of the animals, calm as the cat curled into his body. Within moments his eyes had closed and blessed sleep claimed him.

'Messire...' a hand shook him gently and the cat mewed, luring him from slumber, his attention at first tardy but then rushing upon him like a flood-tide.

'Brother Hugo...' he scrubbed at his eyes.

'I'm about to ring for Matins. Dawn is not so far away and you said you wanted to leave early.' The monk carried a candle in one hand and with the other, he picked up the cat and looped it over his arm where it languished, eyes half-closed. The priest's rough wool robe had a streak of loose cat hair down the front and the cat's green eyes dared Guillaume to say that the hair shouldn't be there.

'I thank you,' he said to Brother Hugo. 'I couldn't sleep and walked the yard, visited the horses and sat with your cat. Whereupon it appears I fell asleep.'

The novice bobbed his head. 'I must ring the bell.'

'Father Jerome?' Guillaume called after him.

'The same…'

Guillaume watered and fed the horses, Diavolo tearing at the hay as if his throat might be cut. The mule took a breath, about to caterwaul, and Guillaume forestalled it by shoving an armful of hay in the animal's direction and then walked to the fountain as the bell began its crazed ringing. He washed his face and rubbed at the cat hair and hay over his clothes, knowing full well that to the Gigni he would represent a peasant in appearance, if not in manner and intelligence.

Brother Hugo stood at the gates to farewell them as they passed through, leading their horses single file. Guillaume halted next to the novice, his mount pushing against him, eager to be on the road. Gone was the threatened mizzle of night, the air dawn-crisp and the lower sky a washed blue and gold bleeding upward from the forest canopy.

The novice seemed smaller than yesterday, younger, shifting his calloused feet in worn sandals as the priory cat sidled up to him. He held out a woven flax bag. ''Tis bread freshly made. Brother Francis baked it overnight to thank you for the monies.'

Guillaume took the bag. 'You are kind, young monk, and have no fear. Your situation and that of the village and your fellows within the priory will receive due attention. I swear to you in God's name.' He pushed the sack into his saddlebag, gathered his reins and mounted. His horse seemed eager as Guillaume watched Adam give Tobias a leg up before taking up his own reins and mounting Diavolo. The horse snorted and stretched his neck and Guillaume raised an eyebrow at the way Adam had calmed the horse.

Thus they began to move onward and Toby looked back, raising an arm to wave to Brother Hugo who stood watching them, the cat now in his arms.

'The perfect embodiment of Pangur Bán. You know the poem?'

'No,' said Adam, his hand running back and forth through Diavolo's mane, 'but I'm sure you're about to tell us.'

Tobias had a beautiful voice – mellow with a clarity of diction that was pleasing on the ear. The horses, content to be on the move, walked calmly, ears twitching and eyes bright. For once Guillaume let his grip open on the reins, his body swaying to the rhythm of the horse's stride and Tobias' words.

'This was written by an old Irish monk maybe three hundred years ago. All about his cat and his life.' And he began…

'I and Pangur Bán my cat.
'Tis like a task we are at.
Hunting mice is his delight,
Hunting words I sit all night.
Better far than praise of men
'Tis to sit with book and pen…'

Tobias shifted in his saddle, lifting his head as if he spoke to a vast audience – a presence that defied his size. He could hold whole halls in his sway and he relished the skill and one could hear the enchantment as his voice dipped and rose.

'Pangur bears me no ill-will,
He too plies his simple skill.
'Tis a merry task to see
At our tasks how glad are we,
When at home we sit and find
Entertainment to our mind.
Oftentimes a mouse will stray
In the hero Pangur's way;
Oftentimes my keen thought set
Takes a meaning in its net.
'Gainst the wall he sets his eye
Full and fierce and sharp and sly;
Gainst the wall of knowledge I
All my little wisdom try.
When a mouse darts from its den,
O how glad is Pangur then!

O what gladness do I prove
When I solve the the doubts I love...'

Guillaume had no trouble envisaging the monk at his scribe's table as the cat pounced on mice in the scriptorium. He recalled the bible in Adam's saddlebag, with its vivid inks and simple, delicate illumination. The bible of the heretic. He was glad when Toby's voice broke through his rumination, turning him from the convoluted path he had been on for days now.

'So in peace our task we ply,
Pangur Bán my cat and I,
In our arts we find our bliss,
I have mine and he has his.
Practice every day has made
Pangur perfect in his trade;
I get wisdom day and night
Turning darkness into light.'

Around them, the hills of the Forez rolled out like billowing woollen cloth, the forest thick with umber, browns and ochres. Some trees were bare, the canopy of branches twisted and turned and here and there with the deserted nests of forest birds. The waysides were thick with damp brown mulch from beech and oak and the hoofbeats thudded a dull tattoo on the cushioned track.

'Very nice,' commented Adam.

'And of course, I believe you,' Tobias replied. 'Ah well, it would be an odd world if we were all aesthetes.'

'Keep a civil tongue in your head, Toby, or you can buy the next round back in Lyon and it will cost you a pretty penny for us all, I can tell you.'

The two continued to jest and Guillaume listened lightly, smiling at a scored point. Eventually though, he clicked his horse to a trot, the day having lightened to a soft morning glow. Like Tobias' poetry, they moved forward with rhythm, thump, thump, thump, thump on fallen leaves and moss. Occasionally, they would cross a patch of dried bracken and the noise would change to a crackle and swish, but then back to the forest mould and the dulcet beat would reassert itself.

Adam led the way, Diavolo well settled, and Guillaume rode rear-guard, his Gigni mount calm, head swaying slightly from side to side. Tobias in the middle, intermittently missed the two beat of the horse's gait and would bounce hard in the saddle, causing he and the horse discomfort, so that the mount would toss its head and lose a stride.

'Just sit down in the saddle, Toby,' called Guillaume. 'Deep down. It will be more comfortable for you and the horse. You're tense and the horse senses it.'

'All very w…' As he called back over his shoulder, something swished between he and his horse's neck, crashing into an adjacent trunk.

'Crossbow!' he yelled as his horse stalled and then reared, Toby hanging onto the mane. 'Crossbow!'

Guillaume leaned low and kicked his horse into a canter, crashing into Toby's horse as he sped forward. The horse reared again, spun and bolted back the way they had come.

Guillaume had to let him go, spurring behind Adam as they sharp-turned off the track and into the forest, Adam dragging at his sword whilst trying to control Diavolo.

They stopped where they could see the road, the horses dancing on the spot, nervous, excited, snorting. Guillaume pulled his bow from his shoulder as they heard shouts and footsteps on the track. Nocking an arrow he said, 'How many?'

'Three, maybe four?' Drawing his sword, Adam hushed the horse, 'Settle boy, settle now. How many arrows do you have?'

'Six.'

'More than enough…'

They both saw the crossbowman at the same time, as he pulled up on the track and bent to re-arm his bow. With the soft creak of a tree in a breeze, Guillaume drew his bow and loosed. The arrow sighed away, catching the bowman deep in the chest. He reeled back, arms outflung and before he hit the ground, Guillaume loosed another arrow, catching a further bowman in the side of the head.

'Two down, two to g…' but before Adam had finished, another arrow had flown away, catching a third man deep in the thigh. The man shrieked as blood oozed around the shaft. To pull it would cause an almost instant death, but to leave it there, he couldn't run. He knew he was a dead man in either case and backed away to a tree, whimpering as he slid down the trunk.

The fourth man, if there had been one, had vanished and Guillaume threw himself off his horse, dropping his bow and pulling his sword from its scabbard.

'The fourth?' he whispered.

Adam nodded his head toward the trees. 'Go right,' he whispered. 'I'll go left and loop back...'

They edged away to catch their prey, the injured man unconscious against the tree. Guillaume listened for a break in the silence, the cry of a bird, the crack of a trodden twig.

Nothing...

But...

What was...

The man dropped on top of him, crashing him to the ground in a tangle as a knife cut into his arm. He heaved, crunching back with arm and fist, hitting something soft and there was a pained grunt.

A neck?

A face?

He had time to roll away and pull himself to a crouch, sword raised. Opposite, a muscle-bound man with short hair and a now broken nose laughed at him, wiping the blood away.

'Come on, turd,' the fellow sneered. 'Let me break yours.'

But Guillaume stood his ground, no advance, no words, no expression – studied indifference that was like salt to the wound of the man before him. Behind the fellow, he caught a glimpse of Adam's red hair and so he remained rooted to his spot. Confusion drifted through the felon's eyes and as quickly left as he muttered 'Pig shit!' and came low at Guillaume, swinging his knife.

Knife against sword was no real challenge and so Guillaume played with him, stepping back, letting the fellow's impetus carry him on to trip on a root. As he turned, he dropped his knife and drew a sword. 'Come on now, whore's son. He didn't tell me you was a coward. Said you was a crusader.'

He?

But Guillaume again stood rock solid, as the attacker advanced, blade raised, bringing it down hard, an opening gambit. Guillaume met it, a block that sizzled up his arm.

Strong...

But still he stood, merely flicking his sword round in his hand, an insouciance designed to aggravate any opponent.

Again a thrust.

A loud parry. Then two quick swings left and right surprising the attacker, the point of Guillaume's sword cutting neatly across the man's chest. Blood oozed and swords hammered, Guillaume beginning to turn the man away so that a vulnerable back would face Adam.

Guillaume considered it an easy fight. He had faced much worse in Outremer; he hated the *kilij* and the skill of the fighting Saracen. This fellow was a thug with a blade, no finesse, just strength and anger.

Two more left-right swings and he had driven the man to the trees, allowing him just the occasional forward step to think he was winning against a tired opponent. Then Guillaume made a pass, the man laughed, stepped back, caught his heel on a fallen branch and fell onto Adam's sword. The look on his face changed to horror as the force of the fall drove the blade back to front.

Adam pulled his sword out and the felon slumped to the ground, blood seeping from his mouth, his eyes staring beyond Guillaume to the forest canopy. 'That was easy,' Adam said as he wiped his sword clean on the attacker's tunic.

'Speak for yourself,' Guillaume wiped his own blade and sheathed it, allowing battle fever to carry him along for a moment, knowing when it stopped that his legs would barely hold him up and that his hands would tremble.

Vaguely he heard a voice shouting and he stood, head cocked.

'It's not Toby,' Adam said. 'Christ, his horse has probably bolted back to Lyon.'

'I think I know the voice…' Guillaume walked back to his horse, picked up the bow and shouldered it and mounted.

'You do?' Adam grabbed Diavolo's reins and swung up, the horse jogging momentarily. 'Settle, you daft thing, settle!' he said and then rode up next to Guillaume. 'Who?'

They rode out onto the track just as a dark-haired, richly attired individual withdrew his sword from the wounded man's chest. He swung around as he heard the horses, his face opening into a relieved grin.

'Guillaume! Thank the Virgin! I saw this…' he swept his arm round the macabre scene and then wiped the sword on the cloak of the man he had just despatched. 'And I thought the worst. I asked him where you were, ordered him but he wouldn't answer, refused me outright, so I finished him off. God, but I am glad you are safe. Are these *your* arrows? I thought … no, I hoped…'

'Luzio,' Guillaume said. 'Well met, my friend. How came you here?'

'To greet you, of course. My uncle said you left Lyon yesterday so I thought I would meet you and we could ride on to the *domus* together.' His frank gaze slid to Adam.

'This is my Master at Arms, Adam of London.'

'Your Master at Arms?' Luzio grimaced. 'Has there been more trouble?'

'On the contrary. Adam works for my brother and comes to us from Venezia for a time. Your uncle knows that I bring him to the hunt. I also bring a minstrel, but his horse bolted when we were attacked.'

'A minstrel! It seems in the short time I have been gone that de Clochard has climbed the ladder. I bow to you, my friend!' He swept a low and elegant bow. Tobias would have approved … if he had been here. 'Adam of London, welcome to the Forez.'

'I thank you, Messire Luzio. May I be so bold as to ask you a question?'

Guillaume glanced at Adam. He knew that clenched expression of old, when the square jaw stiffened and lines indented deep from nose to mouth. That Adam didn't like Luzio was obvious to any who knew him. To Luzio? Guillaume hoped he had no idea.

'Ask whatever you like, Adam.' Luzio sheathed his prettily damascened sword in the tooled scabbard. Guillaume had always thought him effete, but watching the calm with which he had withdrawn his sword from the felon's chest and the cool way he handled the aftermath, he revised his opinion. Luzio could have been a hardened routier if one didn't know the truth, and surely better as a friend than an enemy. He hoped that Adam's question would not offend…

'Messire, why did you kill him? He was valuable. We may have learned much.'

'*Mea culpa,* Adam, I agree.' Luzio's reply was gravely honest. 'But when I saw the arrows, it was too much of a coincidence for it not to have been from Guillaume's bow and a fury came over me. When the fellow wouldn't answer me, such rage as I haven't felt for an age caused me to draw my sword.

He was dying anyway and I helped him along the way. Besides, God forgive me, he deserved it. How *dare* he attack my friends!' Luzio took a breath. 'But I am sorry, you are right, Adam. I *was* too precipitate. I didn't think.' He walked up to Guillaume, rested a gloved hand on the horse's neck and looked up. 'Truly, Guillaume. I have grown to like and respect you so much in my time in Lyon. If I did not have your friendship and that of de Clochard, I think I should kill myself in the tedium of the Gigni house. Can you forgive me?'

What could one say? Whilst Adam obviously boiled at the fellow's insouciance, Guillaume took the path of diplomacy. Besides, his half-brother, Guy, had a saying – *'Keep you friends close and your enemies closer'.* But then Luzio was hardly an enemy – a woman's man yes, a man's drinking friend to be sure and generous with it, but not an enemy.

'Luzio, there is nothing to forgive.'

'Good.' He retrieved a bay mare, as pretty as he himself and Guillaume was not surprised. 'Then shall we move onward? My uncle waits with excitement for the arrival of all his guests, especially you, Guillaume.'

Me? Why? I am but a lowly merchant manager…

'How far away are we?'

'Not far. Two leagues. It's a pleasant ride.'

Was he glad that Luzio would ride with them?

No.

He wanted time, needed time, to digest this latest attack. The *'He'* that was mentioned changed the nature of the event from accidental to deliberate. Was it Crispianus or was it Alexandrus Gigni? Besides, they must surely wait for their minstrel to catch up. Adam thought the same.

'But,' Luzio said, 'if he follows this road, it leads to the Gigni *domus*. He will not be lost.'

'You misunderstand, Messire.' Adam spoke between gritted teeth as Diavolo sidled about in the presence Luzio's mare. 'Our minstrel is no rider. He could be unhorsed, lying injured.'

'But you say he is on a Gigni horse,' Luzio replied. 'They are most tractable. Women with child can ride them. Now if he was on yours, Adam from London, I would say he has a problem. You should give your man credit, Guillaume, for his care of your other servant.'

Guillaume almost spat in the face of such a patronising tone and words. Instead, 'The men are not my servants, Luzio. They are my equals. We *all* work for my brother's interests and are perhaps *his* servants.'

'God save me from opening my mouth any further! It seems I can do no right today,' Luzio replied with equanimity. 'It makes little difference anyway. We are three men missing another. We can stand here amongst the death and gore, or we can retrace steps and look for him. Or we can ride on and meet your host who waits with expectation. What say you to the idea that if your minstrel has not arrived by None, we send a search party to find him?'

'It would be easier and less discommoding to the Gigni to search now,' Adam persisted.

'Guillaume?' Luzio asked.

'Adam is right – we will search now and I will just have to apologise to your uncle. In the face of this...' he waved his arm around, 'I suspect Messire Alexandrus will understand. At the very least, he may have to send some men to bury these felons.'

Luzio said nothing as they mounted and turned back along the track, for it was barely a road like those leaving Lyon. At the top of the first hill, they stood, shading their eyes from the morning glare, examining the road as it laced down between copses of trees and tilled fields and stubble.

'There!' exclaimed Adam and yelled, waving his arm like a banner. 'I see him. Stay here, I will go down. Better yet, you ride on to the *domus* and we will follow more slowly.' He closed his heels on Diavolo's flanks before they could reply and cantered toward a far distant figure who walked in their direction, leading a horse.

'A good idea,' said Luzio brightly, watching Adam. 'Nice beast.' He turned his horse and Guillaume followed suit.

'It's a livery horse.'

'You say?' Luzio's mare tossed her head up and down fretfully. 'My Bella is obviously taken with him. Tell me, my friend, do you think you were mere roadside victims today?'

Guillaume glanced at Luzio but his expression was open and the Pisan met the scrutiny honestly. 'Perhaps you might tell me,' Guillaume said. 'You know the Forez, I presume.'

'Methinks there are criminals everywhere and the Forez has a reputation for hiding its share.'

'Then we are indeed accidental victims.'

They passed the bodies again and began to trot. 'As soon as we reach the *domus*, I shall send a party of men to bury them. They will smell very quickly and it is not at all good for the hunt guests, if they see this before them.'

They passed through the copses of trees and continued on up hills and then down until Luzio halted his mare. 'See that?' He pointed to a stone building poking through a rolling forest. 'That is Choizey. The *domus* of the Gigni.'

'It's a chastel…'

Luzio shrugged. 'The noble family whose domain it was have decreased to one unmarried knight who became a Templar. His property, as one would expect, became the Templars' and they make money by renting large tracts of their assumed lands to those who can pay. My uncle can.'

'Obviously his mercantile business thrives.'

'Oh, he doesn't just deal in trade, Guillaume. Did I not tell you? He has a force of routiers that he hires to any who need them. It's a good business.'

Guillaume could only think of the routiers who had killed his mother and stepfather. To him, routiers were the lowliest of human life, God rot them!

'Come on, let's race to the gates. H'yar!' Luzio clapped his heels to Bella's sides and she shot to a gallop, sending up clods of dirt. Guillaume touched his own horse, now dancing as the mare left and was soon pounding up behind Luzio. The mare was fractious, unhappy as the gelding gained on her and soon she was pulling sideways and Luzio at odds to hold her. Guillaume urged the Gigni horse faster, hoping for no rabbit holes in the ground. The wind tore through his hair and for one wonderful moment, all concerns dissolved in the slipstream of air, the horse's thundering hooves a wonderful free-ing sound. He gave the horse its head, his hands up the animal's neck as they passed Luzio, Guillaume laughing at having beaten his friend's pomposity into the ground.

He slid to a dust-filled halt at the open gates, the Gigni horse blowing hard, its sides puffing in and out and he jumped off and loosened the girth, leading it back and forth as Luzio pulled his mare to a stop. He too dismounted and loosened his own girth.

'You won by default, my friend,' he called out. 'I will pay you back!'

'I won by rights, Luzio. No default about it. No quarter given and none taken. My horse ran the better race, admit it!'

'Damn you!' Luzio laughed. 'You're always right!'

'Messire Guillaume!' That smooth voice from days past called from the gateway. 'Welcome to Choizey. I sincerely hope my nephew had no money on that race. You would be the wealthier, if that was so.'

'No bets, Messire, and thank you for your invitation. I am in awe of your forest home.' Guillaume bowed to his host. The man had shed ten years since leaving Lyon – his hair blew in a breeze and his body was clothed in fine crimson wool – a knee-length tunic with a border of gold and blue. His girdle was tooled leather and a purse hung on one side, a sword on the other and his leather boots were halfway to his knees. He looked every inch the hunstman.

Guillaume scanned his own dusty, hay-seeded clothes. 'I apologise for my appearance; it has been somewhat of a journey.'

'Uncle,' said Luzio. 'Guillaume was attacked and there are four dead men to be buried in the forest.'

'No! You say? And you killed four men singlehanded? Guillaume, it is my turn to express awe!'

'Not at all,' said Guillaume. 'I killed two with a bow and arrow, my Master at Arms killed one with his sword and Luzio did away with a nuisance fourth.'

'Christ God. I know we have felons in the Forez, but when my own guests are threatened… I can only apologise…'

'Please,' Guillaume said. 'It is one of the dangers of travelling on the roads. We accept the dangers or else we would sit locked behind city gates forever.'

Alexandrus Gigni patted Guillaume's back. 'I am glad you see it that way. My men shall deal with the bodies and I will inform the authorities. Please, come this way and I shall show you where you will sleep and where you may wash.' He stopped, looking back to the track. 'But your Master at Arms – you said he would accompany you.'

'He follows with a minstrel I thought might entertain your guests.'

'Then when they arrive at the gates, I will have them taken to the servants' quarters…'

'Ah, but Uncle, they are Guillaume's *friends*.' Luzio grinned at Guillaume as he spoke. 'Friends just like me. They are not his servants.'

It was these times with the Pisan that made Guillaume want to knock him down.

Friend not enemy…

'Then,' said Alexandrus Gigni with barely a beat. 'They may sleep in the *dorter* where Guillaume will sleep. It is a decent chamber with room for all. Come Guillaume, get rid of the dust and the day's trials with a good wine and some clean water.'

Gigni's manner was like marble – cool, smooth and with a deep vein of something else that Guillaume had yet to plumb. Nerves tickled his belly as they turned toward that gates of the *chastel*.

The lion's den…

They walked through gates let into a circular tower that was the feature of the building, along a corridor and then into a hall.

'Luzio has told you? The Choizey family ceded the lands to the Templars. If the last Choizey had not become a Templar, the Forez family would have taken back the land – like Pommiers en Forez and much else besides, it is in their demesnes. But the Templars seem sacrosanct…' he shrugged. 'So I rent the *chastel* from them. They have a commanderie not many leagues south of Lyon, at Marlhes, but we rarely see any of them.'

'I fought under Grand Master de Sablé at Arsuf…' Guillaume hated saying the man's name but something prompted the admission. A confirmation that he *had* fought in the Crusade? A warning that he, Guillaume, was not someone with whom to trifle?

'You say? A fierce fighter by all accounts. You must tell us about the Crusade. Perhaps tonight?'

'I rarely speak of it, messire. Some may glory in the deed. I do not.'

'Of course.' Alexandrus pushed his grey hair behind his ear and studied Guillaume. 'It is hard for men to come home from war and rejoin life. I hear it from routiers all the time.'

'Luzio told me you hire mercenaries. Vastly different to trade, I would think.'

'Not so different. The routiers are a commodity, just like anything else. They are in demand in this troubled world of ours. I service the demand. But enough of that.' He waved an arm around the large stone hall. 'As you can see, the place is big and somewhat dour. There are only so many tapestries one can hang, or fires that one can light. And yet, we are more relaxed here than in our headquarters in Lyon.'

'Do you miss Florence?'

'Sometimes. I miss the sound of Latin, I miss the carillons of bells, but trade is the same everywhere and my family, including Luzio, make up for it.'

'But he is from Pisa.' Guillaume tried to puzzle out the man before him. Calm, erudite, welcoming, even open and honest.

Or good at play acting. Tobias would know…

'Indeed. He is related by marriage to me as you know. And there have been others of his family who worked for me.'

They walked through the hall where a massive side hung fireplace was set with what appeared to be whole trees. The floors were paved and servants were busy pulling trestles and benches from against the walls for the approaching meal.

'We eat simply today, my friend, a quiet meal and conversation. But tomorrow after the hunt, we have a banquet. I think you will enjoy yourself.'

Servants stood on ladders lighting torches and others set flagons and mugs on the trestles. Candle trees were carried into corners to shed more light on the cavernous space. From beyond a doorway, instruments were being played and voices exercised in a sound that was at once musical and not.

'You hear? Your minstrel will be well-supported. Although I warn you, we have some of the best.'

'Then I am sure our minstrel will feel at home. He has sung for Queen Eleanor and was a troubadour in the courts of Richard Plantagent. He counts Blondel as his friend and is well respected across Europe.'

Alexandrus Gigni stopped in his tracks and turned to Guillaume. 'You are a curious young man. There are depths to you that I am going to enjoy exposing.'

'Expose is such an aggressive word, Messire…'

'My apologies. I should say *revealing,* perhaps. You seem to know people that…' he shrugged his shoulders, perplexed.

'I am a mere manager, Messire Alexandrus. For a small trading company. There is little else to know.'

Gigni considered Guillaume's words and then laughed. 'I do enjoy an enigma, it makes life so interesting. Oh Lord! The noise!' Children ran wild around them, yelling and crying and he looked on helpless before catching sight of Luzio walking toward them. 'Luzio, get your cousin my daughter, and tell her to round up the children if you will.'

Luzio bowed and ran up the circular stair of the tower that was the *chastel's* foremost feature as they had galloped toward it this day.

'For the hunt, we have many guests. I am trying to make it an autumnal tradition.' He stopped at one of the trestle tables and took a flagon, pouring rich wine into two pewter goblets. 'Here, quench your thirst. My wine is excellent.'

Guillaume lifted the wine to his lips and drank deep. It slid down his throat and he was glad, feeling its warmth flow to his veins, relaxing tense muscles. 'I thank you again for this invitation.'

'Nonsense,' Gigni sipped and made an appreciative little mew. 'I repay a debt, 'tis all. I told you … you befriended Luzio and I am grateful he has found someone who is as levelheaded as yourself.'

'Some say not so,' Guillaume replied. 'Messire, may I speak with you about the Pommiers en Forez priory we stayed in yesternight?'

He explained the situation, stressing the role of the Archbishop and the Forez family, speaking of the distress of Brother Hugo. 'He is a novice, immature, has no idea what will happen to he and Brother Francis when Father Jerome dies. They seem to have been forgotten, along with the whole village…'

Gigni listened. That he took in every word there was no doubt; he gave Guillaume all his attention. 'Members of the Forez family will be here tomorrow, but I will send a message to Archbishop Renaud as a matter of urgency. It is a sad story…' He placed his empty goblet back on the trestle as a servant walking backward with a folding stool knocked him. 'Steady now – we want no injuries before the hunt,' he put out a hand and righted the man who apologised and hurried away. He examined the interior of Guillaume's goblet. 'You are done? Then let me show you your quarters. It is not unlike a religious *dorter*. Single men to the left of the hall through that door, single women to the right through there, you see? And of course, married couples up there in chambers.' He nodded to the higher levels of the building. 'Do go and choose a cot. One of my men is behind you as we speak, with your saddlebags…'

Guillaume had a moment's panic, wondering what he possessed that may be vulnerable to inspection and then thought that Adam needed to keep a hold of his own bags on arrival. Suddenly he wanted Adam and Tobias for moral support. He felt as if he had been soaked in the cloying sweetness of honey and needed his companions to keep him sharp. Between the three of them…

'Guillaume?' Alexandrus Gigni enquired.

'Yes? Oh, my apologies. I was trying to remember what doors go where.'

'I said, trust me in respect of the priory and the village. I hate distress. I go now to write a note to Reynaud de Lyon.'

The two bowed to each other and Guillaume took his saddlebags from the servant, heading for the left door.

It had the atmosphere of a *dorter* crammed full of pilgrims and travellers. Some chatted loudly and some laughed, some were playing dice. All turned when he walked in.

'Greetings,' he said and scanned the chamber for an empty cot.

'There's four left,' said a man of middle years. 'Grab one there.'

'I thank you,' said Guillaume, unhooking the bow from his shoulder. As he laid his bags on the cot, the smell of rue drifted up. He had no doubt that every mattress in the *chastel* would have been refilled and that no insect would survive the mission.

'I'm Henri de Montbrison.' His neighbour said and held out a hand. Guillaume met the firm grip with his own.

'Guillaume de Gisborne,' he replied. 'from Lyon.'

'But only recently, I suspect. You have the look of a man from elsewhere.'

Do I?

Guillaume half-smiled. ''Tis true. Before Lyon, I came from Venezia where I lived in my ... family's house.'

'You don't look Venetian...'

'There is a look? I did not know,' he parried as calmly as he could. He hated questions of any sort. Especially from strangers.

Henri de Montbrison laughed. 'Ignore me. I am old and testy and bored with the goings-on in this chamber and long for a meal and sleep so that I may get out to this infamous hunt as fresh as a wildflower!'

Guillaume flipped open his saddlebag and took out a clean chemise and tunic. 'Is there somewhere to wash? I am travel-stained.'

'A small *lavoir* in the yard but you will fight with the servants whom Madame Gigni has ordered to wash anything that stands still in the *chastel.* Interesting bow...' Henri picked it up and turned it this way and that, drew the string and let it go with a twang. 'Outremer I presume.'

'No. My stepfather gave it to me when I was a boy.'

'Do you hunt with it?'

'Yes. Henri de Montbrison, I must beg you to excuse me. I must find my friends, wash and change and then we can talk.'

'Of course. Go, go!' The man made shooing motions and then lay back on his cot and closed his eyes.

Guillaume debated the danger of leaving his possessions on the cot but decided trust was a virtue and thus he walked out, carrying only clean clothes and longing to find Tobias and Adam somewhere.

The yard was busy – horses being led here and there, dogs barking, children again making noise, but the afternoon light had eased and long shadows had been cast by the high walls of the *chastel*. The *lavoir* was as Henri had predicted. Busy with women washing laundry whilst men washed faces and torsos. He squeezed in and knelt on one knee, dragging the water to his face and body, rubbing hard with his dirty chemise and apologising silently to Ariella who would wash it on his return. He slipped on the clean linen chemise and then followed it with an ebony wool tunic, embroidered in blood colours on the hem. Ariella had stitched it, contriving a griffin pattern in repetition. She had found the design on a piece of cloth sent from Byzantium and had studied it carefully. From his purse, he removed the comb she had insisted he bring and he pulled it through his hair now, ripping at the slipstream knots from his race with Luzio. It fell sleekly to his nape and if he passed for a nobleman, he gave thanks to the woman who waited, back in Lyon.

The women working in the *lavoir* chatted like a flock of birds, laughing, beating clothes on the long stone trough that held running water from the stream which looped past the *chastel*. The back wall of the *lavoir* was incorporated into the curtain wall of the building, with a shingled roof giving shelter to those using the space. Children splashed at one end, yelling until one of the women reprimanded them and as Guillaume watched, he realised the Gigni estate had an extraordinary sense of family – that everyone seemed happy and excited. It floated on the air like seeds released by the breeze.

'It's a nice scene, isn't it?' Toby sounded from behind him.

He swung round. 'I was wondering where you'd got to.'

'My horse threw a shoe and thus it was a slow and cautious journey. I felt a certain responsibility to the animal, given that he belongs to your host. Where is the great man?'

'Inside, I imagine. Talking to his many guests.'

Adam walked up alongside. 'There's money here, Guillaume. If they are not noble, then they're as near as dammit. And where's the lovely Luzio?'

Guillaume looked around, concerned that someone might have heard the heavy sarcasm in Adam's comment. He needed to talk to his companions but wondered where they would have peace and privacy.

'He's no doubt inside with his uncle, doing what he does best which is enjoying the good times. You are sleeping with me in a *dorter*. But I suggest you clean up now, before we go inside. Otherwise you'll have to walk back out here after dropping your bags…'

The three turned into the *lavoir* and Guillaume waited whilst they washed and changed tunics and chemises, Adam shaking his head to allow his fireball hair to fall free, Tobias, taking out a small comb and pulling at his black hair. He had shaved in Lyon and together with his dark girdled tunic, looked every inch a troubadour, the lute gleaming as he pulled the leather strap onto his shoulder. The *lavoir* had emptied, women placing baskets of washing on their hips and heads and calling their litters of children, decamping to find drying places. It seemed as if most of the guests had wandered into the *chastel*, as the only people in the yard were servants with a sense of purpose.

'Quickly, we have the *lavoir* to ourselves. Firstly Adam, the contents of your bag – it's not safe in the *dorter*…'

'It's safe where I have left it…'

'Not the horse stalls, surely…'

'No…' he leaned over and whispered to Guillaume, 'halfway up the hill where I met Toby. There's a rocky overhang. We rested Tobias' horse there and it occurred to me … well, exactly what you have just said. So between the three of us, we know where it is. Now, your friend…'

'You don't like him.'

'No. My skin crawls. It's usually a good sign.'

'In what way?'

'It usually means trust is in short supply.'

Guillaume had lost faith in everyone since the crusade and yet, he trusted

Luzio. Adam was surely too circumspect. 'Adam, he has never done anything to indicate he is not to be trusted and *I* barely trust anyone, as you know. If you want my opinion, I think he is too self-absorbed to care about anyone else.'

They heard footsteps and watched as a man led a lymer across the yard. The animal moved with insidious, lithe grace and for some reason, Guillaume had a vision of Luzio.

'But I hear what you say and will be on guard. As I have said before – the lion's den. Or so it feels.'

'Lord,' muttered Toby dryly. 'This is just too exciting and enervating for words. Are we done?'

Adam hooked his saddlebag over his shoulder and said to Guillaume, 'Lead the way.'

They walked along the cold passage, lit by nothing but light at the end. Noise drifted from further afield and Guillaume said, 'Sounds as if everyone is in the hall. We'd better hurry.'

The *dorter* had emptied. All except for one man, Henri de Montbrison, who was pulling a crushed chemise over his head. His back was broad but covered in a welter of scars and he turned as they entered.

'Ah, Guillaume de Gisborne, we'd all better hurry. The call for the meal has come.'

'We are ready. My friends need just claim their cots... This is Adam of London and ...'

He realised that they hadn't discussed Toby's identity at all nor whether it was necessary for him to even assume a different identity.

What would Guy wish?

For Toby to be anyone but Toby. Simply because minstrels could find cracks in places that others could not. By their very nature – charming, urbane and adored, they plumbed the dark secrets of many lives. The Gigni house was no different...

'And this,' he said, indicating Tobias, 'is...'

'I know you, don't I?' Henri remarked. 'I have heard you sing. Now where? Let me think.' He studied Tobias' face intently. 'I remember! Montpellier! That's it. Some time ago. You're from Spain – you're Di Dia. Ah, I was much taken with your voice.'

Tobias fell into the role of a lauded troubadour with ease, his accent

206

tumbling out of his mouth. 'Sens di Dia at your service, messire. And yes, I have sung in Montpellier. May I ask whom I am to thank for the compliment?'

'De Montbrison. Henri de Montbrison.' He clasped Tobias' arm and said, 'What a pleasure. And good even' to you, Adam of London. Thank the saints there are at least three men with whom I can enjoy myself. Are you done? Come – let's eat and drink at our host's pleasure.'

They entered the hall – a wave of sound rolling toward them like an endragoned sea, crashing upon rocks. Nothing but men's voices, a grumbling roar that made one search for the soft ameliorating face of any woman at all.

And there they were in their fine wools of *carsey*, *celestrine* and *cramoisy* and with crisp white veils. They sat between their men, looking at each other across the trestles so that Guillaume could almost see their thoughts: *'Let us speak'. 'Why do you have to shout?' 'Show some respect for what is before you?'*

Ariella would have spoken anyway. She would have engaged with the men on either side of her – earnest discussion that covered any subject of which men might think she knew nothing. His hand moved to his purse where had rested the ring. Despite that she knew little of the field of war – of the cut and thrust and fear as man fought man, she knew enough about subterfuge off the battlefield. She knew about York. She knew about the suspicion in men's eyes when they gazed upon Jews. He examined the women briefly and saw none equal to Ariella's smouldering appearance and he took comfort from the fact and held it to his heart.

But this was a men's occasion and quickly, the three Gisborne companions and their new acquaintance found seats well down the hall, just as Messire Gigni stood up at the high table. Guillaume guessed that tonight he had only his family seated with him – two daughters and their husbands, that much he knew. And the older woman at his side, would surely be his ladywife, a woman he had never seen. And then there was Luzio, lounging in his chair, one hand holding a goblet, the other playing with his dagger. Even from this far back in the hall, it was possible to discern the flush of the grape on his face and disappointment seeped into Guillaume's bones. When he saw that flush in any man, he knew it was wise to keep a distance and he wondered what had caused it.

In Lyon, Luzio had never been so drunk that he was a danger to remonstrate with. Nothing less than the gentleman, always the good friend. A servant reached down from behind Guillaume, placing a flagon of wine on the trestle and Henri took it, filling his own mug and passing it on to Adam. Slowly the rumble of men's words faded to a whisper and then to quiet and Gigni finally spoke.

'My friends. Welcome to Choizey and I thank you for accepting my invitation. Tonight we sup plainly and will retire early, ready for my hunt on the morrow. Before dawn, my men will be out in the forest with torch and stick, herding game to one of the forest's best corners. Messire Le Comte de Forez, who will be hunting with us on the morrow, has offered a purse for whomever brings down the largest deer…'

The hall erupted into noise as mugs were banged on the trestles and men cheered but Gigni held up his hands and the noise sank swiftly.

'And I,' he continued. 'offer a purse for whomever brings down a boar.'

The hall exploded with excited sound, men standing and applauding. Even Luzio, Guillaume noticed, until his cousin's hand pulled him down and he sat unsteadily. When the hall had quieted again, Gigni added,

'And God help us, there is a boar in the forest who has already killed two fine men. He is murderous when cornered and swift on the attack, so beware. Suffice to say that if anyone is successful in killing him tomorrow, they will not only earn the purse, but the thanks of those who live in the Forez. Now, my musicians will play whilst we eat, but tomorrow at the banquet, we will have much more entertainment and of the highest calibre. We have a famed troubadour in our midst and I have heard that he will sing ballads that will tear at your heart. So – shall we eat? And then I wish you good night and will see you in the yard at dawn.'

'A good speech,' Henri said as a trencher appeared before him. 'He has the gift of the word. I suppose he talks of you, Messire Sens di Dia – our troubadour.'

Toby had wadded his cloak as a cushion to allow him to sit higher at the table. 'I suspect he does and that's perfectly fine. For you men are hunters and I am a singer. We all have our talents.'

'I confess,' said Henri. 'One or other of the purses would suit me. What think you, Adam of London?'

'A purse'd be good,' the Master at Arms said as he chewed on some pie.

'And you, Guillaume,' said Henri. 'You're very quiet…'

'I care nothing for the purse to be honest. I just want to come back alive. The boar sounds … interesting.'

They talked as they ate. Henri de Montbrison had met Gigni in Marseille as the southerner was returning from Outremer. The two had travelled for some distance with a group of merchants.

'I confess I liked him,' Henri admitted. 'He seemed to be one of those few men who are sincere. And I was done with insincerity. I saw a lot of that in the Holy Land.'

'Huh. You too?' Adam muttered.

It appeared that Gigni had asked Henri to the hunt well in advance of the event, admitting quite openly that he wanted a crowd at Choizey and wanted to make it an annual event amongst those he liked.

'What can one say? I find I am at a loss as to what to do with myself currently. I am tired, disenchanted and thought the hunt may fill in some time. Besides, I heard that Gigni has a force of routiers he hires to those who will pay.'

'You would join?' Guillaume said. 'After the Holy Land?'

Henri sighed. 'I have no family, no monies, nothing but a sword, a horse and some skill. Why not?'

Guillaume shrugged. 'I saw too much to ever fight again…'

Henri agreed. 'But show me what else I can do to survive and I shall do it. What are your skills?'

'I was a fletcher and bowyer. Then an archer. Now I manage a merchant company for my noble half-brother…'

Henri's eyebrows lifted and he huffed and Guillaume could see a long line of questions emerging from the sharp and interested mind of the man next to him.

'It is a long story, Messire Henri. Let's eat and toast tomorrow's hunt and leave the past behind.'

The meal was simple, good stews and pies, fresh bread and cheese and platters of autumn fruit and nuts to end the meal. The wine kept coming although Guillaume suspected that as the evening deepened, so the wine was watered more and more. Gigni would surely want alert hunters on the morrow, not those for whom the night before had taken its toll. He looked to the high table and caught Luzio's eye and the Pisan waved, before leaning to his uncle and speaking. Gigni's head nodded and Luzio stood to leave the table, but Gigni had one last word and Luzio stood still for a moment, then seemed to agree with his uncle and stepped down from the dais, moving round the edge of the hall toward Guillaume and his companions.

He slapped Guillaume on the shoulder. 'Well, my good friend, what think you of Choizey and my uncle's hospitality?' His words slurred faintly but it seemed he had control of himself and Guillaume replied with sincerity.

'Impressive, Luzio. I think there are nobility who could look to your uncle for manners and style, and most certainly generosity.'

'He has all of that, I will grant you. But wait till tomorrow. This is nothing by comparison.'

'You say,' said Toby in his best Spanish accent. 'I am agog.'

Luzio looked down at Toby. For a moment he seemed at a loss but then he leaned against Guillaume, addressing Tobias, 'So you are the minstrel, I suppose. Might you be the troubadour of renown of whom my uncle bragged?'

'I think I might be. I am Sens di Dia, troubadour of some note with the Plantaganet court, and a friend of Blondel. Greetings.' Toby bowed his head and then met Luzio's insouciant gaze.

But the Pisan replied tidily. 'And I am Luzio, Guillaume's best friend and servant. And I think I am now yours as well, Messire Sens. There is nothing I like better than to sit with good wine and good friends and listen to the best of the world's minstrels. Shall we weep when you sing?' he asked. 'Will there be ladies who need my shoulder upon which to dry their tears?' He grinned, once more the wicked and amusing man with whom Guillaume was familiar. 'I do hope so.'

Tobias laughed. 'If that is what you wish, Messire, then I shall contrive it so.'

Luzio turned to Guillaume. 'I like your Spanish friend, Guillaume. And I have already met Adam of London who is staunch and no doubt as strong with a sword as he is with a frown. But who else might I meet here? Sir?'

He referred to Henri and it was a matter of moment for introductions to be made. Around them chatter had begun as the meal had ended but it hummed like a bee chorus rather than the seastorm roar of earlier. Men were organising themselves into teams for the hunt tomorrow and Luzio encompassed the four men with a smile of blinding and complicit brilliance.

'Let *us* form a team for tomorrow. Why not?'

Tobias answered. 'An excellent idea if you exclude me, Messire Luzio. I am an appalling rider, hate the sight of blood and would prefer to meet the ladies, sing a little and compile a list of songs for the banquet. I would slow you down sorely.'

'Then you are excused,' Luzio replied. 'But the four of us? A good team I think. What say you?'

The others agreed and despite that Adam did so quietly, he shook Luzio's hand to seal the deal.

'Then I think we should to bed,' Luzio said. 'The hunt is fast and requires a clear head. I must, according to my uncle, go clear mine own. Till tomorrow, then.' He began to turn away as groups drifted from the hall. 'Oh, and Guillaume? It's good to have someone I trust and whose friendship I value here with me.' He smiled the mercurial smile and walked away, lost in the crowd and leaving the group the less for the loss of his brilliance.

'Saints and sinners,' said Toby. 'He's rather charismatic.'

'Charming,' Henri replied. 'It must run in the Gigni family.'

Guillaume and Adam added nothing to the commentary, stepping over the bench seats to follow the rest of the men and women to their various cots. Tobias and Henri walked ahead, Toby chatting, Henri answering back, all very benign, but Guillaume had no doubt Toby was building a mind-load of facts. Adam and Guillaume followed behind, the last to reach the passage.

'Still doubtful?' Guillaume asked.

'Don't know. Not sure,' Adam answered. 'I'll sleep on it.'

CHAPTER TEN

×

The *dorter* rattled in the pre-dawn as swords were buckled and daggers slipped into neat scabbards at the girdle. There was mumbling and swearing as those who had wineheads from the night before, tried to shake the fogginess away. Some sucked greedily on costrels, as if some more of the same might banish the ache. Some ran outside to find a corner to puke in or to relieve themselves.

Adam, Henri and Guillaume checked their weaponry with mercifully clear heads whilst Toby watched from the warm comfort of his cot and a cocoon of cloaks.

'Good luck, my friends. Stay safe. I shall think of you as I languish here with a *chastel* full of lovely women…'

'Shut your mouth,' Adam muttered. 'Or I won't bring you back a lucky hare's tail.'

'If it's bloody I don't want it,' replied Tobias. 'Besides, am I not already wily and a survivor? It's hardly likely that a hare will help.'

'Right then, no hare's tail. But don't languish either. Your fame has spread and this crowd will expect the best after a long day's hunt.'

Tobias sat up, his hair at right angles to his head, stubble across his chin and his eyes still heavy with sleep. 'You doubt me?'

Guillaume grinned. 'As you look now? Yes. Like the village idiot.' He picked up his clutch of arrows. 'Three's not going to go far…'

Adam held out three more. 'Here, we pulled them from the felons yesterday on our way past. I cleaned them for you.'

The ash arrows were fletched with a hawk's flight feathers. In their own

213

way unique, a kind of signature. The bodkins glistened coldly in the weak torch flames. Thanking Adam, he took them, bunched them with the others, and rammed them through his girdle at the back, then swung his cloak over the lot, before shouldering his bow. It was as if a little piece of Anselin sat with him, and he kissed his thumb and pointed surreptitiously to the heavens. If the others noticed, they said nothing, just joined in the file of men who walked out to the yard to harness their horses.

As they walked down the corridor, they could hear Toby singing,

'In a forest realm lived a great boar
that the king rode out to slay
While among the ancient oak bent and hoar
The king's mastiffs would bay...'

'Lazy sod!' chaffed Adam.

The yard was lit with torch and brazier and lines of horses had been saddled, men standing with reins hooked over their arms, calling to each other, joking baldly about the day's outcome. Beyond the *chastel*, the sky had the faintest blush of dawn, a brazen cock crowed and the hounds bayed and fretted at their chains, their handlers holding tight.

Alexandrus Gigni strode out and was handed a dark grey horse of bearing, an arrogant animal but steady as a rock. He climbed a block and slid into the saddle, joined by his wife on a palfrey and sundry other female guests on small, sturdy horses of varying quality. It was the signal for all to mount and the sound of hooves shifting, leather creaking and metal bits chomping filled the yard. Luzio, astride the beautiful Bella, squeezed in beside Guillaume, looking brighter than it was fair to be after his copious drinking bout the night before.

'You see that entourage entering the gate? It is Messire le Comte de Forez, Archbishop Renaud's brother,' Luzio whispered. The family fed into the yard on horses of quality, riders' faces lit with expectation and interest. 'The Forez family did well when Renaud became archbishop. In order to maintain a good relationship with his extended family, he transferred his wealth and holdings to them. Ah, such brotherly love...'

Guillaume watched the meeting between the Gigni and Forez, waiting for the former to defer to the latter. But there was no deference; one could almost be forgiven for thinking they were on an equal footing.

'You sound scornful, Luzio. Or if not scornful then patronising.'

'Not at all,' the Pisan replied. 'I'm merely acknowledging the power of politics. Renaud is as much a God-fearing archbishop as I. This is purely a family wanting power, so they channel such strength from the Church by pushing one of their own into the position.'

'What would your uncle think of such a bald view?' Guillaume was surprised at the look that passed across his friend's face – the scorn was like chipped marble.

'I'm not sure I care,' Luzio replied. 'I watch. I make deductions and then I plan how to live *my* life so that I don't get caught in any nets hooked and set for *me*.'

Maybe we are not so dissimilar, Luzio. Who would have thought?

'Ah well,' Guillaume said, 'That aside, my friend, this is a prodigious sight.'

It was a frosty morning and the mists had begun to rise, allowing seductive glimpses of a Virgin-blue sky above the skeins of vapour. Horses danced on their toes, blowing down their noses, their breath white with cold. The riders sat easily, even as their horses neighed, ear-splitting shrieks that rattled their whole bodies. As if they screamed a battle cry to all those that would be hunted.

The strengthening light illuminated a plethora of earth colours – mud, umber, crimson, forest green and yellow amongst the crowd. Some had elaborate saddlery upon their mounts, others were plain and unembellished, as if the riders mounted on those unadorned horses really meant business.

Dogs ranged around the edges of the crowd, held firm by handlers on foot – some of the dogs were the oyster colour of the moon, some as black as Hades and some a fierce brindle that defied any artist's pigment. They were sleek and beautiful but filled with a terrifying power which set Guillaume's nerves tingling – that this was business showed in the spiked collars, in the lengths of chain and leather and in the shrill commands from the hunting horns.

Gigni lifted a gloved hand, his fur-trimmed sleeve falling back to reveal a snowy chemise. And then his hand dropped, dog-handlers and hunting packs away – a purposeful lope that had the waiting crowd shortening reins and which prompted horses to snort, to sidle, to give small anxious half-rears.

'Well, team,' Luzio said glibly to Adam and Guillaume. 'Here we are, like the Wild Hunt. Let's make a killing!'

The mounted hunters began to canter at a discrete distance, allowing the hounds to pick up the scents of the earlier drive. Their yelps and bays filled the dawn air, drowning the sounds of birds, and they began to tug hard on their restraints. The handlers released the lymers who took off in a streak of moonshine and black thunder, their very howls sending thrilling echoes up Guillaume's spine, the horn calls directing dogs to follow a line.

Once the dogs were loose, men galloped with abandon, facing their horses at any obstacle that appeared, whooping as they cleared it, shouting to each other with the women following behind and skirting the bigger logs and hurdles, but gamely clearing the lesser ones.

The sun had burned the mists away and the sky had cleared to a profound blue, beams of light glancing off metal buckles and bits, off sword grips and daggers. Guillaume sensed images streaking past as his horse pecked over a log, and he thought how Tobias would have loved the colour, the sight and the sound and how it would make such a ballad.

Guillaume's heart sang with the freedom of the gallop. For one brief morning in time, memories and anxieties left him as free as the air rushing through his hair. He focused his gaze between the horse's ears, feeling the unpegged joy of the animal itself as it stretched out, mane flying, ears slicked back.

He didn't hear Luzio calling immediately but the Pisan rode up beside him yelling 'Stop!' and he pulled on his reins, sitting down hard in the saddle, the animal slowing to a canter and then a bouncy trot. Its fury as it watched the rest of the hunt stream ahead was obvious as it swirled in an angry circle, snorting and tossing its head.

'Steady, boy, easy,' hushed Guillaume. 'Steady now...' He turned to Luzio. 'What? What's wrong?' And then he noticed Henri and Adam cantering back to them. Diavolo was already dark with nervous sweat and mouthed his bit with a fretful clinking.

'Friend Luzio!' Henri shouted as the hunt disappeared into the trees and tracks of the Forez. 'This is not the way to win a purse!'

'On the contrary!' Luzio laughed. 'Do you think our wily boar will allow itself to be baled up in the depths of the forest? Do you not think there are deer who have escaped the beat and are behind us? Or to the side of us? And hares and wild fowl too? I think we should leave the rest to their orchestrated day and we should hunt elsewhere. What say you?'

Adam made no reply, just looked down at his reins, waiting for Guillaume to speak.

'What would your uncle say?' Guillaume asked.

'If we kill the boar and bring down meat for the table, I think he will admire our ingenuity.'

Guillaume could hardly disagree but before he could reply, Henri jumped in.

'I say you're right,' his eyes were bright with excitement. 'The purses can be ours! Do you know the forest well?'

'A little. Which way do you think the breeze blows?'

Guillaume sucked on a finger and then held it in the air. 'It's a barely-there zephyr. But if it's anything, it is blowing from the southwest.'

'Then we loop around the back of the track and return behind the beasts. What say you?'

'You think there will be quarry where we have just thundered through?' Adam spoke quietly but Guillaume could detect the incredulity.

'Yes,' Luzio could not be swayed. 'Listen. Can you hear the hunt?'

The apparent silence around them whispered with a far distant sound, maybe a league or two – the hunt, moving away, fainter by the heartbeat.

'The beasts in the forest can hear it too. Moving fast and away. They will settle, move around to forage, enjoy the morning sun. *And,* what's more, I think we should progress on foot. Think about it – we'll be quieter, taking any quarry by surprise.'

Guillaume knew he was right. How many times had he and Anselin moved through the woods of La Flèche as if they floated on air, quietly tracking, always returning with a kill. The power of silence and sharp observation…

'Done!' said Henri, swiftly dismounting and pulling some rope from behind his saddle. He grinned. 'For trussing a kill. But we can tie up the horses with it for now and come back to retrieve it when we are successful.'

Luzio jumped off his horse, smacking Henri delightedly on the back. 'You are a kindred spirit, Henri de Montbrison, and I say that you and I work in one direction and Adam and Guillaume the other. Come, you laggards, we must beat the hunt's return.'

The horses settled, happy to graze and rest in the sun. Even Diavolo stood with his hip angled, his ears twitching less fractiously.

The men moved into the forest proper, agreeing to meet back at the horses when the sun was at its zenith. Almost immediately as they followed unknown trails, Guillaume spotted a deer track – a hoof imprint embedded in damp soil. And another. They could neither see nor hear Henri and Luzio, so intent were they on the ground, Adam bending frequently to touch an imprint, a pile of droppings.

'It's fresh, Guillaume,' he fingered a hoofprint. 'A good sized buck, I think, and close. I say we split. You go ahead and I shall skirt around and come at it from the other direction.'

Guillaume nodded. He had done this before with Anselin. One would move in front of the beast and send it flying back along the trail upon which it had come, to be greeted by a huntsman…

Adam left like a phantom, not a sound from his movement and Guillaume liked that he was accomplished and a proficient hunting partner. For all that Luzio was a friend and Henri a new one, neither were restrained and Guillaume thought they would scare their quarry with their unbridled enthusiasm. He nocked one of his hawk-feathered arrows, moving forward slowly, giving Adam time. Around him the forest was still, except for the unconcerned chittering of birds – and a small crack of a hoof on a twig.

A young buck of good proportions, well-fed and muscled, grazed upon grasses in the clearing ahead. His coat had thickened with the approach of winter and he had the antlers of a male that had just entered adulthood, and he wore them proudly. He had bulk, a perfect beast, and as Guillaume stood behind a tree, something caught the deer's attention and his head flew up, looking away from Guillaume. He sniffed the air, took a few steps forward, still alert. The silence was thick with promise and Guillaume could barely breathe as he watched. Then the buck turned toward the archer, shaking his head gently from side to side before beginning to graze in peace.

The arrow sighed away.

Never was a shot more perfect.

Straight through the animal's skull.

The beast looked up in surprise at Guillaume, gaze meeting gaze, pain flashing across the one's eyes and then echoed in the other's. The buck grunted, falling to his knees before crashing onto his side.

And all Guillaume could think was 'Shame…'

He hated himself afresh, as in Outremer.

His hands loosened on the bow and it fell to the ground as a wave of sweat swept over him and he trembled. The deer's hind leg kicked out and pulled him from deep within a tainted soul and he grabbed his *misericorde* and hurried to put it out of its agony.

But it was dead, its eyes staring right at him like pointed fingers.

As dead as those…

He knelt on one knee, running a shaking hand over the winter hide, dreading the moment when he must retrieve his arrow.

'Adam!' he shouted. 'To me!'

He can pull the arrow…

His fingers lingered over the ears. They were smooth, like a puppy's ears, velvet, so soft…

A sound filled the copse behind him – bellicose and fraught and his blood froze, eyes closing, hand tightening on the slim little dagger.

Mary Mother, help me. My bow…

But it lay where he'd dropped it. Useless.

An arrow…

He pulled at one of those that remained tucked into his girdle as another snort reached him, guttural and impatient. There was little point in turning around.

You would let it take you in the back? You would meet it like a coward, as if you had been running away?

Christ God, he thought. I need no conscience voice now. He levered himself slowly off his knee, crouching low. Feral breath puffed in and out, punctuated by a belligerent snort and then the boar gave a high-pitched squeal.

It's moving, thought Guillaume. Gaining speed.

He leaped over the carcass of the deer, spinning round, using the body as a shieldwall between he and tusks that could eviscerate. He held the arrow hard, bodkin facing the animal, awaiting the impact.

A bone needle would be as good…

The animal lifted its front legs up to clear the deer carcass and in that brief moment, Guillaume punched the arrow into its belly. The animal grunted, bent and tossed its head and caught Guillaume's arm with a tusk, ripping though velvet, silk, tendon and muscle. The beast ran on then, squealing like a hundred pigs at slaughter but skidded to a halt at the edge of the clearing, crashing into a tree and spinning around.

Guillaume grabbed at another arrow, finding only one left in his girdle, no time to see where the others had fallen.

The boar's rage filled the sunny morning as it went to crash over the deer again, its foul breath hitting Guillaume in the face as he lifted a bloody arm to strike, impaling the arrow close to the other. It ran on, a shorter distance this time, before spinning again and Guillaume had nothing, no weapon beyond the needle-sharp blade of the *misericorde*. The arrows were little more than a bee sting on leather and had merely served to further enrage. The dagger would be no better.

A vision of the boar spears carried by the huntsmen flashed through his mind along with images of Ariella smiling, Ariella laughing, Ariella slipping the Byzantine sapphire onto her finger. He'd avoided death in war. How it irked him to think death would come on a hunt that held little or no meaning and by a feral beast of all things. All his life with Anselin they had courted boars in their forest, killed one or two with boar spears made by Anselin and Jean One Eye. And now…

Ave Maria, gratia plena, Dominus tecum. Benedicta…

An arrow whined past his face, slamming into the skull of the boar and as the beast slowed, its tusks lowered for a lunge, a boar spear slid over his shoulder and through its chest, positioned right above the heart. The animal shook on the end of the weapon, screaming wildly. Guillaume grabbed at the spear, not turning, holding on tight as the animal fought against its death.

Further words ran through his mind, *Benedicta tu in mulieribus, et benedictus fructus ventris tui, Iesus…* but he didn't speak aloud, just held on until the juddering slowed and the animal's snorts became less, its eyes flattening.

Finally, 'Christ God, Adam…' he turned, but it wasn't Adam. 'Luzio! Christ, the saints and Mary Mother! I owe you my life.'

Luzio let the spear go and the animal sank in front of the deer. 'I should think you do, Guillaume. And I think I may have won the purse as well. A good day.'

Guillaume glanced at his arm, blood dripping freely. He clasped his hand over the top of the wound, pressing hard against the pain that had begun as the fear that had been rampant began to ebb. It was different to battle fever where one was carried along on a tide of kill or be killed. This time it had felt as though he could do no more, that the die had been cast and he had lost the game.

Still a coward then? Just like the time you walked away from Arsuf?

Luzio pulled the arrow from the deer's skull, then the other from the boar's skull. He held them out, blood dripping from the bodkins. 'These are yours?'

'Yes.'

'And this is your bow?'

'Yes – you are a good archer, Luzio. I didn't know.'

'No. You didn't. A pity. Tell me, do you fletch you own arrows?' He wiped them on the grass and ran fingers back and forth over the hawk feathers. Idly, like the indolent that he was.

'I was a fletcher in times past. Yes.'

'And do you normally use hawk feathers? It is unusual, surely.'

Guillaume heard something in his friend's voice and looked up from his wound. But Luzio just focused on the feathers, running those slim, well-tended hands back and forth.

'It is something I have done for some time. It reminds me of my father…'

'You have never told me of your father. Why do the hawk feathers remind you of him?'

Guillaume shook his head. 'It is not something I talk of, Luzio. Where are Adam and Henri?'

'But if we are friends, you should tell me about your life.' He dragged a linen square from his purse. 'Here, let me bind that for you.' He ripped the kerchief and with the strips, bound the wound tightly. 'As to Henri and Adam, I think they must be tied up. Perhaps on their own hunt. Who knows? Does that feel better? Good. Now – about your father. Did he live in a place called La Flèche in Anjou?'

Guillaume blinked, startled.

'Ah, he did. Well, well.' Luzio's voice had changed. At first Guillaume thought he was drunk, but he spoke with such cool, concise clarity…

He thrust an arrow into Guillaume's hands, passed him the bow and then dragged the spear from the boar and turned to face Guillaume. The camaraderie of the past had vanished. In its place, calculation.

'You see. I know La Flèche,' he said. 'I went there. Perhaps whilst you were in the Holy Land. I had to retrieve something my family had lost.' He toyed with the spear, a feint here, a feint there. 'Do you know what my family lost, Guillaume? Can you guess? Especially as you know I am from Pisa…'

Realisation flooded through Guillaume. His throat closed tight, knowing that he now faced something vastly more dangerous than a boar.

'I see you can guess. My brother and his friend were murdered, Guillaume. I had to find out where they were for my grieving parents. The interesting thing is that they were found by some travellers with hawk-fletched arrows through their skulls. What do you think of that? La Flèche's local priest saved the arrows and closeted them away but money opens many things. Especially crusty old priest's caskets.' He thrust the boar spear at Guillaume, allowing it to press into the velvet of his tunic, pushing a little harder and gazing at Guillaume with such hate. 'You killed my brother.'

'Your brother and his friend,' Guillaume said through clenched teeth, 'raped and killed my mother and slashed my father's throat. The priest knew this.'

'The priest had an accident. Besides, your parents were peasants, like you. My brother was not. So who cares?' Luzio thrust again, a little harder and the tip pushed through the nap of the velvet, piercing the linen of Guillaume's chemise and touching his stomach.

He jumped away and drew his sword, his arm weak. 'I cared,' he shouted. 'They were innocent people going about their business. Your brother had already caused havoc in the village, threatening my friend's daughter. He had no moral creed, a common routier!'

'And so you became the villager's saviour. Look at you! The righteous avenging angel.'

'Look at *you*, Luzio. What are you? A warrior bent on revenge? A killer of priests, for God's sake? Don't stoop to your brother's level. You were my good friend.'

'Don't stoop? *Don't stoop?* Jesu, you pile of hog-shit. And you say your *friend?* Christ, you jest.' He lunged with the spear and Guillaume caught it on the edge of his sword, the sound ringing round the copse.

'Luzio!' Guillaume blocked another stab with the spear, clapping it down with the flat of his sword.

Luzio retreated to the far side of the copse, playing with the spear and as bright and dangerous as naptha. 'Do you know,' he said, 'I decided you were my brother's murderer long since.'

'How so?' Guillaume tried to enter Luzio's mind.

What is your next move, my friend? To swagger?

'Once, not so many weeks after we met, I came to de Clochard to urge you to drink with me. Mahaut said you were in the stables, fletching. *'He's a fletcher?'* I honestly laughed when she said that, but she answered me sourly back. *'A common artisan, he is.'* And she hoiked and spat. So I moved to the entrance of the stalls, your back was to me, and I watched you with your precious arrows and when you took up hawk feathers, I was stunned. I turned and left and as I passed through the gates, Mahaut was leaving and so I walked with her…'

'He's an excellent artisan, Mahaut. I wonder where he learned the trade. I knew he was an archer during the crusade, although he speaks little enough of it…'

Mahaut spat again, all her hatred of Guillaume concentrated in the furious action. 'In Anjou,' she said. 'Madame de Clochard said he was the son of a bowyer and fletcher. I say he is not good enough for the family I tend.'

Luzio touched her arm. 'I am sure he means no harm. So you say he comes from Anjou?'

'Oc. A village called La Flèche. I wish he and that devil woman had stayed there.' Her bottom lip jutted out and Luzio wondered if she could look any more horrendous if she tried.

'You don't like them?'

'No.'

'Do you walk to the Cathedral, Mahaut? I will accompany you, if you like.' Her head shot up and she studied him. Then blushed. 'If you want…'

'And so I heard all about your Jew woman, Guillaume. Mahaut hates Ariella even more than you. She says the Church will make amends by ridding de Clochard of an unbeliever. You know, the venom coming from someone who wants to be a nun is astonishing. Ariella needs looking after, but sadly you won't be around to do it.'

Ariella!

Guillaume's heart pounded. He had a sword and Luzio had a long boar spear. The odds were stacked…

'And as I walked to the Cathedral with redoubtable Mahaut, everything fell into place.'

'And yet you helped us when de Clochard caught fire. Were you keeping your enemies close, Luzio?'

'Ah, you see? You think like I. It's probably why we became friends in the beginning. Either that or some Divine irony was being played out.' He pushed himself away from the tree-trunk and tapped the boar spear on the ground, looking up at the glittering head and then, with speed that took Guillaume's breath away, ran forward and thrust the weapon at Guillaume's stomach.

Guillaume jumped sideways. Another thrust and he jumped the other way. The linen around his arm dripped blood and his grip on the sword began to slip again, so he grabbed it two-handed.

The idea of defeat hovered on the edge of his mind but Anselin and Cateline deserved so much more, and he bent his knees, glad that he was supple and fit.

As supple as Luzio?

On the next thrust, he crashed the sword, *forte* edge down, onto the wooden handle of the spear, splinters flying. But Luzio dragged the spear back and thrust again, the lugs catching on Guillaume's tunic. Luzio growled, a rising crescendo of frustration as he shook the spearhead free.

Guillaume swung again with his sword, two hands, thrashing down, the blade slicing into the already weakened handle of the spear, splinters flying again, the haft breaking, the spearhead falling to the ground. But Luzio was quick, throwing the wood end of the haft at Guillaume and stooping to pick up the spear end, lunging forward.

Closer now, Guillaume with the advantage. Luzio's confidence shone a little less brilliantly and he panted. On his forehead was a scar Guillaume had never noticed before. Always that carefully groomed hair and meticulous appearance. It hid so much. Maybe now that the odds had reduced in Guillaume's favour, Luzio fought harder, thrusting the spear under Guillaume's guard.

He jumped to the side, landing on the deer's hoof, falling, the sword slipping from his hands, his wrist cracking underneath him as he landed.

Mary, Mother of God!

Luzio looked down at him. 'Three carcasses together. What an end to a hunt, don't you think, my friend? And to be honest, the purses pale significantly now. Do you want to die quickly? As quickly as my brother did? Maybe I should push the spear through your skull and honour my brother in the doing.'

'Honour him? A rapist and a murderer? Christ, Luzio.' Guillaume spat the words, pain from his wound, from his wrist, from grief and fear for Ariella. He was so filled with fury, it flooded like hot oil through his body.

But Luzio's smile was as soft as an angel's, his perfect face lit by the midday sun, his hair lifting in a slight breeze. He drew back the spear. 'An eye for an eye. God will understand.'

He raised the spear to hammer it home and Guillaume yelled, drawing his leg back, kicking out his foot. It erupted from him in a cry of rage and Luzio gasped as his shin cracked under the force.

He began to fall forward, spear in hand and Guillaume rolled over the deer's leg, as Luzio toppled, crying out, a wretched sound.

'Christ God!' he screamed. And then nothing but a short, panting whimper. 'Guillaume … help me…' His face was buried in the deer's belly, his body lying over that of the boar and its eviscerating tusks. 'God, please…' Blood had begun to seep from under him to mingle with that of the hunted beasts.

'Please…' he tried to push himself up but shrieked and collapsed down again.

Guillaume stood, divided by pity for a man who was dying and a ferocious need to hate him.

Let him die in agony, like my mother…

Luzio's wretched crying filled the copse and a kinder man may have slit his throat to save his agony. Wouldn't they? thought Guillaume. The bloody, dusty colours of the Holy Land flooded his memory.

But I am not like kings on the battlefield and I am not de Sablé, caring for nothing but the fight.

He took a step…

'Don't touch him…' Adam's voice sounded behind him and he turned. 'See? Even as he dies, the bastard has the spearhead and would use it.' He strode forward to tug it from Luzio's hand and it was possible to see that there was a gash where blood coursed freely down the Englishman's neck. 'You vainglorious, pretty piece of shit,' he spat at Luzio and cast the spear to the side, wiping at the blood on his neck. 'He did the same to Henri as me, only Henri's is worse. We'll pick him up with the horses.' He pulled at Guillaume's arm. 'Leave him, he's dying. Let's go.'

'I cannot leave him like this, Adam.'

'You can. Come…'

'I said no! We must help him and allow him to die with some sort of grace, facing God, not with his back turned.'

Adam scoffed.

'Help me pull him off or I shall do it myself.'

'With that arm and wrist? Christ's toenails! You're a fool, Guillaume.'

'Indeed. But it is what I would do.'

Adam huffed out a sigh and bent down to break off a solid twig. 'This will hurt, messire. Bite…' He shoved the wood into Luzio's mouth. 'On my count, Guillaume. One, two, three…'

The scream filled the copse and Guillaume wondered if the hunt heard it, so loud and agonised was it.

How to explain this to Messire Gigni…

'He's fainted,' Adam said as they laid Luzio on the ground. His tunic was sodden and Adam unbuckled the Pisan's girdle and eased his tunic and chemise up. The wound may have been smaller if Luzio had fallen straight down, but when he scraped forward in the fall, the tusk ripped through his belly like a plough through soil. Through the one jagged tear a grey loop poked out and so Adam dragged the chemise and tunic back over it and wiped his hand on the grass.

'Not a hope in Hell.'

'Now or later, think you?' Guillaume asked as he knelt by Luzio.

'Soon. He bleeds inside and out. See his colour?'

Luzio's eyelids fluttered and the gloriously feminine black lashes opened. He groaned and licked lips that were bloody with seepage.

'Wine?' Guillaume asked and Luzio sucked greedily on the costrel held for him. 'I liked you, Luzio, I really did. But if I had known you were of the family who killed mine, we would have come to this point sooner…'

Luzio smiled. Christ Jesus, Guillaume thought, even with approaching death he is beautiful. How can it be?

'But I win, Guillaume. Even now…' he coughed and cried out.

'You say?' Adam sneered. 'And yet we stand here and *you* meet your Maker.'

'I win because Mahaut and Brother Crispianus conspire against what remains of your life, Guillaume. Your little Jewish whore…'

Guillaume went to smack him across the face but Adam grabbed his hand as the life fled from Luzio's eyes.

Other things filled the glade around them. Motes on sunbeams, birdsong, the sound of a bee enjoying the last of the autumnal sun before settling in a skip somewhere for the cold months – the stuff of life.

'I must fetch Messire Gigni,' Guillaume said, cradling his arm against his chest.

'Damn the Gigni! Let's get you bandaged, get the horses, get Henri and leave this place.'

'Adam, I would leave Luzio here to rot and fester as I hoped his brother would. I would love to think that he was ravaged by forest creatures, that worms would crawl through his eye sockets. I despise *his* family for my family's deaths. And I would return to Lyon swiftly because of his threats. But I am the de Clochard representative and a guest of the Gigni. Unfortunately for them *and* for us, this is their nephew,' he indicated Luzio's body. 'I must do the right thing.'

'The right thing is to leave the sod where he is and let the uncle deal with it when he finds him!'

'And that should do our reputation good, you think? Listen, de Clochard is Guy's and Saul's as much as Amée's and its standing must be protected. Whatever I do must and will reflect upon the whole house.'

Adam sighed. 'Then tell Gigni nothing of what passed between you and the pretty boy. Let him think his nephew died from the boar, protecting you. And to add to the embroidery…'

He picked up the broken spear head and slammed it into the boar's skull, grunting as he pushed it with all his body weight.

'It is a good idea,' Guillaume said. 'Except that Alexandrus might know of Luzio's plans and might share the plan for revenge.'

'Then you'll have to gauge that as you speak with him. Either way – my advice would be to leave the body here and return to Lyon immediately. Since you won't do that, you had better ask God to be on your side. Come now, we cannot leave Henri lying for too long.'

They began to walk away and Guillaume would have given anything to leap upon a horse, ride to Lyon and spirit Ariella to Venezia and to Hell with

Guy's investments. To Hell with Saul's as well. Ariella was worth everything and he knew her father would agree.

The horses were dozing and barely lifted their heads when they reached the tether. Adam reached into his saddlebags for a roll of linen strips whereupon he washed the slash on Guillaume's arm.

'This is deep and I worry for its cleanliness. I think you must see a physician as soon as possible. I shall not stitch it, Guillaume. There are layers here that I don't know how to deal with and if it is open, we can keep it clean until told otherwise.' He bandaged the wound in clean linen, and then splinted the broken wrist with two small sticks before wrapping that as well. 'You know – it is my lot in life to doctor you. I hope I never have to wrap you in a shroud.'

But Guillaume barely heard him as he went over in his mind how to read Alexandrus Gigni. It was essentially the difference, he thought, between life and death.

Henri lay against a tree trunk, his face pale and blood oozing down his forehead. 'Thank the Lord,' he said as they tied the horses to branches. 'I thought you might leave me to my Fate.'

'No, I would have liked that to happen to Messire Luzio, but Guillaume has other ideas.'

'That little fringe-eyed bastard!' Henri winced as Adam doused a pad in wine and patted the cuts and bruising in amongst his hair. 'I've just puked last night's banquet onto the ground because of him.'

'He knocked you out,' Guillaume said, unsurprised.

'Me first and then I suspect he found Adam. But he didn't hit Adam as hard or I imagine, Adam would not be so bright-eyed and able. Luzio tried to hit me from behind but I heard him and swung round to defend myself and he caught me here…' He fingered the wound and winced. 'As God is my witness, when I find him, I will kill him.'

Adam wrapped the last of the linen strips round Henri's head. 'The boar beat you. He's nicely dead.'

'You say?' Henri tried to turn round. 'Ouch. Careful how you go, friend.'

'Very dead. Guillaume has now to inform his uncle.'

'Making all of us a team, separating us from the main hunt.' Henri stood and leaned against Adam. 'He had an agenda and I think it might have been you, Guillaume.'

'You think?' Guillaume asked wryly. 'Why?'

'I lay on the ground pretending a faint, and he muttered something…'

'What? We are all ears,' said Adam.

'*Two down, one to go.* And then he ran as if the Devil pursued him.'

'In a way the Devil did,' said Adam.

'Might I be told?' Henri asked. 'I feel as if this…' he indicated the bandage, '…gives me a vested interest.'

Adam looked at Guillaume and gave a small nod.

So, my friend, you like this man and trust him. You read Luzio right, so maybe I need to follow in your footsteps…

Guillaume told him the story of Anselin and Cateline and what he had done to avenge them. Of how Luzio had discovered him – how Luzio himself had called their meeting a Divine irony as Guillaume's identity was revealed.

'Divine irony? Christ Jesus! I should think that all the saints and angels are sitting laughing at the turn-up. That you should both meet in Lyon of all places! Leagues from La Flèche and so much time having passed. Somebody in Heaven doesn't like you, Guillaume, for it to turn that way. Have you thought of taking Holy orders to be safe?'

'And end up sharing my life with the likes of Brother Crispianus? I think not.'

'Brother who?'

Adam broke in, 'A story for the journey home. Guillaume, we must make haste if you want to speak with Gigni before we return to Lyon.'

As they rode back through the forest, listening for the sounds of the hunt, Henri hung on grimly. 'Christ, I need to lie down. I am feeling the worse for wear. That shit of a Pisan! I'm angry at myself as well because I liked him and was convinced by his charm, God help me. I liked his enthusiasm for life which was like a breath of fresh air after the Holy Land…'

Guillaume had mounted from a log, sliding gingerly into the saddle and holding the reins with one hand. 'If it makes you feel less like an idiot, Henri, I liked him too and I am not given to easy friendship. What a fool I was. Only Adam could see the rot.'

'There are those with attributes that are real whom one knows one can trust,' Adam said. 'You were both blinded by the easy charm, 'tis all. I'm a natural cynic and Luzio was too oily, as if he greased his way into everyone's ambit. And he knew how I felt. That's the other thing. People such as he, those who are cunning and sly, have sharp intuition, knowing very quickly who will fall for their blandishments. Guillaume, before you bleed yourself dry with Mea Culpas, let me say that I think he caught you when you were vulnerable. Nothing more, nothing less.'

They halted for a moment to listen for the hunt and heard horns calling dogs and men close to Choizey.

'They have returned. God's breath!' Guillaume shifted in the saddle. 'Ah well, it may be easier to talk with Messire Alexandrus in the *chastel.*'

'It may be,' Adam said. 'In any case, Henri must lie down on his cot for a time to resume his equilibrium and I will wait in the yard. We will have to take men and a cart back to the copse, I am sure.'

The sun had begun to slide to mid-afternoon as they passed through the gates of Choizey. In the yard, ostlers led sweaty horses away, and guests laughed and chatted as they headed for the main door. Of Gigni there was no sign, and Guillaume asked a passing servant as he eased himself warily onto a mounting block of cut stone.

'Messire Alexandrus?'

'Inside, messire,' answered the servant, eye-ing the blood and bandages. 'Perhaps in the hall.'

Guillaume cursed. He'd hoped his host was in a private chamber, somewhere away from the crowd. He pulled his tunic down with one hand, adjusted his girdle, realised his scabbard was empty and walked after the crowd into the hall. Guests were being served watered wine and sweet treats. A servant offered Guillaume almonds concealed within plump eastern dates and he took one, examining it.

How do I recognise rot carefully concealed?

He leaned against a wall, surveying the crowd, trying to identity his host when a voice said at his side,

'Guillaume! God save us, what happened to you?'

He turned, crushing the date into his palm. 'Messire Alexandrus…'

The man was alone, his hair tossed from the gallop, his tunic smeared with blood. 'Did my nephew entice you away from us on some ridiculous hunt of his own? I despair! And you have missed a good day,' Gigni's face was flushed with colour and his eyes danced. 'We have a number of deer, some hares, some wildfowl and Messire le Comte brought down the boar!'

'We killed a buck, messire, and a boar…'

'You say! Then I am glad, for it was hard to entice you away from your business. I would not like to think it had been for nothing. We shall have tales to tell over our banquet. Come my boy, you look as if you need our *medicus* to check your arm. What happened?'

'Messire, may I speak with you privately?' Guillaume could see nothing of the rot yet, but he was forewarned.

Gigni frowned, looking toward the mingling guests. 'It is not convenient at this time.'

'Please…'

There was a moment's hesitation and then, 'Come. This way.'

They entered a small alcove with a bench seat. People walked back and forth but they were left alone.

'What worries you, Guillaume? You seem ill at ease…'

'Luzio…'

'Has he disgraced himself again?' Gigni sighed. 'It would not surprise me. You are my hope for him, you know. You have a quiet strength, a dignity and goodness about you.'

'Messire, he is dead.'

Gigni frowned again, opened his mouth, perhaps to argue. But then he studied Guillaume with a head slightly turned and a perplexed expression moving over his fine, elongated face. 'Dead?'

'The boar, messire. I was attacked,' Guillaume indicated his arm, 'and Luzio leaped in with the boar spear, but it broke in two before it could pierce the beast and instead, the boar impaled him. Adam and Henri killed the animal with the broken end as it gored Luzio. Both were flung around and have small head injuries from crashing to the ground. I am so very sorry…'

CHAPTER ELEVEN

×

He hated lying but he scrutinised every move, every flicker from Alexandrus Gigni. In such scrutiny was life or death. The man sat so still, no clue to his thoughts evident at all, not a twitch, and then he stood and excused himself, asking Guillaume to remain where he was and that he would return imminently.

He hailed his wife and navigated the chamber toward her, stopping to speak words with those who took him by the sleeve, smiling, clapping men on the back. Consummate behaviour. And Guillaume began to try and puzzle the man out. A merchant, and successful at that, privileged, with the ear and indeed friendship of nobility. He would not want this great hunt, this *event* for which he would be notable, to be affected in any way. This day would continue smoothly, Guillaume would bet his life on it.

Gigni's wife stood with their daughter, who held a young child in her arms. He towered over both women and his wife basked in her husband's elegance and notoriety in a quiet way, as she smiled at him. If such genteel expression was the measure of a person then Guillaume might say he would like her. Her veil was skewed and she had a dash of mud down her cheek, which Gigni rubbed with a linen square. He bent toward her and whispered and she drew back, her mouth forming an 'o', but he bent again and she comported herself. Then people stood in front of Guillaume and he leaned back against the wall, his broken wrist throbbing with a fierce ache that almost matched the beating of his heart.

Then the people moved and he noticed Madame Gigni nod, Alexandrus picking up her hand and kissing it. It was not the polite kiss of a man and a woman in society, but the intimate kiss of lovers who trusted each other. He touched his daughter's arm and stroked his grandchild's cheek and then turned back against the excited flow of guests, once again the host of autumn's most social event.

Eventually,

''Tis done. My family will host the banquet and shall be my proxies. The excuse is that difficult but worthy business has called me away and everyone knows I am a proud and successful merchant, so all is well. I do not want a pall over this...' he waved his hand. 'Least of all because of Luzio...'

Guillaume grabbed hold of those words. Truth? Or a shield against the truth. He himself second guessed every view of the man.

'But you must give me a moment,' Gigni continued. 'I must speak with Messire le Comte de Forez and make my apologies and ask him to accept the seat of honour tonight. I will meet you in the yard, Guillaume, and you may guide me to my nephew.'

He left Guillaume breathless with the smooth and indeed unemotional way the man had handled himself and yet it was difficult to be surprised and so Guillaume made his way to the *dorter* where Henri lay, almost asleep. Other men were in stages of dress and undress, cleansing the mud and sweat, the noise rising with the expectation of a good meal and entertainment.

'And?' asked Henri.

'It went well, although I am confused with the man's cool acceptance of the news. Strangely though, I trust him. Adam will no doubt chastise me for the thought but...' he shrugged his shoulders. 'I wonder where is the minstrel?'

'He was here, dressing into his finery, and I was able to tell him the news in peace and then he left, saying he would see us anon.'

'Did he make comment?'

'He said Luzio does not surprise many people. And then he cursed Pisans as the scum of the earth. Do you know why?'

'It is a tragic story for another time and perhaps,' Guillaume said thinking of Mehmet's words, 'it is for him to tell. There is more to him than you yet know. In any case, it may be we must leave here without him. In fact, methinks you should both follow on the morrow because Adam and I must leave immediately this next is done. To rest will give your head a chance to settle and it allows our musical friend to do what he must. In the meantime, Adam and I will go and show Messire what he wishes to see. *Valete*, my friend. Sleep well.'

Henri smiled vaguely and his eyes closed, leaving Guillaume to hurry to the yard and the *lavoir* where he washed himself as well as he could with one hand. Adam waited across the deserted yard with the horses and presently two men emerged from the stables on sturdy rounceys and another followed with a horse-drawn cart. Guillaume took his reins from Adam and used the mounting block again, gritting his teeth at the ache in his wrist, conscious of the bandage on his arm becoming damp and dark in the last of the afternoon sun. A breeze had begun and the horses' manes lifted, straw skirling across the hard-packed ground. Above them, palest grey clouds drifted across the sky, suggesting a weather change.

The servants talked quietly together and Adam and Guillaume waited, Adam listening to what had happened in the hall.

'You trust him,' Adam said. More of a statement than a question.

'I believe so.'

'So Luzio is not an apple from the same tree?'

'I would say not...'

Gigni rushed out the door and was handed his grey mount again. 'My apologies,' he said as he climbed the mounting block. 'I could not leave swiftly; it would have been rude and might have aroused undue curiosity. I want this handled with utter discretion. We shall take the body to the priory at Pommiers en Forez. It will be a slow journey but I will pay them well for caring for my nephew and I will have him buried there. What think you?' He nodded to his men and they moved out the gate.

'You must do what you think is right, Messire Alexandrus. It is not my position to comment,' said Guillaume.

'Nevertheless, I ask because I am impressed with you, Guillaume. I have been since you first took over the management of de Clochard from Madame Amée. You have handled yourself with a firm, quiet dignity of which I approve. If Luzio could have behaved so, I would have been well pleased.'

Guillaume thanked Alexandrus but said nothing more.

'You think I speak ill of my nephew now that he is dead? Nothing changes. When you visited me that first time, I told you he was undisciplined, I think. But there is more to it...'

Guillaume shifted his reins, and rested his arm against his chest.

'Your wrist hurts, and yet you do not complain. That is what I mean. You are strong. Luzio was a weak, self-opinionated fool. His family had difficulty with both he and his brother and they sent them to me to try and make something of them. His brother became a *routier* and joined the crusading force. Like yourself, I understand.'

Guillaume sat straighter. So Luzio's brother would have travelled to the Holy Land if he had lived? By God...

'But he died in Anjou as he rode to Marseille, waylaid by thieves perhaps, in the forest. It is sad for his family that both their sons have died, but I compare those men with my daughter's husband, with you, even with your Man at Arms,' he nodded at Adam, a complimentary glance, 'and they were a half, a quarter of you all. They were indulged, had no discipline and the family found them an embarrassment, I suspect. Pisa is a small town. They could be embarrassing elsewhere.'

They rode on in silence for a few strides, the late afternoon birdcall filling the air and removing the negative taint of the words that had dropped into Guillaume's lap.

'I don't mourn him, Guillaume. I would not have you think I am a hypocrite and will indulge in months of wailing and woe. Luzio died on the hunt. Better that he died in action protecting his friend, than in a back alley, stabbed for fornicating with some man's lover as was his want.'

Guillaume's soul curled with the lies he had told. He liked Messire Alexandrus a little more with each word he spoke but he knew that if the truth emerged, his own and de Clochard's reputation would be ground down to nothing in a heartbeat. He risked a glance at Adam, but the Londoner looked straight ahead along the track, ducking his head to avoid a low-hanging branch.

They reached the copse, the cart a little way behind and a pair of crows which had been stalking the edges of death, marking the carcasses for a feed, flew up, cawing their maudlin cries to the world. Luzio lay where he had been left, a little more wax-like, his eyes staring wide. Guillaume wished they had closed them immediately he had passed away but such things had not been thought of. The boar lay almost atop the deer, the broken spear piercing the skull down to the lugs, and the fine buck was frozen in death – the tableau had not changed at all.

'Lord have pity…' Alexandrus said and dismounted. He walked to Luzio's side. 'Astonishing that he can be as handsome in death as life. Few can claim the skill.' The cart rumbled in and he began to order the proceedings, a woollen cloth laid out, Luzio lifted onto it and wrapped gently before he was lifted into the cart. The servants then trussed the boar and the deer and loaded them onto the two saddled rounceys, whereupon they began to walk back to Choizey leading their macabre burden.

Alexandrus mounted his horse from a log and stared down at Guillaume and Adam. 'Go back to Choizey and enjoy what is left of the day and perhaps see my *medicus*. I thank you for … for this,' he said and looked at Luzio's shrouded body.

'Messire, we would leave now to return to Lyon and would stay overnight at the priory to which you take Messire Luzio. Perhaps we may accompany you if you will allow,' said Adam.

Gigni smiled tiredly. 'I would welcome your company at this time. It assuages the nasty taste I have in my mouth.'

The priory was as drear and tired as when Guillaume, Adam and Toby had reached it the day before. But Brother Hugo answered the call at the gates and pulled them wide for the cart to enter. The cat lay in his arms and watched, its tail swinging from side to side. Guillaume introduced Messire Gigni to the novice and the two began a conversation on how to proceed with the difficult task. It would seem that Father Jerome was lying even closer to death and would not be able to conduct a Mass.

'May I interrupt?' Guillaume asked. 'Brother Hugo, I am sure you know the necessary words. If Adam and Messire Gigni's man can dig the grave, may you not conduct a burial service?'

Hugo looked panicked. 'But I am not ordained.'

'A prayer is a prayer, is it not?' Guillaume said kindly. 'And Death and the Hereafter will not care. Neither will God, I think. As long as He can receive Messire Gigni's nephew into His embrace. By facilitating this, you will put Messire Gigni's mind at rest.'

Brother Hugo debated with his conscience and the cat arched its head and butted his chin. 'I will do it then. Would you have it done this night or on the morrow?'

'This night, if you please,' Messire Gigni said. 'My nephew deserves to rest in peace. He died protecting my friend here from a wild boar. He was a brave young man…'

'Right then,' said Adam. 'Brother Hugo, show me where are the tools and where is the graveyard and we shall dig the grave. Messire Guillaume and Messire Alexandrus, why do you not go to the refectory and have some refreshment? You must be tired…'

'We have little to share,' Brother Hugo said apologetically.

'I will make sure that from now on, Brother Hugo, your needs and those of this little village are met. I have already spoken with Messire le Comte de Forez and he will speak with his brother, the Archbishop. I thank you for putting yourself above and beyond what must be considered your duty just now and would avail myself of a drink of wine, if you will, and then your chapel, where I might pray for my nephew's soul.'

And so at dusk, and with a fading light and the sad cries of the forest birds carolling the oncoming of night, Luzio was laid to rest. Guillaume felt nothing but a relieved dislike, crossing himself when required, but longing to leave Messire Gigni behind and make haste to Lyon.

'*In nomine Patris, et Filii, et Spiritus Sancti. Amen…*'

He jerked from his ennui and crossed himself once more and then returned with the others to the small, dilapidated buildings of the priory. They ate and drank with Brother Hugo and Brother Francis, in dour silence, as befits a religious house, and Guillaume was glad for he had little to say. And finally, as the cracked bell rang for Compline he lowered his tired, tense body to the mattress of his cot.

'Guillaume,' said Alexandrus, before the candle was snuffed. 'I thank you. When we return to Lyon, we can perhaps move beyond this day, but I want you to know that I consider de Clochard a worthy competitor and you a man to admire.'

'You are kind, messire, but I have only done what is right in the situation and what any man might do. In any case, I look forward to passing the time of day with you in Lyon, perhaps sharing a wine. Goodnight, messire, and thank you for the hunt. I regret the outcome with all my heart.'

'Leave it now,' said Alexandrus. 'As shall I. Life moves on. Good night to you, my friend.'

The *dorter* rumbled with snorts, farts and snoring. Gigni's servant had a broken snore, a kind of whistle which would stop and then begin again with a gasp. Gigni himself snored without ceasing. Guillaume tested the depth of their sleep by coughing loudly but neither stirred.

Pain, the noise and the events of the day kept him awake until he could stand it no longer and eased himself from the cot. They had fallen into bed fully dressed with no clean attire into which to change and he picked up his boots as Adam rolled over and held a finger to his lips. He slipped out of his bed and joining him, crept quietly from the chamber. The snores faded as they moved further away along the cloister toward the stalls.

'Jesu,' Adam whispered. 'I've slept with noise in my time, but those two…' he blew out a relieved breath.

He saddled the horses in the dark, cursing as he twisted a strap and then they were done, leading the animals to the gates, opening the groaning timbers and squeaking hinges, on through – pulling the gates behind and setting off apace to beyond the village. They mounted by the light of a watery moon on the far side of a filthy night sky, and somewhere, an early bird called. As they pushed the horses at a smart walk along the track, the cracked bell rang for Matins, announcing to all who slept, that dawn was coming closer.

'Well?' Adam said. 'Gigni?'

Guillaume shrugged. 'Against my better judgement, I can find no fault but we know my better judgement is not good. What think you?'

'Different,' said Adam.

'You say? To my view?'

'No. To Luzio. I think he is a good man. Intelligent, sharp and fair. Christ knows how he managed his nephew. It would have been no easy task.'

'Then we can cross him off the list, can we not?'

'So it seems. Although I might yet be proved wrong but I doubt it.'

'Methinks Luzio started the fire, Adam. Or at the very least paid to have it started and I think Mahaut opened the gates and I think Brother Crispianus colluded with him with the assistance of that ugly bitch. He told me he spied me fletching my arrows with hawk feathers, that his brother had been killed with an arrow very similar. He apparently asked Mahaut about my background and it was she who told him I was from La Flèche where his brother was murdered…'

'Ah, I missed that,' said Adam. 'In fact it seems I have missed a lot. Let me guess. *You* killed his brother…'

'He raped and killed my mother and my stepfather.'

Adam pulled up his horse. 'Guillaume, I am bereft for you.'

Guillaume halted. 'I swore over my mother's ill-used body and over my father's…' he looked down at his hands, surprised to see them resting unclenched upon the pommel. 'They slit his throat, Adam. Almost beheaded him and I swore revenge. Finding out who did it in a place the size of La Flèche was easy. They were loud, drunken *routiers* who had made their mark, and in trying to defend herself, my mother tore Luzio's brother's sleeve. The rest was simple. But I think God watched and then took His time, making sure that eventually I would pay for such a crime. And it happened. I met Luzio. And he saw me fletching…'

Adam clicked his horse on. 'Such is life, Guillaume. Don't look back now, look forward. I heard a little of what Luzio said at the end and we still have work to do. We need to get back to Lyon and soonest. It's getting lighter, can you canter?'

Guillaume dug in his heels and his mount sprang to a steady, even stride and he and Adam sped through the tracks, past the tilled fields where crows were already pecking at worms. They stopped regularly to spell the horses, but had no food and had finished their costrels of wine long since. Once, they chanced upon an apple tree and found wrinkled fruit which they picked and ate, offering the cores to the horses.

And then their final run was upon them, approaching the gates of Lyon, seeing the city in the distance and realising that any breathing space was done, that now they had a monk's zeal with which to contend. Guillaume knew they could expect nothing from the Archbishop and suspected that any confrontation with Brother Crispianus would be covert and all the more dangerous for that.

They reached the gates as the last of the pilgrims, villeins and merchants walked through. As they waited to file in, a shrill hand bell rang like an alarm, cutting through the end of day murmur and rumble of the trickling crowds.

People jumped away, turning their heads, placing hands over noses and mouths as a group of lepers walked from the city. They were clad in travel-stained clothes, with worn cloaks, hoods and straw hats covering diseased faces. Some held begging bowls and others held staves and Guillaume felt in his purse, leaned down and dropped a *livre* in each of three bowls held out.

'Three *livres*?' Adam whispered.

'Adam, that could be you or I, and they harm no one. Unlike the monks and Pisans of this world.'

They rode on, twisting and turning until they came to Rue Tramassal and the Gigni gates.

'Would you call Messire Odo, if you please?' Guillaume asked of the gatekeeper. 'We are returning Messire Alexandrus' horses.'

By the time they had tied up and unsaddled the horses, Odo had hurried across the yard. His formerly neat appearance had changed, a dark green tunic stained with ink, his bluntly trimmed hair awry.

'Messire Guillaume. I was not expecting you, I have been working at my papers all day,' he apologised.

'We had to return early, Odo. If we could prevail upon an ostler to settle the animals, we can return to de Clochard quickly.'

'Is something wrong, messire?'

'One hopes not. But that aside, I suspect Messire Gigni will not be more than a day behind us. He may have quite some work for you to undertake…'

'How so?' The notary looked confused.

'I wish I could say, Odo, because you have been very good to us, but I think it must be for Messire Gigni to inform you of the detail.'

Odo's face creased with concern. 'Is the family well? We hold the Gigni members in the highest esteem, sir.'

'I assure you, the Gigni family is safe and well. But we must take our leave. Will you excuse us?'

'Of course,' Odo walked with them to the gates. 'I took your note to Messire Michael. Fortunately, he was there and I was able to give it to him directly.'

'I thank you. Your loyalty as the Gigni's notary is remarkable and I told Messire Alexandrus so.'

Odo smiled. 'Messire, it is I who am lucky to be working for them in this house. They are generous beyond measure.'

They made their farewells and hurried away along the street and then leaped down the gentle slope towards Rue Ducanivet and de Clochard.

'I think that proves the case,' said Guillaume, holding his arm against his chest. 'I like Odo and I don't believe his loyalty would be as marked if Gigni was rotten. Would you agree?'

'Yes. Which once again underlines our mad monk and the even madder servant. I don't want to make light of what is to come, Guillaume, but it helps me keep things sorted in my own head. If we consider the man mad it makes it so much easier to kill him…'

'Your moral code is one to be examined another time, Adam. I am sure you have thought it through.'

They turned along the river front as dusk lay an ivory sheen across the sky and heavy clouds skirted the horizon. The smell of the water rushed up to greet them and Guillaume could feel a gratefulness for home and hearth creeping upon him. But it could only take full effect when…

'Guillaume?' Michael's voice sounded behind them.

They both swung round to greet Amée's son-in-law. 'Michael!' Something of relief flowed through Guillaume because Michael smiled and if there were trouble of any kind, he would not – surely. 'All is well?'

'Of course. You have only been gone three days.' Michael scrutinised them both, saw the bandages and frowned.

'But things have gone badly for you, I think.'

'Somewhat. Perhaps we should talk inside the gates…' Guillaume walked into the yard, noting the oak tree was now completely bare and the yard swept clean. That the repairs of the barn and storeroom were completed and that the place looked as prosperous as a merchant house should. That the water butts were full. 'You have had rain whilst we were gone?'

'Yes, it rained every day. Which annoyed Amée as she plans her great entertainment for two days hence.'

'What?'

'To repay those who fought the fire for de Clochard. She plans a kind of banquet. With jongleurs and food, and she was hoping Tobias would hurry back to help her plan.'

'I see. And with what does she intend to pay?'

'She borrowed money from Joshua. She has completely changed her thinking about moneylenders now that she knows Jehan had dealings with him. She borrowed against the other half of the monies for the Hohenstaufen purple.'

Guillaume wondered at how quickly things had moved on in three days and took a breath. 'And you think we will still be in profit when we have paid back the debts?'

'I think so. There was a letter from Gisborne while you were gone. He says there are more fine woollens and some heavier cloth on the way here and that if the weather holds, we may receive them before winter. I have my doubts, although this letter was couriered after the goods were despatched. Methinks the letter and the shipment left Venezia only a day or so after we did. But even so, winter is coming. Be that as it may, though, he said the dyeing of the cloth is excellent and there will be colours that will be desired by men and women alike. There is also a length of purple velvet which he knows the Hohenstaufens will want. He said it is rather like already having a casket of monies, so sure is he of the sale.'

'Then my brother is a more courageous merchant than I. What think you?'

'I think he is right but come, let us hear of your doings.'

'Michael, before we go in, is Ariella well?'

'Yes, of course…'

'And who is within the house?'

'Jehanne and Ariella. Why?'

'Where are Mahaut and Amée?'

'The Cathedral.'

Adam and Guillaume exchanged glances.

'Then quickly,' said Guillaume. 'Whilst they are gone, we will tell you what occurred at the hunt. And I beg that you keep what we tell you quiet…'

Ariella flew out the door and into Guillaume's arms and he could barely help a cry as she crushed his arm and wrist.

'I knew it,' she muttered, on hearing the intake of breath, and examining his arm. 'It would be impossible for you to do anything without injury. I must be grateful that you still have a life to lead, I suppose. That is something!'

They all walked inside and she placed a quick kiss upon his hand as they entered the hall where Jehanne sat embroidering a dark green length of wool with scarlet thread. She looked up in surprise.

'A welcome return. But three days early…'

'They have news, Jehanne,' said Michael. 'Urgent news…'

Everyone sat close to the fire and its glow took the chill from Guillaume's words as he relayed the story of Luzio's death – the truth this time, not the gilded lies that had passed to Alexandrus Gigni.

'It was a matter of expediency that we kept the truth from Gigni,' said Guillaume. 'We needed to know he could be trusted in the future as a fellow merchant in Lyon and it seems he can, but even so, I do not want him knowing that *I* killed Luzio's brother and Luzio planned to kill me because of it.'

'*That*, we keep to ourselves,' Adam reiterated 'But what has not been told to you yet is that the fire was started by Luzio and some hired felons, and that all the attacks upon Guillaume, even in the Forez, were because of Luzio. But you should also know that Brother Crispianus has been a willing partner for two reasons – one is because of the Vaudès Bible which was indeed in the house. I found it the night before we left…'

'You say?' Jehanne frowned. 'Do you think *Maman* knew?'

'In truth Madame, I suspect she did not. This is something that your father did secretly for the *Sandalati*. And we took the book with us for its safety and yours. But let me tell of the second reason. We believe the monk partnered with Luzio because of *Dameisele* Ariella, a Jewess residing in a Christian house. He readily passed information as to her whereabouts at crucial times.'

'Then we shall protect her like gold in the future, shall we not?' Jehanne said. 'As to the Bible?'

'Tobias will bring it back on his return and then we must find some of the itinerate preachers. From what we can gather, it is the original Bible that Pierre Vaudès had copied. To the Poor Men of Lyon, it would be like having Christ's shroud within their midst.'

Jehanne placed some more stitches through her fabric and then said, 'Do you feel some kind of moral duty to pass the book on, Guillaume?'

'In a way. I suspect your father hid it within the house for them, with every intention of passing it to a man called Hamelyn who would then take it out of Lyon to Piedmont. Sadly, your father died and with him, the plans for the book's escape. And the truth is, I certainly don't think your mother has any idea at all.'

Jehanne answered dryly. 'Just as well. *Maman* can have a loose tongue and would have brought the wrath of the Church down upon us.'

'But there is one other thing I must tell you,' Guillaume took a breath. 'It is about Mahaut. Luzio said she helped him, opened the gates for his men to light the fire. In addition, he said as he died that he had won, that Brother Crispianus and Mahaut would make sure of it. The fact is that her loyalty is not to this family, Jehanne. It is to the Church and to the monk. She has a twisted zeal that the priest has used to his advantage and she sees no wrong in any threat she puts before de Clochard. She has been subverted well and truly.'

Jehanne sat back. 'But she would not hurt my mother, surely...'

'And yet she opened the gates to allow some firemongers in.' Adam spoke with no ambiguity. 'Your mother may have been burned to a crisp.'

Jehanne snipped her thread with a small dagger and laid the frame down. 'If it wasn't that I spoke with Soeur Marie yesterday, I would kill Mahaut. But by mentioning Mahaut's voice, I may have avoided eternal damnation for myself and for de Clochard. Our gentle Chambress with whom you have dealt for so long, said the Precentrix is always looking for excellence for her choir. There may be a solution here...'

There was complete silence as the five companions sat and revelations were digested. Guillaume's arm ached and he longed for some food and drink and for some sleep. It seemed he had been wakeful ever since the fire and he now began to crave an unbroken night of rest so that he could begin anew. But he was afraid to let go, afraid for Ariella.

She had sat so still during the discussion and now, she took his good hand in her own. 'I am used to sentiment against me. And I have fought for myself and my Faith before. I can do so again. I have made this clear before.'

'No, that is not how it shall be,' said Jehanne. 'You will not have those threats hanging over you, day in day out. We will make sure...'

'You cannot.' Ariella stood. 'Without removing the monk and Mahaut, you cannot.'

'Then that...'

'You cannot indulge in cold-blooded murder. I will not add that to the list of things for which I must beg forgiveness.'

'But it would solve the danger,' Adam said. 'He will bring this house down in his search for the Bible and with his hatred of the Jewish faith.'

They talked around Ariella and over her and she and Guillaume lapsed into silence. But Guillaume knew her silences were like a smouldering coal; that sooner or later, a flame would jump and all the kindling in the hearth would conflagrate. Her hands lay in her lap, the sapphire ring glistening in the subtle light of dusk.

'*If*,' she said quite loudly and everyone turned to her. '*If* I might speak? Thank you.' There was nothing but cool determination in her tone. 'I thank you for your concern, but you must listen to me when I say this. I will not be cowed by one monk's hatred of Jews, no matter how twisted you think he might be. A Jew's life is not an easy path here. Nor anywhere. Phillip Augustus made sure of that when he expelled Jews from Paris and burned many of us at the stake. Nor when he took our property and annulled Christian debts to us.'

She stood, a flaming column of autumnal colours, and began to walk back and forth. 'But we survive. We carry on. And yes, we even do business. You forget I survived York.'

Jehanne went to speak but Ariella undercut her. 'No, Jehanne, you do not understand. My father was not in our house the day that Malebisse, de Fauconberg, Percy and Darell incited York to kill my family and friends. All the Jews fled to the castle keep in the hope of being safe. I was buying fruit and nuts when they ran. I heard the mob and I hid. I found a cellar, pushed my way inside and stayed there till dark. All of York was at the castle walls and so it was no effort to slide from shadow to shadow until I reached the gates. When they were opened next day, I joined a group of pilgrims leaving for the Holy Land and once outside, managed to escape into the surrounding countryside. The pilgrims had spoken of negotiations with our people in the keep, but such negotiation was in word only and our rabbi, Rabbi Yomtob, and one of our senior Jews knew the mob would rape and slaughter everyone. So they slit the throats of the women and children and then killed themselves.'

She looked around at everyone. 'Jews would rather die by their own hand in the face of God and with the blessings of the Faith than suffer the wrath of an incited mob. Can you imagine? And my mother was one of those who gave of her life.'

Guillaume took her hand, holding her back from her agitated pacing but she shook him off.

'In my heart, I knew my father was not in that keep. And I was right. A day later, I managed to make my way back into York. I was a filthy peasant, not a sign of the wealthy Jew's daughter that I had been and I roamed the streets until I found Father, ribs broken and face smashed and him left for dead. I sought help from those who had used our family's services in the past, a Christian family I trusted. De Tourney by name. Good people. They helped us leave secretly and from then on, we travelled from one city to the next until we settled in Venezia. There we were safe. There we healed ourselves and began to prosper with people like Gisborne. There my father salved the harsh cut that is grief.'

She sat then, pulsing with her memories 'So you see, that is why I learned to fight like a she-wolf for myself and those I love. I will leave Lyon when *I* am ready and not by fear or force.' She fixed them all with an amber glare, and pride in her spirit filled Guillaume's heart and soul.

Fear for her filled his mind.

'*Dameisele*,' said Adam. 'You would be a worthy amongst men, but I owe it to your father, the *best* of men, and to Guillaume here, and to you, to make sure you are *never* alone and always protected.'

She grimaced and shook her head.

'*Never* alone,' Adam repeated. 'And if that is all you have to put up with until this debacle is done, then you can thank the Lord … or whomever it is you pray to.'

Guillaume waited for the explosion but it didn't come. Instead she bent down and kissed the top of Adam's head, her fine chestnut and gold locks mixing with his flaming red hair. They could have been brother and sister.

Adam spoke firmly. 'I will have my men primed and on watch, mind, but I tell you, I am disturbed there is to be a banquet, with its associated dangers. Unless we hide you *both* somewhere…'

'That is a nonsense, Adam, and I think you worry unnecessarily,' scoffed Ariella. 'Prime your men, though, if you wish, and I shall be armed as well. The truth is that as a Jewess, I am never not.'

As she spoke, there was the vociferous chatter of the widow in the yard and in moments, she had rolled into the house, cheeks red with cold and a smile of great pleasure upon her face.

'Oh, Guillaume. I prayed for your safe return and here you are! Oh,' she gasped as she noticed the bloodied and splinted arm. 'Did you encounter a boar? Really? Oh, Lord God, how dangerous and exciting! You must regale us...'

Mahaut eyed both Guillaume and Ariella with undisguised hatred and Guillaume thought one could be forgiven for thinking how like a boar she was, with her hairy chin and wide spaced, tiny eyes.

Ariella forestalled any more talk, asking Mahaut to heat water for the men to bathe in the barn, and a fresh round of acid glances shot between them. Amée added to the woman's angst by asking that the wines be the best from their casks, for tales from the Forez deserved a toast, did they not?

'By God,' said Adam as he helped Guillaume pull off his tunic, then his chemise. 'She has had time to fester and rot in three days. 'Tis as well she hasn't taken to poisoning.'

'It is a thought that has crossed my mind frequently. How easy it would be to poison Ariella and myself. I suspect the monk has instructed her otherwise. I am unclear why in my case, but as for Ariella, my mind churns with fear.'

'What do you say?' Ariella walked in as Guillaume sank into the half barrel.

'We talk of Mahaut...'

'Then don't. The very fact that we live with her is trial enough. To talk of her is a step too far. Guillaume, I want to see your arm before you dress and now is as good a time as any. Adam, will you excuse us?'

'Of course, *Dameisele*,' he lowered his blushing face and backed out of the barn.

'You embarrassed him walking in when I was naked, Ariella...'

'Naked? You have half a wine cask over you. And your arm is more important. Hold still.'

She began to unwind the gory bandage, leaving the wrist alone. 'I trust Adam to splint you but this looks like something that needs a physician. Oh...'

The bandage strips fell away and Guillaume looked. There was a wide puncture mark which had torn upward, and even now, blood dripped freely to the floor as his arm hung over the edge of the barrel.

'Does it hurt?'

'Honestly? Yes. Is it clean, do you think?'

'I will flush it myself and then I shall get a physician...'

'No – you do it all. Flush it with wine, flush it and flush it. Stitch it shut and then put honey over it. Then bind it. And if you change the dressing daily, it will heal.'

'And this from the Crusade, presumably.'

'And many other things besides.'

'If you say. I shall get some wine, Amée's best, and some honey and bandages. I won't be long. Adam can help you get out.'

Adam returned within heartbeats, muttering, 'Christ's beard but she's a fireball, isn't she?'

Guillaume agreed, adding, 'I haven't dripped in the water, it is clean for you if you can help keep my arm clear as I get out.'

'Very kind,' Adam muttered and held a cloth under Guillaume's arm as he levered his body out. He patted himself dry with the cloth as Adam stripped off and jumped in. 'By the saints, that does feel good. Thank you, Mahaut, for the water. *Dameisele*!'

Ariella hurried back into the barn. 'Oh, Adam, who cares? I do not.'

Guillaume couldn't help laughing and it felt good. So much tension, one laugh and his limbs relaxed a little. 'Don't tease him, 'Ella. We shall go elsewhere, if you help me...'

'Wrap this cloak around and you may come to the storeroom. I will dress the wound there. Gosse may be asleep but we must manage.' She flung an old cloak round Guillaume, the wool prickling on his bare skin and then she stalked off, calling, 'Until later, Adam. Don't drown!'

Guillaume hurried after her, trying to hold the folds of the cloak around as well as pressing a cloth to his arm. 'You have your bit of fun, you tease!'

'We all need to laugh more. I wish Tobias were back. It is his skill...'

'He will be here by tomorrow. By the banquet at the latest.'

'You do not approve of Amée's idea?'

Guillaume knew that they must repay the kindness and bravery of their neighbours. He had indicated as much when he thanked them after the fire. But timing in life is all and this seemed so wrong and he said so.

'But you know Amée. Once she wants something, then she will get it. I told her it would cost quite a lot of money. Thus we went to Joshua, *with* Herviet and Gosse before you ask, and she put her request, claiming monies coming from Germany would pay him back, and he placed a loan in her hands. It was done in less than a half day.'

Guillaume had no trouble then imagining invitations carried to the neighbours in Rue Ducanivet and La Grande Rue. No doubt even to the Gigni house. The district would be filled with excitement. 'I must accept that it is done then, whether I disagree or not, and deal with it as best we can...'

Gosse lay on his stomach, another snorer, and barely moved as they entered the storeroom now called the guard quarters.

'Ow!' Guillaume grabbed at his arm as she poured wine directly into the wound. 'Ow!' he whispered more carefully as Gosse moved and snorted.

'Don't be a baby,' she whispered back, patting it dry and then beginning to stitch with a double silk thread and bone needle. He ground his teeth so she thrust a piece of smooth wood between his lips. It was tucked into her girdle as if she expected him to cry out and then she began to stitch finely – many stitches drawing the jagged wound together. 'Good...' she said, knotting and then cutting the thread with her dagger. She flushed it again and again until it looked as if a cask had broken open at Guillaume's feet.

He spat out the stick. 'I shall smell like a drunk.'

'Better that than a decomposing corpse.' Her slim fingers ladled honey along the wound, and then she covered it with a square of fine linen, wrapping the arm in creamy white strips. The strips around his wrist were changed and she commented on the startling blue and yellow bruise braceletted between the splints.

'Shall I remove the stitches in your back whilst I am embroidering? It looks messy but it is clean and the stitches have done their work.'

On his agreement, she picked away at Adam's handiwork and then gently lifted the hair on his neck to check that wound as well. 'My poor Guillaume. So much pain – because of a man, a monk ... and me.'

'Luzio being the man,' he said as she slipped a clean chemise over his head.

'Yes. How clever he was to fool us all...'

'Indeed.' Fools, every one of us, he thought.

She pulled a scarlet tunic over the chemise and then held out *braies*. 'Shall I continue?'

'I have no dignity left,' he replied. 'Why not?'

And so she finished dressing him and still Gosse snored and they left him to his slumber to return to the house. He felt clean and cossetted and in truth, the pain felt less because he was surrounded by a strong household whom he knew would stand at his and Ariella's backs. They just needed Tobias and even Henri de Montbrison – after all, Adam liked the man – and they would be complete.

'Ah, they return cleaned and polished,' Amée smiled as Guillaume and Adam walked into the hall accompanied by Ariella. 'Good. Are you hungry?'

'Madame, I could demolish a horse and an ox,' said Adam. 'My stomach roars with hunger.'

'I have meats left from our dinner and we have bread – Mahaut brought excellent wastel from the baker's booth near Rue Tramassal today. There is cheese and some late autumn fruit. Will this fill your belly, Adam of London?'

''Tis a feast, Amée,' Guillaume said. 'After a hard ride, even just cheese and bread would suffice.'

'We can do better than just cheese and bread, Guillaume. It may not be banquet quality but it is wholesome. Now, eat first, think you?'

'Madame,' Adam piped up. 'If I could be so bold, *please* eat first.'

Good man. It gives me time to decide what to say…

Amée sat back, her chin folds billowing over her wimple. 'Then while you eat, I shall regale you with *our* news. Jehanne has told you we have a banquet in two days? Mahaut,' she called loudly through the door. 'You may bring in the food!'

They heard the moody '*Oc*' and Jehanne quickly assured her mother that the returned hunstmen did indeed know of her little event.

Mahaut carried in platters of meat slices, wastel, cheeses, dates, apples and figs. The mutton had been cooked with spices and reminded Guillaume of the ships docking in Venezia. Loaded with such things, when a fresh breeze blew off the water the exotic aroma would drift across the islets as far as Gisborne's villa. It was a reminder of a life to which he wished he could return he and Ariella right now.

'Shut the door if you would, Mahaut. A breeze blows in from outside,' Amée said as the last platter was lifted over Guillaume's shoulder and whacked down on the table. He caught Adam's eye and grimaced as Jehanne called Mahaut back.

'Madame Jehanne?' The servant acknowledged her with deference and let it be said, affection. The shift in her manner was like a weather change –

heavy cloud drifting away from the sun.

'Mahaut, Tobias has told us of the gifted voice you have and that you have always craved to join the convent...'

Mahaut's expression had softened. Even as she stood in front of those she despised at the table. She clasped her hands tightly in front of her. 'To sing for God, Madame. It is my heart's desire. Messire Tobias is kind to say my voice is good.'

'He says more than that. And when we were at the convent yesterday delivering remnants, we talked with Soeur Marie. She will take you to talk with the Precentrix who will want to hear your voice, and if she considers it good enough then they will take you to the Mistress of the Novices...'

Really? You did not say this earlier. Methinks we come to your solution...

'But Madame,' Mahaut looked as if a gateway to Heaven had revealed itself and then the door shut in her face. 'I have no dowry monies. They will not accept me.'

'De Clochard will pay your dowry.'

As Mahaut gasped audibly, Amée turned to her daughter. 'Jehanne! How could you? What shall I do without her?'

'*Maman*, you have me,' she took Amée's hand. 'You may never have a servant as accomplished as Mahaut again, but Messire Michael and I feel that we can compensate reasonably well. More importantly, Mahaut has a Divine gift, and it would be wrong for her not to lay it before Our Lord. It would be even worse if we prevented her from doing so.'

Both Mahaut's and Amée's mouths opened and closed but nothing emerged and Guillaume had to fix his attention upon a windfall apple from which a dried leaf hung.

One danger removed into the arms of God. There is an irony there, if I had the time to unpick it...

'And so tonight is your last night with us. Take yourself off now, and do whatever you must to prepare.'

'Madame!' Tears slid down her fat face and she rushed to Jehanne and kneeled by her side, grasping her hand and holding it to her cheek. 'I cannot thank you enough but I will miss you and Madame...'

'Yes, yes. And we will miss you. Now go to prepare.'

The servant looked nonplussed, as if her mind could not process what she had heard. That her life would now change completely. That she would be a servant of God, a Bride of Christ. If it were possible for her sallow face and pig eyes to alter at all, one could almost say she was radiant. Guillaume, however, decided it was a trick of the light. He tried to imagine her robed and singing with other nuns behind the screen at the convent services.

He could not.

As she stood, she caught his eye and then her gaze slid to Ariella and she seemed confused. 'Do you mean, Madame Jehanne, that after tomorrow I shall never return here?'

Christ but she's dimwitted…

'Yes.'

Mahaut's eyes rested on Ariella as if she were in the midst of a dilemma and then she quickly pulled herself back from whatever murky place she had retreated to and said 'Thank you. Madame Jehanne, I am in your debt.'

As she walked to the door, Jehanne's voice followed her in what was almost a warning. 'Perhaps you are, Mahaut. As we have been in yours for some time. But this is our way of showing gratitude to you and to God. Perhaps you can give your voice to God as a form of gratitude as well. Go now, with our thanks and fondness.'

Chapter Twelve

×

Guillaume was in awe of Jehanne.

That she felt such warmth to the family servant was an untruth and he doubted that she and Michael spoken with Soeur Marie to such a degree. If they had, then the two showed great foresight and he knew then that de Clochard could only go from strength to strength under their aegis. It seemed that as soon as Amée's little occasion was done, there would be little stopping Ariella and himself leaving Lyon.

'Well played, Madame,' said Adam.

'Well played?' snorted Amée. 'You have removed my right hand and I am aghast!'

'*I* am your right hand, *Maman*. And Mahaut's voice *is* angelic. One of the most renowned troubadours has said so.'

'But a dowry! How can we afford this?'

'In the same way that we will pay for your banquet. It has been organised so. Now, let us hear what Guillaume and Adam have to tell us.'

Guillaume had decided what he would pass on to Amée. It would be cut as neatly as Ariella might cut her cloth. Snip, snip and the edges would disappear. He relied on Adam to follow his lead and for the others to underline it with subtlety. It was perhaps fortuitous that Amée had been so shocked with the speed of Mahaut's approaching departure that she listened quietly, slumped in her chair.

Finally,

'Oh,' she uttered, tears filling her eyes. 'He died saving your life. What a courageous and brave man. Poor Luzio. And my heart breaks for his family and for poor Messire Gigni.' She dabbed at her cheeks. 'I gave an invitation to their notary this morning. But even if they returned in time, it would be unseemly for them to attend.'

Guillaume told of Luzio's burial and explained why he and Adam had returned immediately it was done. 'We could not stay. Luzio saved my life and died for it. I would not rub salt into Messire Gigni's wounds with our presence. He is after all a perceptive and generous man and I would not want to disturb he and his family.'

Amée nodded. 'I presume this must be kept quiet until the family returns?'

'Yes, *Maman*,' Jehanne impressed upon Amée. 'We must respect the Gigni family in this and show that we are sensitive to their distress.'

'Perhaps we should we cancel our entertainment?' Amée asked.

'No,' Guillaume replied. 'We must go on as usual. People will wonder otherwise. This is Gigni news that must be made public by them, not us. Which they will do in their own time. So the plans don't change.'

The evening began to wind down with yawns and blinking as Amée recalled moments with Luzio. Guillaume cursed the name and as the women carried the detritus of the meal to the kitchens and the men stood at the hearth, they talked softly.

'You really spoke with Soeur Marie?' Guillaume asked Michael.

'I did not but Jehanne did.'

'To the point of placing Mahaut within the convent?'

'Ah, that was news to me as well. I suspect that Jehanne may have been quite manipulative tonight and will be like a duck on water tomorrow. Calm on the surface but paddling furiously underneath as she tries to organise for the Preceptrix and Mistress of the Novices to move to her tune rather than the convent's and rather quickly if I may say. I did tell you she was strong.'

Guillaume smiled. 'And we are grateful.'

'One down, one to go, think you?'

Adam grimaced. 'Badly chosen words, Messire Michael. We heard almost the same yesterday as Luzio chased after Guillaume.'

The women returned and Jehanne said with a sharp edge of delight, 'Mahaut cleans everything in our kitchens. She said she would not leave what has been her family until she has done so. And listen…'

Faintly, through the stone and timber walls, they could hear the melody of *Carmina Qui Quondam* filling the air.

'Lord be praised,' Amée said. 'Tobias is right and I never knew.'

Adam excused himself as Jehanne, Michael and Amée wandered to their chamber. Guillaume and Ariella remained sitting in the glow of the dying fire, the candles having expired.

'Are you in pain?' Ariella ran her finger down his arm.

He shook his head but laced fingers through hers. He was sure they were bound by something immeasurable, something beyond their faiths – or lack thereof in Guillaume's case. As her fingers lay meshed in his, he knew for a certainty that Saul would agree to this marriage. There would be a caveat no doubt – *Thy people shall be my people and thy God my God.* If it meant that he could share a life with Ariella, he would say it. God was God after all. He had seen too much to argue the point.

Saul and Ariella had been nomads born of Faith and fear. Venezia was a burgeoning city – a place of disparate beliefs and people, where they could be safe. It was a place that had begun to challenge the old societal order as a powerful merchant class developed and Venezia's trading name launched ships and men.

Lyon's violence was not such a shock after her past life, but it may well have been a surprise after Venetian domesticity and he said so.

'In a way,' she mused. 'But one never forgets past injustices and as I've often said, one remains alert. It is the way of it.'

'Then what would you say if I suggested we leave after Amée's celebration? The business is in good hands now, and I see no point in confronting Brother Crispianus further.'

She looked down at the sapphire ring and twisted it round her finger. He was sure that somewhere in the Jewish Talmud, the giving of a ring was a binding betrothal.

'The suggestion has merit. I miss my father greatly. But Guillaume, you know I wanted to become a merchant of my father's ilk. Not in his shadow, but using my own wits…'

'And have you not done that here?'

'Yes … to a degree.'

'Well, you have little to prove, do you? Besides, there is no reason for you not to travel to markets beyond Venezia. We would go together as husband and wife.'

'You make a perfect case.'

'Then?'

'After Amée's so-called banquet.'

'After. And I am glad.' He kissed her forehead and then stood, bidding her goodnight. Outside, the night sky lowered at him, as if chastising.

It is the right thing to do. She needs to be safe...

As he lay in his cot, the threaded ropes creaking, he could have laid on hot coals and slept, so tired was he. He had gone for longer periods in the Holy Land without sleep, but one was primed, a visceral fear that kept one moving through exhaustion. It had taken months for that fear to ease enough for him to give in to proper sleep. Gradually, as Gisborne's Venetian villa wrapped its soporific and watery peace around him, he dropped his guard and found he slept for two hours, maybe three or four.

Since the fire, however, the fear had risen like a phoenix and he remained alert for hours at a time. But tonight was different. That he was exhausted was a given, but the knowledge that Ariella was safe, that he had Gosse, Herviet, Adam, Raol and Michael to share the load made it easier for sleep to advance its dark hand toward him. He sighed – in that one breath, so much tension released. He sighed again and as the mule answered with a halfhearted snort, sleep finally claimed him, body and mind – a dreamless slumber where he lay on his back, his damaged arm lying loose by his side.

He woke the following morning to the sound of rain on the roof and to the cluck of Amée's disconsolate fowl at the barn door as they heard the drops falling to the ground. The horses shifted their hooves, turning their rumps to the entrance. But the mule just hung its head over the rails and stared at Guillaume in his cot.

He stretched, loosening muscles that had bunched and stiffened as he slept the sleep of the dead. Thinking such a thought, he uneasily made the sign of the cross, his fingers touching his forehead, his chest and his shoulders. He could almost hear Alain's immature voice saying *In Nomine Patris et Filii et Spiritus Sancti. Amen.*

Protect us, Alain…

And then he lay still – the oyster light of a grey day seeping under the door. He listened to the rain – a tattoo, like someone playing a *tabour* with agile fingers rather than a stick. He couldn't hear anything from the house – no Amée, no ugly Mahaut. Nothing to disturb his peace as his cot enticed him further down into its warmth. A few moments more, he thought, wanting to ignore what Amée might want them all to do this day. The cot had a mother's warmth, cosseting and loving, but in such a thought lay deep sadness and so he fixed his gaze on the door, urging his mind to stay empty of thought for a few moments longer.

But the door was eased open and the mule turned its head curiously, its flop ears lifting to momentary attention as a hooded figure stepped in.

'You're awake,' Adam noted, throwing back his hood. 'Good. We need to talk before the house wakes.'

Guillaume frowned.

And so we begin again…

'Come in, Adam. You are up early?'

'Gosse and Herviet came in from their nightshift and I had to wake Raol for his shift. I will join him shortly. Godawful day for it. We have been lulled into a false sense of ease till now with the weather. But just a quick word, if you please.'

Guillaume sat up, swung his legs over the bed and asked Adam to help him slip on his tunic and boots. He had slept in everything else – too tired and too disabled to manage the rest.

'I am going to be of little use to you as a guard, Adam. I can fight with my left hand if pushed but I am essentially right-handed…'

'I am not concerned. We have five able men and when Toby returns we will have seven because I suspect Henri might stay for a time. Thank the stars that Mahaut will be gone, because another two to add to the household and I think she would have set fire to us all! What a blessing that she will be pushed sideways into the Church. Ha! I would like to see the monk's face when he hears that!'

'Don't laugh too hard, Adam. It may be that he is losing an *espie* here, but that will only make him all the more rabid. Imagine when Tobias turns up again. Brother Crispianus will see a Jewess, and a malformed imp. If there was any doubt before that this was a heretic's house, then it will be a surety in his eyes now.'

'Which is why I wanted to quickly talk with you about this banquet Madame de Clochard has initiated. It's filled with danger, of course. But the only thing in its favour is that it actually takes place within our yard and that we will have seven able men to defend the space and its inhabitants. I am thankful she didn't go ahead with the idea to have it on the Pont du Change. I remember she wanted to emulate La Fête des Merveilles. Imagine on the bridge!'

Guillaume had never seen the Fête but had been informed it was a gory Church event where white bulls were pushed into the Saône and then fought until killed. The remains were then pulled ashore, butchered, cooked and then eaten. The white bull was a symbol of redemption for tardy souls wishing to enter Heaven.

If there is logic in such a belief, I cannot find it…

But he was grateful Amée had been persuaded away from a *fête* on the bridge or even at the convent on Presque L'ile– so much scope for a vengeful attack on onlookers and participants and he said so, pulling a leather girdle from the floor and passing it to Adam to sling around his waist.

'But even so,' the Londoner said. 'Even though it is a small space here, danger can lurk at the end of a knife in a crowd. And every man who enters the gates will have a knife with which to eat. Can you find out how many folk Madame has invited? Forewarned, you see.'

'Of course. Is there anything else?'

'Nothing beyond more of the same. On guard always and *Dameisele* Ariella goes nowhere unaccompanied.'

They left the barn and hurried through the rain to the house, noting that candles were lit in the kitchens and that Mahaut moved about. Far away, at the Cathedral, the bells rang for Prime.

'By the Virgin Mother, but I am glad she will be gone,' Guillaume said in a low voice. 'Sometimes I think she presented more threat within the house than the monk without. Ariella was menaced all hours of the day and night.'

Adam snorted. 'I tell you, if anything will make me return to God, it is that.'

When they entered the hall, the fire was burning, candletrees had been lit and the remains of the bread, fruit and cheese had been placed on the long table along with jugs of fruit wine. Amée greeted them.

'I couldn't sleep. I thought about Luzio and about our banquet and so I left Michael and Jehanne in peace and came down to the fire to plan what we must do for tomorrow. Will you both sit?'

They sat as ordered and Adam pierced an apple and began to peel as he liked to do, with a trail of red falling between his knees to the floor.

'I will need trestles, Adam. But in lieu of those, Soeur Marie has agreed to lend us planks that the convent use when it is market time. We can use our own casks as supports. If you would be so kind as to take the mule and cart and collect them? Soeur Marie says it is payment for the cloth pieces we give her and that the Archbishop's notary need not know. Damn the wretched man to perdition.'

She crossed herself and Guillaume smiled. Such a little firebrand when she wanted.

'I have asked the baker from whom we collect our bread to set up a stall in the yard,' she continued. 'Ariella and I will go to the market this morning and collect more eggs, fruit, nuts, almond meal and sugar and we shall cook fritters and *darioles*, maybe some *gaylede*. Custards perhaps,' she sighed then. 'Mahaut had a hand as light as a wisp of river mist with custards. Ah well, we shall have to make-do. Oh! Of course! Jehanne and Michael go with Mahaut to the convent as soon as they have broken their fast, so perhaps they can take the cart and collect the planks. Tuh! Mahaut's departure happens so quickly I can barely think straight.' She stopped then, as the remains of last night's bread found its way to her mouth, the fire popped and cracked and the trickling sound of wine being poured into a mug by Adam softened the edge of silence.

But,

'God and the Saints!' Amée blurted through her chewing. 'I forgot the meat! I have ordered a pig and some fish from the Golden Fleece. It can be collected after midday with a cask of their second best wine and some of their fruit wines. So will you do that, Guillaume, please? Oh, I tell you, this is exhausting. But we owe it to those who saved de Clochard and I think we must show we are a successful merchandising force as well...'

'Amée,' asked Guillaume. 'How many have you invited?

'All those from Rue Ducanivet and Rue Tramassal. They are the ones who fought the fire. I even asked old Matthieu, for all that he will cough his way through the entire proceedings.'

'How many?'

'Twenty? Perhaps a little more. But less than thirty, I think.'

'So many? Then I hope not too many more because that is a squeeze into the yard,' Guillaume said.

'I know. But Michael persuaded me the convent grounds would displease the Archbishop, even if the Abbess agreed. And he said the Pont du Change was beyond our capabilities as we would have the whole of Lyon wanting to be entertained. He said this way, we can oversee everything.' She grabbed the end of her veil and tugged absently. 'Excuse me, I must get some food for the others. I think Mahaut's head is in Heaven today if she thinks that this is enough for us all to break our fast.'

She waddled off, counting the eggs she thought she might need for preparing the feast and Adam muttered, 'Well done, Michael!'

'Indeed.' But Guillaume wondered how they would guard anyone or anything when all were packed inside the yard like sardines in a fisher's pail.

Restraint coloured the household farewell of Mahaut. The drizzle persisted and the sky still frowned upon Lyon. Guillaume and Ariella stood back, watching the servant as she turned a cold back upon them to grasp Amée's hand.

'Madame, forgive me…'

'For leaving me? I should, but…'

'No…'

'Mahaut,' called Jehanne. 'It is time to go. The Precentrix will not wait.'

Michael edged out from behind Ariella and Guillaume, whispering, 'Given that the Precentrix has no idea we come with a potential choir member, that is an understatement.' He raised his eyebrows at his friends and grasped the mule's bridle. The mule hung its head, unimpressed with the idea of walking out in the rain.

Amée's face crumpled whilst Mahaut's completely subsided.

'You *must* forgive me,' she whimpered as Jehanne took her arm and guided her after the cart and through the gates.

'I had thought she would skip to the convent with joy,' Ariella said.

'She seeks to right her wrongs before she enters the convent. I pity the other novices because she has a vicious streak. Life in the convent will either beat it out of her or make it worse.'

Amée walked back to the house, her face red with emotion. 'I shall miss her. She was a good servant…'

'She was. Of that there is no doubt. But shall we go to the markets now? It might help to brighten your day,' Ariella said. 'After all, you are about to throw a banquet that will make a mark for de Clochard. What think you?'

'Oh yes. We must. This is to go down in the history of de Clochard – *if* the sun ever shines! Jehan would have loved to be a part of the event. He had many good friends…' She almost wept again but Ariella swept her up in good cheer.

'And his wife is no different. Nor is his daughter. This is the chance to introduce Jehanne and her husband to our neighbours. Show them just what leadership exists within this house and this company. Now – did you have flour on your list? The supplies are low in your granary.'

The two walked into the house discussing lists and food, as baskets and cloaks were collected. Guillaume hurried to his cot to fetch his own cloak and as they emerged, he said, 'I shall come with you. An extra arm does no harm.' He did not look at Ariella as he spoke.

The drizzle had weakened to a fine mist that settled on their clothes like dew on spiders' webs. Ariella's hair curled around the edge of her hood and Amée's veil hung limp and lifeless around her wimple. For all that she looked doleful, her spirit began to improve as they turned into La Grande Rue.

'We must stop at the Cathedral, if you will. I must ask God to bless our day. I missed Mass and will be too busy to go tomorrow until the banquet is done.'

'Can you not ask God for a blessing whilst you sit under the oak tree? Or open your window and speak to the Heavens before bed?' Guillaume asked.

'You are so facile about God, Guillaume. As I have said before, it will come back to bite you one day.'

'And I replied that God and I have an understanding. Do you remember?'

He could see that this day would be overlong as Amée built herself to fever pitch over the morrow. But he was with Ariella and it was all that mattered.

As they walked, he enquired of business whilst he was gone.

'Good,' said Ariella. 'Some sales of woollen cloth and Messire Ricard's wife came to look at some cloth for her husband. She had to match it to some leather with which he has asked she trim the hems. The idea has merit, but embroidery would be better. Nevertheless, the customer is never wrong and she left with a fine length of mud-brown wool. Such is life.'

They reached the Cathedral doors and as Amée informed them she would be swift, Guillaume examined the square, as was his habit – looking for trouble to come walking toward him.

'So,' said that acid voice he hated. 'You choose to stand with a Jew rather than enter God's house.'

He swung round to Brother Crispianus. 'I do, monk. But then God and I have an understanding.'

'She is evil,' spat the monk, his yellow face turning a florid shade. 'Did not Saint Jerome say that in their synagogues, the Jews blaspheme the Christian flock and thus they will wreak their own destruction in the eternal fire?'

'And did not Paul say,' Ariella spoke clearly, standing in front of the hissing priest who grasped his crucifix and held it toward her, 'that Jews are still loved by God, loved for the sake of their ancestors. Further, did he not say that God never takes back His gifts or revokes His choice. Yes, Brother Crispianus. I know the words of your church. I wonder, do you know the words of mine?'

'I do not need to.' His ire fountained like flame from every pore. 'You are the personification of evil and worship words of the anti-Christ. You should be burned at the stake.'

Guillaume grabbed the priest by the folds of his foul-smelling habit. 'If you so much as touch her, priest, I shall kill you. With the blessing of my God.' He pushed the monk away and grasping Ariella's hand as Amée joined them, pulled the women in his wake.

'Guillaume!' said Amée. 'That was dangerous. If you had an enemy before, 'tis now thrice as large.'

'He threatened her with burning,' Guillaume walked with speed and the women hurried behind him.

'Oh,' gasped the widow. 'He didn't!'

'Amée,' Guillaume slowed down as they reached the row of market stalls. 'We have decided to leave Lyon after the banquet. That monk has set himself at Ariella and it is as safe for you to have us leave as much as for us to go. You have Michael and Jehanne now and our work is done.'

'Oh my dears. I am losing everyone, but I can understand. What if I petition the Archbishop?'

'Archbishop Renaud is weak. He sits behind the walls of Pierre Scize, counting whatever monies that poisonous notary procures and cares little for fairness nor Christian charity. Now, let us find what you need and return to Rue Ducanivet. I find the atmosphere close to the Cathedral quite poisonous.'

The women shopped – exchanging words with the stall-holders, and gradually their moods lifted, until he heard Amée's belly laugh and Ariella's delighted chuckle soon after. He was glad, but his own mood strayed into dark alleys and corners. He would kill that priest as soon as look at him and wouldn't ask God for forgiveness in the process.

They walked back to the house via Rue Tramassal, noting the quiet pervading the Gigni house. But as they passed the gates, Odo ran out, calling to Guillaume, and he turned.

'Messire, I have had a note…'

'I see,' Guillaume replied.

'He died saving you, I understand.'

'Yes. How does the family?'

'Messire Gigni did not say. The note was to inform me and to have me prepare the house accordingly. I am not to relay the sad news to the household servants until the family returns. They are due tomorrow. Messire, I think he will be grateful for your discretion. It was kind.'

'That discretion continues, Odo. Be assured.'

'I thank you, messire. Mesdames, have a safe and happy day tomorrow.'

He turned and walked away from them, his shoulders bowed with his responsibilities and they walked on with their baskets.

'So sad,' murmured Amée and was quiet for a moment. Then, 'Do you know I had thought to make savoury *darioles* but I think we shall fill them with almond cream. What say you, Ariella? By the saints, we must cook all day today and tonight! Until we drop!'

For once Guillaume was glad of her short attention span.

The sky lightened as they walked along Rue Ducanivet to the gates. A shaft of weak sun pooled on the river and it glistened. Almost immediately, birdsong became louder and the waterfowl clacked and splashed in the water. And from the yard came the sound of a song of a different kind…

'Toby!' Ariella hurried through the gates, holding her baskets carefully so as not to break eggs and drop almond meal.

'The lovely Ariella! Ah, my dearest lady, what a sight for sore eyes you are! And you, Madame Amée, I have missed you.' Tobias took her hand and kissed it, looking up at her and winking. 'Still beautiful, I see. And what is this I hear about a grand banquet. I trust I am to sing?'

Amée swept Toby up in her wake as she and Ariella made for the kitchens and Guillaume turned back to the gates to tell Adam of his confrontation with the monk.

'If the fire wasn't already lit, Guillaume, you and the lady have damned near set the taper to it yourselves.'

''Tis true. But I would not stand and let him threaten a woman, whether she is a Jewess or not. In any case, we leave the day after tomorrow. Now that the Bible has come back to us with Toby, we shall take it and return to Venezia via Piedmont. I shall find Vaudès' preachers there. It is their homeland now.'

'Guillaume, that is two days hence. You walk a fine line between now and then.'

'Then we are forewarned. Where is Henri? Have you told him your true identity?'

'I have and in answer to your question, he's in the storeroom. But there is no spare cot...'

'Find another and put it next to mine in the barn and he and Toby can sleep there. I shall sleep in Mahaut's cot in the kitchens. 'Tis not putting too fine a point on it when I say we are now more a military establishment and less a merchant house.'

'Guillaume, on that point. When you leave, I shall travel with you. I am content that the men we leave behind can care for this place under Messire Michael's able guidance. I suspect Tobias and Henri will leave as well.'

'If you say, then I am happy. It will be like old times with us together and I crave the return to somewhere quieter and more civilised than our stay here has been.'

'Methinks you need time to heal...'

Ah yes, Adam. But heal from what?

'Guillaume!' Henri clapped him on the back. 'How does your arm? The better for being back here, I'll be bound. I like your men – methinks I might stay until my wanderlust moves me on.'

'Henri, welcome.' Guillaume clasped his arm. ''Tis good to see you here. But we move on after the banquet that Madame de Clochard is holding. We return to Venezia. Methinks you might like to come with us. My brother has a business that might fit you well.'

'You say? Then I am all ears…'

'Later perhaps. And then think on it whilst de Clochard pays its friends what it owes.'

Aromas of the east drifted out into the yard, or so Tobias said.

'Constantinople floats on a cloud of such fragrances, doesn't it, Jehanne? I remember you gave me wine with spikenard once.'

'I do recall that, Toby. And yes, spices are part of the lifeblood of the city.' Jehanne and Michael had returned with the planks and Herviet and Raol set up the casks beneath them and the table stretched over three quarters of the whole yard. Amée clapped her hands and danced on the spot when she saw it.

'So exciting!' she chirruped.

Guillaume and Michael retrieved the pig carcass, the fish and the wines from the Inn of the Golden Fleece and the women set to, cutting, mixing, and cooking. Amée's spice chest was removed from her chamber and unlocked, its contents resembling a Venetian noblewife's and she employed it with great subtlety and skill.

'I will not overpower good food,' she said. 'Nevertheless, I would have Lyon informed that my kitchens rival those of the great houses. If we are merchants, then we shall have a name as reputable as the Gigni's. This shall aid such notoriety,' she said as she sprinkled a handful of cinnamon across the top of an apple tart. 'Michael, will you pepper and salt the pig? I need someone with a long arm.'

The pig roasted over the fire, its fat hissing and spitting with vicious regularity. Guillaume had great difficulty not thinking of Mahaut as he watched the skin crispen. This was what she would have done to the house of de Clochard, if Luzio and the priest had played their hand right.

And so, pepper, saffron, cinnamon, ginger and nutmeg turned the house from a cloth merchant's to a spice merchant's and anyone walking past would know that something of great import was to happen in the yard where the gates had been closed to prying eyes.

If anyone slept before Matins it was unlikely because still the women worked and the men grabbed what crusts and cores they could, seizing a moment's sleep here and there as the sky thought to lighten before dawn. Often, if they dragged fingers through sweet mixtures, Amée would rap their hands with the flat of a knife blade.

'Leave it or you shall have none on the morrow,' she said, not realising that the morrow was upon them. Her wimple and veil were filthy, her *bliaut* covered with flour and dried almond paste, with blood and juices. But her face glowed with a contented tiredness so that when she finally sat for a moment and asked Jehanne about Mahaut, she took the news well.

'Her voice charmed the Precentrix. The Mistress of Novices took her straight through the door and it was the last we saw of her. We paid her dowry to the Abbess and it was done, Mahaut is a novice from this day.'

'Shall we see her at all?'

'Not immediately. She has some adjustment. Soeur Marie will send to us when you may see her. But *Maman,* she is doing what she has craved all her life. It is much more than most women are allowed in this man's world.' As she said this, she and Ariella exchanged a complicit look.

The women cooked and as the men set up seating in the yard, Guillaume explained Gisborne's business to Henri.

'An *espie*…' Henri's eyes widened and a slow grin emerged. 'And I would be paid for this? I would have somewhere to live?'

Guillaume nodded. 'It is a large waterside villa, and a good group of men. Tobias is one such. And Adam, and many others besides. I think you would fit. My half-brother was one of the Lionheart's knights. A favourite. I may not have said…'

'The Lionheart! They say he is to be ransomed in the New Year.'

'I care not what happens to Richard of England. I have an abhorrence of nobility. And yet my half-brother is noble.' He shrugged his shoulders. 'But somewhere on the journey to the Holy Land my brother lost his way and his enchantment, and in favour of his little son he absconded from Richard's court. The same description of my half-brother fits many of us – we are disenchanted with what we have seen and done.'

'Then I shall think on it.' Henri de Montbrison flipped a lock of his brown wavy hair behind his ear. 'Christ Jesus, Guillaume. Is it ever quiet here? There has been nothing but chittering from the women since we arrived…'

The day's dawn arrived softly with gentle colour and clear air – the apricot and milky *amethystus* of early morning. Amée woke from a brief sleep and clapped a knife on a pan, waking the house. Apart from Herviet and Gosse on the gates, all had subsided where they stood, Guillaume in a chair in the hall, dead on his feet. If Ariella had slept, she did not say, instead appearing fresh and bright as all in the house were chivvied to their duties for the day.

Within moments, it was mayhem, men and women moving about, the yard swept, wines laid in jugs along the table. The midmorning bells rang out from the town's churches and suddenly the guests would not be far away so the hall too was swept, a fire laid, fresh candles placed in the candletrees. Jehanne filled an enormous pitcher with branches from an apple tree – the last of the red leaves holding on robustly. She placed it on the massive linen chest against the wall and stood back, breathing rather than admiring. As Guillaume walked past, she said,

'Is this worth the effort and expense, Guillaume?'

He stood for a moment before answering. 'I believe so. De Clochard was on the cusp of success when the fire hit us. Messire Gigni will tell you that all of Lyon viewed your family's business as one to watch with interest. The fire created an uncertainty, the *foire* reclaimed some of that certainty. If today finishes well, you will inherit a merchant house worth caring for, Jehanne. In addition, I would say that Guy and Saul would not have invested so much in the company if they thought it should fail. Now tell me, have you seen Ariella?'

'Yes, she was heading into the yard with pitchers of fruit wine.'

He left Jehanne to seek Ariella. To just touch her hand and wish her well for the day. Her role was as big as anyone's. The neighbours all liked her. It was well known.

The yard looked perfect now that daylight had settled on the confines. Pigeons alighted along the ridge of the barn and began burbling at the activity below them – at the trestle seats set out, the wine, the laughter of the men as excitement began to build. The baker had set up a make-do stall and was unloading bread and the smell drifted around the yard to lift beyond the eaves of the barn so that the pigeons rubbed their shoulders together with anticipation of a feast to come. In the oak, blackbirds sang, a melodic song that said *Life is good.*

Guillaume searched the yard, finally calling to Henri. 'Have you seen Ariella?'

The man from Montbrison turned, resplendent in a knee-length green tunic of fine wool weave, dark hose and short boots.

'Yes, she went to the gates a moment since.'

Guillaume looked toward the gates which were open and where Raol leaned, yawning. He hurried toward the guard. Ariella was no doubt looking at the river – it was a favourite pastime she said, reminding her of the watery stretches of their Venetian home.

'Raol, where is *Dameisele* Ariella? Have you seen her?'

'*Oc,*' the big man said. 'A child came with a message and she paid the child and hurried off.'

No...

A chill surged across his neck. 'Did she say where she was bound?'

'The Pont du Change.'

'Alone?'

'No. Messire Tobias went with her, dressed in court att...'

'Raol, why? What was the urgency?'

'Joshua the moneylender had collapsed at his premises on the bridge. He was asking for her.'

Guillaume's blood froze to crushed ice.

No! Lies! Joshua has a wife and daughter. He does not need Ariella...

'Was Tobias armed?'

'No.'

God have mercy...

'Wait, yes! He had a dagger at his girdle.'

Guillaume started out the gate. 'Find Adam! Tell him to come to the Pont du Change.' He began to run, calling back, 'Go, Raol. It is urgent!'

He ran with the Devil behind, feeling no pain in his arm or wrist. He ran round folk, through groups, no apologies, with fear pacing alongside him, step for step. He knew with a fatal instinct that the monk had scored a point and as God was Guillaume's witness, he would make the priest pay.

The road onto the bridge was filled with carts and people and customers for the moneylenders and the foodstalls. A black kite soared high above, its shriek piercing the noise of a populace living life, moving from the city to Presque L'ile and back again. The waters of the Saône formed ugly rapids, moving beyond the whisper over the autumn shallows near Rue Ducanivet to a fractious quarrel at the bridge. The river glittered – a sparkle of life and energy, not at all like further backstream where it seemed to slow over pebbles and stone bars until the thaw of spring.

Guillaume scoured the crowds, searching for the flaming hair through which he longed to run his fingers, looking for a friendly face who might know her, might have seen her. But there were none and then he was on the bridge, Joshua's premises at the far side, closer to Presque L'ile and locked. No one there. He began to run again, but intuition pulled him back.

Slow down and search. Look. An empty building, an alley…

He had never noticed before that one slim building on the town side of the bridge was closed, the double doors chained, nor that it sat separate to its neighbour with a narrow strip of pregnant shadow running back from the road to the parapet. So dark that one could barely see, except…

'Toby!'

The minstrel lay slumped, his forehead bleeding.

'Wake, Tobias!' He slapped him hard on the cheek and Toby groaned, trying to sit up before lurching onto his elbow and puking till nothing but yellow froth emerged.

'Find her, Guillaume. In there…'

'Where?'

'There…' But then Toby fainted and Guillaume propped him away from the vomit, turning round, heart leaping, sweat prickling under his arms. A door faced him, barely open.

He pushed into an empty room where dust motes swirled in the slitted lightbeams that slid through cracks in the double doors, and an odd smell of cattle drifted on the air.

Stairs!

He leaped up them to the second and third floors.

Empty…

And then he heard it. A faint sound, a scuffle, a muffled cry, barely there. He drew his *misericorde* and crept up the final stairs…

Brother Crispianus had her on the floor, her *bliaut* and cloak folds lifted and he had crouched over her, legs either side. Her mouth was stuffed with a rag and he had hold of her arms, pressing down. She bucked like a frenzied filly, but he said, 'This is what God would have good Christian men do to evil Jewish whores. You taint our houses, you taint our men. Ursurer!' He kneed her hard in the side and she coughed. 'Whore!'

Guillaume took two strides and with the monk oblivious, he slid his dagger to rest against the wretched neck so that a drop of blood pooled. Crispianus shrieked and jerked back, letting Ariella's hands go. She grabbed the gag from her mouth as the monk snarled.

'You would injur God's messenger doing what God commands?'

'God commands me otherwise, you bastard!'Guillaume grasped one scarred and pitted arm and twisted it back, pulling him to his feet. His wrist screamed as bones rattled and jumped together but his anger was so raw he cared nothing.

Ariella jumped up, the folds of her clothing falling back to her ankles and she ripped off her girdle, passing it to Guillaume to tie up the priest. Then she drew her dagger – a slim sharp blade not unlike the needle with which she embroidered, but longer. Capable of reaching a heart or deep inside the skull. She thrust it toward Crispianus hissing, 'I will kill you!'

Guillaume grabbed the man's arms but he fought with all his strength, one hand flying to his waist and then swiping hard beneath Guillaume's cloak.

'God's hand smites unbelievers!' Crispianus hissed, his mouth stretching to a corpse's grin.

But Guillaume smashed his jaw with his good hand, a fierce thump that jerked the man's head sideways, teeth catching on lips that were instantly split. Guillaume hauled at the arm that had hit him, bashing it against a timber post until the dagger the priest had held fell to the floor whereupon he kicked it to the stair and it dropped, one step after another – clink, clink, clink…

'You are *Nephilim*!' Ariella burst out. 'Guillaume, did he strike you?'

'No!' He sucked in air against the pain across his body, but it was an old friend, such a thing, and one he had been used to for days now. Holding his breath, he twisted the scarred arms, bruising them more as he jerked the girdle so that it cut in hard, trussing the man like a chicken.

'I curse him. He is filth…' She advanced with her knife.

The priest spat at her, a gobbet that sat at her waist like scum and

Guillaume growled, 'No, Ariella! Leave it! Just tell me – did he harm you?'

'No.' She breathed hard, an avenging angel. 'His intent was to rape…' The look she gave the priest smacked of triumph. 'He failed.'

'Move, priest.' Guillaume pushed him to the stair, down to the third and second floors and finally to the ground floor. 'Kneel.'

'You think I am afraid?' Crispianus spoke through swollen lips, blood creeping from the corner of his mouth. 'I who have martyred myself daily for God? Whatever you do I suffer in God's name…'

Guillaume thumped him between the shoulder blades and he tumbled to his knees as Guillaume whispered in his ear. 'Can you swim?'

The monk's head jerked up and the whites of the jaundiced eyes showed large.

'Ah, I see you do not. Good.' Guillaume grasped a ring in the floor and pulled and a trapdoor opened. Far beneath them, the Saône swirled green and angry as it leaped over boulders and stones. 'This is a kind of baptism, Brother Crispianus, don't you think? A cleansing before you stand before God to be judged. Certainly kinder than burning the feet of a gentle man whose only fault was to believe in the love of God. Likewise, slitting the throat of another, cutting out the tongue of a third, trying to kill me, trying to rape an innocent woman. God has a lot to think on.' He grabbed the priest by his hood and shook him. 'Do you know what this trapdoor is for? Can you smell bull shit? This is where they drop the bulls for La Fête des Merveilles. They are driven through the double doors from the bridge and then they are herded one by one, down through the trapdoor. The river falls off deeply from the shore here. Can you hear it hitting the boulders and pontoons?'

The priest coughed against the tightness of his cowl, whining as he wriggled on his knees trying to back away from the opening. 'There is time for you to repent, archer, let the whore go through the trapdoor. You will be forgiv…'

But before he could finish, Guillaume walked behind him and kicked him so that the monk hung off the edge, teetering. Guillaume kicked him again. So quickly – not a moment's hesitation and even he was surprised at the unconscious speed with which he acted. The monk screamed as he fell, hitting his head on a large boulder jutting out from the wavelets, then rolling loosely into the current to float downstream.

An eye for an eye…

Ariella sucked in a breath, looked at Guillaume and with tears pooling in her eyes, asked, 'Was he dead, think you? Will he drift far before he is found? Would people have heard him?'

'He was unconscious. By now he will be drowned. And yes, he will drift and it will be some time before they find him. And no, there is a crowd on the bridge, and the river makes a noise through here. Do not fret.' He wrapped his arms around her shoulders. 'He would have killed us, Ariella. We knew it was to be this way.'

'I know. I am sorry...'

'Never apologise. Not to me. You are shaking, let us get Tob...'

But the door was shoved back and Adam flew in, sword in hand. 'Where is he? Where is the piece of shit?'

'Gone to meet his Maker, Adam.' Guillaume straightened his back – by the Saints it hurt. That monk had hit him near to the old wound. 'It is done. Find a handcart. Ariella is shaking and we can take she and Tobias back...'

Adam cursed. 'No loss and the Church better for it. Wait a moment...' He hurried outside and they could hear him shouting at someone on the bridge.

Ariella still trembled like leaf in the autumn breeze and Guillaume was surprised, this woman who had survived so much. He longed to wrap his arms round her and hold her till she relaxed, but Adam burst back in.

'I have one. I've told the chap that Toby was drunk and fell and hit his head and that you, *Dameisele*, are with child.'

Guillaume and Ariella looked at each other and a smile managed to break free. But Guillaume would say that it didn't reach her eyes.

'How fares Toby?' she asked.

'He might sing the occasional flat note but he can still sing for his supper this day. And you, *Dameisele?*'

'*I* shall listen to him sing. Come. I need to get home and change.' She pushed past them and out onto the bridge, climbing into the handcart next to Toby and wrapping her cloak tight around – a cocoon protecting her.

'Guillaume?' Adam looked back.

'Yes,' Guillaume said, 'I am coming.' And he pushed himself away from the wall against which he leaned, recognising the profound lethargy that settles after battle tension. It had been part of every day in the Holy Land. The shock was that it should be repeated so often away from the field of war.

They turned into the gates to find the yard had filled with guests. Toby levered himself off the cart, muttering about the state of his tunic and that Devil men who had no respect for the fine clothes of this world deserved what came their way. *'Filthy scum!'*

Ariella climbed from the cart, lifting her head and sucking in a deep breath. 'Guillaume, we must change, we smell and you have blood on you from that mongrel. Put on the *murrey* tunic I made, and I will see you anon.' She kissed his cheek quickly. 'Adam, can I prevail upon you? There are things…' She indicated the kitchens and the tables and then hurried away.

Guillaume watched her, in awe of her fortitude. No one would know what she had been through, so well did she conceal things but he knew she wanted to strip all that had happened from her body, if not her mind.

'Excuse me, seems I'm needed.' Adam shrugged and winked. 'Must go and help the firebrand! By the saints but she handles things well, does she not? You'll be alright?' But it was rhetorical question and he hurried after her.

It was as if tides had swept around Guillaume, dragging people away. As though life was moving on without him – Ariella to *her* place within the house, Adam to his, Tobias gone and although he knew it was impermanent, the pain cut through him like a knife.

Such irony – a knife…

He paid the man with the handcart who stood examining the celebrations with evident curiosity, and sent him on his way, and as he closed his eyes for a moment, dark flashes pulsed and he took a breath, reaching out a hand to steady himself.

Barn…

He pushed himself away and walked between the men, waving to Amée and Jehanne, smiling at old Matthieu who was seated on a stool, quaffing wine of some sort and coughing between mouthfuls.

Guillaume entered the barn and shut the door behind, walking to his cot, to the chest which he opened and from which he pulled an old chemise. He ripped the linen, gasping as the sharp action tore at his back. But he ripped again and again until he had wadding. Then he laid hose on the cot and began to feel where he thought the wadding should go. Feeling the slip and slide of slimy blood. He held the linen against the massive slash and grabbed the hose with a free hand, laboriously positioning it and trying to wind it so the linen would be kept in place. Round once and a half, so he tucked the end in and then grabbed the other hose and wound that until the wound felt secure.

Groaning, swift quick exhalations, and he pulled off the stained tunic and the chemise and rolled them into a ball, stuffing them into the chest, slipping on a fresh chemise. Somehow he managed to drag on the *murrey* tunic, despite the bones in his wrist moving over each other and which made his stomach writhe till he thought he would vomit all over the cot.

No worse than battle...

He checked his hose for splatters and decided they would suit and then contrived to swing the cloak back around his shoulders. But a wave of something beyond weakness tore at his body so that he could feel nothing, his senses day to night in a blink.

He collapsed to the cot.

Maman, *Papa – not yet...*

He could have lain there for hours, he did not know, but slowly his senses returned.

Hearing – the crowd roaring with laughter and chatter outside, Amée's delighted shriek above everyone else's.

Touch – the pillow Ariella had made for him under his cheek.

Taste – the unwelcome iron flavour of blood as he coughed. A dribble in the corner of his mouth.

Smell – the food, the spices, but overall, horse, mule and fodder.

And finally sight. He opened his eyes and saw the barn and was glad.

So much better than the Long Sleep they talked about around the fires at Nahir Al-Falik, or at Acre.

Not yet...

'Messire Guillaume, are you within?' Herviet rapped on the door.

He pushed himself up from the cot, wiped his mouth and licked his lips, smoothed his hair and opened the door. 'Is aught wrong, Herviet?' he asked.

'There are two men at the gate asking for you. They won't enter.'

Guillaume followed after the guard, pushing himself to stand straight and tall, to indicate that nothing at all was ill. He glimpsed Ariella in a peacock blue *bliaut*. He remembered that silk – she had worn it to the farewell banquet at the Venetian villa, when her father had valiantly held back tears as he toasted her. She stood behind Adam now, directing he and Raol as they carried the enormous roast pork to the table. She would not touch pork, which was why Amée had thoughtfully provided fish, fillets of which already lay on pewter platters. Tobias' voice rang out, singing some bawdy song to welcome the pig but it was a mélange of noise and he needed to concentrate.

Acknowledge, wave, thank…

He stepped through the gates and looked toward the bridge across the Saône. Messire Gigni stood holding the reins of his horse, deep in conversation with another man who fiddled with a strap on his mount's bridle.

'Messire Alexandrus,' he said and the merchant swung round. 'You asked for me?'

Gigni frowned. 'I am sorry to intrude upon your celebration, sorry too that we cannot attend. But you understand, I know. Come, I wish to talk to you…' He took Guillaume by the shoulder and led him across to the stone wall from which they could look out over the Saône.

'Guillaume, I think you have met someone called Hamelyn, have you not?'

Guillaume's senses cleared swiftly – the acute tension of battle once again upon him; that state that dulled pain and made one forget that blood flowed. Could he trust Gigni? He said nothing.

'My companion,' said Gigni. 'He is *Sandalati*. His name is Joffroi and he and Hamelyn travelled from Piedmont together.'

'I don't understand, messire…'

'I am not a Poor Man,' Gigni continued. 'As you can see. But neither do I dispute their message. It is a good message that our Church would do well to contemplate with humility. For a long time now, since Pierre, my very good trading friend, left his wealth behind to preach, I have provided safe and subtle shelter for the Poor Men. Even my wife does not know. Only Odo. When Hamelyn and Joffroi arrived, they told me they would collect the Vaudois Bible which had been placed in Jehan's care by Pierre Vaudès. But Hamelyn has disappeared and with his vanishing, so too the exact hiding place of the Bible.' Gigni called to the preacher and the man came, leading the horses. Guillaume studied his face and had a vague recollection of him from the tavern, the day Hamelyn had squeezed his shoulder.

''Tis true, I did know Hamelyn,' he admitted, proceeding to inform them of the manner of Hamelyn's death and of the priest's role. 'And we have the

Bible and would be glad to pass it on. It has been of great concern to us to maintain its security.' He staggered a little and Gigni grabbed him, a hand across his back.

'Guillaume? What ails you?' Receiving no reply, he withdrew his hand and looked down at his palm. 'You are injured...'

'I am, but...' he coughed and wiped at his mouth with the back of his hand, an action Gigni noted with distress.

'Joffroi, help me get him onto your horse. Guillaume, come to my home. Methinks you don't want a fuss here.'

'No...' In truth he was too tired to argue and merely said, 'I need to speak with Herviet first.'

Joffroi held out cupped hands and Guillaume placed a foot therein, sliding into the saddle as Herviet was called. He gave him a concise order. 'Tell Adam to come to the Gigni house immediately, and bring the book.'

The horses walked carefully but somewhere between Rue Ducanivet and Rue Tramassal he fainted, knowing nothing until he was laid on a soft bed. Gigni pulled a cover over him as he shivered, despite the warm and dulcet light in the room. When Gigni saw his eyes open, he said,

'My *medicus* comes. He will know what to do.'

'Messire,' Guillaume's breath rasped. 'He can do nothing.'

'But of course he can. You will see. Ah, Yusuf, you must help my friend. He has been wounded...'

Yusuf wore the pristine white robes so favoured by other Arab doctors of Guillaume's acquaintance. He ordered Guillaume to be rolled on his side and his hands were long-fingered and gentle as he unwrapped the temporary bandage.

'How long ago did this happen?'

'This morning,' Guillaume answered.

He swabbed the wound, cleaning, probing, saying nothing and Gigni huffed impatiently. Guillaume coughed again and the *medicus* quickly passed him a wad of linen to catch the blood.

'Thank you,' Guillaume finally managed, his throat hoarse. 'I know another Arab physician like yourself, sir.'

'Yes?' said the man.

'Mehmet Al Din. He is a close friend.'

Ysuf began to re-bandage Guillaume. 'I knew Mehmet once. I studied with he and his brother. They were good men.'

'Indeed…' and Guillaume swooned away as they rolled him back. This time the dark shadow was a welcome reprieve.

But he woke quickly, pulling himself back from the abyss. Enough time to hear Gigni ask, 'Well?'

Yusuf looked at Guillaume, noticed he had regained consciousness and said, 'Guillaume, your wound is infinitely deep. I do not know how you have survived this long. Much damage has been done.'

'I know and I know you cannot help me.'

'I can make you comfortable but it is a matter of time. Make peace with your God, my dear friend.'

Amée's voice rang around his head. *You are so facile about God, Guillaume. As I have said before, it will come back to bite you one day.*

And suddenly the door flew open and Ariella and Adam rushed in.

Guillaume looked at Gigni and the merchant answered the unspoken question. 'I felt she needed to be here with you.'

She said nothing, just kneeled by his bed as Adam passed the Bible to Gigni. She reached for Guillaume's hand and held it softly, like air caught in wool.

Gigni said 'We will give you peace. Yusuf will return with some poppy for you in a moment, Guillaume.'

'I thank you, Alexandrus…'

''Tis nothing that I wouldn't do for any of those I respect, my friend.'

The door closed and there were just the three in the room.

'He sent a message,' Adam said. 'And all of the house knows you are hurt. Even Amée, who has remained remarkably controlled. It was decided to follow the Gigni example of the hunt and continue on with the celebrations. Tobias is singing and playing his heart out and Henri is being a good second to Michael. It all goes well, you needn't worry.'

'I am glad.' His voice sounded husky and distant, even to his own ears. 'Ariella, can you get me some watered wine. Just a little. I am so thirsty…'

She kissed his hand, and went to the door. 'I will be but a moment…'

He waited till the door closed. 'Adam,' he said urgently 'I am dying. Listen to me – take her back to Saul. Take Tobias and Henri and all three of you must guard her as if she is worth more than the Holy Roman Empire's fortune. Heed me…'

'You need not ask. It is done. Guillaume, could the *medicus* not…'

'He can do nothing. It is…' he coughed and filled the wad with blood. 'It comes fast…'

He closed his eyes against the enveloping blackness and then opened them again.

'I shall fetch the *Dameisele,*' Adam said kindly. 'And leave her with you. I shall wait outside.'

'You are a good friend, Adam. I thank you…' His chest tightened as he spoke, a crushing sensation, as if he had run from Lyon to the Forez without stopping and then Ariella came through the door, a flash of blue with tumultous hair hanging down her back. He loved her fierceness, her verve but this time it made the tightness worse.

She held a mug to his mouth and he swallowed a sip and lay back.

'Of all the men I have met, you are so quietly stubborn, Guillaume. And so very brave and I find I love you for it.'

He marked her beautiful hair and the thickness of her eyelashes. The freckles across her nose, and her glorious eyes – did they not say one could see a person's soul through their eyes? Her soul was so valiant. She took his hand and rubbed it with her own, bringing it to her lips and kissing the knuckles one by one as Adam left the room. He counted the kisses – one, two, three…

But then he thought he heard the door open again and when he looked, young Alain stood behind Ariella's shoulder and he knew for a certainty that it was indeed time and that nothing he did or said could make a difference. Alain uttered Ambrosius' words and he knew how true they were.

'Where a man's heart is, there is his treasure also.'

And then he let go…

LA FIN

$\mathcal{A}$UTHOR'S $\mathcal{N}$OTE

✕

Guillaume was a natural follow-on to *Tobias*, the first book of *The Triptych Trilogy*. Guillaume's place in the Gisborne house was something of an enigma and it seemed natural, as I had told Tobias' story, to then expand on Guillaume's own.

At the time of the story, 1193 AD, Guillaume lives in Lyon, a thriving commercial town at the confluence of the Rhône and Saône rivers and benefiting from being a gateway for goods travelling north from the exotic east via the seaport of Marseille. Thanks to its Roman foundations, Lyon was a reasonably sophisticated town. But Lyon's twelfth century history is only glanced upon by historians, even though one of the greatest reformist thinkers of the time, Pierre Vaudès, lived in the city. The paucity of detailed fact of course, plays to a fiction writer's strengths, but there *are* details which can't be overlooked.

I have been fortunate to have an excellent researcher in Lyon, Monsieur B. Cobb – one who has the ear of various historians in various institutions. Between them all, we have been able to create a factual world in which the fictional de Clochard house and business exists. Street names have changed of course, but much of my setting still weaves its way through Lyon.

The *traboules* are a case in point – stone tunnels from the Saône to the upper reaches of the city, created by the Romans when Lyon was Lugdunum, and which enabled goods to be carried from the river to the town under cover. They allowed free access between streets, but had locked doors off them, leading to chambers above and cellars and river access below. They are still very much in evidence today.

De Clochard was imagined to be a riverside property in a street called Rue Ducanivet, evidenced by a fourteenth century map, the earliest map to which I was able to gain access. The home of the Gigni (a fictional family) in medieval times was situated in Rue Tramassal. It became Rue Tramassac in later years. It should be noted that in fact, there existed a Florentine trading family in Lyon called the Guardigni. But as the information about them was lean, I chose to create my own Florentine family. Thus the Gigni were born.

The small priory in the Forez, at *Pommiers en Forez,* was later to grow into a substantial religious house. In the twelfth century however, it would have been small and intimate. The forest *domus* of the Gigni, situated not far from the priory and which I named Choizey, is in fact a fictional *chastel* for the purposes of the narrative.

There is no extant evidence of *lavoirs* in Lyon, however, one historian with whom my researcher spoke, (Monsieur M. Locatelli) indicates that *lavoirs* existed throughout the Rhône valley and that large fountains existed within Lyon and were used for laundry and other public activities. It was therefore decided that it was within the realm of possibility that a *lavoir* might have existed, potentially just outside the clergy walls of the Cathedral of Saint Jean. Rue Tramassal (Tramassac) is close by, so the idea fitted the story well.

The village of La Flèche existed in the twelfth century and is a thriving town today. It is situated between Maine and Anjou and there are two meanings to its name. One rather plainly states 'rock in the ground'. But the other fitted my character, Guillaume, and his background as a bowyer and fletcher as if tailor-made. *Flèche* also means arrow in French and so I took that meaning for my story – that the most gifted bowyers and fletchers in Anjou lived in the village and that it had a reputation for providing the finest bows and arrows – something that Richard Lionheart heard about whilst in Chinon, before leaving for the Third Crusade.

There are references to actual historical personages in the narrative. Guillaume has personal contact with King Richard I who is in Chinon as Guillaume leaves for the Third Crusade. Whilst in the Holy Land, Guillaume has an ugly confrontation with the Grand Master of the Templars, Robert de Sablé. On his return to Europe and whilst in Lyon, Guillaume deals with courtiers from the Hohenstaufen court. And he has significant dealings with the Archbishop of Lyon at the time, Renaud de Forez.

There is very little information available on Archbishop Renaud. However, one point is that he spent more time in the fortified Chateau Pierre Scize in Lyon than in his own episcopal palace. I took a certain amount of licence with this fact, assuming that he was afraid for his safety. I also assumed that such fear came from the fact that he and his episcopal staff had nefarious dealings around the town. And thus my ugly episcopal notary, Brother Crispianus, was born.

Renaud was Archbishop at the time of the Waldensians and so I began to see an overlapping thread – my story about merchants and trading included the wealthy merchant Pierre Vaudès. Vaudès became a reformist thinker and gave up his wealth in favour of following a simple path as laid out in the Gospels. He had the Bible translated to the *Lengua Romana*, so that the common man might understand that God's love was not dependent on money and plenary indulgences. His preachers, of which there were many, became known as *Sandalati* because of their simple footwear. But more particularly they were known as The Poor Men of Lyon. We know them as the Waldensians.

The Church of which Reynaud was part, declared the *Sandalati* heretics and the preachers and followers were forced into hiding, in fear of their lives, eventually leaving France for the hidden valleys of Piedmont. But did they leave that most famous (or infamous) translation of the Bible behind? I decided that Jehan de Clochard, merchant and friend to Pierre Vaudès, would take the Bible into safekeeping until the *Sandalati* could retrieve it and transport it to Piedmont.

The theme of trade pulses through Guillaume's story like lifeblood. Ever since I read my first facts on medieval trade, particularly from places far east, the hairs stood on my neck. Everything that we conceivably value today was traded throughout Europe. Doors to the Mahgreb had opened long since and the spice and silk routes were now being explored through doorways with Byzantium. Two of my favourite books throughout this journey have been *Power and Profit – the Merchant in Medieval Europe* by Peter Spufford (Thames and Hudson, London 2002) and *The Great Sea – a Human History of the Mediterranean* by David Abulafia (Penguin London 2011). The merchant class was now on the cusp of arrival and societal change was heading Europe's way. It made for quite heady reading.

My characters often swear, mostly using body parts of God and Christ. For this excursion, I was led by Melissa Mohr, from her book *Holy Shit – a Brief History of Swearing* (OUP, Oxford 2013)

I welcomed Tobias back to this novel. He and I share a special relationship and in what is the venal world of trade, he invited the inclusion of poems and lyrics in the novel, something for which I have always admired the late great Dorothy Dunnett. I would love to have asked DD (as she is affectionately known by her aficionados) how she found her worthy pieces, what techniques she used to decide which piece went with what character and action.

Earlier this year, I heard the song *Carmina qui Quondam* (http://www.classicfm.com/music-news/videos/boethius-song-1000-years/) and fell in love with its beauty. As it dates from the eleventh century, I felt it would most definitely appeal to a minstrel of Tobias' standing. And there are other pieces throughout the novel. The song, *Women*, is from Luminarium. (http://www.luminarium.org). *Somer is Y Comen* is from *Medieval English Lyrics 1200-1400* (Penguin London 1995) And the poem on hunting is from https://www.stormfront.org/forum/t639657/.

I should also mention that velvet features in this novel. There are many schools of thought about the existence of velvet in the twelfth century. Sharon Penman was forced to retract the view she held that velvet did exist although I believe she specifically referred to velvet in England. I scoured books and the web for information and came across a most unlikely source – http://artisanssquare.com/sg/index.php?topic=4023.0 – which said: *'Moorish Spain was a second major centre of velvet production; it had been manufactured there since 948 AD, and various velvet-weavers' guilds and organisations served to ensure the industry's prosperity.'* My characters are textile traders. They trade with Arab merchants from all parts of the Mediterranean, Adriatic and further afield. To me it seemed logical that they would source something as valuable as velvet, in the same way that they had sourced the dye, Tyrian Purple, in Constantinople and which was the key element in the story of *Tobias*.

I would also like to acknowledge a particular poem that I love and which I have used in the novel. This year, the most beautifully illustrated book came into my possession. It is called *The White Cat and the Monk*, by

Joe Ellen Bogart and Sydney Smith. (Groundwood Books, Ontario, 2016) It is based on the nine century poem **_Pangur Bán_** which was written by an Irish Benedictine monk from Reichenau Abbey in Germany. I sourced the online translation of the poem by Robin Flowers (https://www.ling. upenn.edu/~beatrice/pangur-ban.html) and when Guillaume, Tobias and Adam stay at the small priory of _Pommiers en Forez,_ they are cared for by Brother Hugo, who has a white cat. As the three men leave at dawn the next day, Tobias turns back to look and what he sees reminds him of that ninth century poem. Now do you see why I love Toby?

I would just like to conclude my notes by saying that I am fully aware that some words (like fart) are not twelfth century. But where words are required and set the scene, I use them with painstaking care, trying to avoid overtly anachronistic language when possible.

ACKNOWLEDGEMENTS

×

Claire and Brian Wallace – my parents. They taught me to love literature and to apply myself to whatever I wanted to achieve.

My husband – always.

My diligent and respected researcher and friend in Lyon, Brian Cobb – *Merci, mon ami.*

Rebecca for sourcing information on the Jewish faith.

My beta-readers, Jane and Pat, for never being afraid to pull me up.

My editor, John Hudspith – for strong guidance and advice.

My e-formatter, Daniel Gillan, for swift and professional delivery.

My cover designer, Clare Batten, for putting up with her mother.

My muse – my Jack Russell dog who tries so hard to understand why a computer takes me away from his side.

To SJA Turney – thank you for believing in me.

To Ziggy, Louise and Libby M for always being there and saying and doing things at just the right time.

And to my legion of friends online – at The Review on Facebook and HNS-Australasia on Facebook. Thank you for erudite posts and comment during the writing of *Guillaume*. It's appreciated.

If you liked this book, please consider posting a short review on Amazon and/or Goodreads. Honest reviews help others decide whether they might like to read the novel.

You can always find up-to-date lists of this series and other books I have written, with purchase points on *www.pruebatten.com*

Please feel free to connect with me:
Via my blog at *www.pruebatten.com*
Via Facebook at *www.facebook.com/prue.batten.writer*
And for a visual treat that will inspire your journey
through my books, go to *www.pinterest.com/pruebatten*

www.ingramcontent.com/pod-product-compliance
Lightning Source LLC
Chambersburg PA
CBHW030627110726
47901CB00002B/347